S imon worked so hard on not seeing what he saw that he almost missed the start of the attack. The HUD painted the figures hanging upside down from the tube ceiling green as he turned the corner.

Other twisted and misshapen figures lay in wait behind the overturned cars of the tube train. Once he saw them, though, Simon knew they were Darkspawn.

"Ambush!" one of Derek's men yelled in warning.

Out of habit, Simon reached for his sword and the Spike Bolter. He spotted Leah behind him in the HUD view. Backing into her, he growled, "Get to cover." Then he had the Spike Bolter up in his fist and was firing. A string of detonations ripped away the quietness inside the tube.

The palladium spikes ripped into one of the Darkspawn hanging from the ceiling, pinning the creature to the stone surface. The demon yowled in pain and anger as it tried to rip itself free. Its thin body whipped and twisted, tearing the wounds in its flesh even larger.

Upon closer inspection, Simon saw that on the ceiling the demons had woven a web of cargo netting they'd undoubtedly scavenged from the overturned tube cars. They'd worked awfully quickly to have set the ambush up on the Templar's return.

A moment later, the Darkspawn Simon had nailed to the ceiling braced its feet and pulled through the spikes. Dark blood ran freely from the wounds. Snarling, the demon landed only a few feet in front of Simon. It lifted a weapon and took aim.

HELLGATE LONDON®

BOOK ONE OF THREE
EXODUS

MEL ODOM

POCKET STAR BOOKS
New York London Toronto Sydney

Pocket Star Books
A Division of Simon & Schuster, Inc.
1230 Avenue of the Americas
New York, NY 10020

This book is a work of fiction. Names, characters, places, and incidents either are products of the author's imagination or are used fictitiously. Any resemblance to actual events or locales or persons, living or dead, is entirely coincidental.

Copyright © 2007 by Flagship Studios, Inc. Flagship Studios and Hellgate: London are trademarks and/or registered trademarks of Flagship Studios, Inc.

All rights reserved, including the right to reproduce this book or portions thereof in any form whatsoever. For information address Pocket Books Subsidiary Rights Department, 1230 Avenue of the Americas, New York, NY 10020

First Pocket Star Books paperback edition July 2007

POCKET STAR BOOKS and colophon are registered trademarks of Simon & Schuster, Inc.

Cover art by Blur Studio
Interior design by Davina Mock-Maniscalco

Manufactured in the United States of America

For information about special discounts for bulk purchases, please contact Simon & Schuster Special Sales at 1-800-456-6798 or business@simonandschuster.com.

10 9 8 7 6 5 4 3 2 1

ISBN-13: 978-1-4165-2579-0
ISBN-10:   1-4165-2579-3

This book is dedicated to my sons Shiloh and Chandler,
who play video games with a vengeance.
(They get that from their dad.)
Can't wait till *Hellgate: London* comes out
so we can kick butt together!

ACKNOWLEDGMENTS

Thanks to editor Marco Palmieri, who helped me figure out the world and how best to approach the novels.

And to the novel review guys at Flagship Studios: Bill Roper, Chris Arretche, Matt Householder, Tyler Thompson, David Brevik, Ivan Sulic, and Phil Shenk, who have helped me stay on the path and provided encouragement.

Thanks also to Steve Goldstein at Flagship Studios (www.flagshipstudios.com) for shuttling the material along.

HISTORIAN'S NOTE

This story begins eighteen years prior to the events depicted in the *Hellgate: London* video game.

PROLOGUE

The winged demon sped out of the darkness without a sound until it was almost on top of its prey. Then it screamed, a bloodcurdling, high-pitched shrill of terror. The razor-sharp claws of its lower appendages were open to grasp and slash. It looked like a cross between a wedge-headed cat and a flying lizard packed into a vaguely feminine form. Glittering silver-gray scales covered the creature from head to tail. Sulfurous odor trailed in its wake.

The demon was a Blood Angel. And the prey was Thomas Cross, who had witnessed a similar such creature—maybe the same one—gut a fellow Templar standing beside him only a few moments ago.

Thomas stood in the shadows of St. Paul's Cathedral. He kept the stone wall to his back as he turned to face his hellish opponent. If he hadn't been walking so close to the structure, the demon probably would have taken him on its first pass instead of missing by inches.

The trees blotted out some of the moon, blunting the full moonlight that would have made him easier to see in the night. The heads-up-display (HUD) inside Thomas's helmet made the adjustments to bring his opponent into sharp relief.

"Lock," Thomas commanded.

Instantly the computer-augmented systems built into the armor tagged the demon. Even as the creature flew away, the helm's viewplate kept it marked, tagging it with a blinking red triangle that indicated direction. Digital numbers relayed the distance between the demon and Thomas.

"Target locked." The computer's voice was that of Thomas's father, copied from records Thomas had of Tregarth Cross before he'd died. The voice was the most calm Thomas had ever heard.

All around Thomas, his fellow warriors fought and died. Dozens of Templar littered the ground already, their armor beaten and broken and shredded. Hundreds more would join them before morning came.

When High Lord Patrick Sumerisle, the Grand Master of the Templar, had called them to action tonight, none of them had believed they would survive. In fact, survival would have meant failure.

Even though he'd prepared all his life to shed his blood to protect the world from the demon hordes, as his father and grandfather before him had, Thomas still hadn't been prepared to watch his brothers-in-arms die. His own likely imminent death left him shaken despite his grim resolve, but the bloody carnage that lay where brave men and women he had known had once stood attacked his very faith.

And they had died. Singly, and—now—en masse.

As the demon came at him, Thomas threw himself to one side, hitting the ground and rolling back to his feet. The armor thudded against the ground, absorbing the shock so that he barely noticed the impact.

The Blood Angel's claws raked the cathedral's stone side, unleashing a torrent of sparks, and its wings rustled above Thomas. Wheeling, Thomas brought the great broadsword up before him. Emerald-green energy, a blending of Nano-Dyne technology and arcane forces, sparkled along the blade.

The demon flapped its leathery wings and heeled over,

coming back on target with the speed of a swooping falcon. The bigger ones, and more powerful, had taken out some of the British special forces jets within hours after the Hell-gates had opened two weeks ago. Thomas had watched in helpless horror as the aircraft had dropped into Central London and taken out whole city blocks. Only carnage and rubble had remained.

Come on, you blackhearted hellspawn. Tonight's a dance of death, and devil take the hindmost.

Thomas knew he'd never live to see morning. They'd known that—all of them—when they'd left the Under-ground to bring a final battle to the demons that had in-vaded their earth.

But Thomas hadn't been able to turn away, not even knowing that. He was a warrior. More than that, he was a Templar, a knight who had pledged to follow the Rule. He was Seraphim of the House of Rorke. As the First Guard of the House, his loyalty and courage were unquestionable.

He stood clad in the armor his father had helped him make in the eldritch forges beneath London, in the hidden tunnels of the Underground the Freemasons had started building back in the seventeenth century. Pewter-gray and black, the armor yet sparked with the arcane energies Thomas had pounded into the metal when he'd cast it. He'd also layered in NanoDyne upgrades that turned the armor into more of an exoskeleton, powering him up rather than merely protecting him. He'd forged his sword as well, crafting a Negotiator.

Made from an arcane alloy of palladium, strengthened by the holy energies Thomas had called to his cause all those years ago, the sword was a fierce weapon. It was light enough to be employed with one hand and sharp enough to slice through an engine block.

Yelling, Thomas raced forward to meet the beast, hoping to strike quickly enough to throw the Blood Angel's timing off. Thomas attacked, swinging with all the considerable strength the armor lent him.

The demon stretched forth one of its lower extremities, intent on seizing Thomas's head. The sword met the demon's clawed foot in a spray of green sparks. The keen blade sliced through the demon's leg, lopping the limb off near the body. Black ropes of blood hit the ground and cathedral wall. The dark, viscous liquid hissed and smoked.

Angry and in pain, the Blood Angel squawled and turned toward the dark sky.

Thomas followed the creature, moving to take advantage of the scant cover afforded by the trees along the outside of St. Paul's Cathedral. Fires already danced along the top of the building, promising complete destruction if they weren't put out.

A few weeks ago the London Fire Brigade might have been able to arrive in time to save the cathedral. But most of those brave men and women were dead now, and the ones that hadn't fallen in battle or to a disaster had other tragedies to deal with tonight. Death walked through the city on cloven hooves and clawed feet.

The Blood Angel glided to the high branches of one of the nearby trees. It held the stump of its maimed leg in its taloned hands. The crimson runes burned into the demon's skin glowed fiercely. Abruptly, the severed stump stopped bleeding. Turning its baleful gaze on Thomas, the nightmarish creature launched itself into the air and attacked again.

Spinning to his right, raising his armored left arm to provide some protection from attack, Thomas took a fresh grip on his sword.

"Down, Thomas!"

Thomas reacted instantly to the familiar voice of command, dropping into a crouching position. Armor scraped against his own as someone took up a position at his back. Then he saw the squat, ugly body of the six-barreled Spike Bolter thrust before him. Instantly, the pistol barked and jerked in the mailed fist.

Palladium bullets with sharpened tips erupted from the barrels as it whined to life. The rounds impaled the Blood Angel, opening up bloody craters and furrows in the scaly flesh. Crossing its arms before its head, seeking to protect its face, the demon veered away and gained altitude. The Spike Bolter kept whining. Holes opened up in the demon's wings and allowed the moonlight to shine through.

Relieved, Thomas turned to the Templar behind him. He instantly recognized Guy Wickersham's distinctive royal purple-tinted armor. Guy was older than Thomas, in his sixties now, old enough to be Thomas's father. He had helped train Thomas, and had even helped Thomas train his son.

Thomas grinned but didn't dare lift the faceplate on his helm. "Thanks, Guy."

The older Templar nodded. He leaned heavily against the wall behind him. "Don't mention it."

"Are you all right?"

"Just . . . just trying to catch my breath . . . is all. It's . . . been an eventful . . . night."

Thomas put his left palm against the other man's breastplate. Deep grooves showed where a demon's claws had almost penetrated.

"Scan," Thomas ordered.

As soon as the connection was made, information pulsed into Thomas's HUD. Medical readouts about Thomas and Guy pulsed across the screen. Guy's heart rate was up but the blood pressure was dangerously low.

"What happened?" Thomas surveyed the other man, turning him slightly and finding two deep slices that had penetrated the armor covering Guy's back. Something had cut through the armor and deeply into the man.

"Carnagor." Guy sagged against the wall. The Spike Bolter dropped from his nerveless hand.

Thomas knew about the Carnagors. They were fierce monsters, as large as an elephant and as strong and unstoppable as a rhinoceros. They were equipped with tusks, hundreds of teeth in a gaping maw, and hands—not paws.

"Came up out of the ground behind me," Guy gasped. "By the time I saw it, I was too late. It . . . killed Davy, Wallace, and Morton."

All of those men had been friends as well. Thomas's heart ached with the loss. For a moment tears blurred his vision. He had not been friends with these men all of these years to lose them in one night. It wasn't fair.

"See you . . . on the other side." Guy slid down the wall to a seated position.

Thomas didn't need his armor's onboard systems to tell him Guy was dead, but he used them anyway. Leaving someone behind wasn't something he was prepared to do.

All of Guy's life signs were gone. Thomas's HUD showed flatlines across the board.

Pushing his grief aside, Thomas turned back to the battle. There was still his own death to attend. He scooped up Guy's Spike Bolter to replace his own lost sidearm.

He hadn't gone more than a few feet when he felt the ground trembling. Sprinting toward the corner of the cathedral, he turned back and watched just as a Carnagor burrowed up from the ground only a few feet from Guy's body.

Mounds of displaced earth formed and tumbled aside as the demon burrowed up. Thomas knew what it was because he'd seen them throughout the battlefield. Such demons could easily dig up through the pavement and buildings of Central London's High Streets.

Cautiously, the blunt snout shoved through the hole and scented the earth. A snake-like tongue whipped out as it licked its eyes. Thomas didn't know if the demon had continued to track the other Templar by sound or if it was another Carnagor that had just arrived.

Satisfied that it wouldn't be attacked at once, the Carnagor heaved itself up from the ground. Earth fell away from it in clumps. It shook and shivered for a moment like a dog.

The creature was huge, taller than Thomas at the shoulder and as broad across as a lorry. The hideous mouth between the tusks gaped open large enough for a grown man to step into. Moonlight and reflected weapons fire glinted off the rows of razor-sharp ivory teeth.

Thomas didn't know where the demons truly came from. That was one of the things the Templar researchers, the Ophanim—which were the intelligence agents within their ranks—tried to find out with all their investigations. With the disparity between the creatures, there was some conjecture that they didn't come from the same world. Some of the older Ophanim suggested that many of the creatures were subjugated species, ones that had been altered by the demons' awful magic.

The Carnagor sniffed the air again for an instant, then launched itself at Guy's still body. Its gigantic hands raked at the dead knight's armor, stripping it from him as if he were a shellfish. In the time it took Thomas to lift the Spike Bolter, the Carnagor had gulped Guy's remains down as if they'd only been an appetizer.

Then Thomas held the trigger down. The Spike Bolter fired, the six barrels whirled, and spiked bullets whistled into the side of the demon's head.

The creature turned toward Thomas, snuffling in fear and anger. It raised a stubby arm in front of its huge, ugly face. Bloody gashes opened up in its scaly flesh. Roaring, it jumped toward Thomas, taking away half the distance between them in a single bound.

Thomas felt the earth shake when the massive beast landed. Throwing its head back, the Carnagor loosed an echoing roar. Its fiery eyes fixed on Thomas.

Steeling himself, trusting his armor, Thomas holstered his sidearm, then took a two-handed grip on his sword. With a fierce war cry of his own, he raced at the beast, unwilling to let it go unchallenged after watching its unholy repast.

October 31, 2020

My Dearest Simon,

    First of all, I want you to know how much I've always loved you. I know I've been a harsh taskmaster. There are days, I'm sure, that you were certain I'd never be satisfied in your training. But you mastered everything I'd taught you. In fact, you surpassed me in your skills. I knew you would. You've always had more than a little of your grandfather's strength in you. And he was a fierce, grand Templar.

    But you outstripped my skills long before I thought you would. Perhaps that was the reason that we had so many conflicts over the last few years. It was hard, my son, letting you grow up, seeing you go out into the world to make your own mistakes. The world was a far harsher environment at your age than it was at mine. These days, it seems there's no forgiveness for the unwary.

    Now there may not be a hope for survival.

    At the time I'm sending this, we're preparing to go into battle against foes that all of us have trained to stand against all of our lives, but few of us truly ever expected to see. We won't be returning unless there's some miracle from Providence.

Tonight, I'm afraid. Truthfully, I'm afraid for myself. I always told myself that when the time came to lay down my life to protect those I swore to defend, that I would do so gladly. Tonight, I find that I am not glad, and that I'm more fearful than I should be. But I'll go forth when Lord Sumerisle leads us into battle.

Mostly, though, I'm afraid for you and for this world. What we knew of the demons pales in comparison to what we have learned. And we still don't know everything we need to know.

[cont'd]

The Carnagor lunged forward and snapped at Thomas. Ready for the move because that was a basic striking pattern for the creature, Thomas vaulted. His left foot landed on the Carnagor's right tusk and he centered his balance just as it jerked its head up to snap at him again.

Propelled by the Carnagor's efforts as well as his own, Thomas sailed into the air. The NanoDyne technology used in the armor spun through the mini-gyro systems and helped him stabilize. The armor not only increased his physical resistance, but it amplified his strength as well.

Thomas landed on the Carnagor's head. "Anchor," he ordered. Immediately, short spikes popped out of his boot soles and bit into the demon's scaly hide.

The Carnagor roared, but whether in pain or just the effrontery of the human standing on its head, Thomas didn't know. He reversed the sword, pointing it down, then rammed it home with all the strength he had at his command.

For a moment, Thomas didn't think the sword was going to punch through the thick skull. Then, with a dull, grating *thunk,* it did. He bore down on the weapon, shoving it all the way to the hilt.

Blood and gore spurted out around the blade. The Carnagor roared in pain then. It reared and battered itself against St. Paul's Cathedral.

Holding tightly to the imbedded sword, Thomas managed to stay atop the frenzied creature. He knelt, his left arm snaked around the sword to hold on.

"Knee anchors," he ordered.

The suit responded, driving another group of spikes from the metal knees to bite deeply into the Carnagor. Further locked into place, Thomas drew his right fist back. "Right hand hammer."

The gauntlet, powered by the NanoDyne technology memoryware, curled into a fist and became hard as an anvil. Raising his fist, Thomas bashed it against the Carnagor's skull beside the sword over and over. Unable to hold against the unflagging effort, the demon's skull fractured.

Bone turned sideways in the mass of ichor and gore at the top of the Carnagor's head. Thomas unlocked his fist just as his sword slid free. He slapped his left palm against the demon's head and triggered the anchors there. Locked into position again, holding on for dear life, the Templar reached deeply into the open cavity he'd created in his opponent's skull.

His fist crunched through the broken bone. He tore the Carnagor's brain out by the handful, emptying the skull. A moment later, the demon's movements became awkward and unbalanced. The Carnagor sagged against a tree, and uprooted it from the ground before collapsing, shuddering a final time, and lying still.

Bruised and battered inside the armor, feeling nowhere near triumphant, Thomas got to his feet. "My sword," he said.

Immediately, the HUD flicked a light on inside the 360-

degree view and revealed that the sword was behind him. He released the anchors and leaped from the Carnagor's back. His heavy weight drove his feet several inches into the blood-covered ground.

He drew the Spike Bolter as he crossed the ground to pick up his sword. He fisted it, then turned to look for his next opponent.

There were more demons than Templar remaining. In the distance, smoke blew across the urban landscape. Only a few days ago, London's citizens had shopped and eaten and worked in the area. Now it was little more than masses of rubble.

Tanks, armored cars, and other military machines the British Army had employed against the demons and found lacking lay abandoned, burned-out, and overturned in the streets like a child's broken toys. Conventional warfare hadn't even dented the demons' armament.

[con't]

Simon, I don't know how this news will reach you. Or when. I know only that it will come at an ill time. Bad news always does.

I remember when you left, how angry and proud you were. So full of yourself. I wasn't at my best. I apologize for that and hope you'll one day choose to remember the good times rather than the bad.

Just know that I don't begrudge those feelings. They're a young man's feelings. Most of us, myself included, have to feel wronged in order to separate from our parents. I know I did.

Maybe things would have worked out differently if your mother had lived. We'll never know. I'll never know. But remember that she loved you. You were the apple of her eye.

I know that you felt all the training we did here in the Underground was for naught. You argued that on more than one occasion. And when you wanted to enter the extreme sports field to glory in your physical prowess, I forbade it. That was my conditioning. As Templar, we're supposed to remain in the shadows, live quiet lives until such time as we are needed.

Well, the time is now, my son. I feel I'm being selfish by wishing that it hadn't happened in your time. But that would only have meant wishing this horrible act onto your children, or their children.

None of us should have to pay the blood price that's going to be required to see this thing through to the end. But that's what I swore to do, and I'll see it done.

The demons have arrived, Simon. They've come to London through the Hellgates, magical and technological openings between our world and theirs, and fulfilled the ancient prophecies. They're bigger and stronger than we ever thought they would be.

As I write this letter, as I prepare myself for the battle that lies ahead, I know only that you're in South Africa. I've tried the phone numbers that you left, but everyone there says you're off in bush country and won't be expected for a few more days as yet. I knew it had to be something like that since you didn't call when the demons first openly attacked. But several of the communications satellites have been destroyed by the demons as well.

The Templar may contact you, my son. If that's even possible. Or perhaps other Hellgates have opened around the world. I'm afraid I don't know. There's even a chance, and acknowledging it makes my heart heavy, that you'll never see this—my final letter to you. I pray that isn't so. A father should have a chance to tell his son a final good-bye.

If the Templar do speak with you, they'll want you back here, to fight and die in the battle to rid the world of the hellspawn. I don't know what your answer will be. With the odds so stacked against us, I don't know that there is a wrong answer. Fighting means dying, if not today, then tomorrow. The same for running.

I pray that there is a weakness in the demons, something they've overlooked, something that we may yet learn. And I pray that you stay safe and whole until I see you again.

I love you, Simon, with all my heart as I ever have.

> *Your Father*
> *Thomas Cross*
> *Templar Knight*
> *Seraphim of the House of Rorke*

Thomas ran. Not for his life, but that of another. Six Stalkers harried a female Templar. Her blue-tinted armor blazed azure sparks as the teeth and fangs of her attackers made contact. She wielded her sword with skill, causing ruby sparks to fly as she attacked. In the end, though, there were too many of them. Her attackers depended on numbers.

The Stalkers were small and wiry. Their lean, wolf-like bodies were covered in a mixture of fur and scales. Jagged, razor-edged claws stuck out from their forearms and backs. They had long, predatory snouts that opened up to rows of serrated teeth.

Thomas struck from behind, never thinking of giving

quarter. Stalkers were jackals, preferring to mass on a victim and strike when their prey wasn't looking or was already overwhelmed. Bringing his sword down in an overhand swing, Thomas cut and smashed through the Stalker's spine.

Instantly, the demon howled in pain, but then attacked Thomas. It dragged its paralyzed hindquarters behind, slowing it. Still, though, it went for his groin, looking for vulnerable areas. Thomas slammed the hilt of his blade against the creature's head, breaking teeth and crushing the skull. Twitching, fighting death every inch of the way, the Stalker collapsed to the ground.

The other Stalkers hadn't given up their attack on the female Templar, though. Although many in number, they worked with single-minded purpose. One of them leaped to the back of another, then vaulted onto the Templar's back.

Unable to stand against the assault, the Templar went down. Fangs and claws ripped at her armor, finally tearing it away.

"*No!*" Frantic, Thomas redoubled his efforts. He lopped the head from another Stalker just as the woman Templar put her blade through the throat of a third. No longer able to work with the sword as the Stalkers covered their fallen prey, Thomas abandoned his sword and drew the Spike Bolter.

Knotting his mailed hand in the scruff of razor-sharp tines across a Stalker's shoulders, Thomas pulled the demon free of the pack. It turned on him, lunging for his face. Thomas shoved the Spike Bolter into the demon's mouth and squeezed the trigger. Spikes erupted through the back of the Stalker's head as it continued to try to bite Thomas's hand off.

Thomas threw the carcass away. He put the pistol at the

back of another Stalker's head and pulled the trigger again. Spine severed, the demon went down in a mewling heap.

The surviving two Stalkers reluctantly sprang away, hissing and snarling challenges. They took up positions behind trees only a few feet away and called to others of their kind.

Thomas knew there wasn't much time. The Stalkers would re-mass at any moment. He picked up his sword and knelt to the woman.

Blood covered her armor, and it was the good, rich blood of a human, not the foul pus of a demon. Judging from the amount of it, Thomas doubted he'd arrived in time.

"Who . . . who are you?" The woman's weak voice echoed inside Thomas's helmet.

"Thomas." As long as he was in contact with the woman, a hand on her armor, he knew she'd hear him. "Thomas Cross."

"The Seraphim . . . of the House of . . . Rorke."

"Yes."

"I know you."

Thomas felt bad that he didn't know her.

"I'm . . . Kathleen. A knight. Of the House . . . of Stratham."

"We need to get you some help, Kathleen." Thomas kept his voice calm, as if they were only discussing crossing a busy street.

"Too . . . too late."

Somehow he knew she'd be smiling beneath her featureless mask. His hand against her armor told him her life signs were dropping. And there was nothing he could do.

"Die well," she whispered.

"I will."

She reached for his hand and he took it. Then the strength and the life fled from her.

Gently, Thomas placed her hand beside her. He thought about Simon again, about how this war—this unholy war—was going to be left to his son. *So few of them.* Levering himself to his feet, he surveyed the battlefield around St. Paul's Cathedral.

The demons were winning. Just as Grand Master Sumerisle had believed they would. The Templar were there to struggle and die, to shed so much blood that the demons thought them all dead.

Here and there, though, the Cabalists—the strange group that had allied themselves with the Templar to fight the demons—were in evidence. They fought not to die, but to better understand the enemy and to scrape up whatever weapons or even body parts the demons left behind. Thomas feared they had their own agenda, though, and it wouldn't be discovered until it was too late.

Remembering the woman he'd met, Keira Skyler, her strange clothing and the horns that jutted through her skin along her jaw, the writhing tentacles of hair, Thomas knew that those people could be a threat as well. If they had met under other terms, without the arrival of the demons through the Hellgates and the fate of the world hanging in the balance, Thomas knew they would not have been allies.

A raging, deep roar behind Thomas nearly froze the marrow in his bones. Locating the new threat on the HUD, he turned to face the demon, lifted his sword, and took aim with the Spike Bolter.

The demon towered fifteen feet tall, made even more huge and fearsome by the clustered spikes atop his reptilian head. Corded muscle stood out along his sinewy neck. Pointed fangs filled his huge, gaping maw. The broad expanse of his thick shoulders made his head look small by comparison. Broad-chested, clad in a gray-green chitinous growth as tough as Templar plate mail, the demon stood on legs thick as tree trunks. The scales picked up the light from the fires dancing atop the cathedral.

But the most fearsome thing about the demon was his left arm. It was impossibly huge, dwarfing his entire body. His right arm was thin and spindly, as if it would only take one good tug to yank it free.

"Shulgoth." Thomas didn't mean to say the demon's name. There were some who maintained that naming a demon aloud gave it strength. Thomas didn't know if he believed or disbelieved that.

But he knew this demon. He'd seen it crush the British military's finest weapons. Shulgoth had waded in among them fearlessly. Armor-piercing rounds and even sabot rounds fired by British tanks only bounced from his impervious hide. Single-handedly, Shulgoth had lain waste to tanks, armored cars, and self-propelled guns. He'd left only carnage in his wake.

Snarling in a harsh grating language Thomas didn't understand, Shulgoth opened his mouth and breathed out a cloud of vapor. Thomas ducked to the side but couldn't evade all of the thing's volatile breath. The gray steam slicked over his right arm and right side.

Instantly emergency lights flared up inside his HUD.

"Warning," the calm male voice said. "Outer integrity of armor has been breached on—"

"Cancel warning." Thomas ran, aware that Shulgoth raised his massive fist to slam down like a hammer. The Templar threw himself forward, rolled, and regained his feet as the blow struck the ground where he'd been.

Whirling, Thomas swung the sword into one of Shulgoth's legs. The keen blade, further enhanced by the magic the Templar had woven into the weapon, bit deeply into the demon's flesh. The acidic blood hissed and spat.

"Warning. The sword has taken—"

"Cancel warning." Thomas could already see the damage the sword had taken. The palladium alloy was the hardest substance the Templars had to work with. Even it wasn't impervious to the demons' powers. Or their blood. He yanked the sword free.

Thomas dodged two more blows, then pulled the Spike Bolter up and fired at Shulgoth's exposed eye. Rounds tracked along the side of the demon's head and glanced from the spikes, but none of them struck home.

In the next instant, Shulgoth swept Thomas up in his harsh grip. The Templar felt his arms and legs break, heard his armor splinter. His ribcage and the armor's torso became a vise over his lungs. He couldn't breathe, but if he had been able to, he would have screamed in pain. He tried to fire the Spike Bolter, but he knew then that it was too late.

Shulgoth lifted Thomas to face him. The demon grinned. The long tongue slathered through the horrible fangs.

Thomas wanted to shout defiance at the blasphemous thing, to let it know that he wasn't afraid. But he was afraid, and he knew he was dying. His crushed lungs wouldn't let him make a sound.

Opening his jaws wide, Shulgoth breathed out a noxious breath. The purple-gray mist coiled against Thomas's helm. In the next instant the HUD's display lit up with warnings. Pitting scarred Thomas's vision.

Then, mercifully, everything went black. But his last thoughts were of his son, of Simon, wondering if they would see each other again.

ONE

Loud gunshots woke Simon Cross from a too-short slumber and threw him directly into the path of a killer hangover. He sat up in the tent, automatically reaching for the hunting rifle beside his sleeping bag. He tried to figure out where the gunshots had come from, but had to admit that he might have dreamed them.

Or hallucinated them. He groaned and cursed as he forced himself to his feet. *You know better than to drink like that, you stupid git. Especially while you're out in the brush.*

Bright sunlight lay in wait outside the tent and the mosquito netting. No one else was up and about. The three other tents comprising the group of vacationing tourists he'd brought out to view the flora and fauna of the Fynbos grasslands for the last two weeks hadn't stirred.

Simon listened intently but the gunshots weren't repeated. *You dreamed it. Go back to bed. Get what little sleep you've got coming to you and be glad of it. With all that alcohol in your system, you're going to be sweating your bleeding guts out today.*

With a sigh, he turned back to the sleeping bag. Last night Saundra had joined him. Sometimes she did, but she liked to be out of his tent before their clients got out of bed.

Saundra McIntyre was long and lean, five foot ten if she was an inch, but he still towered seven inches above her and made her look small because he was so broad-shouldered.

She wore her long auburn hair pulled back in a ponytail. Freckles spattered her cheeks and nose.

He held a great affection for her, but it wasn't love. He'd been truthful about that. They'd been conducting safaris in the South African wilds together for the last sixteen months. Long enough to get to know each other really well. And to develop great affections for each other.

Neither one of them wanted to risk continuing the relationship anywhere else. Simon, if he ever went home again, lived in London. Saundra lived in Sidney, Australia. Both of them had family ties.

Simon figured he could leave his family—his father was it, more or less—behind easier than Saundra could, but he was unwilling to do that at this point. He preferred an . . . *extended* absence from England, he supposed, rather than a more permanent separation. That was the kindest way to put it. Saying it like that didn't feel so grim and so final.

He sighed. *You're thinking way too much. Dreaming strange things you've no business dreaming about. Imagining things. Then there's that huge hangover you're going to have to pay for last night's festivities.*

That had been a definite mistake. He'd told everyone when they'd left Cape Town that there weren't to be any unnecessary items in their gear. He and Saundra hadn't checked their clients' gear. If they hadn't been getting paid so well, Simon might have pressed the issue and looked to see who carried contraband. But they hadn't.

Jarl Klinker, the photographer from Dusseldorf, had brought in bottles of Russian vodka. He was part of the film research team. The other two claimed to be a director and a writer.

Simon put the hunting rifle down and climbed back into the sleeping bag. It was cool now, but the day would be hot.

"You're awake?" Saundra mumbled.

"Only just." Simon closed his eyes and lay back. Saundra snuggled up against him.

"Can't sleep?"

It was true that sometimes he couldn't. Too many unresolved complications, he supposed. "I can sleep."

"Are you sure you want to?" Saundra's voice held a throaty giggle. She kissed his ear.

Simon rolled over to face her. "Well, I still think that sleep is overrated. And no one is up, so—"

Two quick gunshots cracked the quiet morning again.

Saundra's eyes widened and Simon knew he hadn't imagined the gunfire. They both surged up from the joined sleeping bags. Three more gunshots followed.

Simon dove for his khakis and pulled them on. "How far away, do you think?"

"A half-mile. A mile." Saundra pulled her sleeveless shirt on. Worry pinched her face. "Too close."

Simon nodded. He stepped into his calf-high boots and quickly laced them. "I'll go investigate. You take care of the camp."

"Be careful." Saundra leaned back and pulled on her brush pants. Her stomach muscles corded up. "Take a radio."

Another two shots rang out.

Simon cursed the shooter as he shrugged into a beige t-shirt. He picked up the rifle and one of the small radios he carried for short-range communications. He dropped the radio into the backpack he slid over one shoulder. First rule of the wilderness was to never go anywhere without supplies.

"Take care of 'em." Simon unzipped the tent flaps and pushed through. "I'll be back quick as I can."

"I will."

Outside in the open area, Simon checked the compass built into his watch. The shots had come from the east, toward the interior and away from the coast.

"Mr. Cross." Rupert Dalton's balding head poked from one of the other tents. "Were those gunshots?"

"Yes."

"I thought you said it was illegal to hunt in this area." Dalton was in his late forties, a wiry man with an awkward way about him.

"It is," Simon assured the man.

Another couple of gunshots echoed over them.

Voices came from the other tents now. That was good. Saundra wouldn't have to wake everyone, and she'd have help waking those who were reluctant.

"Then whoever is doing the shooting must be a—"

"Stay with Miss McIntyre, Mr. Dalton." Simon took the rifle in both hands and headed out of camp at a jog.

Perspiration quickly covered Simon as the grasslands grew hotter with the rising sun. It peeked through the rose and cream mass of clouds to the east.

His head and stomach protested the strenuous exercise at first, but—as always—his body became regulated and he moved effortlessly. Once again, all the harsh conditioning his father had compelled Simon to do came to his aid.

When he'd been younger, he'd enjoyed the runs and the martial arts, especially the sword training. But that had been back when he was a boy and still believed that demons lurked somewhere out in the world just waiting for an opportunity to take it over again.

He didn't believe that anymore. One of his main problems was that he didn't know what to believe. All his life he'd been brought up to fight demons, trained in arcane ways and even taught limited mystical abilities. None of which could be talked about outside the Underground labyrinth where the Templar skulked in the shadows.

Simon had tired of all of it. Two years ago, at twenty-three, he'd left the Templar, his father, and all of London.

Talking about the training he'd received, about the cult-like atmosphere he'd been brought up in, would have done no good. Few left the ranks of the Templar, and only those who knew to keep their mouths shut escaped a date with the loony bin.

Simon pushed those thoughts away and concentrated on running. No hunting was allowed in the grasslands these days. He and Saundra carried hunting rifles only for self-protection and to protect their charges. Occasionally a lioness that had gotten too old to hunt and had been abandoned by her pride developed a taste for blood. But the biggest worry was from poachers.

Only minutes later, something less than two miles from camp, Simon found the shooters.

There were five of them. They were a scruffy lot, from their early twenties to their forties or fifties. All of them had the permanent sunburned look of men who had spent their entire lives in the bush.

They drove two four-wheel-drive Land Rovers strapped with extra tires, jerry cans of fuel, and water. Evidently they'd settled in for the long haul.

Five adult elephants lay on the sun-baked scrubby ground. Blood leaked into the dry dust. Overhead, vultures circled, waiting for the predators to leave.

A baby elephant tugged pitifully at its mother, wrapping its trunk around its mother's head and crying out. One of the hunters raised his rifle to his shoulder and fired. The baby elephant dropped in its tracks.

The killing happened before Simon knew it would. If he'd had a chance to stop it—

You don't know what you'd have done, mate. Simon concentrated on the men, working on seeing through the death. Settling into the shady protection of a camel-thorn acacia tree, he shrugged out of his backpack and watched the poachers.

He took a pair of expensive MechEye digital binoculars from his pack. His father had given them to him on his tenth birthday. And they were far better than those that any other guide he knew carried into the bush.

Depressing the power button, Simon zoomed in on the men as they went about their brutal business. They used handsaws to cut free the elephant tusks. Even with the recent decision to issue licenses to kill off a few hundred head of elephants after it was deemed their populations had grown too large to sustain them, ivory remained valuable on the black market.

The men worked with grim alacrity, tossing their bloody prizes into the backs of the Land Rovers. One of them stood guard, a rifle braced on one hip. His sunglasses reflected the orange coal of his cigarette as he smoked.

Simon captured images of the men and their grisly profit. The binoculars came fully equipped with a surprising array of software.

Okay then, you vicious cutthroats, you're going to pay for what you did here.

During the last sixteen months, Simon had gotten to know the Cape Town police and the gamekeepers that worked in the Fynbos Biome. The area was protected by international law.

Someone will know you.

Simon captured a few more images, then watched in silence as the corpses were stripped of their tusks. The radio vibrated in his pocket.

Leaning back, Simon shook the earpiece out and shoved it into his ear. "Yes."

"I just wanted to make sure you were all right." Saundra sounded worried. "I heard that final shot—"

"Wasn't me." Simon quickly explained what had gone on.

Saundra cursed when he'd finished. "We can't let them get away with this."

She had very strong feelings about preserving wildlife. As a result, they'd never guided hunters while working together. She knew that Simon did, when the price was right and the interest was there, but they never talked about that.

"I've got pictures of them. They won't get away with it."

The circling vultures dropped from the sky and alighted on the carcasses. Their hooked beaks and cruel talons tore into the elephant flesh.

"What are you going to do?" Saundra asked.

"Wait here. Watch them. Make sure they don't come your way. Get our tourists out of harm's way. I'll catch up to you quick as I can."

"All right."

Simon took his earpiece out and dropped it back into the radio. He pocketed the radio and pressed the Velcro tab closed on his thigh pocket.

Almost twenty minutes passed. The poachers worked quickly. So did the vultures.

Simon knew the blood scent would draw other predators. It always did. But he didn't expect the Cape buffalo that came up to the scene and stood in the scrubland on the other side of the kill site.

The buffalo was huge and black, with the wide, curving horns of its kind. This one looked near to six feet at the shoulder and weighing more than a ton. The face was massive, all bone and muscle. Most of the gamekeepers Simon knew regarded Cape buffalos as the most dangerous animals in the region. A single lion couldn't bring a Cape buffalo down, and it took a pack of hyenas to do the job.

Since it was alone, Simon guessed that it was a "bachelor." Older bulls were usually cut out of the herds by the younger bulls. People every year died on the horns or under the hooves of Cape buffaloes. They died hard, and most of them didn't die alone.

The poachers noticed the Cape buffalo, too. They pointed at the animal. The older men in the group got more wary. Even a Land Rover wasn't always the best protection out in the open. Cape buffaloes were quite capable of overturning vehicles.

One of the younger men brought his rifle to shoulder.

An older man shouted, "No!" but that happened at the same time the younger man fired.

The first bullet caught the Cape buffalo between the horns, knocking a chunk of hide flying. The buffalo staggered, throwing its head back. As a result, the second and third bullets hit the animal in the chest.

With an angry bellow, the buffalo broke cover and charged the poachers. Simon watched, hoping the buffalo would get them all.

The poachers scattered. The more seasoned among them ran to the elephants' bodies for refuge. The dead elephants were bigger and heavier than the Land Rovers.

Never breaking stride, the Cape buffalo slammed into the side of the lead Land Rover. The impact echoed under the acacia tree where Simon sat. Incredibly, the Land Rover came up on two wheels and rolled over onto its side with a *crunch*.

Still in motion, the animal sped into the trees and tall

shrubs. It disappeared almost immediately. The young poacher got his nerve back and tried two more shots that Simon doubted hit anything.

The older poacher crossed to the younger one, grabbed the rifle barrel, and backhanded the other man to the ground. Then he turned the rifle on the younger man, who threw his hands up in front of him and tried to scoot away on his back. For a moment Simon thought the man was going to kill the younger man.

"That was stupid." The older poacher lowered the rifle, then finally tossed it onto the younger man. "Do something like that again, and I'll kill you." He turned and walked away.

Simon settled back into the shadows. The radio vibrated in his pocket and he took it out. "Still not me, love," he whispered, then explained what had happened. "Are you out of camp?"

"Yes. About two miles west. We're headed for the coast. I think the tour's over. At least for the moment." Saundra didn't sound happy about that. She hated being stuck in Cape Town with nothing to do. She couldn't make money in town.

"There are a few campsites we'll have to visit between here and there," Simon pointed out. "Maybe we'll convince them that making an early retreat isn't what they really want to do." Personally, he didn't care. He enjoyed Cape Town. At least it wasn't London. And he didn't have to hear any talk about demons.

But it meant being around Saundra when she wasn't happy. That wasn't a pleasant prospect.

"I don't want to go back," Saundra said.

"I know. Something will come up." Simon sighed, watched as the poachers gathered by the overturned vehicle and pushed it upright once more. "In the meantime, I'm going to be a little late."

"Why?"

"Got to track down that buffalo bull. Can't let it wander around out here to hurt someone. And it shouldn't be left to linger and die of infection." Simon listened to Saundra breathing over the radio connection. He knew she was frustrated and concerned.

"Go," she said finally. "Just take care of yourself."

In spite of the dire circumstances, Simon grinned. Saundra didn't like to hunt, but he did. And the wounded Cape buffalo was a danger he didn't want to leave out in the wild.

Cautiously, Simon made his way through the brush. He angled around the kill site where the poachers concentrated on the condition of their vehicle, then took up the trail of the wounded animal. A few minutes later, he found the first few bright crimson splatters on leaves where the Cape buffalo had vanished into the scrub.

Judging from the amount of blood, the animal had been severely wounded. Left to its own, it might die anyway. But that might take days. Wounded as it was, it was also dangerous.

Simon slung the hunting rifle over his shoulder and took up the trail.

TWO

The Cape buffalo stood in a stream and drank noisily. Two hyenas cowered in a tangle of broken rock and brush. Blood pulsed down the buffalo's chest, but from his position behind a thick-boled acacia tree Simon could see that the wound had slowed.

He felt badly for the animal. The wounds would never heal properly in the wild. Infection would settle in around the bullet and turn gangrenous. He focused on the fact that it would have a hard death ahead of it if he didn't kill it.

Of course, there was also the possibility the buffalo would kill him.

That made Simon smile, and he knew if Saundra had seen him she would have taken him to task for it. So would his father.

But that bit of uncertainty to life was what drove Simon. It had been that draw to the daredevil side of his nature that had made him the skateboard champ he'd become for a while. With the LiquidBalance technology available to the boards, he'd gone faster and higher—especially since those boards had limited hover ability—than anyone had before.

Then his father and the Templar Grand Master had made it plain that extreme sports weren't going to be in his future. Too many people had come around asking too many questions. Then there'd been that base-jump from Big Ben. He'd done that one after getting in trouble for doing the one from the Tower of London. Just to throw it in their faces before he left London. If the police had caught him, Simon would have served time for that one. He'd gotten out of London just in time and made his way down to South Africa.

Quietly, smoothly, Simon slipped out of the rifle sling and the backpack. He laid both to the side.

For the last hour, he'd tracked the buffalo, watching as the blood trail had thinned but had never completely gone away. For all he knew, the poachers might have gone, or they might not have noticed a round going off somewhere else.

On the other hand, they might be only a short distance behind him and might wonder if he'd seen them killing the elephants. Especially since he was trying to kill the Cape buffalo one of them had wounded.

He reached into his backpack and took out one of the expanding punching daggers he'd bought shortly after he'd arrived in South Africa. The daggers were deadly weapons, modeled on the Indian katar, also known as the Bundi dagger.

Collapsed, the weapons were easily stored, but the segmented blades sprang out of the forearm brace and provided twenty inches of razor-sharp steel. The Roman army had conquered the world with eighteen-inch blades.

Simon strapped the punching dagger onto his right arm, took a final quiet breath to focus his mind, then eased through the brush toward the Cape buffalo. He moved in a crouch, like a tightly coiled spring.

The old bull wasn't foolish, though. It had gained experience over the years, and—wounded as it was—it was especially wary. Shoulders rippling, the bull swung about just as Simon emerged from the brush.

Simon froze. The punching dagger hung loose and ready at his side.

Beneath the rocks and brush, the hyenas laughed in anticipation, as if they knew they were going to be eating in a few minutes one way or the other.

Breathing easily, Simon stood his ground. He locked eyes with the buffalo, wondering if it was simply going to run away again. He didn't want to have to chase after it.

Without warning, the bull charged. Its hooves tore into the earth, cutting free clods that sailed in its wake. Tremors raced through Simon's feet and legs. He waited till the last instant, then dove and rolled to the side.

The Cape buffalo's horn sliced a groove in the ground only inches from Simon. Pushing himself to his feet again, Simon whipped around, seeing only then that the huge animal had spun on a dime and was once more right on top of him.

This time Simon launched himself into the air, barely getting over the bull's horns. Tucking himself into a roll, he landed on the animal's broad back for just a moment, then slid off its glossy hide. He dropped to his feet, finding his balance only just in time to save himself again.

Spinning, seeing that the bull was faltering now from its exertions and that the wounds had opened up again, Simon gave chase to the animal. When he closed to within a few feet of it, he vaulted onto its back.

The bull went insane, throwing itself into the air as it sought to rid itself of the unwanted passenger. Simon tried to hold on with his knees, but the thick expanse of the Cape buffalo's back was too broad to properly manage. He knew he was going to fall; it was only a matter of time.

He threw himself forward and roped an arm around the bull's neck as far as he could. He strained to hang on, to keep his balance. As he watched, the radio came free of his thigh pocket, landed on the ground, and was crushed beneath one massive hoof. When the bull's foot lifted again, only pieces remained.

Setting himself as best as he was able, Simon drew the

punching dagger up, then shoved it between the Cape buffalo's ribs and into its heart. For another moment, he hung on desperately, not trusting the fall or his ability to avoid the rampaging hooves. In the next, the buffalo suddenly gave out and fell, a mountain of rolling flesh that dropped at the edge of the stream.

Stunned, Simon sprawled beside the great beast. Shafts of sunlight slashed through the trees overhead. He lost consciousness briefly, scared because he wasn't sure if he was paralyzed or if he was breathing.

When Simon opened his eyes again, one of the hyenas was almost on him. The scavenger's nose was wrinkled back to expose sharp, yellow teeth.

Simon moved out of instinct, slashing the hyena's throat with the punching dagger. Blood sprayed, but the animal ran until its life fled.

Drawing a deep breath, Simon levered himself to his feet. The other hyena ran off, barking with insane laughter. Simon looked down at the Cape buffalo and saw at once that it was dead. He felt bad for it. Just like the elephants the poachers had killed, the buffalo had simply been in the wrong place at the wrong time.

After washing the punching dagger in the stream, Simon went back to survey the damage to the radio. It was immediately evident that the radio was a total loss.

So much for impact-resistant.

Returning to the tree where he'd left his gear, Simon collapsed the dagger and put it away. He hefted the backpack and his hunting rifle, took out his good compass to check the direction, and started back toward camp.

Back at the campsite, Simon knew things had gone badly wrong. He'd known they would when he started tracking the tire marks left by the poachers' vehicles and found they headed toward the campsite.

For a little while he'd let himself hope that the poachers wouldn't find the campsite. But as soon as they'd gotten into the area, Simon knew the men were hunting them too. Tire tracks cut through the abandoned campsite, rolling through the gray ash of the campfire.

Simon cursed himself and surveyed the terrain. The poachers hadn't had any problems picking up Saundra's trail. Saundra hadn't had time to hide her tracks, and with tourists in tow, that hadn't been possible.

There was little doubt that the poachers had probably overtaken Saundra and the others by now.

And what will they do? Kill them for possibly being witnesses to their poaching?

The possibility flushed ice water through Simon's veins. He redistributed his pack across his shoulders and pushed himself into a jog. He'd lost over two hours tracking the wounded Cape buffalo. His sweat-drenched clothing clung to him. His muscles protested, but he pushed himself forward.

Four and a half miles later, as best as Simon could guess, he found where the poachers had overtaken Saundra and their group.

Hyenas savaged Dalton's and Carey's bodies, growling at each other as they claimed their meals. Both men had been executed, a bullet between the eyes and powder marks to show the proximity.

Breath burning in his lungs, Simon dropped to his knees beside the men and checked their pulses even though he knew he wouldn't find any. He closed their staring eyes and got up again.

Why did they kill you? Did you resist? Simon couldn't believe that. *Or to make a point?* That felt more right even though it was ultimately more wrong.

He swung back to search the ground, barely holding the panic within him in check. There were footprints and tire tracks everywhere. He figured that the poachers had found Saundra and the tourists in the brush, flushed them toward the trail, then killed Dalton and Carey and loaded the survivors onto the Land Rovers.

Saundra's alive. The others are alive. Simon chose to concentrate on that instead of the dead men. Despite his fatigue, he sipped water from his canteen and ate an energy bar as he walked. When he finished, he began to run again.

"What are they going to do to us?"

Calming herself, Saundra turned to face one of the women in the group. It was a struggle to remember the woman's name. Saundra hated that; she prided herself on getting the names of her charges sorted out promptly. She was a perfectionist. Simon teased her unmercifully for that.

Simon. She wondered if he was still alive. So far the poachers hadn't said anything about killing him. He couldn't be dead. She wouldn't let him be dead. She'd never known a man more alive than Simon Cross. But he wouldn't have given in to their captors either. She knew that as well.

"Miss McIntyre? Did you hear me?" The woman whispered more forcefully.

"I heard you." Saundra made herself speak calmly. She was anything but calm. The poachers had tied their hands behind them with rope, then tied them together around a tree. At first Saundra had tried to break free, but her hands had quickly gone numb from lack of blood circulation.

"Well?"

"I don't know what they're going to do."

The woman was young, probably in her mid-twenties, the same age as Saundra. But she hadn't seen as much of the cold callousness of life that Saundra had. The woman lowered her head as she wept. Tears ran down her dusty cheeks, leaving muddy furrows behind.

Saundra's first impulse was to tell the woman—*Cherie,* the name just popped into her head—that everything was going to be all right. But she didn't. One of her first rules, one she'd had to teach Simon, was not to ever promise a paying client something you couldn't deliver.

So she let the woman cry. One of the others, Denise, leaned in to her. They whispered in French, and Saundra only had marginal French. The two women came from France, somewhere outside of Paris, Saundra thought, but she couldn't be sure now. They'd come on a grand adventure, hoping to meet men that would make them forget about boring jobs.

They're not thinking about work now, Saundra thought, and she felt guilty as soon as the thought had manifested. She scanned the camp.

Night was coming, lengthening and deepening the shadows. As soon as the sun dipped below the horizon, full dark would be upon them for a time before the moon rose. It had been full last night, but Saundra couldn't remember if that had been the second or third night.

The men sat around the campfire eating the supplies Saundra and Simon had outfitted their clients with. They'd also found the vodka left over from last night.

In the flickering firelight, Saundra thought she recognized two of them. She knew that wasn't good. If she knew them, they probably knew her. They wouldn't want any witnesses talking about what they'd been doing. Gamekeepers would find the elephants' bodies soon enough, and they'd be looking for the people responsible.

You're a witness, she reminded herself. *That's like an inch away from being dead.* She pulled at the ropes again, but she still couldn't feel her hands or the ropes. The others were all in the same shape. Even if they'd been able to sit back to back without getting noticed, they wouldn't have been able to untie the ropes.

Worn and weary, caked in dirt and dried sweat, Simon knelt beside an acacia tree and peered through the open sights of his hunting rifle. It was a bolt-action .375 Weatherby Magnum. Even as quick as he was, he could only get off one round, perhaps two, before the poachers reacted. By then the survivors might try for hostages.

The rifle wasn't the way to do this. And if he'd been a regular wilderness guide, he wouldn't have been the man for what he had to do.

He put the rifle to the side and reached into the backpack again. Taking out both punching daggers, he strapped them on. Then he crept deeper into the shadows, getting closer to the poachers.

The men didn't think they were being followed. Otherwise they'd have posted guards. More than that, they wouldn't have been sitting around the fire where they'd be highlighted so easily and ruining their night vision with full dark coming on.

Even as he worked his way toward them, Simon kept his eyes averted from the fire and used his peripheral vision. In darkness, direct vision suffered. It was what was seen from the corner of the eye that was seen best.

He counted all five of them. He could smell them now, too. Even over the smoke from the fire, he scented their unwashed musk and sour odors. Saundra often told him he had the keenest nose of any man she'd ever met. She also said that about his hearing and eyesight.

That was due, in part, to the training Simon's father and the other Templar had put him through. Even down in the Underground, there had been combat zones and tests and trials. He'd been shown how to use all his senses in battle.

"—some kind of craziness goin' on over the radio an' the television," one man said. "I heard there was some kind of alien invasion going on in London. Said some kinda beasts just beamed down from a mothership of some kind."

"That's a bunch of crap if you ask me," another man said.

Simon moved out of the brush, crouched down, and eased one foot in front of the other. He couldn't believe what he was hearing. His first thoughts were of his father. But aliens weren't demons. Then he was behind the closest Land Rover, inching his way forward, trying to figure out how the men would split once they knew he was there.

"Nobody asked you," the first speaker growled. "So just keep your trap shut."

The second speaker made a rude comment.

"What kind of aliens?" someone else asked.

"From another world," the first speaker said. "What kind of other aliens is there?"

"Like those aliens out of *Alien*? Or like the ones out of *Predator*?"

"How should I know?"

"You said you seen 'em."

"On tri-dee."

"When?"

"Few days ago. While we were back in Cape Town. Before we got ready to come out here."

"Did they say where they came from?"

"No."

"That would be interestin'. I wouldn't mind baggin' a few aliens."

The other men laughed.

Hunkering down beside the front of the Land Rover, Simon took fresh grips on the punching daggers. He shoved all the questions and extraneous thoughts from his mind and achieved the focus his father had trained him to have. He took in a deep breath and let it out.

Then he moved, as quick as he could, going for the man closest to him. The poacher sat in a collapsible canvas chair that Simon thought he recognized from the gear their clients had brought. There was no hesitation in Simon as he attacked, no forgiveness. Seeing Dalton and Carey had drained that from him. If he was going to save Saundra and their clients, he couldn't be merciful.

Except for quick deaths. And that was more a tactical choice than out of compassion. A dead man couldn't get back up at an inopportune time.

Still crouching as he closed on the nearest man from behind, Simon rolled his right arm forward, twisting his hips and getting his shoulder behind the blow. The katar sliced through the canvas back of the chair, then sank deeply into the poacher's back and punched through his chest.

Kicking out, Simon yanked the dagger from the dead man and knocked him forward into the fire. The smell of cooking flesh and burned hair filled his nose. He whirled, going back behind the Land Rover as one of the poachers pointed a rifle at him and fired.

THREE

The rifle shot jerked Saundra's attention back to the poachers. She'd drifted off to sleep, never knowing when she'd given in to the fatigue that clung to her after spending tense hours traveling in the hot Land Rovers.

A dead poacher lay in the fire, one of the younger men, not their grizzled leader. Flames embraced the body, quickly catching the clothing on fire. The four other men were up and moving, bringing their rifles and pistols to bear on an unseen target.

For a moment Saundra thought perhaps they'd started arguing among themselves. Then she realized that all four surviving men were circling the Land Rover, obviously pursuing someone or some *thing*. She couldn't imagine the predator that would so brazenly attack the men.

A flurry of movement erupted from beneath the vehicle. A long blade flicked out across the back of a man's legs. Blood spurted as the man screamed and went down. He tried to hang on to his rifle.

Simon Cross shot out from under the back of the Land Rover as the three other men turned to their fallen comrade. Saundra's heart thudded to life in her chest, but it was more out of fear for Simon than in any hope he might rescue them. She'd seen him fight before, in bars when someone got physical, or to protect her from a drunk that wouldn't take no for an answer.

But that was different. The poachers wouldn't hesitate for a moment to kill him. Saundra was certain they'd kill her and her clients before it was over with. The only thing that had forestalled that up till now had been the possibility of ransom.

In the darkness, Simon looked huge and dangerous, like some big cat. He was six feet five inches tall, broad-shouldered with a narrow waist, no spare flesh on him anywhere. His dark blond hair gleamed in the firelight. Even though she couldn't see them, Saundra knew his eyes were pale blue fire.

He moved like a dancer, hauling himself up onto the back of the Land Rover, then throwing himself forward before the poachers could react. Saundra got a brief glimpse of the two blades he wore on his hands. She'd noticed them in his backpack, and a few times she'd seen him working out with them when he'd thought he was by himself. Reaching the top of the Land Rover, he threw himself forward.

"Up there!" the fallen man roared.

The three poachers still standing turned to meet the threat. Before they could fire, Simon was among them, landing with the grace of a skilled gymnast. His blades flashed. One shot through the throat of a poacher, sending the man stumbling backward. The poacher forgot about his weapons and wrapped his hands around his slashed throat.

A second man wheeled on Simon, pointing his pistol and firing at almost point-blank range. But Simon wasn't there when the shots arrived. The bullets drilled holes into the Land Rover.

Saundra watched, unable to do anything, certain Simon was going to be dead in seconds.

* * *

Two men dead, another incapacitated, and two to go, Simon thought grimly. He furled the katars in against his body, spun back into the man with the pistol, then blocked the weapon up with the back of his right hand. Whirling in, Simon drove his left-hand katar into the man's exposed ribcage and pierced his opponent's heart.

As the newly dead man dropped, Simon went after the last man. Bullets sparked from the katar blades as Simon held them up defensively. The movement was sheer instinct. There'd been no hope that the blades would fend off bullets, but one of them hit and ricocheted and the others went wide of the mark.

The poacher tried to run and shoot at the same time, and didn't succeed at either. As a result, Simon blocked the man's efforts, then swept the man's legs out from under him with his own. When the poacher fell on his back on the ground, Simon pinned him there with the katar.

Surprised and scared, the poacher reached for the blade, wrapping his fingers against the sharp steel and cutting himself to the bone. Another breath, though, and he was past caring about the new injuries.

Simon watched the man's eyes dull, the pupils broaden and relax. Before tonight, he'd never killed another man. Now he'd killed four of them in under a minute. It was unreal. Nothing his father or the other Templar had trained him to do had prepared him for this.

"Simon!"

Saundra's voice drew Simon from his reverie. He put a foot on the dead man and yanked the katar free, then whirled to face the man whose legs he'd sliced.

The poacher had his rifle in his hand and was trying to bring it to bear. Simon ducked to the side and kicked. His foot connected with the rifle and sent it spinning away. In the next heartbeat, his blade was at the man's throat.

Closing his eyes, the poacher threw his hands out to his sides. "Don't kill me! Please don't kill me!" His eyes fluttered open and closed, as if he was afraid to look but was afraid not to look.

Simon thought about the way he'd found Dalton's and Carey's bodies, left out for the scavengers to have their way with. The poacher didn't deserve to live. The Cape Town authorities weren't going to be lenient with them.

But it was one thing to kill a man when he was capable of defending himself, and another to do the deed in cold blood, when he was helpless. Surprisingly, Simon thought—if the circumstances warranted it—that he could do it.

The poacher must have seen that too. "Please." His voice was a hoarse whisper.

Simon knew it would only take one quick thrust to cut the man's carotid arteries. He'd bleed out in seconds and it would be relatively painless. Not at all what Dalton and Carey had had to endure.

"Simon." Saundra's voice was calm. "He can't hurt anyone. Don't. You've done enough." She paused. "Simon. Do you hear me?"

Feeling cold and distant, Simon looked at the man. "You're lucky." He lifted the blade from the poacher's neck. "Feel free to go ahead and try something stupid, though."

The poacher lay back, his chest heaving. He closed his eyes and swallowed.

Simon got to his feet and unstrapped one of the katars with his teeth. He picked up the man's rifle and threw it into the nearest Land Rover.

"I'm not going to move," the poacher declared. "I'm going to lay right here." His accent sounded German or Dutch. Simon's ear hadn't developed enough to tell the difference.

Without a word, Simon walked to the captives. He cut Saundra free with the katar, then gave her his boot knife to free the others.

Simon found the stream only a short distance from the campsite the poachers had chosen. He'd left Saundra in charge of the clients. He could have gotten them organized, but none of them wanted to be around him much.

Last night he'd been the life of the impromptu party. Tonight he'd killed four people.

Be fair, Simon chided himself. *They saw two of their own get killed today, too. It might not all be you.*

While on safari, Simon had seen three people get killed. Thankfully none of those instances had been through any fault of his. One had been gored by a Cape buffalo. Another had been taken by a crocodile when he waded too far out into a river. And the third had been killed in a knife fight with another man.

Each of those incidents had left their marks on him. He knew their clients wouldn't soon forget their own experiences.

He knelt at the water's edge, feeling the wet mud soak into the khaki pants. Across the stream, a four-foot long crocodile lay half-buried in the mud and in the water. It watched Simon with cold eyes that looked bluish in the moonlight.

Other nocturnal birds and rodents drank from the water or went hunting. Some of them preyed on each other.

Leaning forward, Simon scooped up water in both hands and splashed his face. Cuts and scratches he'd collected while scrambling under and over the Land Rover stung. Before he knew it, he was sick, throwing up into the water. It lasted for only a short time and he tried to keep it quiet, but it left him drained and shaking.

"Are you all right?"

The voice belonged to Saundra. She stood somewhere behind him.

The slow current floated the sickness away. Simon leaned forward and splashed water in his face again. He hated the taste of bile trapped at the back of his throat.

"I'm fine."

"Did they hurt you?"

"No." Simon wished she'd go away. He'd come out here to be alone.

"What you did, Simon—"

He turned to look at her then. "What I did was kill four men. That's pretty horrible, don't you think?" He realized he was speaking louder than he'd intended.

Saundra didn't back away from him. Instead, to his surprise, she came to him and dropped to her knees. She looked him in the eyes.

"Yes," she said softly. "It was pretty horrible. And if there'd been another way, I wouldn't have wanted you to kill them. But there wasn't another way. I know that. Our clients know that." She paused. "And you know that."

Simon didn't say anything.

She leaned into him and took him into her arms, holding him tightly. "I was afraid for you. I thought they were going to kill you. I didn't know you could do that."

"Honestly, neither did I." *I was trained to fight monsters, not men.* But he couldn't tell her that, of course. He remained quiet, leaning into her, feeling her heat against the cooling night and the loneliness around him.

Back in the camp, Simon got out one of the tarps they used to set the tents up on. He placed it on the front of one of the Land Rovers, then grabbed the dead poacher lying in the fire by the feet and dragged him out of the coals.

The fire had burned away the man's hair and his face. Only a grinning blackened skull remained. The stench was stomach-churning and seemed to hang in the air all around the campsite.

Simon used water from the stream to put out the smoldering clothing that had melted to the dead man's upper torso. When he was certain the fire was finished, he dragged the dead man to the tarp. Then he went back for the next one, grabbing him by the boot heels and depositing him with the other.

At first, no one else moved. They only watched in silence. Then Saundra helped him with the third while two of the male clients dragged the fourth over to the tarp.

"What are you going to do with them?" Blaisdell asked. He was an American, working on a book, he'd said.

"Take them back to Cape Town." Simon grabbed one end of the tarp and folded it over the corpses. Saundra took the other end and helped him.

"Why? So they can have a burial?" Anger edged Blaisdell's words. "They don't deserve that. They should be left out here. Let the animals get them."

Simon started to reply, but knew he was going to be heated about it.

"Then those animals might develop a taste for human flesh," Saundra interrupted calmly. "Furthermore, seeing these men come back in this condition might give pause to anyone else who might try something like this. We're not doing them any favors. They're dead. They don't care anymore."

Blaisdell dropped his head and backed away. "I'm sorry. But I liked Dalton. He didn't deserve what happened to him. Neither did Carey."

Simon silently agreed.

When he and Saundra had finished wrapping the dead

men, they wrapped them in ropes and secured the grisly bundle to the Land Rover. It was too much like a big-game hunter's trophy kill to suit Simon, but there was nothing to be done about it.

Picking up the remains of Dalton and Carey was worse. Simon and Saundra fired shots into the air to scare off the larger predators that didn't give way to the lights from the Land Rovers. The smaller carnivores ran and hid at once.

Simon took another tarp and a large flashlight. He also wore one of the pistols he'd taken from the poachers. Then he went after the remains.

Carey's body was mostly intact, but Dalton's was scattered. They had to pick it up in pieces. Saundra got sick and finally could no longer help. Simon pushed himself through the queasiness and made himself complete the task.

Dalton had a wife and children. They'd want to bury as much of their father as they could. Finding everything he could took Simon the biggest part of an hour.

At midnight, miles from the campsite and well on their way back to Cape Town, Simon stood guard while Saundra took care of the clients. He kept his hunting rifle across his knees.

Most of the clients were quiet. If left to their own devices, Simon felt certain they would have eventually gone to sleep in the tents. But Saundra had insisted on heating some of the soup stock they'd brought.

After their clients were taken care of, she brought a bowl of soup to him. It was crowded with chunky vegetables and beef, a substantial meal. Despite the scent of death that still hung in Simon's nostrils, the soup smelled divine.

Saundra sat cross-legged across from him with her own bowl of soup. They ate in silence for a while.

"I don't think we can count on any return business with this group," Saundra said. "Nor any good word-of-mouth from any of them. Not even the travel writer."

Simon nodded. She was just talking. He knew that.

"You feeling any better?"

Glancing at her, Simon nodded. "I'll feel even better when we get back to Cape Town."

"That should be by tomorrow afternoon now that we have the Land Rovers."

Simon shook his head. "I didn't think to check the fuel." He started to set the bowl aside.

"I already did. We've got enough."

Some of the tension unwound from Simon's stomach. Saundra was bright and capable. It felt good that not everything was riding on his shoulders.

"How's our other guest?" Simon referred to the surviving poacher.

"Hurting. Scared. I think the bleeding's finally stopped. I thought we were going to have to cauterize the wounds." Saundra ate some of her soup. "He's worried that he could be crippled for life."

"With the court system, he won't live long enough to get through rehab."

Saundra looked at him. "You sound different."

"Different how?"

She hesitated for a moment, then shrugged. "Cold."

Simon thought about that. His father and the other Templar had taught him that about life. When he'd grown up, he'd trusted little outside of the Templar. Most of his life had been spent down inside the Underground in London. For the first few years he'd been homeschooled there. He hadn't gotten out into the real world until he was a teen.

And he'd never been able to make friends. He couldn't bring those people back to the Underground and show them the dojos and training schools that were set up there. He hadn't been able to have fights, either. The first time he had, he'd nearly killed the two boys who had tried to hurt him. He still didn't know what Grand Master Sumerisle had had to do to get him out of trouble. But he hadn't been allowed out of the Underground complex for a month afterward.

"I just want to get back," Simon said finally. But he also wanted to talk to the poacher, to learn more about that supposed invasion of London.

The man was sleeping in back of one of the Land Rovers. He lay atop a pallet of tusks. Simon hadn't gotten rid of those because disposing of them would have been useless. Someone would have claimed them. And they were valuable. The money gleaned from the sale could help pay for Dalton's and Carey's funerals.

"Wake up," Simon growled.

The man opened his eyes and looked groggy. Saundra hadn't mentioned giving him painkillers from the med kit, but Simon suspected that she had.

"What?" Fear and suspicion tightened the man's voice.

"What did you hear about the London invasion?" Simon stood with his arms folded across his chest.

"You woke me to ask that?"

Simon reached out like he was going to grab one of the man's heavily bandaged feet.

"Don't," the man moaned. He bent his knees and pulled his feet up toward him.

"Tell me about London."

"There's not much to tell. We heard about it in a bar before we left Cape Town. They had some vid, too, but it looked like a bunch of crap if you ask me. They showed these images of these . . . *things*. I don't know what else to call them."

"What did they look like?"

"I don't know. The vids they had on the news weren't very good. Said that only a few people had made it out of London at the time. These *things* had some kind of weapons that made it impossible for most people to leave. Either that, or they're all dead. The reports said a lot of people have gotten killed over there."

"How did they get there?"

The poacher pinched his nose. Simon knew it was the painkillers. He'd had to take them in the past for injuries he'd received skateboarding and base-jumping. A lot of them had made his nose feel numb and tingly at the same time.

"Don't rightly know. The newsmen were guessing that they mighta beamed down. Other people guessed that they opened up some kind of dimensional portal and stepped through."

"What about the British Army? Surely they're dealing with this."

"They're dead," the poacher said. "Most of 'em, anyway. I seen lots of footage of them getting killed."

Simon stepped away from the poacher and headed back to where he'd left Saundra standing guard. Things his father had told him kept coming back to haunt him. Thomas Cross had always claimed that when the demon forces came to the earth, no human without special training and weapons would be able to stand against them.

"Well?" Saundra asked.

Simon shook his head.

"Didn't he tell you anything?"

"Enough that I wish we were in Cape Town right now."

"You've got family in London, don't you?"

"My father."

"What about your mother?"

"She died from cancer when I was three. I barely remember her." That was something Simon had never gotten past when he'd learned of it. His mother had died in one of the hospitals where the Templar were cared for. Simon didn't believe the hospital was as sophisticated as the ones in London proper had been. He didn't see any way that could be true. They'd never taken her anywhere else for treatment.

And because the Templar were so prideful and paranoid, his mother had died without him ever having the chance to get to know her.

"You must be worried about your father," Saundra said.

"Not really." Thomas Cross had always been able to take care of himself.

Simon stretched out on the ground and tried to make his mind be quiet. He didn't know what he would do if the demons had finally returned to the world as the Templar had always claimed they would.

In the end, he suspected he wouldn't have to do anything. After all, his father and men like him had trained all their lives to handle just such an occasion. What could go wrong?

But he couldn't escape the nagging feeling that something had. Hadn't the poacher claimed that the British Army had been destroyed? Or was that the truth being stretched? A last jab at Simon's peace of mind?

After a long time, Simon finally slept, but the dreams were all bad, brought on by all the warnings and fearful stories he'd learned as a child. He kept seeing the Monster, the winged demon, that the Templar kept on display at the school. His father had said that it had been created from what they'd understood of the demons and placed there so no one would ever forget why they were there in the Underground, and what they trained for.

Years ago, the Templar had been ostracized by Philip IV as devil worshippers because they'd tried to build a demon's skeleton from bones they'd known weren't human. They'd intended to study the bones and get a better understanding of the demons. Instead, the king had used the opportunity to seize Templar lands and fortunes.

Simon had long ago stopped thinking the demon had ever been real. It had just been a prop the Templar had used to scare their children with.

Hadn't it?

FOUR

"Don't you think you might come away from the window, sir?"

Detective Chief Superintendent Alfred Hyde lowered his binoculars and turned toward the speaker. The superintendent was actually a little unnerved because he hadn't heard the man enter the dark room. And what with all the . . .

Hyde sighed. Despite everything he'd seen, he couldn't bring himself to call the improbable beings that had established a beachhead at St. Paul's Cathedral demons. Although it would be fitting, given what he'd seen them do, naming them as such didn't quite seem sane.

The room was black with shadows. Only a sliver of moonlight touched the floor, and the chief superintendent made certain none of it touched him. They were on the fifty-ninth floor of the Bishopsgate Tower, one of the newest buildings in London. During the battles against the invaders, the building had taken several direct hits. So far the enemy hadn't seen fit to destroy it.

"Who are you?" Hyde asked. He knew the man wasn't one of the personal guard that followed him around. Nor was he worried about the man's presence. His team would have verified his identification. More than that, the man looked human. Not like . . . the others.

The young man snapped to attention in a way that belied his casual dress. All of them had learned not to wear the uniform of the Metropolitan Police Service. The creatures that had invaded the city harbored especial ill will toward anyone in uniforms.

Hyde didn't know if that was because of the attack by the British military forces in the beginning, or because of the knights.

Calling the armored men knights somehow didn't quite seem sane either, but the men who'd survived in the ranks called them that despite edicts from on high. Given the mode of dress those men wore and the heroic way they'd laid down their lives fighting the enemy, there was no way they were going to be called anything less.

"Officer Krebs, sir. William Krebs." The young man saluted smartly.

"No salutes, Krebs," Hyde said. "It's one thing if you go off and get yourself killed, but I don't want you identifying me as a ranking officer to one of those bloody . . . *things.*"

The young man looked embarrassed. "Yes, sir."

"And stop calling me 'sir,' confound it." Hyde was in his fifties, a fit, solid man with white hair and mustache. He wore round-lensed glasses.

Krebs wisely remained silent.

"I suppose you didn't show up here just so I could yell at you."

"No, s—. No. Dr. Smithers asked me to fetch you."

"Oh?" Dr. Smithers was one of the coroners that worked for the MPS. He was a good man, and a friend.

"They've identified one of the kn—one of the armored men."

"Really? Who is he?"

"Dr. Smithers didn't tell me. He just asked that I bring you to the morgue straightaway."

"All right." Hyde wasn't fond of the idea of traveling

anywhere in the city. It wasn't safe. The monsters that had gutted the city hunted almost fearlessly in packs.

For the moment, he and his group—part of the small number of police officers that had survived the initial attacks of the enemy—had taken up residence under Bishopsgate Tower. The building was one of the newer structures in the city and had been built to stand forever. Supposedly.

Personally, Hyde doubted it would last through the month. The enemy was enlarging daily the area they controlled. It reminded Hyde of the stories his grandfather had told about the Nazi occupation of France and the air raids over London.

Turning back to the window, Hyde lifted his binoculars again and looked in the direction of St. Paul's Cathedral. The black, roiling mass of the Hellgates—that's what some of the shortwave radio reporters were calling it, and Hyde saw no reason to disagree—glowed and flickered.

The meteorological effects of *whatever* it was were growing more and more every day. Hyde had daily reports of the devastation the manifestation was causing. Over the past few days, since the massive attack by the kn—*armored* men on All Hallows' Eve, even the River Thames had become affected. The water level was dropping at an alarming rate.

Night stretched all across London. Hyde doubted the city had ever been so dark since World War II. Back in those turbulent years, the men and women who'd stayed had lived with the darkness at night because it was their greatest defense against German bombers.

Now, though, the invaders had somehow gotten into all the power grids and shut them down. The tubes had gone silent, no longer ferrying people throughout the city, and no lights were possible save for oil lanterns and candles. Even those burned at the peril of their owners. The invaders moved at night, seeking out humans and killing them where they found them.

Grudgingly, afraid that he might miss something in his absence, Hyde turned from the window and accompanied the young officer.

Hanging out over a fifty-plus-story drop wasn't a pleasant experience. DCS Hyde hung on to the ropes around the cage they used to navigate the building.

Since the power was out, they'd had to jury-rig an elevator system. Since adding more weight to the cage only meant more dead weight for the men muscling it up and down to manage, the builders had elected to go with a skeletal frame and ropes. The platform swayed sickeningly and Hyde's stomach lurched.

Gradually, the platform descended the empty elevator shaft in a controlled fall. Hyde hadn't made up his mind whether it was worse descending or ascending. Descending felt like one long fall but didn't take long. But ascending felt like a multitude of short, very quick falls. His heart lurched with every one.

Finally, though, they arrived at the basement level. Going to the lobby was too dangerous because it forced them to go directly out onto the street.

In the basement, one of the armored riot cars that had so far survived the attacks waited. Scars tracked the metal sides and spiderwebbed fractures lined the windows. The snouts of small cannons and machine guns peeked out of gun ports.

The side access panel opened and a young man stepped out. "Chief Superintendent."

Hyde nodded.

"Mind your head, sir. She's low."

Ducking his head, Hyde stepped into the vehicle and

was promptly shown to a chair. The armored car was packed with hard-edged men and weapons. From the look of them, they'd all spent time in the killing fields. Haggard and often unshaven, their eyes looked haunted. Hyde didn't even want to guess what horrors they'd seen.

"Buckle in, sir." The young man took another seat while Krebs took one beside him.

"Where are you taking me?"

"Orders are to take you to the Central Library. You'll be met there by Dr. Smithers."

"I wasn't aware that Dr. Smithers was there."

"Recently relocated, sir. They had to have a new morgue."

"What happened to the old one?"

"It filled up, sir."

"Oh." Hyde sat back in his seat and felt the armored car lurch into motion. The morgue had filled up, and that was only with the dead they'd recovered. There had been plenty more that they hadn't.

The armored car's transmission engaged smoothly and they accelerated.

Hyde's anxiety increased because he couldn't see out of the vehicle. He wouldn't know if they were attacked until it was too late.

"How have the evacuation efforts been coming, sir?" the young officer asked. He spoke as calmly as though they were out for a Sunday drive.

"We've established staging areas," Hyde answered, grateful for something to take his mind off being exposed in the streets. "But it's not doing much good, I'm afraid."

"Really?"

"There's no way to send the people we get together." Hyde hated discussing the futility of the exercise. Great Britain was an island kingdom. In the past, that had been a strength. Now it worked against them.

"What about the Chunnel?"

The Chunnel was the thirty-one-mile underground railway that ran under the English Channel and linked Great Britain to France.

"The . . . invaders seemed to have concentrated some of their forces there," Hyde said. "They've executed the last few caravans we've sent that way."

"No headway has been made toward reclaiming the airports?"

"No." Heathrow had all but been destroyed in the initial attack. Gatwick and Stansted had been destroyed. No one knew exactly what shape Luton Airport was in.

"Pity. It would be better if we could get the noncombatants out of the area."

"Yes," Hyde said. "Yes it would." Privately he worried that most of the citizens would not escape. Not unless some miracle occurred.

The man tapped the earpiece on the side of his head. "Hold on, sir. We're about to clear a rough spot."

Hyde was aware of the armored car's acceleration. He reached down and took hold of the armrests.

A moment later, the sound of machine guns and cannons roared to life. Then something struck the side of the armored car hard enough to rock it up on one side. Still, it churned through whatever lethal encounter it had run into. The vehicle accelerated violently again, then executed a series of right and left turns.

"Watch it, Joey! Over to your left!" one of the men yelled. "*No!* Your other bleedin' left, mate!"

The gunners worked diligently, shifting and jostling as they tracked their targets.

"I hate them ones that can fly like that."

Hyde got a momentary image of the flying creatures that he'd spotted on several occasions. Only two days ago, he'd seen one scoop a child from the street like a falcon taking a hare. Hyde didn't know if the creature had killed the child or if it had been the bullets his men had fired. The child was never seen again.

"You're not hurting it," one of the men said. "You're just making it madder."

The driver jerked the armored car through a series of quick turns. The vehicle jumped and jerked as it scraped along the side of a building. Then everything went quiet again.

"All right," the officer said, visibly relaxing. "We're clear."

But only for the moment, Hyde couldn't help thinking. *They're still out there.*

They stopped at another underground parking garage and Hyde was ushered out of the armored car. A group of plainclothes officers awaited him. All of them carried heavy weapons and wore bulky riot gear that only slowed the creatures but didn't stop them.

"If you need a ride out of here later, sir," the young armored car officer stated, "we'll be happy to assist."

"Thank you." Hyde shook the young man's hand. "Keep safe out there."

The officer gave him a cheery thumbs-up. "Always."

The doors of the armored car closed like some monstrous beast. Then they were off, streaking for the exit.

"If you'll follow me, sir."

Hyde fell in with the group waiting for him. Even though they fairly bristled with weapons, the men of the group were wary.

Their footsteps echoed in the cavernous parking garage. They took a flight of steps down to the next level. Guards stood at attention in front of the opening. Bright light blazed through the doorway.

"Detective Chief Superintendent to see Dr. Smithers," one of the men announced.

The guard glanced over Hyde's ID and handed it back. He nodded. A half-healed wound tightened his left cheek and promised a terrible scar in the future. If the man lived to see it.

Hyde had to blink several times as he entered the makeshift morgue. The lights were incredibly bright. He felt the heat from them, too. The warmth seemed to intensify the smell of death that permeated the room as well. Despite his years of experience with the Metropolitan Police Service, Hyde felt almost unnerved and queasy. He parted his lips and breathed through his mouth to lessen the stench. It didn't help much.

Several steel tables had been brought into the garage area, but even as many as there were, there were several body bags around as well. They lay stacked like cordwood, awaiting their final fate.

What are we going to do when we run out of body bags? Hyde wondered. Two weeks ago, he would have been shocked and slightly sickened that he'd even thought such a question. Tonight, however, he realized that it was a real concern.

Dr. Smithers was in his sixties, a withered bone of a man with ill-fitting false teeth and deep eye sockets. The heavy magnification of the lenses made his eyes appear too big for his skull. He wore white scrubs streaked with blood.

"'Ello, Alf." Smithers spoke in a whispery, sandpaper voice. "I 'eard you 'ad a close call on the way over."

"A bit. None the worse for wear. It happens often enough now that I don't think about it much after it's over." That wasn't exactly true. He had nightmares nearly every time he slept. Hyde offered his hand.

Smithers held up both of his. His gloves were covered

with blood and gore. "Not a moment for niceties, I'm afraid."

Hyde dropped his hand back at his side. "You sent for me."

"I did." Smithers waved Hyde over to a body against the wall.

The body was different from most of the others. This one had on the strange armor of the men who'd helped out when the British military had faltered in the streets.

And who had died by the hundreds at St. Paul's Cathedral just a few days ago, Hyde reminded himself.

Another man stood by the table where the dead man lay. The man was in his late thirties or perhaps early forties, tanned and fit. He wore a turtleneck, slacks, and a trench coat. His head was smooth-shaven and so was his jaw. Black-lensed sunglasses covered his eyes.

Hyde stared at the man, awaiting introduction. After a moment, he decided that Smithers wasn't going to give it. He held out a hand and announced his name.

The man made no move to take Hyde's hand. His face remained neutral. He said, "We're aware of who you are, Chief Superintendent."

Feeling foolish, Hyde withdrew his hand. "Who are you?"

"No one you need to trouble yourself with."

"Then maybe you'd like to wait upstairs."

The man smiled at that. "I think not."

Hyde glanced at Smithers.

"'E won't give me 'is name either," the coroner said. "But 'e's some kind of 'igh muckety-muck. 'E's got a letter from the prime minister's office what says so."

"I have . . . connections," the man said. He focused his sunglasses on Hyde. "I was told you could identify this man."

Despite his anger, Hyde's attention was drawn to the dead knight on the table. Why would anyone think that he knew—

But he did know the dead man. That stunned the chief superintendent into silence for a moment.

"Do you know him?"

Hyde nodded. "I do."

"And he is?"

"Thomas Cross." It was hard to recognize Cross in the shape he was in, but the features were remarkable, not overly handsome, but definitely a man Hyde remembered. Cross looked like he'd been parboiled. His flesh was ready to fall off the bone.

"Who's Thomas Cross?"

"A man I got to know in connection with a bit of investigating I did."

"You arrested his son for base-jumping two years ago."

That surprised Hyde, too. He wondered where the man was getting his information. "I did. For base-jumping from Big Ben."

"That's how you got to know Thomas Cross and his son Simon?"

"Yes, but I don't see what that has to do with—"

"What do you know about the father and son?" the man interrupted.

Hyde curbed a sharp rebuke. As chief superintendent he wasn't used to being treated in such a cavalier fashion. He took in a deep breath and let it out. "Nothing."

The man didn't say a thing, but even his silence was insulting.

"The fine was paid," Hyde said. "The young man did his community service. Then he got out of town."

"Out of London, you mean?"

"Yes." Hyde didn't know how much clearer he could be.

"But not before he staged another jump from the Tower of London. Right before he caught the train. Before we could put a hold on the flight, he was gone. He was cheeky."

"Where did he go?"

"Who?"

"Simon Cross."

"South Africa. Cape Town, I think."

"Why?"

"I don't know."

"You're sure Simon Cross went to South Africa?"

"Yes. His father"—Hyde nodded at the corpse—"asked me to facilitate things for his son."

"Why?"

"There was some problem with the son's passport."

"What was the problem?"

Hyde stared into the blank lenses and saw ghostly reflections of himself. "It wouldn't pass inspection."

"You overrode it."

"Yes. Those things happen every now and again. All I did was verify that he was a citizen and he was on his way."

"Why did you take the trouble to do that?"

Hyde nodded at the dead man. "Because I liked him. The father. I know what it's like trying to raise a high-spirited young man. Simon Cross was twenty-three years old. It was time for him to stretch his wings. Either that or drive his poor father mad."

"Simon Cross has been gone from London for two years?"

"I don't know. He might be back."

The man regarded Thomas Cross in his metal shell. "Did you know this man was one of these people?"

"You mean the knights?"

The man frowned, obviously displeased. "They are *not* knights."

Anyone who would put on armor and go tilt at monsters has my vote, Hyde thought. "I didn't know about the suits, no."

"Would it surprise you to learn that prior to his son's arrest for base-jumping, Thomas Cross didn't exist as an official British citizen?"

"Yes," Hyde responded honestly. "It would surprise me very much."

"My people—"

Hyde couldn't help automatically wondering who the man's "people" were.

"—performed a thorough background check on Thomas Cross after we found him in that suit. As it turned out, his image and his fingerprints were on file in a case that you handled as chief superintendent."

Hyde waited for the other shoe to drop. He'd been in the politics of police work long enough to know that it would.

"Prior to that time, neither Thomas Cross nor Simon Cross existed. Our boys in computer forensics backtracked the trail the hackers left while putting Thomas and Simon Cross's identification into the system."

The news caught Hyde off-guard. "I don't understand."

"This isn't the first armored man who has fallen into our hands," the man said.

Hyde knew that was true. The rescue services had gotten several of them from around St. Paul's Cathedral.

"But this is the first one we've been able to identify. The others were able to escape." The man's face soured. "Or they were dead and couldn't tell us anything."

Anger stirred within Hyde. He'd liked Thomas Cross. The man had brimmed with integrity, and he'd loved his son in spite of the legal difficulties they'd dealt with. "Why are you treating this man like a criminal? He laid down his life trying to—"

"Get himself killed?" The man's eyes curved upward in a smile.

Hyde said nothing.

"Trust me, Chief Superintendent: whatever these people are doing, they're doing it to suit themselves. Not out of any altruistic reasons."

"I heard some of the knights were there when the military first engaged the invaders."

"The *demons* you mean?"

Hyde firmed his jaw. "Yes."

"How do you know," the man asked, "that these people weren't the ones who brought those bloodthirsty things into our world?"

That wasn't a new thought to Hyde. As a police officer, he was trained to be suspicious of everyone. The first witness, usually the person who called in to report a crime, was always the first suspect. The knights had fought the demons, pouring everything they had into the effort at St. Paul's Cathedral. He just couldn't see them as villains.

"You see my dilemma, don't you, Chief Superintendent?" the man asked.

"No," Hyde replied. "Nor do I see your interest. You've offered me no credentials as to who you are."

"Can't."

"You mean you won't."

The man shrugged. "To the best of your knowledge, Simon Cross is still in South Africa?"

Hyde hesitated, then nodded.

"Splendid. Can you identify this picture of him?" The man held up a file and opened it to a picture of Simon Cross's booking photo.

Simon Cross looked young and innocent and worldly at the same time. Hyde wondered how the young man would take the death of his father. Not well, he thought. Children who warred with their parents were often as not very close to them. Hyde had the feeling that the two were close, just in different places in their lives two years ago. They shared the same strong features, the same hint of . . . nobility. That was the word that came so readily to mind.

"Yes," Hyde said. "That's Simon Cross."

"You mean, the man you knew as Simon Cross."

Hyde didn't respond.

The man closed the file and tucked it under an arm. "Have a good day, Chief Superintendent. Stay safe." He turned smartly on his heel and walked away.

Four men of average height and average weight stepped away from the back wall and fell in behind them. While they'd been still, they'd almost blended into the room. But now that they were up and moving, they felt dangerous.

In that moment, Hyde knew them for what they were: part of a special operations group. MI-6 or perhaps something even more clandestine.

Occasionally in the past Hyde had encountered such men. Usually at the scene of violent death. Sometimes they'd even committed the murders. But in the end it didn't matter. A quiet letter would get issued from the prime minister's office and the men would disappear as if they'd never existed.

But why were they investigating the knights when the streets were filled with terrifying creatures? And what did they want with Simon Cross?

After the entourage had gone, Hyde turned his attention back to the dead man. "What can you tell me about him, Smithers?"

"Very little, actually. 'E was in good shape. Until 'e ran into whatever it was that killed 'im, of course." Smithers grinned and looked crafty. "I think you'll be better served tryin' to figure out where the armor came from. I'm sure it's more unique than the man."

As Hyde watched, circuitry within the armor pulsed electric blue and died. The armor was amazing, but the chief superintendent didn't think the man who died inside it was any less remarkable.

FIVE

Armed policemen and soldiers blocked the road into Cape Town. One of the policemen held up a white-gloved hand and waved Simon over to the side of the road.

His headlights cut through the night, but the big klieg lights on the back of a nearby flatbed truck plucked him out of the darkness like he'd been set on fire. Simon slowed and pulled over to the side of the road.

"What's going on?" That was from one of the clients, packed in the back with the corpses and the elephant tusks. The smell inside the Land Rover had turned ripe. Traveling during the heat of the day hadn't helped.

"I don't know." Simon peered through the bug-encrusted windshield as the policeman, flanked by two soldiers carrying assault weapons, closed on the Land Rover.

"I need your papers." The policeman was middle-aged, carrying a gut and a no-nonsense approach. His gray-flecked beard stood out against his ebony skin. He kept his hand on his holstered pistol.

As he handed the papers over, Simon felt Saundra tense against him. They sat three abreast in the front seat. None of them had enjoyed a comfortable ride.

One of the men with the assault rifles played his flashlight through the windows. The light kept reflecting from the side mirror into Simon's eyes. It didn't take the man long to find the tusks. He spoke to the policeman rapidly. The bits and pieces of the dialects Simon had picked up over the last two years weren't enough.

But he knew what was coming when the policeman freed his sidearm and pointed it in Simon's face.

"Out of the vehicle." The policeman signaled the other men to close in.

Simon opened the door and stepped out. One of the men grabbed him and slammed him up against the Land Rover. He felt the muzzle of a gun burrow into the back of his neck. Confusion swept over him. He'd never been stopped outside the city like this before, and papers were seldom checked inside Cape Town except for foreign vendors and merchants.

It was bad enough when they'd found the tusks, but when the soldiers found the bodies, things really got ugly.

"That's quite a story, Mr. Cross."

Seated across the long table from a lieutenant in the Cape Town Police Department whose name he hadn't quite gotten, Simon massaged his bruised wrists. The men who had brought them in for questioning hadn't been gentle. "I don't know if I'd believe it myself."

The lieutenant smiled, but he looked tired and worried. "Luckily, you have the corroboration of several witnesses. And these men you killed were known poachers."

Simon nodded. He'd been in holding for hours, crowded in with several other stinking, sweating prisoners. He'd kept his clients separated from the riff-raff and out of harm's way. Then they'd brought him in to be questioned. He hoped his clients were still all right.

"Those witnesses aren't used to jail," Simon said.

"I understand. I had them taken from holding shortly after I sent for you. Their statements will be taken, identification confirmed, then they'll be released. Just as you are."

Getting released sounded good. Simon wanted a bed in a semi-adequate hotel and a few beers and shots to tuck him in.

"Why was there so much security along the road?" Simon asked.

The lieutenant's forehead furrowed. "How long were you out in the bush, Mr. Cross?"

"Nine days. We were scheduled out for two weeks."

"I see. Then you missed all the furor."

Fear tightened inside Simon again. During the long drive back to Cape Town he'd almost convinced himself that the poachers had taken a small story and blown it out of proportion. No one had talked to him at the police station, and none of the prisoners they'd been jailed with had been overly friendly after Simon had knocked two of them senseless for trying to intimidate his clients.

"What furor?"

"Apparently aliens have landed in London," the lieutenant said. "The story is all over the news."

Aliens. "Are you sure they're aliens?"

The lieutenant looked at Simon curiously. "I haven't seen them myself, but I've seen them on the news channels. I'd call them aliens. What would you call them?"

"I don't know. But it just sounds . . . strange." Simon sat back in the straight wooden chair and wished he were home. He had no doubt that if he told the lieutenant what he suspected, though, he'd be kept for observation and not let out around sane people.

"There's not much footage of them beasties," the bartender said.

Simon vaguely remembered that the man's name was Flynn. He was an Irishman, but he'd come to Cape Town as a mercenary nearly twenty years ago, lost a leg, and fallen in love with an Xhosa woman. They'd started Walter's, a bar that catered to the locals and tourists, and provided back rooms for mercenaries.

They were watching old footage on CNN on the tri-dee over the bar. According to the anchorman, nothing new had come out of England for the last fourteen hours. All electronic communication in the area had been cut off.

Simon felt the need to get up and move, to be *there* instead of Cape Town. He'd already called the airport, but no one there knew when flights would be headed into Europe. So far, everyone wanted to stay home.

And that was where Simon wanted to be: home. It surprised him that he felt so strongly. He hadn't been back in two years, and hadn't missed it. He'd made more friends and had more freedom in Cape Town than in London.

The bar was a mixture of recycled, mismatched furniture. None of the pieces looked like they fit together, but the place was packed. Servers hustled between the tables and beer was served in bottles and cans.

After leaving the police station, Simon had checked on Saundra's whereabouts and discovered she was still giving her statement. He'd left a message that he would be at Walter's.

As soon as he'd hit the street, Simon had heard bits and pieces of the stories of the invasion that had taken place in London. If everything was to be believed, nearly everyone there had been killed and half the city destroyed.

Simon kept his eyes glued to the tri-dee holo broadcast above Flynn's head at the bar. Two channels were playing. One showed the news and another covered the soccer championships being played in Rio de Janeiro. Unbelievably, most of the bar's patrons were involved in the soccer game, not the news.

"Does anyone know where they came from?" Simon asked.

Flynn shook his head. "A mothership, I suppose. Though nobody's saying."

"Why invade England, that's what I want to know," the heavyset man sitting next to Simon said. He was black and had a German accent. "They wanted to cripple the planet, they'd go after the United States."

"The United States is too tough," Flynn said. "You know they'd go nuclear over something like this. It's a wonder they ain't done something already. Mark my words, those aliens make a move to cross the Atlantic, them Yanks will put every British Isle at the bottom of the North Sea."

Simon didn't doubt that. The U.S. had involved themselves in a lot of wars and hadn't won much international support. But they had to be respected. Or feared. Simon still wasn't sure which way he'd call it.

In the tri-dee presentation, a British fighter plane battled a flying demon that Simon recognized from the ancient texts he'd been forced to study. *They're real.* That thought kept slamming into Simon over and over again. *They're real. That's a Blood Angel.*

On tri-dee, the demon looked bigger than Simon had imagined. Its wingspread was huge and bat-like.

The demon landed on the jet's nose and began tearing through the metal shielding. A few seconds later, it shattered the canopy and reached inside for the pilot. Arms wrapped around its hapless victim, the demon leaped into the air and unfurled its wings only seconds before the jet ripped across the top of London Bridge in a shower of sparks. Chunks of stone tore free under the impact, then the aircraft went down in what Simon believed were the India Docks. An explosion immediately erupted, throwing flames and debris high into the air.

The scene shifted back to the anchorman for brief commentary, then moved into another scene of street carnage that Simon had seen before. This time, a huge demon strode through the gates at Buckingham Palace. One of its arms was withered, while the other was massive and had a huge fist.

Tanks rolled to attack, firing on the go. The shells burst against the demon's chest, knocking it back, then it lashed out with that huge fist and tore the turret from the top of the tank. It breathed acidic vapor into the crew compartment, killing anyone who might have survived.

A pack of blood zombies, looking like they'd been flayed alive so that muscle and bone stood out in sharp relief, trailed after the great demon. They devoured all the fallen soldiers that tried to protect the palace. Bullets had little effect on them and hardly slowed them.

"Can you get in to England?" Simon asked.

Flynn looked at him as if he'd sprouted a second head. "Whatever would you want to go to that place at this time for?"

Simon sipped his beer. "I've got family there."

Without a word, Flynn reached under the bar and brought out two clean glasses. He poured two fingers of Bushmills in each one. Hoisting one of the glasses, Flynn said, "To the saints what watch over us and them far from us."

Simon clinked glasses and sipped the whiskey. "Can I get to England?"

"All the commercial flights into Great Britain have been held up," Flynn answered. "They've declared a quarantine over the whole area. Something about alien bacteria. Even got stories about the dead rising up and walking." He looked at Simon and his normally hard gaze softened. "Sorry, mate."

Glancing at the tri-dee, Simon watched men, women, and children running through the rubble-strewn barriers that had been set up long ago. The demons chased them, running them down in the streets.

It was horrible to watch.

But more than anything, he needed to be there. He sipped his drink again, feeling the burn at the back of his throat. Then soft fingers touched his neck. He turned and looked up at Saundra.

"Hey," she said.

"They let you go."

"Finally." Saundra grimaced as she looked up at the tri-dee. Worry tightened her eyes as she looked at him. "Are you all right?"

"Yeah. Just tired is all." Simon glanced back up at the nightmares taking shape on the tri-dee. He wasn't just tired. He was feeling scared and guilty. He should never have left London. He should never have doubted his father.

Saundra pulled on his arm. "I've got a room. Let's get out of here."

Simon nodded. He tried to settle his tab, but Flynn waved his money away. The bartender even threw in a bottle of Bushmills.

"It'll keep away the nightmares," the bartender said.

Simon didn't think it would, but he took the bottle anyway.

In the modest hotel room, Saundra showered first while Simon ordered room service. Normally they'd have shared the shower, but they hadn't talked much. Simon wasn't sure if it was the fact that he'd killed the poachers that had created the barrier between them, or all the news about London. Either way, he wasn't a big fan of personal contact at the moment, either.

He stood under the shower under the hottest water he could stand, letting it almost scald him. He scrubbed with soap and shampooed, but didn't feel clean. Visions of demons, his father's patient voice, all kept bouncing around inside his skull.

He kept repeating the process till Saundra knocked on the door and told him the food had arrived.

Wrapped in a towel, seated on the bed, Simon ate from the tray. Saundra sat beside him as they watched tri-dee. The segments kept looping, showing the same horrific images over and over. They drank Bushmills with the meal, and Simon felt the alcohol and the food drain the energy from him.

"I can't believe this is really happening," Saundra whispered.

"Neither can I," Simon replied. *And I've been told it would all my life.*

"Your father lives in London."

"Yes." Simon made himself eat. He needed his strength. He was a warrior, trained by warriors, and he'd slipped back into that mind-set far easier than he'd ever thought he would. He would eat when he could eat, sleep when he could sleep, and fight every chance he got.

"He's probably all right." Saundra ran her fingers through Simon's hair.

"If he was all right, he would have called." Simon made himself say that, to remind himself what he was probably facing.

"They say the communications systems were taken out early on. Either they were destroyed or some kind of damper was put over them. Maybe he couldn't call."

"They have shortwave radios." When he saw the stricken look on Saundra's face, Simon knew he'd spoken too forcefully. He softened his voice. "Hey. I'm sorry. I didn't mean to snap like that."

"It's all right." But she looked away from him.

Simon sighed. They'd both stayed away from family stories. He knew she had a mom and dad in Australia, and three younger siblings, a brother and two sisters, or it could have been the other way around. But he didn't know all the little anecdotal stories for them.

He'd mentioned he'd had a dad, and that his mother was dead, but nothing much beyond that. There was no way he could have brought up the Templar upbringing. Although after the way he'd dealt with the poachers, she'd wanted some kind of explanation but hadn't been rude enough to ask for one.

"It's just . . ." Simon hesitated. "You'd have to know my dad. He'd get a message out. Shortwave radios don't depend on satellites or anything, and you can broadcast halfway around the world on one of those."

"I know about shortwave radios. I grew up in Australia, remember? Long way from anywhere if you didn't grow up in one of the bigger cities. My dad still has a base radio. But who would your dad broadcast to? Does he know where you're staying?"

Simon thought about it only for a moment, then shook his head. "No."

"Nowhere to send the message, no message," Saundra said. "I don't have a message from my dad, either." She paused. "And I'm scared, too, Simon. I want to be home."

"I know." He turned to her and put his arms around her, just holding on. "We'll find a way."

SIX

On his knees in the wrecked supermarket with a dozen other scavengers, Warren Schimmer *felt* the demon before he saw it.

All his life, he'd had *feelings* about people, situations, and things. He could generally tell when someone meant him harm, and no one could lie to him. He knew when a street was dangerous at night, whether because of muggers or because of motorists. When he held objects, he sometimes got intimations about the past history of a particular piece.

Sometimes, if he concentrated hard enough, he could guess which sports team to bet on, or which horse at the track. He'd never had enough money to make a big profit with a bookie or at the track. Money in his life was hard to come by. It always had been. But not being able to be a big winner allowed him to score a good bet every now and again that helped tide him over. But generally, he had to watch his finances.

That was why he was out scrounging for food now instead of staying at home hiding from the demons and hoping the military units would find a way to evacuate them from London. There simply wasn't enough food in the flat to last an extended stay. And his instincts told him the demons were going to be in London for a long time. He hoped to be evacuated soon. He had no feelings about that.

Not that Warren had anywhere to go. He'd lived his entire life in London. He'd never even been to France or Scotland or Ireland on a lark. On what he made working at the bookstore, there hadn't been enough money.

He'd barely made enough to keep his three flat mates from putting him out on the street. If they'd been able to make enough money between them—at the very least control their spending habits—or had been able to pick up another fourth to share the rent, he was certain they'd have gotten rid of him.

For them, he was too creepy or too strange. Too silent and withdrawn. They called him Weird Warren behind his back and didn't think he knew that. Although they didn't know it, they had few secrets that he didn't know after living with them.

Personally, Warren thought of himself as taciturn. He didn't like the company of others, and that usually bothered others. Instead of being glad he wasn't trying to continually get into their business, they looked on him with resentment and suspicion.

They hated the fact that he always had his rent ready at the first of the month without fail, and sometimes had a little extra to cover someone who was short. Instead of being grateful that he had it and was generous enough to share, although he'd been forced to do that through circumstance, they had speculated that he was involved in something illegal, which wasn't a lot of fun for Warren, either.

As a result of their suspicions, they'd sometimes tried to follow him. They also went through his things in his room and occasionally nicked any money he might have left lying out. He was creepy, but lucky, and everyone knew it.

That was why he was one of those that got sent out tonight to get rations. Because he was lucky.

Only now he knew that he had a demon sniffing him

out. There was a fine line between good luck and bad luck, and all his life Warren Schimmer had experienced tons of both.

Warren cowered in the back of the small convenience store. He knelt flattened against the refrigeration unit along the back wall. Nothing inside the unit was cold any more, of course. When the power had gone out, the refrigeration had died as well. The meat and vegetables were bad, but much of the cheese was processed and would keep at room temperature for weeks. Soda, juice, tea, and other beverages would keep as well. He'd hoped to get some of those.

Kelli, the more sane of the two women in his flat group, started to move. He seized her wrist. She was blond and pretty, but had mean eyes and a small heart when it came to taking care of others. She worked mornings at a pastry shop and Friday and Saturday nights at a gentlemen's club. Not as a dancer, but as a hostess.

Her blond hair made her stand out in the darkness, but Warren knew he was almost invisible. At six-two, he was more than a head taller than she was. He was twenty-three, a couple of years younger than she was. He was long and lanky, dressed in black jeans, black motorcycle boots, black turtleneck, and a long black duster. With his black skin, he was a shadow among shadows.

"Don't move," Warren whispered. That warning tickle still exploded inside his brain. It was everything he could do to keep from running away and leaving her there. If she put up much of an argument or a fight, he was going to do exactly that, though. He still wasn't sure why he wasn't doing that now.

"What's wrong with you?" Kelli demanded, yanking her hand free. She reached for the door of the refrigeration unit.

"We're . . . not . . . *alone.*" Warren breathed the words into her ear.

"No, we're not." She whispered, too, hooking her fingers in her long hair and pulling it back from her face. "This place wasn't empty when we came here."

The other scavengers were busy with the canned foods. All of them worked as fast as they could to gather everything they could safely carry.

Warren and Kelli had brought pillowcases, doubling them to increase the strength.

"Listen to me," Warren said desperately, locking eyes with her. He'd found over the years that making eye contact with people he wanted to persuade was somehow more effective than simply voicing a logical argument. "There's something out there."

Kelli hesitated then. Warren had gone out of his way to get her from the club one night four months ago. He'd convinced her he'd had a premonition that something bad was going to happen. Only minutes later, a jealous boyfriend came in and shot his girlfriend and nine customers. The girlfriend and two of the customers had died.

"What makes you think that?" she asked.

"I just know it. We need to get out of here."

"We need food," Kelli argued. "We're running out of things to eat."

"If we don't leave," Warren told her, "we may not be going home tonight."

She stared into his eyes. "Are you sure?"

Warren nodded. "I'm sure."

Kelli glanced around, but Warren knew he had her. "All right," she said.

Warren took a fresh grip on his pillowcase. It was less than half full, but he'd scored peanut butter, which would make George happy.

Lights suddenly flashed against the broken windows of the convenience store.

"Coppers," one of the other scavengers groaned.

Immediately the scavengers began dumping items they'd stolen from residences onto the floor. For many of the scavengers, looting was a natural outgrowth of survival. Maybe they couldn't at the moment sell the jewelry, tridees, or individual entertainment systems they'd boosted, but they believed everything would return to normal soon. Then they planned on making small fortunes selling their stolen goods.

George was doing the same thing when he went out to forage.

The policeman entered the convenience store and shined his flashlight around. Illuminated by the beam, the man looked tired and old. He wore riot gear, bulky and stiff. He carried an assault rifle in his other hand.

"You people need to get out of here," the policeman said. His beam fell across the scattered jewelry and other items on the floor that clearly didn't belong in the convenience store. His face hardened. "And stop that bloody thievery. Don't any of you have a conscience? You're out there robbing the dead. Or people that have been scared out of their homes."

"Don't lecture us," a big man snarled. "We might not even get out of this. And if we do, we aren't going to have much. Insurance isn't going to cover our losses. I didn't have any alien insurance. Did you?"

"They're not aliens," someone else said. "They're demons."

"What do we have here?" the first man asked sarcastically. "Did the parson leave the vicarage long enough to come down and loot with the rest of us heathens?"

"Don't talk like that," someone else said.

"Get moving," the policeman said, "or I'm going to run the lot of—"

A shadow unfurled in the window, swinging down into the window from above and smashing through the glass. The policeman tried to turn and bring his assault rifle into play. He had his finger on the trigger and was firing in a heartbeat.

But it didn't last long. In one stride, the demon was on the policeman. It closed one hand around the policeman's head and yanked.

Warren heard the man's spine snap even across the store. By then Warren had Kelli by the wrist and was dragging her into motion. He ran for the back door, slamming through the alarm bar.

Immediately the alarm filled the night.

Forgot about the batteries, Warren chided himself. Alarm systems would have a secondary power source in case the primary one was shut down.

The cobblestone alley ran in both directions, but the way to the left dead-ended at a tall fence topped with barbed wire. Kelli immediately took off to the right.

Warren started to follow but the warning tickle fired through his brain again. This time it bordered on painful. He stopped short, tightening his grip on Kelli's wrist.

She cursed at him. "Come on." Her voice was tight with desperation. "That thing is going to be coming!"

People ran past them.

Warren held his ground and maintained his hold. "No. We can't go that way."

"Let me go!" Kelli jerked, trying to get free.

"Don't! If you want to live, don't—"

The first of the scavengers fleeing the convenience store reached the end of the alley. Something huge and monstrous burrowed up from under the street.

Warren had never seen anything like the creature. It was as huge as an elephant with a gaping maw.

The lead runner vanished into the hole through the street. The demon reached out and captured another person—things were so confusing that Warren didn't know if the victim was male or female—then bit down. Stumps of legs fell to the ground like crumbs.

The other scavengers tried to reverse their direction, but it was too late. A line of mastiff-sized demons vaulted over the back of the first demon and dropped onto the scavengers, taking them to the ground in their jaws.

Warren pulled Kelli into motion again, heading for the dead end. He halted at the bottom of the wall and formed a stirrup with his hands.

"Up you go."

Kelli stepped into Warren's hands. Thankfully she was slight of build. He had no problem propelling her up. She grabbed hold of the top and rolled over.

Warren leaped up after her, managing the top on his first leap, then pulling himself up. He flung himself over the top and pushed off. He landed and threw himself forward, seeing that Kelli already had a good speed worked up.

SEVEN

Something smacked into the wall behind Warren. He glanced over his shoulder and saw a wedge-shaped head with ruby eyes hang on the barbed wire for a moment, then it slipped back down to the other side.

The fence is too tall, he told himself, and hoped that was the truth.

Then something—or several somethings—kept smashing against the wall. Wood splintered and gave way. By that time Warren had caught up to Kelli. They reached the street together in four more strides.

"Which way—"

Before Kelli could finish her question, Warren felt the warning itch increase again. He threw her down, covering her with his body. The broken window of the Italian restaurant ahead of them showed the menacing reflection of a feminine-shaped demon with wings. She missed them by inches.

Pushing himself up, Warren hauled Kelli up and started running again. She couldn't keep pace with him despite her best efforts.

Run! Leave her behind! Warren knew that was what he should have done. But he couldn't. He didn't truly care about his flat mates. They had all shown too much disrespect over the last few months for him to trust them. But there was no one else in the world that he even came close to caring for.

The door of a comic book shop that Warren sometimes frequented stood open ahead. He ducked inside, pulling Kelli after him. She was out of breath, gasping hoarsely, all but undone.

Two of the hound-looking demons charged past the door.

Slowly, not wanting to attract their attention, Warren guided Kelli to the back of the showroom. Posters of superheroes with amazing powers covered the walls. Those worlds—not the impossible things that happened in them, but the way most things ended happily—seemed a million miles away. The heroes in those magazines weren't afraid of death. But Warren Schimmer was. He'd seen it close up, had taken a life before and knew how easy it was.

"Quiet," Warren breathed into Kelli's ear. He tried to keep his fear out of his voice but doubted he succeeded. "Just stay quiet and we'll get out of here."

She was tense, shaking against him. She didn't believe him. But that was fair; he didn't believe himself.

One of the demons turned toward the comic shop and thrust its snout into the air.

Does it scent us? Warren didn't know. He reached the back of the sales floor and went through the open door to the stock room. He'd never been there before. Too late, he saw that there was nowhere to go.

Boxes lined the shelves. A table occupied one end of the room. Thankfully the room was dark.

The demon approached the door and threw its snout into the air again.

Warren willed Kelli not to speak or make a sound. And he wanted her to obey him without him having to give instruction. She let him guide her like a child, dropping to the floor and crawling under the table.

Outside, the demon's footsteps drew nearer.

Kelli almost screamed. Warren put his hand over her lower face. *Don't,* he thought at her. *Don't make a sound.*

She quieted, but her heart throbbed against his arm thrown over her body.

In the darkness, the demon was barely visible, but Warren made out its feet. They were gnarled and misshapen, nowhere close to anything human. But they were corded with muscle and sharp talons curled over the toes.

You can't see us, Warren thought at it. Then he corrected himself. *You can't sense us. We're not here. No one is in this room.*

A moment later, the demon thrust its ugly head under the table. The slavering jaws were less than a foot from Kelli's head. One snap of those powerful jaws would tear her face away.

You can't sense us. We're not here. Go away. We're not here. Warren's unspoken words felt like hammer falls inside him. A massive headache suddenly throbbed between his temples. He clung to the words desperately, and he clung to Kelli because she was shaking so hard there was no way the demon wouldn't see her.

A moment later, unbelievably, the demon withdrew. Then it left the room. Stunned, Warren listened as the footsteps receded and finally disappeared.

Long minutes passed. During that time, Warren felt Kelli's tears rolling across his fingers, felt her shaking as she silently cried. He also heard the screams and cries of those who didn't get away.

After a while, he heard only silence.

"Stay here," he told Kelli. "I'm going to go look."

"No." She caught hold of his shirt and tried to keep him with her.

"Let go," Warren said automatically. His voice was more

harsh than he intended, but his head ached so severely that he wanted to lie down and sleep.

Kelli let go.

Getting to his feet, Warren went to the door and peered out. He saw no demons. At the door, gazing out onto the street, he saw a few scattered fires, but no sign of the demons.

"How did you do that?"

The woman's voice startled Warren. He drew back quickly enough to collide with the door frame and trigger a new onslaught of pain to cascade through his head.

A thin woman stood at his side. She looked emaciated, and like she'd just crawled out of a bin at a medical examiner's office.

"Who are you?" Warren asked. The warning itch squirmed like a worm on a hook inside his aching head. He curled his fists, ready to lash out. He'd learned to fight while he was growing up in state-sponsored homes, but he'd never been very good at it. Others had always hurt him more than he'd hurt them.

"Calm yourself," the woman said. She took a step back and averted her face as if he was shining a bright light into her face. "You are raw, boy. Has no one trained you?"

Warren didn't know what she was talking about. He backed away from her, toward the stock room where Kelli was.

Upon closer inspection, Warren thought the woman was in her late forties or early fifties. Her skin was pale as milk, but the shadows blended with the tattoos that covered her, making them hard to identify. They looked like the sigils and symbols that had drawn Warren's attention in the library. Some of them seemed to burn with a green fire. But her most astounding features were the stubby horns that jutted out of her forehead.

"What are you?" Warren demanded before he had a chance to think about what he was going to say.

"A human, if that's what you're wondering."

It was, though Warren didn't want to admit that.

"My name is Edith Buckner," she told him.

"Warren," Warren replied automatically, then stopped himself before he could give his last name. He hadn't wanted to answer, but his first name was off his tongue before he knew it.

"Well, Warren," Edith said. "It's a pleasure to meet you."

Staring at her, Warren noticed the dark, shapeless cloak the woman wore. It also had sigils, but these were sewn in black thread.

"What are you doing here?" he asked.

"Much the same as you are." She smiled. "Trying to survive in difficult times. But I'm also trying to learn. As you should be. Not everyone has our talents." She waved a hand in front of him. Yellow highlights dawned in her eyes.

Something coiled and twisted inside Warren. Although the woman wasn't touching him, he could feel her hands on him. The sensation made him feel uncomfortable, almost sick. Without thinking about it, he pushed back.

The tattoos on the woman's forehead and cheeks momentarily flamed lambent green. The effect was gone so quickly that he might have believed it was his imagination playing tricks on him. If he hadn't felt her touch inside his mind.

She staggered back as though struck. Glaring at him, she took a deep breath. "Where did you learn to do that, boy?"

"I didn't do anything." Warren turned from her, intending to go get Kelli and get home.

The woman caught his arm. "Don't turn your back on me, boy."

Warren yanked his arm from her grip. "Get off of me."

"You knew you had this power," Edith told him in a calm, cold voice.

Warren didn't say anything, but memories of his stepfather and mother flashed through his head.

You've been spending our money on that crap again, haven't you? his stepfather yelled.

It isn't crap, his mother replied. *I have power, Martin. I have the kind of power that they haven't seen very often.*

You're a stupid, girl, Tamara. Very stupid. People as stupid as you pay for being stupid.

Stay back! Don't!

The sound of the gunshot that had ended the screaming match exploded inside Warren's mind again . . .

"Did you have this power before the demons came?" the woman asked.

Walling off all those painful memories again, Warren ignored her. She had brought that memory to the surface with her mind-touch. He wanted to break her for what she'd done. He hadn't thought about his parents and that night in months.

"You knew you could turn that demon, didn't you?" the woman demanded.

Warren hadn't known that for sure, but he wasn't going to tell her that, either.

"If you had the power before the Hellgates opened," the woman said, "the power is only going to grow stronger. If you don't learn how to harness it, it may well destroy you."

He felt her fingers inside his mind again, poking, probing.

. . . the smell of burning flesh and blood . . . the iron taste of blood in his mouth . . . the raw burn of power that made him feel ripped apart . . . his stepfather's final screams . . .

"Stay away," Warren said hoarsely. He pushed against her with the angry force that had resided within him since the night his parents had died.

Staggered, the old woman shrieked and shrank back. She was sick for a moment, throwing up on the sidewalk in front of the comic book shop. She wiped her mouth with the back of her hand.

"You need someone to teach you," the woman said. "Someone to guide you. Before you hurt yourself or someone else. I can help you."

Warren wheeled on the woman then, standing half a head taller than the tips of her horns. "I don't want your help. Don't you understand that? I don't want anything to do with you or your kind. If you try to touch me again, I'm going to hurt you."

The woman took a half-step back, obviously afraid of him. "You need us, Warren. You need someone to help you grow in your power before it burns through you like an electrical short and kills you."

"That's not going to happen."

"You don't know that. A lot of us have gotten stronger since the demons came into our world. We're going to get stronger still. You need to know what to expect before you get caught up in it."

"I don't want your help."

Noise came from down the block. More sirens ripped through the night, punctuated by rapid gunfire. Warren assumed the police officer had had support teams show up. For all the good that would do. The sirens would draw the demons.

"I'm leaving," he announced. "Get out of my way."

"There's a group of us who have been meeting for years. We've noticed how more accelerated the power is in individuals since the Hellgates opened. We're helping them."

The woman reached into her cloak and took out a pen and pad. "We could help you."

"No."

Edith wrote anyway. When she finished she held out a piece of paper with an address on it. "If you ever want to know more about what you're experiencing, come see us."

Even though he told himself he didn't want to, Warren took the piece of paper that she pressed into his hand.

"Come see us," the woman urged. "We can help." She smiled. "We can help you get stronger. Strong enough even to survive what's about to happen to this world."

Warren heard Kelli calling out to him. He turned back to the comic shop to let her know he was there. When he turned back around, Edith Buckner had vanished. Only smoke and fog drifted through the street.

Slowly, Warren thrust the note with the address into his jeans pocket. Then he went to get Kelli.

"I heard you, you know."

Back at the flat, Warren looked over at Kelli. They laid their precious cargo out on the table. George and Dorothy were out, presumably still searching for food as well. Warren wondered if they'd both make it home alive.

"Heard me what?" Warren smiled a little as if she were working a punch line.

"Send that monster away."

Warren took out two jars of peanut butter and six tins of salmon. Those were going to be delicacies for George for the coming week.

"You were imagining things," Warren insisted. "You were scared and disoriented. You only thought you heard me send the demon away."

"No. I heard you."

Remaining quiet, Warren sorted the food. They'd made

a good haul. Most of the stuff would keep for weeks or months. But they were still short on water. Water was the hardest to haul because it took so much of it to get them through a day and because water was so heavy and bulky to transport.

"You're delirious," Warren said. "You were scared out of your wits."

"I heard you," Kelli insisted. "Only you weren't speaking. It was like you were hardwired into my head."

Irritated, Warren turned from his work. "Would you listen to yourself, Kelli? You sound mental. Like you're ready for the loony bin."

Her face tightened. Now that she no longer had to be scared for her life, she could be angry. "I know what I heard."

"No, you don't."

"How do you know how to talk to those creatures?"

"I don't."

"Why do you want to lie about it?"

"I'm not."

Kelli looked like she wanted to argue further, but she closed her mouth and walked away from him.

They lived in a converted warehouse area in Manchester, a two-story affair that had been converted into lofts. The area comfortably fit them, though Dorothy's paintings tended to overflow into the main room.

Kelli climbed the ladder up to her private area. She pulled the sheets that served as their walls, shutting him out. A few minutes later, the soft, sad chords of her acoustic guitar pealed within the loft.

Warren continued sorting the food. He'd been the one who had come up with the idea of inventorying everything they salvaged from the city so they would always know what they had and what they needed. He'd learned how to exist—he couldn't call it a life—organized and small while living in the state homes. Now those skills served him in good stead.

When he'd finished, with Kelli's soft playing still present in the background, he went to his own living space and pulled the sheets. He knew he needed to go back out. They hadn't gotten any water, and they needed water. That had been one of the primary objectives of their foraging tonight.

But he lay back on his bed. Even in the middle of chaos, with demons roaming loose in the city, he'd made his bed. Every day, as soon as he got up, he always made his bed. Nothing else could take place till that was done. He'd learned that habit from a family he'd stayed with whose father was a Special Air Service member, a drill instructor.

Shelves held his comics, favorite books, and DVDs. The DVDs had been the hardest to hang on to while living with flat mates who tended to borrow things. In the end he'd made them *untouchable*.

He didn't know what else to call it. He'd learned the skill while in foster homes. All of his life he'd been small and sickly, easy to take advantage of. But he'd learned to fight back in his own way.

He could manipulate people. As long as they didn't know they were being manipulated. Tonight Kelli hadn't noticed because she'd been so scared. Fear had been her overriding emotion. She hadn't even felt him tampering with her mind.

Through trial and error, he'd learned that he could gradually manipulate others he lived with to leave his personal effects alone. It worked on things like DVDs and books, but he couldn't keep them from taking his money. They'd simply wanted the money more than he'd been able to control them.

Tonight Kelli had wanted to be safe. She'd wanted to believe him. She'd been easy.

But the demon . . .

He truly hadn't known he could do that. That had been pure fear. Just the way it had been the night his parents had . . . died.

Reluctantly, he took the piece of paper from his jeans pocket and looked at the address. It wasn't too far away.

Fear ached within him. He didn't know if it was a warning from that mysterious power within him, or a reluctance to embrace the beast he felt certain lived somewhere trapped within him.

EIGHT

For two days, Simon searched for some means to get out of Cape Town. All the commercial airlines refused to go that direction. He was getting desperate enough to attempt to go by boat when he heard about a mercenary pilot who'd been hired to fly English citizens back at least to France.

The man's name was Horner, and he'd set up in a back room in Walter's. The bartender, Flynn, sent word to Simon by one of the boys who hung around outside the bar to run messages no one wanted to use the phone for.

Horner was a big man. Tanned and gaunt, he was sixty years old if he was a day, and had a drinker's road map of burst veins across his nose and sallow cheeks. He wore an old Grateful Dead t-shirt with the sleeves hacked off and a bandolier of rounds crossed his chest. Amber-tinted aviator's glasses covered his eyes beneath an Australian Outback hat with one flap pinned up.

Two armed men sat on either side of the pilot. They held shotguns at the ready.

Horner looked up at Simon. "You Cross?" he asked in a voice scarred by cigarette smoke and booze.

"I am."

Nodding at Saundra, Horner asked, "Who's the woman?"

"My friend."

"I heard you only wanted passage for one."

"I do."

"So who's going?"

"Me." Simon felt sad about that. He'd miss Saundra, and as yet they didn't know if she had a way to Australia. He promised he'd keep in touch to find out. If he could.

"If I'd have known how big you were before we set a price on this, I'd have charged by the pound." Horner grinned.

Simon didn't feel good enough to exchange witticisms. There'd still been no shortwave contact with London. "When do we leave?"

"First light in the morning. Do you have the money?"

Simon took out a packet of bills and passed them over. The price had wiped out nearly everything he'd managed to save while in Cape Town. He'd even had to sell his gear and his weapons.

Horner thumbed the bills. "Looks like it's all here." He tucked the packet into a pocket and gazed at Simon speculatively. "You plan on going all the way to London?"

"Yes."

Nodding, Horner took out a pack of cigarettes and lit up. "I know a man in France. You can get a ride with him on his boat." He waved away smoke from his cigarette and dropped the spent match into one of the empty glasses in front of him. "They're still trying to ferry people out of there. The French ain't too happy about it, but that's how it is."

Simon shook his head. "That's all the money I've got."

Horner sighed and sucked air through his teeth. "Money would have made it easier, but I can still work it out for you. Those boat trips across the Channel aren't safe. Those alien beasts are pursuing survivors all the way to the shore."

"They're not crossing the Channel?"

"Not yet. But the French army is massed up there. Got a skirmish line. I don't think it's going to do them any more good than it did the British. But this man I know, he isn't selling seats to get *into* England; he's selling seats to get *out*. I'll tell him you'll help work as security on the way over. But you can bet he'll put a boot in your arse if you try to come back."

Simon nodded. "All right."

Horner offered his hand. "Then we got a deal. Kiss your friend good-bye tonight and come see me in the morning. Six o'clock. If you're late, me and your money are on our way north."

Horner's plane was an old military cargo transport that looked like it had seen better days, but the props spun smoothly and the engines sounded strong. A blonde in sunglasses and a bikini was spray-painted beneath the pilot's window.

Saundra held Simon's hand as they stopped a few feet short of the gangway leading up to the cargo hold. He turned to face her.

"I guess this is good-bye," he said, feeling terribly awkward. He suddenly didn't know what to say. When they'd first met, it had been like that. Not sure of what to say or not to say. But in the last year and a half, they'd come to know each other well. She was the best friend he'd had, even counting his shield mates—the boys he'd grown up with—back in the Underground. She'd understood him in ways that he'd never thought anyone would.

And he was about to lose all that. Maybe forever.

It was hard to deal with, something that he truly hadn't understood until just this moment. He wavered, thinking that it was already too late in London and that his presence there wouldn't matter. That made the most sense. What could one man do? He'd be better served staying with Saundra and trying to keep his own skin intact.

Except he couldn't do that. His father's constant brainwashing from the time he'd been born wouldn't allow him to do that. He had to go, to see if anything could be done and to find out what had become of his father.

But I don't have to die there. It felt good deciding that.

Saundra smiled at Simon, but the effort looked a little frayed around the edges.

"Not good-bye," Saundra said. "Just 'See you later.' When you get a chance, let me know how you are."

"I will." She'd already given him her father's call signs on the shortwave radio.

"Maybe I'll come see you," Saundra said. "After the military sends the aliens packing. I've always wanted to see London."

Simon thought of all the crumbled buildings he'd seen in the news footage. *There doesn't seem to be much of it left.* But he nodded. Then he took her in his arms and kissed her good-bye.

It was hard letting go, but he made himself. Squaring his shoulders, redistributing his backpack, he squeezed her hand a final time and headed up the gangway.

The cargo hold was jammed with supplies and people. Horner's grizzled payload master took one look at Simon and cursed. "I heard you were a big one, mate, but Lord love a duck." He consulted his clipboard and started moving the passengers around, balancing the weight.

Feeling awkward the way he often did when he got trapped in large groups of people, Simon sat against the side of the plane, taking a seat on the metal floor and dropping his backpack in front of him between his knees.

He leaned back, resting against the vibrating surface. He

hadn't slept much last night. Not knowing if he'd ever see Saundra again had made the last few hours they'd had together even more special—and desperate. A headache dawned between his eyes and he tried to relax. He hated flying with someone else at the wheel.

A moment later, he realized he was being stared at.

Opening his eyes, he caught a glimpse of a young woman seated on the other side of the cargo area as she looked away from him. She acted as though she'd only been glancing around, but Simon knew he'd felt the weight of her gaze on him.

He didn't recognize her. She was tall and slender, athletic, not fragile, dressed in jeans and a simple blouse. She wore hiking shoes and had a backpack on the ground in front of her. Her brunette hair was so dark it was almost black, but it was cut close to her head. Her eyes, Simon remembered, were a deep violet. Striking, memorable eyes. He knew he would have remembered seeing her before if he had.

So why are you interested in me? Then Simon realized he was being paranoid, or maybe even egotistical. Everyone in the cargo area was staring at everyone else.

The man to Simon's right spoke up. "Hello." He offered a hand.

Simon took it, but didn't say anything. He didn't feel like conversation.

"Philip," the man said. "Philip Torrance." He looked like a salesman, dressed in a white shirt and slacks. He was in his thirties or forties, tanned and fit.

"Simon Cross."

"How far are you going? If you don't mind my asking."

"London."

The man frowned. "You do realize the plane doesn't go that far?"

"Yes."

"I'd heard there was a way to get to England from France, but I'm not interested in doing that. Too dangerous. I'm going to take up a support position. They've got a lot of people coming out of England. I want to do what I can to help."

Simon nodded. As he looked around, he wondered how many people were interested in going to London. He was aware of the violet-eyed young woman watching him again.

The engines suddenly whined louder, filling the cargo area with noise. The loadmaster and his three assistants plopped down onto the floor against the wall. The crates and bags behind the cargo netting in the rear of the compartment shook and vibrated. A moment later, the plane lurched forward as the pilot released the brakes.

Laying his head back, Simon closed his eyes and wondered if he was doing the right thing. His father was doubtless dead, and he wasn't sure how he felt about that. So what was there waiting for him in London?

A chill filled the cargo area as the plane closed on the last few miles of the final leg of its journey. When Simon breathed out now he could see his breath, pale gray in the barely moving air.

Wrapped in a blanket, he sat against the cold metal of the bulkhead and tried to sleep. Normally, no matter what was going on, he could at least count on sleep. And all he'd done for the last three days of the flight was stress and worry.

They'd gotten news secondhand for the most part. Radios didn't pick up signals inside the cargo hold, and they were never at the fuel depots much longer than to pick up fuel and sandwiches. Both of which were way overpriced.

Stories continued to filter out of London, but they were tales of horror. The city remained wreathed in smoke, burning constantly.

A short time later, the cargo team passed out self-heating tins of beef stew.

Simon sat cross-legged and pulled the tab that activated the chemical reaction that heated the stew. He breathed the scent of the stew in as he waited for the contents to reach temperature. His stomach rumbled in anticipation.

The cargo team also passed out chunks of bread and bottles of water.

Gnawing on the bread, Simon chewed it thoroughly. If he didn't, he'd found during an earlier meal, the bread would lie like a congealed lump in his stomach. He sipped the water.

The young woman watched him through the fringe of hair that hung down over her eyes. Even though Simon couldn't see her eyes, he knew she was watching. He just didn't know why.

He peeled the stubby spoon from around the mug-shaped can and snapped it out straight. When the stew had cooled sufficiently, he spooned it up, emptying the contents too quickly. He turned his attention back to the bread.

The young woman leaned forward, extending her tin toward Simon. "Are you still hungry?"

Simon didn't say anything, but his stomach rumbled at the prospect of more food.

"I'm through with this."

Reaching forward, Simon took the tin, then offered it to a young mother and baby to his left. He'd watched them during the trip, noting that the mother sometimes looked tired and still hungry after their meager allotment.

The woman hesitated, then nodded her thanks. Simon didn't think she knew English, but he wasn't sure what her native tongue might be. She took the tin from him, darting a quick, furtive glance at the young woman.

The young woman turned her violet eyes back to Simon. "My name's Leah. Leah Creasey."

Feeling a little awkward because he'd taken the woman's offering, Simon gave her his name.

Leah brushed a lock of dark hair back behind her ear. "You're going to London?"

"Yes."

"So am I."

Simon didn't say anything.

"I don't know anyone else who is," Leah said.

As far as Simon knew, no one else intended to go to London. Or any part of England. They were all hoping to find survivors in the refugee camps in northern France.

"Do you have a way to get there?"

"Maybe."

"Can I come with you?"

Simon studied the woman for a moment. She looked slim and compact, more of an acrobat than an athlete. He felt certain Saundra could have taken her hands down in a physical encounter. He knew he didn't want any baggage trailing along after him when he reached London. Or even during the trip there. He was headed into a war zone.

"Please." Leah's voice softened.

Hardening his heart, telling himself that the woman's welfare was no concern of his, Simon started to say no.

"It's my father," Leah went on. Her violet eyes gleamed wetly. "After my mother died, we only had each other." She drew in a quick breath to calm herself. "I got mad at him a few months ago. I had no business doing that. He put me through university, then wondered why I wasn't working at a job I'd trained for. Marketing. I ended up back in the same dress shop I'd worked my way through university in.

Ended up barely making the bills again. Almost starving to death. He told me he didn't see to it that I got all that training only to see it go to waste."

The words hit home inside Simon, cutting deeply. They were a lot like the final words he'd had with his own father before he'd picked up and gone to South Africa. Simon had received Templar training all his life, and his father had rebuked him for squandering it with his excesses in extreme sports. The base-jumping had been the final straw.

"I tried to tell him that jobs weren't that easy to come by," Leah said. "But he wouldn't listen." She wiped at her eyes and wetness gleamed on her fingers. "So I got a job, only it was down in South Africa and he didn't like that, either. By that time I was mad, and I'd already signed off on my flat. All my money was tied up in moving to South Africa and making it in that job."

Simon felt the weight of his own decision settling across his shoulders. It hadn't been easy. And he knew exactly what Leah had gone through.

"That was fourteen months ago," Leah whispered raggedly. "I haven't been back to see my father since. If something's happened to him—" Her voice broke and she couldn't continue speaking.

Simon tried to figure out what to say but couldn't. Leah's fears were his own, and he didn't know how to deal with his own.

Angrily, with a trace of embarrassment, Leah slid away from him and resumed her place on the other side of the plane.

For a while, Simon tried to listen to the plane's engines and the other whispered conversations around him. He wanted something to take away the guilt and fear that plagued him. *She's not my problem.* But he felt like she was.

She'd touched his emotions and made him realize how raw they were.

"Maybe your father made it out of London," Simon said after a while. "He could be in one of the refugee camps."

Leah ignored him. She turned on her side and pulled a worn coat up over her head, shutting him out.

Simon leaned back against the bulkhead and closed his eyes. Her father might have made it out of London. Several thousand had. But Simon knew his father would never leave. Grudgingly, his stomach partially full, he drifted off to sleep.

But the demons waited on him there.

NINE

REFUGEE CAMP
OUTSIDE PARIS, FRANCE

S imon only stayed in Paris for sixteen hours, long enough to secure passage to Coquelles, not far from Calais. A heavy blanket of snow lay over the French countryside. Most of the meteorologists seemed to think it had something to do with the strange weather and power that seemed to gather over London.

On the tri-dee, storms roared through London's streets without interruption, filled with jagged lightning and un-accustomed heat. Some of the reports that got out of the city said that an incredible black fog filled much of the sky and blotted out the sun.

"You're sure you want to go there?" the truck driver asked after Simon had made the deal to help with the cargo in return for them taking him along.

"I need to," Simon said. If he had to, he'd walk through the snow to get to the hell on earth dawning in London.

In the back of a cargo truck filled with supplies for the English refugees, Simon sat still and tried to remain warm. He'd arranged passage by agreeing to help the truck driver and his second with the loading and off-loading of the supplies. It was backbreaking labor, but they'd added sandwiches and wine as well.

The back of the truck wasn't heated. He'd managed to buy a heavy winter coat, gloves, and a watchcap with some of the money he had left. There hadn't been enough money left over to purchase a pistol and ammunition although he'd wanted some kind of armament.

Not that it would do any good against the demons.

His breath fogged out in front of him. Cases and buckets rattled in their restraints as the driver drove. Through the flaps at the rear of the truck, snow continued to come down in thick, fat flakes. Pristine whiteness, lit up by the moon, already covered the landscape.

Without warning, the truck jerked violently to one side. Boxes tumbled across each other and crates skidded across the metal floor.

Simon shoved both arms out, managing to span the rear compartment of the truck and brace himself as boxes fell all over him with bruising force. For a moment he thought the driver was going to lose his vehicle.

When the truck finally stopped, Simon pushed the supplies off and stood up. He stepped over the tailgate and down to the ground.

The driver and the handler stood at the front of the truck, gazing glumly down at the shredded left front tire. The driver cursed beautifully, and with real feeling.

"What happened?" Simon asked in French.

"I don't know. It just went out from under me. Lucky I didn't crash us into a tree and kill us both."

The truck had left the road and plowed through the newly fallen snow. The fluffy whiteness came almost to the top of the truck's hood. A deep path led back to the road.

"Hey." The handler pointed down road at a pair of approaching headlights. "Someone's coming."

The driver returned to the truck cab and brought out a roadside flare. He triggered the ignition and a blaze of sparks carved a hole out of the darkness before settling down to a deep ruby glow. He tossed it onto the road.

Simon waited, but he stood apart from the other two men. There were more good stories to tell at the moment than bad ones, but the tales of thieves and murderers still ran rampant. If the people in the other truck intended to do them harm, Simon felt he still had a chance to escape cross-country. He could survive in the harsh climate.

He stood silently at the truck's side, taking advantage of the shadows. The vehicle was another truck from Paris. The new arrival was loaded up with supplies as well.

Leah Creasey sat inside the cab, but she got out with the driver. She looked swallowed up by the big coat she wore.

The drivers quickly sized up the situation, then the man who'd driven the wrecked truck came back to Simon.

"The truck," the man said, "isn't going to go anywhere. Even with the winch on the other truck, we're more likely to get them stuck as well. Jacques and I will stay with the truck, but the other driver has offered to take you the rest of the way."

Simon studied the older man's face. Everything in Simon screamed to go, not remain stuck here. But that wasn't how his father had brought him up. He'd been brought up to keep his word, and now—in the face of everything going on in London—that seemed important to do.

"I said I'd help you unload the truck in exchange for the ride," Simon replied in French.

The driver waved the offer away. "It will be hours, per- haps days, before anyone arrives to help us, my young friend. You've said you have family in the refugee camps. Go. Go and take care of your family."

Simon didn't argue. He thanked the man and started for the back of the truck.

Instead, the driver of that one waved to him. "Up here. Sit in the cab with us. There is room."

Staring through the frost-covered window, Simon saw Leah looking back at him.

"Hurry," the driver said. "There are people much in need of these supplies."

Reluctantly, Simon opened the door and clambered inside. Leah scooted over, but there was still barely enough room.

"It's going to be a tight fit," Simon said. "I can sit in the back."

"Nonsense. We'll be fine." The driver engaged the gears. "Perhaps a little more warm than we otherwise might have been." He smiled beneath his mustache. "Lucky for you we came along, eh?"

Simon nodded and looked out the window at the two men they'd left with the truck. *Not so lucky for them.* Then he breathed out and the window fogged, erasing them from view.

Hours later, Simon came awake as the truck driver changed gears and pulled off the main road. A sign beside the road announced *Coquelles.*

Leah slept beside Simon. Her head rested against his arm, rocking gently with the sway of the truck.

"Not much longer," the driver said.

Simon looked down at Leah and thought about waking her. In the end he decided against it, thinking there was no reason for her to dread what she was about to find out.

"You're planning to go to England?" the driver asked.

"Yes."

"You have family there?"

"My father."

The driver glanced at Simon. "Things over there . . . they're not so good, you know." Concern showed in his weathered face.

"I know."

"Perhaps your father, he will be in the refugee camp. One can hope so, eh?"

"Sure," Simon said. "Maybe he will be."

But Thomas Cross wasn't at the refugee camp.

The camp was a collection of featureless prefab buildings plunked down all around the small town that lay at the other end of the channel tunnel. For a time the underground and underwater railway line had been nicknamed the *Chunnel* but the name hadn't stuck.

The prefab buildings had been added when the survivors first started coming over from England. From the stories Simon gathered, many of them had come over by the tube, almost reaching the other end from Folkestone, Kent, before the power had gone off. For days, several others had trickled through on foot, till finally the monsters had shut down all egress through the channel tunnel.

Monsters.

That was what they were calling them now. Simon knew the name fit. He'd read about them in the Underground nearly every day of his life.

The survivors were lost and traumatized. Most of them were still awaiting word of family and friends, but hope dimmed with each passing hour. Boats and ships seldom made passage across the English Channel now. More often than not, captains brave enough to take their vessels across the water were getting sunk. And there were precious few survivors left to pick up along the coast. The *monsters* hunted there as well.

With dawn breaking in the east, a golden glow in a vague dirty-cotton sky, Simon found the man he'd been told about. Bolivar Patel was a salvage expert who'd plied his trade in the frigid North Sea and in the English Channel. Tanned and fit, he was in his early fifties, spry and fierce. His East Indian heritage showed in his dark skin and hawkish nose.

Simon found the man in the cantina after hearing he'd arrived less than an hour earlier with a boatload of survivors. Most of them were children whose parents had stayed behind.

The cantina was crowded, serving out soup and bread to hundreds that came up with bowl and mug in hand. They had their choice between tea and water.

"Captain Patel?" Simon called.

The captain turned to look at him.

Simon knew his size made him stand out immediately.

"Do I know you?" Patel stood with a bowl of soup and bread in one hand, a cup of tea in the other. He wore dungarees, a khaki shirt, a thick woolen coat and a winter hat. A burn stood out against his left cheek.

"No, sir." Quietly, Simon told Patel about his need to get to England, and of Horner's message.

"Get something to eat," Patel said, "then join me over there." He waved toward a table in the corner where five men sat hunkered together.

Simon hesitated, then went and stood in line till he was served. He joined the men in the corner.

Patel quickly made introductions, identifying each of the men as part of his crew. Most of them had finished eating and now sat smoking.

"You'd have to be a fool to want to go there." Patel pushed a chunk of bread across the bottom of his bowl to get at the last of the soup.

Anger stirred within Simon, but he kept it tightly under control. "My father is there."

Patel eyed him warily. "Your father—" He sighed tiredly

and wiped at his dark eyes. "You'll have to forgive my bluntness, Mr. Cross. I've not much use for politeness these days."

"I understand."

"I hope so." Patel chewed and swallowed. "But the sad truth of the matter is that your father is most likely dead."

"I have to know."

Patel stared at him a little while longer. "Can you use a rifle, Mr. Cross?"

"I can. And well."

"We'll see." Patel grinned slightly, but there was no mirth in the effort. "These . . . *creatures* are almost unkillable."

With what you're using, yes. Simon ate his soup, finding it warm and tasty.

"If we see them, if we engage them, the guns we have are there only to slow them down long enough for us to escape. If I should be faced with the dilemma of you not leaving the boat to make room for a woman or child when we reach the other side of the Channel, you should know that I will kill you to make that happen."

Looking into the man's cold, dead eyes, Simon believed him.

"There won't be a problem," Simon assured him.

"Then be at the dock an hour before sunset."

"Thank you, Captain Patel."

Scowling, Patel stood and took his bowl with him. "Don't thank me, Mr. Cross. By allowing you to do this, I've very probably just signed your death warrant."

TEN

Conscious of the night around him, Warren stood across the street from the building. The address matched what had been on the piece of paper the woman had given him. Trepidation, confusion, and curiosity warred within him. Curiosity was winning out, but he didn't give in to it easily.

There was so much he wanted to know. And so much he was afraid of.

Remembering his mother's curiosity about the arcane held him back. The interest had transcended, became more than curiosity and turned into obsession. In the end, it had gotten her killed. It had almost gotten Warren killed too.

The gunshots that had forever changed Warren's life echoed inside his head again. The sounds triggered the smell of burned flesh, then a wave of sickness that turned his knees to water. He leaned heavily against the building behind him.

Bloated corpses lay on the sidewalk around him. The legs of another stretched out of a window within his reach. A trio of cats fed on it, safer there than on the street.

In the aftermath of the demonic invasion of London, many of the borderline domesticated animals—such as cats and birds—had turned feral again. During the fitful snatches of conversations he'd had with other scavengers the last few days, Warren had learned that some people believed animals had been affected by whatever evil magic now filled London.

It seemed only fair that the animals turn on the humans, though. The people that had once fed the cats and the pigeons in the park now stalked them for food. The immediate world was turning into a grim place.

You're going to have to turn with it, Warren told himself. *Or you're going to die.* He knew that was true. When no immediate rescue had come with several days now passed, he'd had to give up on it and direct his thinking toward survival.

Days had passed since the Hellgates had opened. There hadn't been an hour that Warren hadn't thought of the note in his pocket. Several times he'd come close by but hadn't approached the building.

The structure was an older eight-story apartment building. Snow covered the street, the eaves, and the windowsills. No lights showed anywhere. If not for the people that Warren saw going in and out, he'd have thought the building abandoned.

There was something more there, though. *Magic* surrounded the building. He could feel it and recognize it for what it was.

But why hadn't the demons discovered it? Unconsciously, he turned to look at the malevolent smoke from the Hellgates that permanently smudged the horizon these days. It was still there, still pulsing against the sky and doing whatever it was doing to ruin the city.

Reaching into his pocket, Warren took out a peppermint candy, unwrapped it, and popped it into his mouth. Then, knowing he really didn't have a choice if he wanted to know for himself, he shoved his hands into his duster pockets and crossed the street.

* * *

"Who are you?"

For a moment, Warren thought the voice had come from the building. Instinctively, he retreated down the short flight of steps leading up to the building's front door.

Then a big, blocky man with no neck and a bowling ball for a head moved out of the shadows and into the moonlight and snow. Cool green fires burned along the lines of the tattoos that covered his face. He'd shaved his head, showing even more tattooing there. Gold hoops dangled from his ears.

"Warren," Warren stammered. "I'm . . . Warren."

"What are you doing here, Warren?" The man had a Scots accent.

"I was invited."

"You?" The man raised an eyebrow, arched sharply in doubt. "Who would be inviting you?"

"Edith Buckner."

The man frowned. "She didn't say anything about inviting you."

"Maybe I made a mistake." Warren started to leave. Before he reached the last step, though, he knew leaving was the wrong thing to do. That itch inside his mind tugged him back toward the building. He stopped and turned around, looking straight up the side of the building.

He felt the power inside the structure. It was strong, but it was unfocused, wavering, rising and falling like ocean surf pounding a beach. It was like a symphony, but rather than being in harmony, the notes were discordant and jarring. The vibration set his teeth on edge.

But he belonged inside. He was certain of that.

With meaty arms crossed over his broad chest, the big man still stared at Warren malevolently. His coat had opened enough to reveal the butt of the pistol he had hidden there.

Heart at the back of his throat, Warren ascended the steps again. He locked eyes with the big man, pushing with his mind the way he'd intuitively learned to do.

"I belong in there," Warren said in an even voice.

"Not without an invitation," the man replied.

Warren took the folded piece of paper from his pocket. He held it out.

"This is the invitation," he said. He put as much confidence in his voice as he could, and he willed the bouncer to see exactly what he needed to see. "It's the best invitation anyone could ever possibly have."

The bouncer reached for the pistol under his coat, then pulled his hand away. He studied the piece of paper harder, then nodded. "Go on in."

"What floor?"

"The eighth."

Without another word, Warren entered the building. His heart pounded against his breastbone as he passed through the door. He couldn't believe he'd gotten past the man. But he already felt stronger.

He took a torch from his pocket, switched it on, located the stairwell, and started up.

On the eighth floor, Warren felt the energy more strongly. It was like a river current, pulling him toward it. Even though he still considered turning back, he knew he couldn't. Whatever lay before him in this life, it lay wherever the energy came from.

He flicked the torch on at the doorway, briefly illuminating the corridor. When he saw the people sitting on the floor in the hallway, all of them looking at him, he was so surprised he almost dropped the torch. The beam danced across the tattooed faces as his hand shook.

Too late, he realized that the light might be seen outside.

He didn't want to draw demons to the building. He quickly flicked it off.

"Sorry," he mumbled, pocketing the flash.

"He can't see," someone whispered.

"Who is he?"

"What's he doing here if he can't see in the dark?"

"How did he get here?"

"Is he alone?"

"How did he get past McCallum?"

Clothing rustled and Warren knew some of the people seated in the corridor had gotten to their feet and closed in on him. His imagination filled their hands with weapons, guns, and knives. He didn't know how they could see him in the Stygian black.

Images of the magic shops his mother had dragged him to as a child filled his mind. Those places had been small, almost having to hide in plain sight so the average Londoner wouldn't see them.

Some shops disguised themselves as magic shops for hobbyists. They stocked marked cards and even a few elaborate tricks for the cursory observer. But they kept the books on the arcane lore in the back.

Other shops declared themselves as New Age boutiques. They kept crystals and tarot cards. But—again—the real knowledge was kept under lock and key.

A few, like the ones Warren's mother frequented, openly displayed their goods. Books on demonology, intricate artifacts modeled on items that had been brought back during the Crusades, and scrying glasses could be found on the shelves. But even they kept the skulls of sages, the bones of saints, and weapons that had soaked in the blood of victims in the back.

"I'm alone," Warren said. He tried to broadcast a feeling of well-being over the crowd gathered in the darkness before him. During the time he'd had the flashlight on, he'd discovered the windows at either end of the corridor were covered in thick cloth that didn't let light in or out. "I don't mean anyone any harm."

"You couldn't cause anyone here any harm, boy," a man's voice promised.

Warren felt someone's hot breath against the back of his neck. He didn't move, not because he didn't want them to know he was afraid—he was sure they knew that he was—but because he was afraid he was going to step on someone and make the situation worse.

"I didn't come here to disturb anyone," Warren said quietly. "I only came because I was invited."

"By who?"

"Edith," Warren said. "Edith Buckner."

"Ah," someone said. "He must be the one."

"The one that Edith talked about," someone else agreed.

"The one who talked to the demon."

"She said he'd be coming to us."

"I don't believe what she's said about him."

"He's here, isn't he?"

Warren couldn't believe the woman had told anyone about him. Or that she had felt certain he'd show up there.

He felt them moving around him in a circle. Every now and again someone's robe would brush against him. Less often, someone touched him, the tactile impression so light that he barely felt it.

"She says he has power," someone said.

"Real power."

"You can see it in him."

"*I* see it," someone said.

"Get Edith."

There was another rustle of clothing as someone left.

Warren stood very still. More than anything at the moment, he wanted to see through the darkness.

A moment later, a voice asked, "Do you really want to see in the darkness, Warren?"

He recognized Edith Buckner's dulcet tones. He tried to face her, but he wasn't sure where she was.

"Yes," he said.

"Then," she whispered, "open your eyes and see."

Warren looked around in the darkness. "I can't."

"You're not letting yourself. The same power you used to talk to the demon will allow you to see in this darkness. You just have to use that power."

"Look," he said, desperate to leave, "I made a mistake." He knew that wasn't true the minute he said that. He hadn't made a mistake in coming there. He just didn't know what he was supposed to do now that he was there. "I shouldn't have come."

Pain lit up the side of his face. Only after his head jerked to the side and the sound of flesh striking flesh did he realize he'd been slapped.

She'd hit him. Or someone had.

"Open your eyes," the woman commanded. "Open your eyes and *see.*"

"I—"

Another stinging slap nearly drove Warren to his knees. For a moment in the darkness, he felt like he was back in the foster homes, wakened from sleep again.

Fear and anger mixed within him. He'd always sworn he wouldn't go back to being afraid like that. Or be bullied. Never again. He was through being helpless. All he needed to do was find the stairwell, then he could—

Someone hit him again. The blow split his lips. He tasted blood. And the rage inside him boiled over.

"Open your eyes," the woman commanded.

Warren did, discovering that the pain had caused him to snap them closed. When he opened his eyes, he found that he could see as clearly in the corridor as if on a moonlit night. The sight startled him, and he thought for a moment someone had turned on a light.

"His eyes," someone said.

"He can see."

"Edith was right."

A man tried to slap Warren, but Warren caught the man's hand and stopped the blow. Warren felt stronger than he ever had. Even though the man was bigger than he was, he'd controlled his arm like it was nothing.

"Stop," Warren told the man.

A paroxysm violently twisted the man's face. His eyes rolled up into his head. Then he dropped to the floor and lay on his back.

The crowd stepped back from him. One of the men dropped to his knees and tried to wake the fallen man. He checked him quickly, holding a palm over the man's mouth and nose, then pressing an ear to his chest.

In disbelief, the man looked up at Warren and the others. "He's not breathing. I can't find a pulse."

"Joel is dead," someone whispered.

"That boy killed him."

ELEVEN

*D*ead.

 The word reverberated through Warren's skull. He stared down at the man.

"He can't be dead," Edith Buckner said. "The boy didn't touch him."

"I worked in an ER," the man kneeling beside the body said. "I know dead when I see it, and Joel is dead."

Warren's face still burned from the slaps he'd received while blind in the darkness. But that was small compared to the confusion and disbelief that he felt as he looked at the fallen man.

"I didn't do anything," Warren whispered hoarsely. "I just didn't want him to hit me again." Memory of his stepfather and mother's last argument came to mind.

"You spent all our money again!" his stepfather roared.

"I'm really close to breaking through," his mother had protested. "I needed things. The money I've spent trying to get in touch with my power isn't going to matter. Once I've achieved mastery over the arcane—"

"Mastery?" His stepfather had never been a patient man. He'd never been a forgiving one either. "You can't even manage a house, you cow! We live in filth! I work hard all day—"

"You're a thief! Don't you go getting sanctimonious with me! I know what you are! You and your friends are just—"

As he always had before, Warren had hidden behind the couch in the cramped living room. His mother's books on magic and lore filled much of the space, but there were also vid components, computers, and other stuff his stepfather had nicked that he hadn't yet fenced.

Usually there was a lot of fighting, some hitting, and drinking that followed. He'd learned that all he had to do was stay out of the way until things got quiet again.

But that wasn't the case that night. He hadn't known it then, but a drug dealer that his stepfather had robbed a few days ago had figured out who he was and was tracking him down. His stepfather could leave London, grass to the cops, or die. The drug dealer had already killed one of his stepfather's accomplices.

The argument hadn't ended routinely.

Trapped by his own fear and anger, his stepfather had pulled out his pistol and shot Warren's mother in the face and chest. He'd killed her, screaming curses at her the whole time, blaming her for the desperation that had sent him after the drug dealer's score instead of playing things safely.

Unable to help himself, only eight years old, Warren had started screaming and calling out to his mother. His stepfather turned the big pistol on him. Warren had known without a doubt that his stepfather was going to kill him.

The first bullet caught Warren in the hip and spun him around. He fell, paralyzed from the pain and the blunt force. The second bullet struck the wall only inches from his head.

That was when Warren had looked at his stepfather and said, "I wish you were dead." And he'd wanted it with every fiber of his being.

Instead of shooting Warren, his stepfather had pulled the gun to his own temple, crying and screaming for help the whole time, and pulled the trigger. The smell of burned flesh, scorched by the pistol blast, had filled the air.

* * *

All those memories spun through Warren's thoughts. Even after fifteen years, they were never far away. A neighbor had called the police. Warren had been transported to the hospital and turned over to foster care as soon as he was well enough to walk out.

But his stepfather had deserved to die. He'd been the most fearful thing Warren had ever known. He still had nightmares about the man.

Warren didn't even know the man on the floor. He didn't even know if the man was the same one who had been hitting him.

Edith Buckner leaned down and laid a hand over the man's heart. "Breathe," she commanded. A shimmer stretched out from her hand.

The man bucked up violently, like someone had seized him by the belt and yanked. Then he fell back onto the floor.

"He's still not breathing," the first man said after a brief inspection.

Edith repeated her command a second time. During this instance, the shadows seemed to recoil from her.

A moment later, the man let out a large breath. Then he sucked it back in again.

"He's alive."

"Edith saved him."

Gathering her robe around her, green light slithering through her horns and the tattooing on her face, Edith looked at Warren. "I'm glad you've come."

Warren didn't know what he was supposed to say. Part of him wanted to leave immediately. Just start running and not stop until he was somewhere out on the street.

"Your arrival isn't any too soon," the woman said. "Another few days, if you don't learn how to mask your ability, the demons will feel you pass by and you'll never be able to evade them again. Your suggestion trick won't work then. They'll hunt you down and kill you."

"But I didn't do that," Warren said, pointing to the man, who appeared panicked and not quite sure of where he was. "He must have just . . . just had a *seizure*."

"That wasn't a seizure," Edith said. "That was power. I've never seen anyone stop someone's heart with a word before."

"I didn't—"

"He did," one of the viewers commented. "I felt the power in his voice."

Warren wished they would shut up as he watched the fallen man wander around shell-shocked, led and comforted by the man who had tried to treat him. *I didn't do that. I couldn't have done that.*

Yet he knew he had.

"Your powers started manifesting themselves when your stepfather tried to kill you?"

Tensely, Warren sat in an overstuffed chair and faced Edith and a man she'd introduced as Jonas. Jonas had asked the question. In his thirties, he was over six feet tall, almost as tall as Warren, and was built more heavily. His eyes were dark but glowed silver with energy. Although no one had said it, he was clearly the leader of the group, but Edith was close behind him.

Like the others, Jonas was heavily tattooed, but he had a number of scars and piercings as well. Several of them looked extremely painful.

"I don't know," Warren answered. After the close call out in the corridor, he wasn't sure what to believe.

"You caused your stepfather to kill himself," Jonas said.

"He had it coming," Warren said defensively. "He'd killed my mother and shot me."

Jonas held up a placating hand. "That wasn't an accusation. Your stepfather sounded like an evil man."

"He was." For the first time Warren saw the strange growths on the back of Jonas's hands. They'd been attached just below his wrists. Even with his improved vision, Warren could barely make them out. Writhing and twisting, they looked like small tentacles.

They were in a small room off from the main one. The building's whole top floor had been mostly converted into one large area. Only four offices remained. Both rooms that Warren had been in featured strange graffiti on the walls and floors. There were also artifacts that he'd never seen before but that seemed somehow familiar.

The robed people sat in small groups. They ate and tattooed each other, working on totally naked landscapes of flesh. Others read from books and scrolls or practiced some kind of meditation exercises.

Others came and went all the time, bringing supplies and news of what was happening in the city.

"It's just that most people don't come into that kind of power at such an early age," Jonas said. "In fact, I'd wager to say that no one in this room can stop a man's heart with a word." He smiled a little, and Warren knew it was to allay his suspicions.

For the most part, Warren knew he could read the man. Jonas wouldn't be able to lie to him. But he could hide things from him. Warren felt those hidden things lurking around behind the man's thoughts.

"You're unusual," Edith said, smiling.

"To say the least," Jonas agreed. He reached into his robe and brought out a coin. Holding the coin in his hand, he looked at Warren. "Can you lift this coin?"

Thinking it was a trick, Warren hesitated a moment, then reached for the coin.

"Not with your fingers," Jonas instructed. "With your mind."

Warren took his hand back. "No." *Of course I can't. That's ridiculous.*

"It's not ridiculous," Jonas said. "Before you came here tonight you didn't think you could see in the dark."

Warren acknowledged that with a nod.

"Many things that you thought of as impossible were possible even before the demons invaded the city," Jonas said. "Reports of those things—out-of-body experiences, precognition, extrasensory perception—were in the news. You've heard of those?"

"Yes." Warren didn't know how many books on the subject his mother had bought and read and reread.

"The problem has always been the plethora of pretenders. There was no way for the public to separate trickery from true power."

Warren had believed that everyone his mother had seen was a grifter only too glad to take his stepfather's money. He'd never seen any true magic.

Not until the night your stepfather blew his brains out.

Jonas licked his lips and turned his attention to the coin. "Plus, before the Hellgates opened, the powers that had manifested had been slight by comparison. Only flashes and glimpses of what would come. Do you know what telekinesis is?"

Warren shifted. "I know what it's supposed to be."

"Indulge me."

"You're supposed to be able to lift things with your mind."

"Do you believe that?"

"No. Of course not."

Jonas smiled at him. "Why?"

"Because it's not real. No one can do—"

Jonas took his hand from beneath the coin. The coin floated in midair. "Some can."

Warren stared at the hovering coin. He felt the power Jonas was using to perform the feat vibrating deeply within him.

"Before the invasion," Jonas said, "I couldn't do anything more than move a coin across a flat surface less than an inch. I couldn't even flip it. Now, that's no problem."

The coin spun on an invisible axis, gaining speed to the point that it looked like a silver ball hanging in the air.

"You'll have to forgive Jonas," Edith said. "He's quite fond of his trick."

"It's not just a trick." Jonas lifted an eyebrow.

The coin shot across the room and embedded in the wall with a resounding crack.

"Imagine a whole handful of coins," Jonas suggested. "Or a handful of pebbles. It would be the equivalent of a shotgun blast. If I'm right, though, this 'trick' can be made even more devastating."

"You're going to fight the demons?" Warren asked.

Jonas shook his head. "We don't want to destroy the demons, Warren. We want to learn to control them. I—and others like me—think there is a lot we can learn from them." He paused. "That's what we want to do. But what do you want to do?"

TWELVE

An hour before sunset, not really rested but still groggy from sleeping on and off throughout the day, Simon showed up at the dock. He caught a ride on a truck with some of the other crewmen he hadn't recognized but who had recognized him.

Snow continued to fall, adding to the thick whiteness that covered the ground. The last rays of sunset splintered through prisms made of frozen icicles that dripped from tree branches.

Simon sat in the back, so cold he was stiff. His breath streamed out in front of him. A short time later, the truck turned to follow the grade that led to the edge of the English Channel. Fog swirled out over the freezing water, as restless as the Channel.

The ship lay at anchor seventy or eighty yards from shore. Men stayed at their posts behind massive machine guns that had been bolted to her decks. Electric lanterns glowed in the darkness, as fragile as soap bubbles.

Seeing the light made Simon feel better. During the last hour, while he'd been shoulder to shoulder with men, he'd started feeling hemmed in, trapped.

After joining the crew in the lifeboat, Simon peered through the fog at the ship. He was constantly aware that an itchy trigger finger would give away their position and attract anyone looking for them.

The ship was long and narrow, a motorsailer that could be powered by gasoline engines as well as wind. It was painted a flat gray and only stood out against the dark water due to the running lights and the sunset. Once the night had turned full dark, Simon was certain that the vessel would scarcely be seen.

Not by human eyes, anyway. The thought was a sobering one.

"We've got guns aboard," Patel told Simon. "Fifty-cal machine guns and two 20 mm cannons mounted fore and aft. And I managed to round up some hunting rifles. Those things will bring down an elephant." The captain looked grim. "But at best, all they seem able to do against those alien creatures is slow them down."

Simon didn't doubt that. Once he was in England, in London, he'd have access to more and better weapons. He was looking forward to that.

Leah Creasey was already aboard *Dauntless*, which was what Patel's men had renamed their ship. Their second choice had been *Foolishness*, but no one wanted to jinx themselves by using that name.

The young woman's presence there surprised Simon enough that he hesitated briefly before heaving himself over the side. She wore winter clothing and had her arms wrapped around herself.

"My father wasn't at the refugee camp," Leah said. "I looked everywhere. I even found Mrs. Baird, she was one of my father's neighbors. She said he helped get her out a few days ago. But he didn't come himself because there were too many women and children."

Simon nodded. Most of the refugees were women and children. "You should have waited," he said.

She gave him a look that would have blistered paint, and

he found that he liked her for that. "Like you waited?" she asked sarcastically.

One of the crewmen called for Simon, then started handing supplies up. Most of the supplies were medical—drugs and bandages, blankets and extra coats, and food. Just enough to help them survive the few hours it took to cross the Channel. Simon handled the boxes easily, stacking them on the deck for other men to carry away.

"We're the only ones who are staying when this boat leaves England, you know," Leah said.

Simon hadn't known.

"If it's all the same to you, I'd rather not be over there alone."

Looking at her, Simon wanted to tell her that there was no guarantee of safety even if she stayed with him. But he didn't. "I'm sure there will be others there."

"Perhaps. But how many of them do you think will be willing to go back to London?"

That was something Simon didn't know. He kept loading boxes and didn't want to answer. He didn't want to be involved. But he knew that wasn't how his father had raised him.

"Do you really want to go into London?" he asked. "After everything you've seen?"

"I'm sure I don't," Leah answered without hesitation. Still, she couldn't quite keep the quaver of fear out of her voice. "But I don't have a choice. Not if my father's still alive."

Simon started to say something, then stopped himself, realizing that whatever he was going to say was more or less what everyone else had told him. And he wasn't letting it stop him. Despite his Templar training, his feelings about losing his father—*If he's been lost*—weren't any different than hers. He wasn't going because he thought he was braver than anyone else; he was going because he was frightened for his father. Just like Leah was.

"And if he's not alive—" Her voice broke. "Well, then I need to know that, too."

"All right," Simon said, and hoped he didn't live to regret his decision. She said thank you, but she didn't look or sound like he was doing her any great favors. He didn't blame her.

Hours later, a gray fog bank rolled out of the north, enveloping *Dauntless*. Simon stood on deck and stared at the swirling mass that seemed to disappear right before it enveloped the ship. But he knew that to anyone fifty feet or more away the ship would have been invisible.

As they neared the coastline, still using the sails so the diesel engines wouldn't alert any creature that might be patrolling, Simon searched the roiling darkness. Patel had warned them that roving parties of the "aliens" hunted survivors as well as ships' crews brave enough to come looking for them.

Simon held a .50-cal Barrett sniper rifle with an eleven-round clip. He wished he had one of the Templar weapons he'd trained with. Headed into battle, he was more accustomed to a pistol and a sword than a rifle.

Patel had control of the ship, handling the wheel with ease. He was stern and hard in the darkness, and occasionally the moon shined down through the fog to paint his features.

A few minutes later, one of the men called out when he spotted land.

Staring at the craggy shoreline, Simon's gut clenched. Waves of cool air and warm air drifted over him, which was why the fog was so thick. He took a fresh grip on the rifle.

At Patel's order, the crew furled the sails and they

dropped anchor less than twenty feet from the shore. *Dauntless* had a shallow enough draw that they didn't touch bottom.

A weak yellow light flickered in the darkness.

"There," one of Patel's crew whispered hoarsely.

"I see it." Patel left the wheel in the hands of another man, then went forward to the ship's prow. "I'm Captain Patel, of *Dauntless*. We're taking on refugees."

A small group of men, women, and children stepped out of the darkness and stood as shadows along the shoreline. "Thank you for coming, captain," a man called out. "We'd about given up. There's talk that the demons killed all of the men brave enough to cross the Channel."

"Not all of us," Patel said. "How many are you?"

"Nineteen, sir. We've got five children."

"I can take sixty. Are there any others about?"

"They're scattered up along the coast, captain. Every day the demons' numbers grow. They hunt us constantly."

"Let's get you aboard. We'll sort out what direction we want to go later." Patel turned back to his crew and gave out orders. He crossed to Simon and Leah. "You have a choice to make, Mr. Cross, Miss Creasey. You can journey with us a while longer, or you can get out here. I don't need the space yet."

"I'm going to take my chances here," Simon said. "If the demons haven't found these people yet, then perhaps it's safe enough for now."

"All right. Miss Creasey?"

"I'll stay."

"Help us get these people aboard, then I'll see to it you're provisioned as we agreed."

Simon helped row an inflatable dinghy to shore, then tied a rope to one of the nearby trees. Shouldering the rifle, his senses alert to the night around them, he helped load the dinghy with the survivors.

He was appalled at their condition. It was easy to see that they hadn't been eating or resting enough. Even the children looked haggard and hollow-eyed, more like stick-people than humans.

The first group in the dinghy was quickly pulled in to *Dauntless* and helped aboard. Then the dinghy was pulled back by rope and the second group was loaded, leaving only three men on the shore with the security crew Patel had established.

The demons attacked without warning.

Simon *felt* them there in the darkness before he saw them. Wheeling around to face the thick copse of trees just back of the shoreline, he saw moonlight set fire to a half-dozen pairs of yellow eyes.

Then the demons vaulted into motion, hurling themselves through the trees without a sound. They were only vaguely humanoid, bipedal, but with tree trunk–like arms and legs and powerful bodies. Their heads were too large for their bodies, but they moved sinuously all the same. Three thick projections flared out from the top of the head and a circle of six eyes flared around a central orb.

Darkspawn. Simon recognized them at once from his lessons. They were Primus caste, driven by curiosity.

Simon didn't bother yelling a warning. He lifted the .50-cal rifle to his shoulder, aimed by instinct, and fired. The heavy rifle thundered and the blowback from the blast hit him in a wave of warm air. His bullet sped true, though, slamming into the center mass of his target.

The Darkspawn tumbled back, hissing in outrage as it went down. Bright green blood showed in the center of its chest. It flailed its arms and pushed itself to its feet.

Squeezing the trigger again and again, Simon hit the

Darkspawn twice more. One of the bullets actually shattered one of the spikes protruding from the Darkspawn's massive head. But it wasn't dead. It pulled out a weapon, threw its hand forward, and fired.

A beam of violet heat blazed by Simon's head. If he hadn't been in motion, the beam would have taken his head off.

Men screamed in pain as some of Patel's crew met their deaths.

Simon ran behind the three survivors still on shore. He shoved them toward the water. "Swim! *Now!*" He considered jumping into the water, but he knew that they'd have no chance.

The three survivors ran into the water and started swimming when they couldn't run anymore.

Leah, Simon was surprised to see, had already dropped to one knee and brought up the H&K MP-5 machine pistol Patel had equipped her with. She fired in controlled three-round bursts. He'd expected to see her frozen in fear.

Or dead.

Even though she was still alive, even though she was still fighting, Simon didn't expect either of them would live through the next few minutes. Only two of Patel's shore party remained. One of them died when the gunners aboard *Dauntless* opened fire, his body ripped apart by a 20 mm cannon shell.

The air suddenly filled with bullets and cannon fire. The 20 mm cannon left man-sized craters in the rocky ground and flaming trees.

Caught between the demons and friendly fire, Simon knew they couldn't stay there. The water wasn't safe either. From the corner of his eye, he saw two of the men burned to blackened husks then sink beneath the incoming waves.

He caught Leah's arm. "Get up. Run." He pulled her into motion, surprised at her strength.

Thankfully she recognized the vulnerability of their position. She fell in behind Simon as they skirted the approaching demon party and ran more deeply into the woods. If they had enough time, he felt certain they could lose themselves in the forest. Darkspawn were scavengers, used to trolling around in the remnants of cities, according to the books Simon had read and according to his instructors. In the wild, he believed they had a chance.

He ran, but he knew the Darkspawn were faster than they were. And probably not as hampered with the weapons they carried. The Barrett was over twenty pounds of serious hardware.

In seconds, the rendezvous point on the shoreline had become a conflagration. Flames twisted up through the branches, sending a steady rain of flames shooting up into the sky. Noise of machine-gun fire and cannon fire thundered along the coast.

Simon kept the Barrett in front of him, wishing he had his sword, wishing he had his armor. With those he at least stood a chance against his enemies.

Unless even those can't make a difference. The stories he'd heard about the dead "knights" that had been seen in London led him to believe that maybe not even those Templar-created items would serve. *They were outnumbered there. They didn't use tactics. They were overconfident.* But he didn't know if he believed that.

Branches whipped at Simon's face. He held the rifle up to ward some of them off, but the effort didn't do as much good as he would have liked. Deadly violet beams from the Darkspawn weapon felled trees and started fires.

A dead tree filled the path in front of Simon. He placed

a palm on the tree and vaulted it, pausing only long enough to glance back, leveling the Barrett automatically.

Leah leaped over the fallen tree like an Olympic athlete, never even breaking stride. Patel's crew member scrambled and hit the tree all wrong. Before he could get over, one of the four Darkspawn that followed him grabbed his head in one massive hand. The demon closed its fist and blood spurted as the man's head collapsed.

THIRTEEN

S imon fired almost point-blank into the Darkspawn's face. He was aiming at one of the eyes and hoping that was a weak point even for the Barrett. The 50 caliber round smashed through the eye, pulping it. The demon staggered back into its mates, holding up the chase for a moment. The wounded one dropped its victim and roared in rage.

In the next moment 20 mm cannon fire raked the forest, toppling trees. Simon felt the vibrations climb through his legs as he turned back toward Leah.

The young woman stood with her back to a tree, peering back at the demons. She changed magazines on the machine pistol. Panic showed in her eyes, but she sounded almost calm as she yelled, "We're not going to make it! They're too fast!"

"Run!" Simon ordered, shoving her into motion. They didn't have a choice.

Leah led the way through the forest, dodging trees and boulders, skidding down leaf-covered and snow-covered inclines that had turned to mud. They barely kept their feet most of the time.

And the Darkspawn pursued.

Without warning, another group came up on their right. Simon spotted them in the darkness, then Leah threw up a hand and shouted a warning.

"Left!" Simon yelled, surging past her and charging in that direction. His breath burned the back of his throat. The fog burned his eyes.

A purple beam blazed a trench in front of him. Unable to change directions, Simon tried to leap across it, but the side gave way and he fell before he could jump. He rolled, hanging on to the Barrett because even though it wouldn't kill the demons, it was at least a weapon.

Something caught Simon's foot and wouldn't let go.

Controlling the panic that soared through him, Simon rolled over onto his back and gazed up at the Darkspawn. Simon kicked twice, trying to free himself, but didn't succeed. His foot simply struck the demon's chest and stopped. Simon's ankle screamed in pain at the impacts.

The demon laughed while it maintained a crushing grip on Simon's leg.

Thrusting the Barrett between them, Simon fired into its face. The bullet ricocheted, coming almost straight back and burying into the ground only inches from Simon's head. He swung the rifle, hoping to use it as a club to break free of the Darkspawn's grip.

The creature swept an arm out almost lazily. The impact ripped the rifle from Simon's fingers and broke the Barrett into pieces. Fingers numb, Simon watched helplessly as the rifle bounced off nearby trees and finally fell to the ground twenty feet away.

"Die, hu-man!" the demon shrieked. According to the ancient texts, the Darkspawn had limited ability to speak, but they'd already picked up the English language. They served as spies and were quick-witted enough to be intuitive about prey and technology.

Simon gripped the Darkspawn's powerful wrist in both his hands. Straining, Simon tried to break free of the inexorable grip. Unable to match the creature in strength,

Simon searched for nerve clusters he could inflict pain to. The scaly hide seemed impenetrable, though. Black comets swirled in his vision. He tried to breathe . . . couldn't.

Then the Darkspawn's grotesque head leaped from its broad shoulders in a spray of green ichors. Simon thought he was hallucinating. He knew from experience that he was on the edge of blacking out.

A mailed fist, dark steely gray with a ruby undercurrent glowing beneath the surface, seized the thumb of the Darkspawn's hand around Simon's throat and pulled. The demon's bones broke with loud snaps that penetrated even the cannon fire.

Simon sucked in a greedy breath that felt like fire to his lungs. He stared up at the armored knight standing over him. The Templar's armor was so shiny while in Engaged mode—with the NanoDyne technology devoting so much of its energy to hardening the shields—that Simon could see his own features in the smooth faceplate.

"Simon?" The amplified voice sounded strange in Simon's ears for just a moment. It also sounded surprised.

It took Simon only a moment to place the voice. He was helped by the fact that the armor couldn't disguise the womanly curves of his savior.

"Giselle?" Simon said, surprised as well.

The Templar offered her hand. Simon took the hand and allowed her to help him get to his feet. He'd known Giselle Fletcher since they'd been children. She was his age and they'd been reared in the same Underground complex.

"Yes," Giselle replied. For a moment she allowed her faceplate to "ghost," turn translucent enough to permit him to see her features. She was a beautiful redhead with freckles sprinkled across the bridge of her nose and her cheeks. Her gray eyes were warm, but they looked more tired than

Simon could ever recall. "Hadn't fancied on meeting you out here, love."

"It doesn't seem like the place to be." Simon's heart leaped and he took strength in Giselle's presence. Looking beyond her, he spotted five other Templar battling Darkspawn with blades as well as sidearms.

A demon lifted its weapon and fired. Giselle blocked the deadly purple beam with her shield. The beam lit up the image of the tall cross with a hippogriff wound round it. Although Simon couldn't see the image, he knew it would be there. He'd watched Giselle make her shield down in the Templar forge.

The energy beam reflected up and away, cutting through trees and dropping branches down.

"Talk later," Giselle said. "Fight now. Take my Grenadier." She hefted the huge Templar sword she carried as she turned to follow her opponent's movements. "Try not to get yourself killed."

Simon ignored Giselle's disparaging remark. They'd always been competitive, always pushing each other to the next level.

He lifted the Grenadier from her hip and readied it. The Grenadier was solid and heavy, an ugly weapon packed with killing power. It fired grenades filled with Greek Fire, the alchemical liquid created centuries ago. Only this version had been upgraded by the latest in Templar technology.

Despite the desperate nature of the situation, Simon smiled grimly. It felt good to have a Templar weapon in his hands. He armed the weapon and stepped into Giselle's shadow the way they'd been trained to do when one of them was wounded or had their armor trashed. While Giselle blocked the purple beams, Simon took aim and fired.

The grenades *whumped* from the Grenadier's stubby

throat and struck their targets with deafening results. The Darkspawn went to pieces, torn apart by the high-explosive rounds that set them on fire.

"At least you haven't lost your touch, love," Giselle commented dryly, as if they were back in the practice arenas their parents had arranged.

Simon took pride in that. Even though he was unarmored and so very vulnerable on the battlefield, he could still kill his enemies. That was what he was trained to do. He searched the area for Leah and found her ensconced behind two large Templar. She looked terrified but moved to stay clear of the attacks.

"Who's the bird?" Giselle asked.

"A friend." That was all anyone needed to know at the moment.

"Well, come on then. Let's see if we can save that ship out there." Giselle strode forward, moving superhumanly fast in her armor. Everything was amplified in the suit: strength, speed, and awareness.

Simon went forward with her, staying behind and slightly to the right so she could offer some protection and he had a fairly clear field of fire. He had to run hard to keep up.

The Templar charged through the night. They carried their swords, preferring them over the sidearms because they'd been trained more for close-up fighting if it came to that in the Underground. And the swords were the most powerful weapon in their arsenal.

A Darkspawn trooper, one of the elite warriors in that class of demon, hurled itself from the darkness and caught Giselle by surprise. Simon knew it had to be cloaked or else the armor's infrared sensors would have picked it up.

The trooper smashed into Giselle and drove her back

with a horrendous clang. She left her feet and nearly fell on top of Simon, who had to duck out of the way. That was the only thing that saved his life.

A rocket screamed seemingly out of nowhere and struck the ground where he'd been standing. The wave of concussive force knocked Simon over and peppered him with rocks and dirt.

Rolling to his knees, temporarily deaf, he yanked his coat up over his mouth and nose to filter out all the swirling debris. If the snow hadn't fallen and the ground hadn't been muddy, dust would have filled the air.

"In the trees!" Giselle shouted as she flipped to her feet and brought her sword up. The Darkspawn was almost on top of her, lifting a huge mallet that looked like it had once belonged to a Templar. The troopers were known to use the weapons of their enemies.

Moving again, knowing he'd heard Giselle only because the suit amplified her voice, Simon skidded on his knees, hooking his toes to slow himself. He raised the Grenadier in both hands and took aim at the figure high in the trees, tracking the purple blasts back to their source.

When he had the crosshairs centered over the Darkspawn sniper, Simon squeezed the trigger. The Grenadier shivered in his grip and three grenades *whumped* to the top of the tree, impacting the demon as it tried to escape.

The explosions ripped the creature free of the branches and hurled it away in flaming pieces. Simon gave a hoarse shout of triumph before he knew it.

"Good job," Giselle said. "Now maybe you could stop celebrating and focus on the work at hand."

Feeling decidedly more confident now, Simon took cover behind a thick oak tree and took aim. The Grenadier was magical in nature, allowing it to generate a nearly inexhaustible supply of ammunition.

He squeezed the trigger again and again, knocking down targets as fast as he recognized them. Most of the Darkspawn died on impact. Few required a second shot.

Giselle and the other Templar fought on, using the incredible strength and their swords to lay waste to the Darkspawn that challenged them. Blades flashed and demons lay stretched out on the ground.

One of the Templar was on the ground, though, and Simon knew from the posture that the man wouldn't be getting back up. His sword lay before him, only inches from his outstretched fingertips.

Clipping the Grenadier to his hip, Simon raced for the fallen Templar's sword. It was a broadsword, much like the one Simon had forged for himself.

Throwing himself forward, Simon slid across the muddy, snow-covered ground. Mud splattered into his eyes and temporarily blinded him. He grabbed frantically for the sword and pulled it from the ground just as a shadow fell over him. Whirling, coming up to one knee, Simon held the sword before him in both hands.

Green energy sparked and winked along the blade's edge.

Feeling more confident, Simon lashed out at the hand. The blade cut through the demon's forearm with ease. The creature's arm dropped to the ground. Before the hand came to a rest, Simon was in motion again, circling around to the right. He launched an attack on the demon, reminding himself that he wasn't clothed in armor.

Simon cut the backs of the demon's legs, hamstringing the creature. It whirled, trying to deliver death, but its unresponsive feet landed it facedown on the ground.

Spinning the sword in his hand, reversing the way he held the weapon, Simon sank the sword through the demon's chest and into the ground beneath. The demon opened its mouth wide to scream. Before it could, Simon kicked it in the head with his boot. The Darkspawn lay there shivering for a moment, then relaxed completely as death claimed it.

"Look out!"

Simon moved as he saw the shadow on the ground lurch toward him. He rolled away from it, picking up cold mud, and came up with the sword in his hands. A Darkspawn flailed for him, throwing a Grappler toward Simon's last position.

The Grappler was Templar magic and technology, too, and the Darkspawn had probably claimed it in battle. Blocky and thick, the barrel an upended rectangle, the Grappler spat a tether made from spun palladium alloy that would wrap around an opponent and pull him into range of the user. If the tether had locked on Simon, he would have been yanked toward the demon.

Roaring in rage, the demon took aim again. Simon surged up from his knees and drove the sword before him, following it with his weight. The blade passed through the demon's stomach, deeply enough that Simon knew it had passed through the creature's back. He felt the spine grate along the edge, then used it as a fulcrum to get the leverage he needed to disembowel the demon.

The Darkspawn emptied in a slithering tangle. Noxious fumes filled the cold air, tightening Simon's breath in his lungs. Almost overcome by the foulness, he stumbled back and lifted an arm across his mouth and nose. He kept the sword ready before him.

As he looked around the broken ground through the trees that still had some of their leaves, he saw that the Templar owned the battlefield. Several Darkspawn lay in unmoving heaps on the ground. Steam rose from the cooling bodies as approaching winter claimed them, too.

Even the gunbattle along the coast had quieted.

Fearing what that meant, thinking of all the women and children he'd helped escort into the dinghy, Simon charged through the trees.

FOURTEEN

Aided by the armor, Giselle quickly caught up to Simon and pulled ahead.

"Idiot," she snapped. "You want to be a hero? Heroes are always the first to get killed." Her voice broke. "We've had enough of those lately."

Before Simon could say anything, she left him behind. He ran harder, but the other surviving Templar passed him as well.

Minutes later, they reached the coastline. Gunsmoke hung in the air, mixing with the thick fog. In the distance, *Dauntless* sped away, climbing the horizon as the ocean rose away from the coastline. Two fires danced on the deck, but even at the distance Simon could see the crew battling them.

Godspeed, Simon thought, and wished them well. Then the ship disappeared over a wave, although the flicker of flames hung in the air for a while longer before the fog swallowed it.

"Going to stand there all day?" Giselle asked.

Simon looked at her.

"There's work to be done, love," she said quietly.

Surveying the coastline, Simon watched as the other Templar walked among the dead and the dying. Most of them were demons, but some of them were human.

A middle-aged man groped feebly. Horror tightened

Simon's stomach when he saw the man's legs had been burned off at the thighs by one of the demons' beam weapons. The cauterized stumps were charred black and bloody.

The sight and smell of battle was nothing like Simon had envisioned. Even what he'd done to the poachers back in South Africa paled before this. This was carnage, raw and vicious.

Giselle went to the man and knelt beside him. She removed one of her gloves and held the man's hand in hers. Her helmet visor retracted, allowing the man to see her face.

"You're . . . you're an angel?" the man asked.

"No," Giselle told him quietly. "Not an angel. Just a woman."

"Not like any woman I've ever seen."

Simon kept his distance, unwilling to go any closer. He tightened his fist on his sword.

Giselle reached into a small compartment built into the armor and brought out a slap-patch.

"What's that?" the man asked.

"A dreamie," Giselle answered. "It'll take away the pain."

"That's good." The man's eyes fluttered. "I don't want to keep hurting."

"You won't." Giselle placed the slap-patch on the man's throat.

The narcotics filtered into the man's bloodstream instantly. The pain and fear drained from his face. "Am I . . . am I going to be all right?"

Giselle smiled at him sweetly and touched his face soothingly. "You're going to be fine."

"I'm glad." The man took in a breath, then let it all out. Every muscle in his body relaxed. His head lolled to the side.

Tears glittered in the moonlight on Giselle's cheeks. Her helmet closed and hid her sorrow from Simon's eyes, but he felt the weight of it in his heart.

Simon looked down at the seven dead humans they'd gathered and laid on the ground. Three of them were the men who'd been left behind to wait on the dinghy, but there were two more men, a woman, and a child that Simon had pulled in from the shallows. He didn't know how many others had been lost to the sea.

"Does anyone know who they are?" one of the Templar asked.

Simon shook his head. Leah did too.

"Captain Patel was just picking up survivors along the coastline," Simon added. "There aren't any regular meeting places, and no communication between England and France. They were just . . . people." *Scared and frightened people.*

"It would be better if we knew who they were. That way we could tell their families." That was from Justin, one of the Templar whom Simon barely remembered from classes. He'd been from another Templar complex, but they had met twice a year in practice matches.

"Their families are probably already dead, too," Devin said. She was a young brunette. She was three or four years younger than Simon and Giselle, and more slightly built. Her face was carved alabaster.

"There's nothing we can do for them here," Giselle said. "We'll take images of them and post them when we can. Maybe their families will find out what happened to them soon enough."

There is no soon enough, Simon thought bitterly. *They're dead. Nobody wants that kind of news.*

In the end they decided to bury them all in shallow

graves, along with the two Templar that had fallen to Dark-spawn weapons. There was nothing else to be done.

"I need to know about my father, Giselle." Simon tramped through the forest beside the Templar.

Simon had outfitted himself with weapons. He would have liked to have used the armor, but all of it was made for custom fit. However, if he'd found a core suit his size—and that would have been nearly impossible given his size—it could be added to, or plate could be replaced from other suits or pieces of armor. The other Templar had salvaged what they needed from their mates' armor. None of it was to be left to fall into the hands of demons.

Giselle faced Simon. "Your father died at the battle of All Hallows' Eve, Simon. I trust he died well."

Even though he'd been expecting the answer, Simon still felt pole-axed. He stumbled for just a moment, then regained his footing.

"I'm sorry," Giselle said. "I thought you knew."

"No. How would I have known?"

"The media broadcasted the battle."

Simon remembered all the footage he'd seen while in Cape Town. "I knew there had been horrible losses."

"Yes. Most of the Templar are dead."

Simon struggled to fathom that and couldn't. All of his life there had been thousands of Templar, men and women, who lived among but separate from the inhabitants of London and England. In the city they lived in the Underground, tunnels that had been lost and forgotten, or built without the city management offices being any the wiser. In the countryside they lived in underground bunkers and complexes.

"Why?" he asked in a strained voice. "Seems pretty bloody stupid to go off and get themselves killed after hundreds of years of preparation. Did they go off like a lot of lemmings, then?"

"No!" Giselle's voice was a whip crack of emotion. "That's not how it was, Simon."

Simon stopped, put a hand against her armor, and shoved. He knew that wasn't what he'd intended, but it was what he did. None of what she was saying was making any sense. Beginning with his father's death. He was angry, and the emotion was almost beyond his control.

"Then tell me how it was!" Simon demanded.

Two Templar started forward. Even though he'd been identified as one of them, he wasn't in armor. Everyone outside the armor was potentially an enemy. Simon had been trained to think that way as well.

Giselle threw a hand up. The Templar stopped.

"Don't you dishonor those Templar," Giselle stated coldly, staring full into Simon's eyes. "They weren't stupid, or foolish, or full of themselves. What they did was the bravest thing they could do. They sacrificed themselves."

"*Sacrificed* themselves?" Simon couldn't believe it. "No. That's not how we were brought up, Giselle. We were told that we weren't supposed to die for our country. We were supposed to make the other guys die for theirs."

"The American general said that. George Patton."

Simon was breathing hard. He fought to keep a lid on the anger and pain and disbelief that crashed through him. It was almost impossible. "My *father* told me that. Over and over again. As I fought. As I learned strategy. That was the main lesson he taught me. For him to do something like what you're suggesting, it's . . . it's . . ." Words failed him.

"They knew they couldn't win," Giselle said in a softer tone. "They had to accept that. The demons came with too many in their ranks. They'd already taken out the British military." She opened her helmet.

Simon saw the pain etched into her features. It humbled him and hurt him in ways he didn't expect. He suddenly felt like he'd swallowed glass, and he didn't trust his voice.

"The demons knew the Templar were here," Giselle went on. "The Templar weren't the only ones who'd prepared. The demons came hunting us. Staged, concentrated efforts. They were digging us out of some of the older Underground complexes."

"How did the demons know they were there?"

Giselle shook her head. "No one knows. Yet. They're smart and incredibly inventive. However they did it, they came into our world, and they began hunting us down."

None of that had been in the news.

"The demons got into some of the Underground complexes, Simon. They found families there. And they killed them. Worse than that, the demons brought the dead back as undead." Tears ran down Giselle's cheeks. "We—I—had to go down there and help destroy a complex that had gotten slain to a man, then drawn back to serve the demons as zombies. We had no choice. We had to burn them out." She took a breath. "When I go to sleep at night, I still see them screeching and trying to get out of the flames. But we didn't let them."

Seeing Giselle's pain before him, Simon found that his own dimmed. He took shallow breaths and focused on her words.

"In the end, Lord Sumerisle and the others felt they had to fool the demons," Giselle said. "Convince them somehow that all the Templar had been killed. At least enough of us so the concentrated hunting would stop and give us time to regroup and make new plans."

"The Templar attacked the demons at St. Paul's Cathedral," Simon said.

Giselle nodded. "All of those who went there died that

day. Every Templar wanted to go, but they drew lots. Some had to stay behind. Your father, some of the other warriors, said that those who stayed behind were left with the hardest task. We have to find a way to live, and to find the demons' weaknesses."

"That was easy for Lord Sumerisle to decide."

She frowned. "Lord Sumerisle died there. His brother Maxim now serves in his place."

Simon thought about that. Everything seemed impossible. "If most of the Templar are dead, how can you hope to succeed?"

"Because that's what we have to do, Simon. We don't have a choice anymore."

"But if they hadn't attacked—"

"The demons would have kept hunting," Giselle said. "They would have killed our future, too. At least this way we can try to figure out what to do next."

Simon wanted to challenge that line of thinking. He couldn't help himself. He started to speak.

"No." Giselle closed her helmet and started walking again. Through the armor's audio pickup, her voice sounded cold and metallic. "This is what we have to do, Simon. There's no other way." She left him standing there.

Simon watched her go. The other Templar walked past him. No one said anything. He felt hollow and empty inside.

Leah approached him, her arms filled with weapons they'd taken from the demons. "Are you all right?"

"I'm fine." Simon redistributed the load he was carrying and started walking again.

FIFTEEN

"We call ourselves Cabalists these days, but that wasn't a name the founders considered for themselves," Jonas told Warren as they observed the gathering of people in the larger room. "We were called that by the Templar, but only in the truest sense of the word."

"In the beginning we had no name," Edith interjected. "The founders of our organization simply knew each other, preferring no name so that they could remain more hidden. They shared an interest in the demons. Their studies brought them together."

"A cabal is a secret organization," Jonas went on.

I knew that, Warren thought. He didn't like the fact that Jonas wasn't willing to admit that someone might know as much as he did, but he chose not to interrupt.

"That we even have a name for something that is supposed to remain hidden is ludicrous. But there you have it," Edith said.

"By necessity," Jonas said, "the early members of our organization were secretive. What we're trying to do isn't understood by many. The few that knew about the demons didn't want anyone prying into their 'unholy' natures, as most claimed—which is a defense the ignorant always mount against things they don't understand. Most historians over the years have linked us to the Jewish *Kabbalah*, but that's simply not right. The Templar knew that when they called us Cabalists. I think they wanted to gift us with as much negativity as they could. The very name inspires mistrust and suspicion."

"The Templar named this organization?" Warren repeated. "The Knights of the Crusades?" Every step he took seemed to introduce impossibility. His mind balked at the notion of the Templar knowing the Cabalists.

"The Templar," Edith said at his side, her horns sparking green fire, "weren't just warriors who took it upon themselves to regain the Holy Lands. There is still a large group of them who train to fight the demons."

"Not as large after All Hallows' Eve," Jonas said.

"Not everyone continued to believe in the demons after the years passed and the Crusades ended," Edith said. "The Templar were eventually ostracized by King Philip IV for promoting their cause and soliciting help against the demons. But no one wanted to believe in the bits of bone and armor they found that they insisted were of demonic origins. Their heirs have kept their beliefs together, and they trained for the day when the demons would try to take our world."

Warren remembered the stories of the armored men who had died at St. Paul's Cathedral on All Hallows' Eve. If they'd trained to fight the demons, he didn't think they'd done a very good job of it.

Instead, he said, "I thought they were all dead. I've heard reports of what happened at the cathedral."

Jonas shook his head. "Not all of the Templar were killed. A great many of them died that night and the following morning. I saw their corpses in the aftermath of that battle. Enough of them died that the demons no longer regard them as a threat. I think that's a mistake, but those that remain serve to test the demons so that we can learn more."

"Our group tried to contact the demons during the Crusades," Edith said. "It was thought that if we learned enough about them, we could bring them under our control."

"Why would you think you can do that?" Warren asked.

"Because we are men." Pride echoed in Jonas's voice. "It's our destiny to become masters of everything. We conquered the land, from the coastal towns to the great deserts. We conquered the sea and even most of what lies beneath it. No predator exists in the wild that we need to fear. We've put a man on the moon." Jonas paused. "The demons are just another facet of the world we have open to us. It will be a matter of time, but we'll conquer them as well."

"Why not destroy them?"

"Because we can learn so much from them," Edith said. "They're a new resource we haven't before encountered. They have knowledge—and powers—that we've only dreamed of. They can help us reach a higher Awakening."

The way she said *Awakening* told Warren the word was in capital letters.

"But they're evil," Warren said.

"Is a kitten evil?" Jonas asked.

Warren didn't answer, knowing there was no way he could reply that wouldn't lend itself to Jonas's argument.

"A child would think a kitten was a loving pet," Jonas said. "Until that kitten took down a beautiful songbird in the backyard. Despite its domesticity, that kitten will never stray from its true nature. In its heart, it's still a predator, a killing machine. Demons have their own mandates they must follow."

"The demons are worse than kittens," Warren said.

"True, but we believe they can be brought into line. Even if they can't, we can cage them and use them to learn about the magic that has entered our world." Jonas smiled. "That's all the Cabalists have ever wanted: the same power the demons wield."

"The Templar get in the way of our ability to do that," Edith said. "We don't like dealing with them when we can help it."

"Although there were some Cabalists who aided the Templar in their attack on St. Paul's Cathedral," Jonas added. "It was important that the demons be slowed somewhat so we can observe them for a period of time. But come with me."

"Stories about the demons have been with us since the Crusades," Jonas said. "Tracking down all the books over the centuries since then has been demanding. The fact that there were so many imitators has made that task even more difficult."

Drawn by the printed matter, Warren gazed at the spines of the books. "H. P. Lovecraft."

"He was on the right trail," Jonas said. "He and Robert E. Howard had conferred on the nature of the demons. There were others, including Clark Ashton Smith and Aleister Crowley. All of these were men who chased the Darkness, wanting to embrace it and learn its secrets."

"But these are just stories," Warren said as he surveyed the books. He'd read all of the authors while he was growing up. Many of the same books were on the shelves in his loft.

"They are," Jonas said, "but their inspiration is based in stories that were handed down from the Crusades. Belief in devils and demons. Belief in supernatural powers. Popular literature is rife with it. It's never gone away."

Searching the shelves, Warren found books he could remember seeing his mother read.

"The legends of the demons never totally left our

world," Jonas said. "Not in legend, and not in flesh. I personally believe they've been here, orphaned somehow from their own world, since mankind has gathered in caves and talked about what lies in the darkness beyond the light of the campfire."

"They originated here?" Warren asked.

Jonas shook his head. "They're from somewhere else. Some other world. Or some other plane of existence."

"Then how did they get here?"

"I think mankind has always been able to sense them. The fabric between the worlds was probably very thin to begin with."

"Till people here learned to fear them," Edith said.

"They're predators," Warren said. "Fear would be natural."

"Would it?" Jonas raised his eyebrows. "The dog was not always man's best friend. It was domesticated. But I'm sure that the beginning of that process wasn't certain."

"Demons are as smart as humans."

"Which means that we have more to learn from them. Don't you see?"

Warren thought about it, and knew that he did.

"We believe that the demons brought magic into the world," Edith said. "As mankind's belief in demons was muted, so was its ability to tap into the arcane energies the demons set loose in the world."

"But now they're back," Jonas said. "And our potential has swelled anew." He looked at Warren. "Of course, there have always been those few that have had more natural ability than most. You were one of those."

"It wasn't because I believed in demons," Warren said. "Until I saw one a few days ago, I hadn't believed in them."

"Your mother did. Perhaps that was enough."

"My mother," Warren said, distancing himself from the

pain and confusion from all those years ago, "wanted to believe in magic. She wanted to believe in something that would enable her to have power over her own life."

"Some just have a natural affinity for magic," Jonas said. "We believe you're one of those adepts. When Edith told me how you'd managed to turn the demon away a few days ago, I knew I had to meet you. I'm glad you came."

Warren studied the man's smile. Jonas was happy for himself, for the opportunity he saw before him. Warren knew he could have seen that without whatever ability he had that allowed him to know the truth when people spoke to him.

"What do you want me to do?" Warren asked.

Seated in the circle in the large room, Warren watched the others in the group. Many of them welcomed him to their efforts, but some of them radiated jealousy and suspicion.

They knew who he was. At least that Jonas and Edith suspected he might be a progeny, even if they didn't know his name.

"We've learned a few things about the opening of the Hellgates and the invasion since it happened." Jonas sat to Warren's left, flanked by Edith. "We believe demons called Harbingers were sent to make the way for the other demons. We think they ended up over here and were trapped, left to die. When they did, the Templar found their bones—at least, the men who founded the Templar—and began ferreting out the demons' secrets. We think the Harbingers arrived before the invasion this time. Prior to the invasion last month, several reports of missing persons were filed. Children and old people . . . disappeared."

Warren remembered that. There were also several brutal attacks by unknown assailants. The occurrences had unleashed a hysteria growing throughout the city. The Metropolitan Police had released several statements that they were doing everything they could.

"A police constable was murdered in Covent Garden," Warren said. "The reports indicated that it was the work of a wild animal." *Only no one ever reported what wild animal that was, did they?* He'd read the story, then promptly forgotten it. None of it had anything to do with his life. At least that was what he'd thought at the time.

Jonas nodded. "The police tried to follow up on that, but by then it was already too late. The Harbingers had successfully used blood sacrifices to open 'tears' in the fabric between our world and that of the demons. More demons poured through. Only a short time after that, the Hellgates opened. According to a text I have gotten a copy of, there may be a way to open a 'window' into the demons' world."

"Won't the demons be able to look back into our world?" Warren was immediately reminded of Friedrich Nietzsche's quote about the abyss. *When you look into an abyss, the abyss also looks into you.* The possibility of looking into the demons' world made Warren nervous, but that was outweighed by the excitement that thrummed through him.

"Even if it does," Jonas said, "it can't come through unless we permit it." He waited a moment. "Are you ready?"

Warren licked his lips. Part of him couldn't believe he was where he was, sitting in the dark but able to see through the gloom, preparing to knock on a demon's door.

"Yes," he answered. Because, ready or not, he had to see if it was possible.

SIXTEEN

Jonas nodded to one of the members he had identified as a Seeker. According to Jonas, Seekers acquired and studied artifacts to further the Cabal's knowledge of the demons. Jonas was a Voice, one of the lieutenants that served the First Seer. They were equals in rank within the Cabal, but were sometimes paired in large groups.

The Seeker walked to the center of the quiet Cabalist circle and placed a mirrored diamond-shaped polyhedron on the floor. The object was roughly the size of a softball.

As the Seeker once more took his spot in the ring, Jonas extended a hand toward the polyhedron. "This is the Eye of Raatalukkyn. It's said that Saladin wrested it from a demon and kept it at Qalaat Al-Gindi, his mountaintop fortress deep in the Sinai Desert."

Jonas gestured. The polyhedron slowly stood on point, rising up. It glowed with inner lavender light that spilled over the faces of the crowd.

"For a time the Eye was brought to Venice at the request of Giovanni di Bicci de' Medici," Jonas continued. "His bank had a client who wanted the Eye. No one knows who the client was, but Sultan Mehmet, known as the Conqueror, sacked Constantinople in 1453 and reclaimed the Eye. He attempted to call upon its powers during his battle with Vlad Tepes, also called the Impaler."

At another gesture, the polyhedron began to spin like a coin.

"The Eye vanished in Wallachia for hundreds of years," Jonas said, "and was only brought to light again six years ago when an archeological find uncovered it. I strove for three years to recover it for the Cabal."

From the corner of his eye, Warren suddenly saw blood on Jonas's hand. When Warren breathed in, he smelled death, and he had no doubts about what it had taken for Jonas to acquire the talisman.

"Before the Hellgates opened, I tried several times to use the Eye," Jonas said. "My attempts before the invasion met with little success. I've been getting better, but I've still not gotten the Eye to open."

The Eye spun so quickly it became a blur. Buzzing filled Warren's ears. A pleasant sensation, like steeping in a tub of hot water in a cold room, filled him.

"With you here, with your power present, I hope to surpass everything I've managed in the past."

Warren stared at the flashing polyhedron spinning on the floor.

"Saladin's journals contain references to the Eye," Jonas said. "With it, he claimed to be able to see the demon he had fought for possession of the Eye. Concentrate on the Eye. Will it to open. Let us see what we may." His voice had turned soft and hypnotic.

Barely noticing Jonas's voice, Warren concentrated on the Eye. But it didn't take long for him to realize that he truly didn't have to concentrate because it was *pulling* at him. He wanted to ask if Jonas experienced the same thing, but he found he couldn't move.

Silver light flared from the uppermost point of the Eye. But it stopped only three feet up instead of reaching the ceiling or diffusing.

Excitement flared through Warren again, but it was quickly tempered by the cold wave that pervaded the room. From the corner of his eye, he saw the frost forming on the walls, covering over the sigils and symbols that had been drawn there. A moment later fissures opened up in the walls. Wind rose out of nowhere and whirled around the room.

Some of the Cabalists abandoned their places, scooting back or standing.

"Stay!" Jonas roared. "Stay where you are!"

Warren wanted to move. He knew he should move. But he couldn't. He sat there like he was made of stone, staring into the Eye.

And he felt certain that the Eye was staring back at him.

More of the Cabalists fell back, breaking ranks carefully.

"Stay!" Jonas yelled again. "You will stay here and help us maintain contact!"

Warren had no idea what the man would do if the Cabalists didn't do as he told them to. But Warren wasn't really interested in that. He was more interested in the Eye.

"It's him," someone whispered.

"He's doing this."

"We've never done this before."

"He's going to get us killed."

"No one is going to be killed!" Jonas roared. "We've trained for this. We're stronger than the demons. We own the Eye. Concentrate on your wards. You will be safe."

Warren felt the resistance to his gaze. It felt like he was asleep and trying to get his eyes open during a dream and couldn't. He redoubled his efforts, willing the resistance to go away.

Molten agony lanced through his body. Before he knew what he was doing, Warren was kneeling on the floor, hands flat before him.

"Who are you, human?" a deep, terrible voice demanded.

Fear gripped Warren's heart then. He felt as scared then—*You'll never be that scared again!*—as he did the night his parents died.

"Speak!" the deep voice ordered.

"Warren," he whispered.

"Do you want to die?"

"No. I want to live."

"Then you're on a fool's errand."

Barely aware of the rest of the room and the fact that the Cabalists were in shock around him, Warren stared at the Eye. Heat raged through him, like the worst fever he'd ever had.

"You have no business here," the voice said.

"Who are you?" Jonas asked.

The light at the top of the Eye flared out into an elliptical shape that kept shifting. The shape was silver as well, but hints of blue figures moved within its depths.

"Arrogance," the deep voice said. "One of the few admirable human emotions. At least it has strength to it, unearned though it may be."

"I am Jonas Wayne. A Voice among the Cabal. You will obey me."

Raucous laughter filled the room, pealing from the walls.

Warren shivered, fearing for his life. His mother had gone on at length about learning to speak with "friendly" ghosts, but the voice that spoke through the Eye sounded purely evil.

"I obey no human."

"I command you to name yourself!" Jonas shouted. His tattoos burned with amber light.

Warren knew that names traditionally were supposed to

give power over a demon. But since he'd never had a true interaction with a demon—especially one of this creature's caliber—he wasn't so sure that was true.

The silver ellipse cleared like a tri-dee with an improved signal. A face, blunt and harsh as a lizard's, covered in red scales and showing scars from past battles, stared back.

"I am Merihim, the Bringer of Pestilence," the demon roared. "Before me, you are nothing."

Growing larger, the silver ellipse showed the demon astride some great beast that didn't fit in the view. It looked vaguely like an elephant covered in scales the size of manhole covers and with massive, curved horns.

Merihim raised his right hand, holding tight to a trident made of green metal that crackled with energy. Shimmering waves passed through the silver ellipse.

Gripped by an invisible hand, Jonas was raised from the floor. He screamed, high and shrill like a woman. He wasn't in control of the situation or of himself. Futilely, he beat his hands against the force that surrounded him. He tried to move his legs and couldn't.

A moment later, Jonas jackknifed like he'd been twisted and bent. His back folded backwards. Bones snapped and shattered.

The Cabalists who were gathered around the circle leaped to their feet and started for the doors. The doors swung shut, trapping them inside. They started crying and pleading for mercy.

Edith made a show of trying to regroup them, but it was a lost cause. Warren felt the fear rolling off her in waves.

The woman ran to Jonas, taking a dagger from beneath her robe. Even from across the room with all the magic already present in the room, Warren felt the power that radiated from the curved blade. It had an Eastern cast to it, like a scimitar.

With his free hand, Merihim gestured again. Immediately demons that looked like gargantuan hounds leaped through the portal and landed in the room. They snarled and snapped, flailing spiked tails.

"I'd been held back so far," the demon said. "Thanks to you, I no longer have to wait for the Hellgates." He caught the edges of the magical window and heaved himself through.

Standing in the room, the demon's horned head scraped against the ceiling. He had to have been at least eight feet tall. Massively thewed, he was as sculpted and built as a dedicated weight lifter. He wore blue-green armor made of lizard scales. A huge sword was belted at his waist.

"No!" Edith shrilled. She threw her hands out before her and pushed.

Waves of shimmering force broke across Merihim's chest.

The demon rocked back silently, then grinned. "Not bad. For a human. But you've no true mastery of the forces you wield." His face looked hideous. "I'll show you power." He gestured with the trident again.

Jonas screamed even though Warren wouldn't have believed the man would have had the capacity to do so. His tattoos burned golden, so bright that Warren almost couldn't stand to look at them. Then, in a twinkling, they turned an angry red, the color of sunset over a dust-filled horizon.

Impossibly, Jonas *exploded*. Pieces of him flew all over the room.

Warren was hit by the gore, then realized how hot it was and had to claw the pieces from his body. He mopped the blood as best as he could from his body.

Giving a strangled cry, Edith lurched toward the demon. Warren was certain she knew she was going to her doom, but she didn't hesitate.

Casually, as if the act were nothing, Merihim flicked his trident at her. The three prongs pierced the woman's chest and propelled her back across the room, pinning her against the wall like an insect on display.

Edith struggled weakly to pull the trident from her chest.

Merihim spoke in a language that Warren didn't understand. Instantly flames engulfed Edith, consuming her and leaving only a stain of black soot on the wall.

The demon spoke again, and the smaller demons launched themselves at the Cabalists. Their claws and fangs tore into the flesh of the men and women who had gathered in the room.

The top floor of the building had become a madhouse. Death filled the room with the stench of blood and burned flesh.

Finding himself suddenly free of whatever had held him, Warren ran toward one of the nearest windows. Maybe the demon's powers had locked all the doors, but if he had to he was willing to throw himself through the window. He thought there was a fire escape below, though.

"Where are you going?" the demon snarled.

Although he knew the demon was talking to him, Warren ignored Merihim and ran for his life. He skirted one of the hound-demons as it disemboweled a man.

At the window, Warren didn't pause. He threw himself into it, one arm over his face to protect his eyes. He hit the glass and broke through.

SEVENTEEN

Everything became a confusing whirl of action. Then it stopped. Suspended by the demon's spell, Warren stared down at the snow-covered alley below him. He knew he would probably have died when he hit bottom, but it was preferable to whatever the demon intended.

But that was no longer an option.

Unable to move, he floated back into the room. When he was once more in the room, he looked around and saw that fires had started in several places. Hardly any of the humans remained alive.

The demon stared at Warren. "You're unusual," Merihim stated. "Why do you wield so much power?"

Warren thought he was too scared to answer, but he found his mouth opening and heard himself saying, "I don't know."

"You humans only had a little power when we first came here," Merihim said. "You believed—truly believed—in so few things until we showed ourselves."

When you look into the eyes of evil, Warren thought, *it's not something you easily forget.*

The demon laughed. "Do you think I'm evil, human?" he asked.

"Yes," Warren replied before he could stop himself.

"I'm not evil, I'm powerful." Merihim held out a hand and set it on fire for a moment. The flames seemed to caress his skin. "Power defines good and evil. The spoils go to the victor. That's the way it's always been. It's not going to be any different this time." He paused. "But I would know more about you."

Warren remained silent, gazing into the malevolent eyes. He gathered all his strength, all that energy that he sometimes used to detect lies and influence others. He focused it on the demon, preparing to strike with everything he had.

But he couldn't help thinking that it would have been better if he'd understood more about what he was attempting to do. Or if he believed he could do it.

The hound-demons gathered at their master's feet. Upon closer and prolonged exposure, Warren realized the hound-demons were more human than beast-like. Keen intelligence glowed in their lemon-yellow eyes.

"What are you thinking, worm?" Merihim asked.

Knowing he'd never get another chance, floating in the air while under the demon's spell, Warren unleashed everything inside him at Merihim. The demon was blown backward by the onslaught, staggering back into the silver portal created by the Eye.

As Warren watched, Merihim fell *through* the portal, pulled by whatever mystic forces were in play there. In the next instant, Warren was released from the demon's spell and fell to the floor. Immediately, he tried to push himself up, aware that the Eye was closing the portal.

Now all he needed to do was avoid the hound-demons. Some of them were hopping into the portal with their master.

"Human!" Merihim snarled from the other side of the portal. He pointed with his trident.

Flames shot from the tines, leaping out of the portal and slamming into Warren. Bowled over by the swirling mass of fire, Warren smashed through the window behind him and started the eight-story drop.

There was no spell to catch him this time.

As he fell, he was grimly aware that he was going to die. He was afraid to open his mouth to scream, afraid that he'd breathe in the flames that clung to him.

When he hit bottom, he landed in inches of snow. But even that didn't blunt the force of the landing. His head struck the pavement and everything went black.

Hours later, Warren's eyes flickered open. Pain filled his world. He realized he wasn't breathing, so he took a breath. He didn't know if he'd been breathing before, but he felt the need to now.

Light filled the world. It was daytime. He'd slept—or been unconscious—throughout the night. He breathed again, certain something was broken inside his chest. His head spun and everything turned black again. His last thought was that he surely must be dead now.

Only he awoke again.

The pain was less, but he managed it better. When the broken bones grated inside his chest, he could bear the ripping agony without passing out.

His clothing was sodden from melting snow, proving that his body held heat. Another—if unbelievable—proof that he still yet lived.

He also grew aware of the fact that his feet were bare. Someone had stolen his boots while he was unconscious. Weakly, he cursed whoever did it and hoped the demons got him or her, then Warren had to wonder why the demons hadn't gotten him.

Moving slowly, he raised his left arm up in front of his face. It was numb. He thought it was from lying in the snow.

Instead he saw that he had probably suffered nerve damage from the intense burns that covered his arm. They were definitely third-degree. Black patches of charcoaled flesh showed bright red blood and pink meat in the cracks.

Grimly, he realized the nerve damage was probably a blessing. Without it he would be in agony. As it was, pain covered him from head to toe.

It took Warren an hour to get to his feet. He knew that because he timed himself, peering through the heat-cracked crystal of his watch. It was 10:43 in the morning.

Conserving his strength, Warren leaned back against the wall and took a few deep breaths. He hadn't been able to use his arm. He still couldn't. It hung numb and useless against his side.

More burns covered his other arm, chest, stomach, and legs. From the stiffness that froze his features in places, he guessed that his face had been burned as well. The smell of burned hair filled his nostrils and made him sick for a moment. He threw up, but it was only a thin, sour gruel.

Wiping his mouth on his burned sleeve, Warren glanced up at the building. Flames had claimed the upper stories and even set the nearby buildings on fire. The snow must have retarded the fire, though, because none of the buildings had burned to the ground. But they were blackened hulks.

Warren wondered how many of the Cabalists had survived. Then he doubted any of them had. Since there were no other bodies lying in the alley where he'd fallen, he assumed that none of them had been able to fight free.

But why didn't the hound-demons track me down and make certain I was dead?

Three guys about his age wandered into the alley. Judging from the bags over their backs, they were scavenging.

"Hey," the one in front said. "Are you all right?"

"No," Warren replied, but he thought, *Do I look all right?* because he knew he didn't.

"What happened to you?" another asked.

"Guy's been burnt all to bloody hell," the third stated. "That's what happened to him."

"I need . . . help," Warren said. "Please." He didn't like asking other people for help. It meant admitting weakness. In his experience, people tended to take advantage of others when weakness was shown.

The lead guy shook his head. "Not me. I'm out. Got all I can do trying to take care of my girlfriend and her kid. The last thing I need to do is take on a gimp. Sorry, mate."

Warren wanted to say "please" again, but his pride wouldn't let him. He just stared at the three.

Silently, the trio turned and walked away.

Feeling humiliated and hurt, Warren ducked his head. He thought tears might come because he felt so bad. But he hadn't cried since the night his mother had died. He hadn't asked anyone for help since that night, either.

But the tears didn't come. He didn't know if it was because of his willpower or because his face was so badly damaged that his tear ducts wouldn't work.

After a while, when he realized no help would be forthcoming, he pushed away from the building, oriented himself, and started home. There was nothing else to do.

Warren was surprised when he reached his apartment building. Even though it was nine blocks away, even though the way was made harder by the accumulated snow and ice, he'd kept putting one foot in front of the other until he stood before the building. His breath kept coming in gray wisps and he followed it.

The loft was a four-story walkup, though.

He paused in the foyer at the staircase, wishing he could simply sit down and rest. But he was afraid to. He was certain that if he sat down he'd never be able to get up and get going again. He also wasn't sure if he was going to die. He hadn't perished so far.

He wished that someone—Kelli, George, or Dorothy— would come out and find him. He could accept their help without losing too much of himself. They were his flat mates. They were supposed to look out for each other.

Taking a deep breath, hearing it whistle through his burnt sinus cavities, he headed up the stairs. Every movement brought renewed pain that throbbed through his body.

Finally, he reached the landing and lurched toward his flat. Taking the key from his pocket, he opened the lock and went in.

The familiar clutter was almost heartbreaking. Everything seemed almost normal, like he could just open his eyes and wake from the nightmare. Coals burned in the heating stove in the corner, filling the room with warmth that would have been pleasant if he hadn't been so burned.

Kelli stood in the kitchen area dressed in a short nightshirt. When she saw Warren, she screamed and stepped back.

"It's . . . okay," Warren said hoarsely. His voice was worse. Speaking took greater effort. Blood from cracked flesh dripped down his burns to the wooden floor. "It's . . . just . . . me."

"Warren?" Kelli took her hands down from her mouth and stared at him. But she didn't approach or try to help.

"Yeah." Warren swallowed. "I had . . . some trouble."

"You need a doctor."

"I . . . know. Don't . . . have one." Dizziness swelled through his head. He had to look around to make sure he wasn't falling over. "I'm just . . . gonna go . . . lie down." He turned and lurched across the floor to the ladder that led up to the loft area.

Climbing up took a long time. Warren couldn't bring himself to ask Kelli for help.

"Are you going to die?" Kelli asked.

"I don't . . . think so." Warren answered while he'd paused to rest halfway up the ladder.

"What happened to you?"

Warren ignored her. Kelli had always been dense and selfish. He climbed to the top of the ladder and swung off. He barely made it to his bedroom area before he collapsed on the bed.

He thought he heard Kelli asking him questions and thought she might even have followed him up. Ignoring her, unable to stay conscious any longer, he was easy prey for the pain that struck again and again within him.

Do you still live, human?

The words echoed in the fever haze that filled Warren's dreams. He knew the voice belonged to Merihim. He also knew he would never forget the demon.

You should be dead, the voice went on.

I'm not. Warren took a savage pride in that. All his life, no one had expectations of him. Other than to fail. Now he had failed to die. He found that humorous. But if this had been real, not a dream, if the demon had truly been talking to him, he knew he would have been scared.

I've marked you, Merihim said. *You can't escape me. But I want to see what you're capable of. So I will let you live. For now.*

The threat woke Warren because it seemed so real. He had to wake and make certain the demon wasn't in his bedroom.

Feverish and dry-mouthed, he rolled from the bed and reached for a bottle of water. Someone had taken all his reserves from beside his bed. He knew his roommates had done it.

Movement on the wall caught his attention. He peered into the mirror hanging there. Although the room was dark with the windows covered, he could still see plainly. Maybe it was the trick he'd learned back with the Cabalists.

The ghastly image that peered back at him from the mirror was his own, but he wouldn't have recognized it if it hadn't been framed in the mirror. The right side of his face was thick, crusty blackened meat that was pulling away from his cheekbone. His hair was singed close to his skull. Swelling half-closed his right eye. As he blinked, blood trickled down the side of his face.

Gazing down at his ruined hand, he saw white bone showing through at the knuckles. His fingers were thick as sausages from the swelling and black as coal. His chocolate-brown skin looked pale around the burned patches. He couldn't close his fist.

Panic set in then, clawing and screaming through his heart, spraying his nerves with adrenaline. Even if he lived, he'd never be the same again. He was going to be a monstrosity. He shivered and shook, feeling too weak to stand as his heart pounded wildly.

Footsteps sounded behind him.

Warren turned as Kelli pulled the curtain back. She looked shocked.

"You're still alive?" she asked.

"Where . . . is my water?" Warren asked.

"We didn't think you'd need it."

He got angry then and took two stumbling steps toward her. "You had . . . no right . . . taking my water."

"We didn't want it to go to waste. We thought you were dead."

"I'm not." Warren focused on her, reaching for that power that had dwelt within him for so long. It felt stronger and more sure than he'd ever felt before. "Bring me . . . my water."

Kelli vanished immediately and returned with a liter of water.

Warren struggled with the cap and finally got it off. His lips felt crusty and thick as he drank. He looked at her, focusing everything inside him on her. "You will . . . take care . . . of me. Do you . . . understand? You will . . . make sure I . . . have food and . . . water."

"I will," she said.

Warren drank more water. Nausea swam in his stomach. He retreated to the bed, hoping to keep the water down. His body needed it. He closed his eyes and hoped he didn't die. But he wasn't convinced he wanted to live as he was, either. He had to heal, but he didn't want to live scarred and incomplete.

EIGHTEEN

S o these are friends of yours?"
Simon glanced over at Leah Creasey seated on a rock only a short distance from him and thought about that question. Were they friends? He wasn't sure. He was cleaning weapons, getting the blood and ichors clear of the actions.

Leah was eating a self-heat can of soup and a freeze-dried roast beef sandwich. Simon had eaten one of the sandwiches and felt certain that the plastic wrap it had come in had possessed more taste.

"I know a couple of them," Simon admitted.

"Giselle."

"Her best of all."

Leah watched the Templars. They'd separated them-selves from Simon and Leah. At first Simon hadn't known how to feel about that, then he'd decided he felt fine about it. He didn't owe them anything, and they didn't owe him anything.

"How well did you know her?" Leah asked.

Simon knew the interest at that point was purely femi-nine curiosity, which almost—for just the moment—made everything seem normal and natural. Like they hadn't just buried seven people in a shallow grave.

"Not that well," Simon said. "Not like that."

Leah appeared to relax a little. "Why is she so mad at you?"

"It's a long story."

Glancing meaningfully toward the east where the sun was painting a golden nimbus at the horizon, Leah said, "I think we have time for a long story. From what I gather from your friends, we're not going to be traveling during the day."

They weren't. Giselle had already informed Simon of that. The demons hunted at night and at day, but with the sun out they could see farther and movement was more easily detected. She wanted to use the night as cover while they traveled.

"I used to be one of them," Simon said.

"You don't look like the type for one of those tin can suits."

Simon grimaced. "That's armor. Made from palladium alloy."

"Never heard of it."

"It's a precious metal. Hard to come by. Even harder to work on a forge."

"You made your own body armor?"

"My father—" Simon's voice broke unexpectedly. He concentrated on cleaning a Grappler until he had control of his voice again. "My father helped me forge it. That's how it's done. That's how it always has to be done. And it's not body armor. Not like Kevlar or anything like that." He nodded at the Templar. "When you're inside that armor, you're more like a tank. It's very high-tech."

"It's computerized? I figured that out from watching it work. And since there aren't any eye slits, I got the idea they'd either been trained by blind monks or there was some kind of imaging system."

"An imaging system. A head's-up display. Way more technical than anything the military has." Simon couldn't help noticing the pride in his voice when he said that. "And magic."

Leah arched her brows. "Did you just say 'magic'?"

"Yeah."

"As in scientific wizardry?"

"No, as in an energy field that can't be accessed through physical science." Simon looked at her, suddenly realizing that so much of the rest of the world was just like Leah. They were trapped in a war and had no concept of what it was all about. "You saw those creatures we fought."

"The aliens, yes."

"They're not aliens."

Frowning, looking a little troubled, Leah said, "The reporters on the tri-dee said they were aliens."

"That's because the media doesn't know what else to make of them."

Leah held her soup bowl in her hands. "Then what are they?"

"Demons."

She took a deep breath. "Like . . . from *Hell?*"

"I don't know where they're from. Just some other place." Simon shook his head. He was tired and bruised, and sad and angry in a way he'd never felt before. His father was dead. The thought kept beating the inside of his skull like a hammer striking an anvil. "The books I studied never named their home. Maybe it is a place called Hell. Maybe Hell was just the name people gave to the place after the demons first started appearing."

"Whoa! Books?"

Simon took a deep breath and tried to be patient. "Where I come from—"

"Where do you come from?"

"London. All my life."

"You were in South Africa."

Simon nodded. "I went there to work. To get away from

here." He paused. "Until this happened, until the demons returned, I didn't believe in them, either."

"What about the books?"

"There are books on demons. The ones we fought back there? They were Darkspawn. Very hard to kill. But they're just shock troops for the more dangerous ones."

"There are more dangerous ones?"

"A lot more dangerous," Simon said.

"Where are these books?"

Giselle interrupted from behind Simon. She'd come up on him without him noticing.

"If you think back far enough, Simon," Giselle said sharply, "I'm sure you'll recall that we aren't supposed to talk to outsiders about our mission."

Feeling guilty, Simon focused on the woman. He felt his rage roiling inside him, seeking to explode. "Maybe you haven't noticed, but things aren't quite the way they were a few days ago. The big secret is out." *My father is dead.*

"But not all of our secrets are." The smooth faceplate of the helmet reflected Simon's irresolute features. "And we prefer it to stay that way. You and your little friend should consider quieting down and getting some sleep. Otherwise we're going to leave you to fend for yourselves."

Simon hated being chastised. Especially when he knew he had it coming. But that was also the only reason he didn't argue. Reluctantly, he nodded. He knew Giselle would do exactly what she threatened to do.

Giselle walked away.

"Wow. She can suck the fun right out of a room, can't she?" Leah asked.

"She's just doing her job."

"So was Louis XVI's headsman. But the peasants still held him accountable when they revolted."

"Don't blame her."

Leah let out a breath. "Okay. I'll work on that. But why is she so hard on you?"

"Because," Simon said, "I betrayed them."

"How?"

"Almost two years ago, I abandoned them. I quit believing in everything I was being told, hated the way I had to live my life, and decided to do things the way I wanted to."

"That's how you ended up in South Africa?"

"Yes. It's also how I wasn't here when they needed me."

Leah's face softened. "I saw those armored warriors on tri-dee. One more soldier—or knight, or whatever—wouldn't have made a difference at St. Paul's Cathedral that night. You'd have died."

Maybe that would have been easier. But he didn't say anything.

The morning brought another mix of snow and fog. Simon lay under a camouflaged lean-to deep within the forest. Giselle and the other Templar had strung warblers around the site, security devices that tracked movement and pinged warnings directly to the armor. Warblers were harder to use in an urban setting.

Simon lay quietly curled up in a high-tech blanket he'd salvaged from the supplies they'd found among the survivors. There hadn't been much. The blanket gathered ambient light through patented NanoDyne technology and turned it into heat.

A dial on the blanket allowed him to choose the temperature. The trick was to leave it cool enough that it didn't melt the snow on the lean-to and warm enough that he'd be comfortable to sleep. The new wave of falling snow made that even harder. He lay quietly, almost warm enough to go back to sleep.

The fresh mantle of snow made the day look even

brighter, but it also made it cleaner. The trees looked naked and vulnerable without their leaves, and the scattered evergreens stood out even more.

The Templar rotated standing watch. None of them asked Simon to take a turn, and he knew the oversight was deliberate and intended as an insult. But there was also the possibility that they didn't trust him. He didn't blame them for that. He didn't know if he'd trust him, either.

Despite the emotions warring within him and the desperate need to get up and do something, he managed to sleep most of the day. He kept a recovered broadsword and a Grenadier close at hand. When he got hungry, he ate some of the power bars Giselle had given him and drank water from a canteen.

The day passed slowly, but it finally gave way to night.

Simon spent four days out in the forest. He traveled with the Templar and fought alongside them, too, encountering two more bands of Darkspawn that had attacked survivors. Mostly the Templar killed the demons where they found them and kept the survivors in motion toward the coast.

"We serve a rotation out here," Giselle told Simon one night. She'd been forced to suture a wound in his back because he couldn't reach it and Leah hadn't had the stomach for it. "Usually ten days out, then twenty days inside London. I think that's to give us a break from what's going on in the city."

"What's happening there?" Simon forced the pain from his mind. He'd learned to do that in his training.

Giselle tied off another stitch. She hesitated a while before speaking. "We're losing the city. The demons are hunting down everyone that hasn't left London. Exterminating them where they find them. Like vermin."

"Just the way the prophecies foretold." When Simon had been young, the Templar prophecies had frightened him. Then, as he'd grown older and bored with constant tales of bogeymen that he'd never seen, he'd stopped believing in them.

"Yes. But there's something the prophecies didn't talk about."

Simon waited, glancing over his shoulder as Giselle slid another piece of nylon into the eye of the curved suture needle.

"They're changing the land," Giselle said. "Starting at the Hellgates—"

"Hellgates?" Simon hadn't heard the word before.

"That's what Lord Sumerisle calls the nexus points that vomited the demons into our world."

"The name fits."

"Yes. Anyway, starting at the Hellgates, the demons have unleashed some kind of force—we still don't know if it's technology-based or magic-based, or some combination of the two—that is morphing the land. Buildings and roads are slagging down, becoming bleak, burned lands filled with lethal chemical pools and acid rain. The general consensus is that they're turning our world into something that resembles theirs."

"Terraforming?"

"That's a term that works as well as any other."

"That would tell us something about them." Simon considered the problem. "Does Lord Sumerisle have any scouts in that area?"

"Yes, but they run a high risk of discovery."

"The demons must already know they didn't kill all the Templar."

"They do. But the Templar who go there often get caught and killed. And we don't have a means of understanding what we've found there. Whatever we learn, it's going to be learned slowly. At great cost. I've no doubts about that."

Simon didn't, either.

"Have you decided?" Giselle asked as she put the medical equipment away.

"Decided what?"

"What you're going to do. Whether you're going to stay or go."

Simon thought about not answering, but he knew that was only due to the rebellious side of him even his father hadn't been able to control. "I'm going to stay."

Giselle's helmet flared open. She gave him a tired smile. "Your father's House will have to agree to that, Simon. And, to be truthful, they may not."

That hurt. Simon tried not to show it. "They would be stupid not to let me stay."

"You already deserted them once." Giselle's voice was soft and held no accusation.

"I didn't desert."

"In their eyes, you did."

Simon knew that was true, and he knew arguing with Giselle wouldn't do any good. He'd have to make his case to his House when he got back to London.

"Why would you stay?" Giselle asked.

To avenge my father, Simon thought bitterly. Then, just as quickly, *Because I don't know anything else to do.* But what he said was, "I was trained to be a Templar, Giselle. Maybe I never believed in the demons until the last week or so, but I've always believed in what the Templar stood for."

Giselle gave him a wan smile. "That's very good. I almost believe you. Keep working on it, though. Master Booth is High Seat of the House of Rorke and won't be as easy to convince. He didn't much care for you before you left."

Terrence Booth was four years older than Simon. When they'd been boys, they hadn't liked each other. There had always been competition between them. When Simon had been fourteen, they'd fought. Simon had beaten Booth even though Booth had had his full growth. It was something that people had talked about for ten years.

"I'll convince him."

"I hope that you do. But he likes you less now than when you broke his nose." Giselle leaned in and kissed Simon's cheek. "Get some sleep. We're heading back to London tomorrow night."

Simon pulled his shirt and coat on. The cold had been so severe that he'd started to go numb, which hadn't been a bad thing considering the wound. Once he was covered and his body started to warm, the pain returned.

"It seems the two of you have made up." Leah stood behind Simon only a short distance away. She leaned a hip against a tree. Dirt stained her face and matted her hair. Scratches scribed one cheek. She'd helped out in some of the battles, choosing to stay back and snipe targets. She had great skill with a rifle, and Giselle had grudgingly made use of that talent.

"I wouldn't go that far," Simon said. He gathered his gear and retreated to the lean-to, which was four inches deep in snow. "Get some rest."

"Why?"

"We're going to London tomorrow night." As Simon crawled under the thermo-blanket, he couldn't help wondering what the city looked like. Nightmares twisted through his mind all night, and he kept imagining the black rot that crept through London. When he got up the next day he felt more tired than when he'd gone to bed.

NINETEEN

The Templar traveled to London by two specially modified Land Rovers that could have doubled as tanks with all the extra armor and guns that had been mounted on them. Getting back to the city took two days. Luckily they missed any demon patrols that might have been in the area.

Coming from the south, they arrived first at Brixton Market. The market was devoid of life. A few campfires burned in the distance. Wrecked cars, some overturned and some smashed and ripped by missiles and beam weapons, filled the streets and created an obstacle course between the buildings. The torn wreckage of a double-decker bus had been shoved through the front of a florist shop.

Seeing the wanton destruction in all directions, seeing buildings lying in ruin that had been so vivid in his mind from when he'd last seen them, shook Simon. It had been one thing to hear about all the carnage that had been unleashed, but it was quite another to view it.

"It gets worse," Giselle said. She sat at the Land Rover's wheel in her armor. She used the armor's imaging system as she drove rather than the vehicle's headlights. "In many parts of the city you'll find the bones of the dead, tossed there by whatever scavenger had finished with them. Most of the buildings in Greater London are damaged in some way, if not outright destroyed."

Guilt coiled tightly within Simon. He'd been raised all his life to help prevent this. Even though he knew his presence in the city wouldn't have prevented the destruction he saw lying all around him, he couldn't absolve himself of not being there. He felt ashamed in ways he'd never thought he could.

They continued on.

The damage grew more intense in Camberwell and Newington. Kensington Park was filled with burned, blackened trees that stood out against the white snow. In Newington, Giselle pulled the Land Rover into an underground garage that was guarded by a group of Templar.

"We'll have to walk from here," Giselle said. "Vehicles draw out the demons inside downtown London. And gasoline is a problem. Once we use up what few stores we have access to, there probably won't be any more fuel. Some of the smiths in the Underground are developing power cells to replace the need for gasoline. Still, the conversion takes time."

Settling his pack over his shoulder, trying to find a position where it didn't chafe his wound so badly, Simon fell into step behind Giselle. The Templar walked in a single file through the tumbled-down buildings and wrecked vehicles.

Every now and again, Simon spotted wary-eyed people watching them from the ruins.

"The survivors," Giselle said quietly. "Usually, as long as you're in numbers, they won't attack you. But after days with little or no food, they'll attack and take what they need. It's not about nationality for them anymore. It's about territory and survival."

Simon spotted a few of the groups that had small children. "Doesn't anyone take care of them?" he asked.

"How?" Giselle's voice sounded tired.

"There's food in the city."

"Going after it only makes them targets for the demons. Bait in a trap. It's better if they leave. The Templar council hopes the civilians leave. That would free us up somewhat on our own course of action."

"The French aren't exactly happy with all the refugees that are piling up on their shores." Simon had heard a lot of resentment about the situation after he'd landed in Paris and made his way to the English Channel.

"Can you think of another thing to do?" Giselle's tone challenged him.

Simon looked away from her and at the dark cloud that hovered over London. "No."

"Then until someone can think of something else, that's the plan."

Simon followed Giselle through the streets and alleys of Newington. Full dark had descended upon the city. All of the electric lights were out, and if there were any oil lamps still to be had, no one lit them. He'd never seen London that dark, though he had imagined it as a child when he'd read about the German night attacks on the city in World War II.

They hunkered down across Elephant and Castle Street from the tube station house. The house was a two-story stone box with arched windows. Some time in the past the structure had been painted dark red, but the paint was blistered and peeling from weapons fire or acid. The windows had been broken out and bodies littered the sidewalk in front of it.

The street had been named for a pub that had been built sometime in the 1700s. It had been rebuilt twice in the 1800s. The name had come from the Indian elephant and the howdah carried on its back, which had looked a little like a castle to early British travelers. But the symbol had been adopted by the Cutlers' Company, which carried the image on their coat of arms. Later it was used by the Royal African Company for the slave trade the Stuarts had taken part in.

"They took out the subways a few years ago," Giselle said as she eyed the street. "It would have been to our advantage if they'd left them."

Simon silently agreed. His father had brought him to the area when he was a boy, familiarizing him with all of London the way Templar were supposed to do with the sons and daughters that would join them as knights. Simon could remember using the underground pathways, called subways in Britain while the Americans called their tube trains by that name, to get across the busy street. Now the streets were more European, featuring street corners and pedestrian crosswalks.

Back then, when the choice had been made to rebuild the Elephant and Castle area, city planners had felt the subways were too unsafe. Simon would have gladly taken his chances with muggers instead of demons.

Simon carried the Grenadier. He'd sheathed the sword down his back. He sat and listened, knowing that was what Giselle was doing.

Every now and again, the wind carried the sound of screams and roars, and the stench of dead things.

"One at a time, then," Giselle whispered. She led the way, using the armor's speed to get her across the street quickly.

Another Templar went next, following the order that Giselle had prescribed. Then Simon ran across with the cluster rifle in his arms.

He took up a position inside the tube station. The moonlight penetrated the gloom just enough to show the debris that had been left by looters and battles that had been fought there. Vending machines lay overturned on the floor. More bodies lay sprawled. The reek of death filled the interior so strongly that Simon had to open his mouth to breathe.

The rest of them crossed the street without incident, but a gliding shadow high in the air attracted Simon's attention. He stood behind one of the broken windows that left him with a clear field of fire.

The movement drew his eyes naturally, and the Grenadier followed. As he watched, a Blood Angel landed on the side of one of the buildings across the street. The demon clung there like a locust or a bat, looking obscene and predatory. Moonlight glistened across the leathery wings.

Simon kept the Blood Angel in his sights but didn't move his forefinger into the trigger guard. He'd been trained not to do that until he was ready to fire.

A moment later, the Blood Angel pushed away from the building, spread its bat-like wings, and took flight. It disappeared almost immediately without a sound.

As he turned around, Simon noted that even the Templar looked relieved. No expression showed on their faceplates, but their body language revealed it.

"They don't come alone," Giselle whispered. "That's one thing you can always count on."

They skirted the vending machines, which had long since been emptied, and the bodies. Simon grimaced when he saw that the corpses had been robbed. He doubted that the demons would have any use for human money, but he supposed there might have been some purpose for wanting personal possessions.

The Elephant and Castle station didn't have an escalator. They took the steps down to the underground rail.

Over half of London's tube system was aboveground. The rest of it was buried in the underground. There were two different levels of underground rail. The subsurface tubes were constructed using the cut-and-cover method, by digging a fifteen-foot trench into the earth, then covering it with concrete.

The Elephant and Castle station connected to the Bakerloo Line, which was one of the first to be constructed as a deep-level line. It had been bored using a tunneling shield and ran sixty feet underground for the most part. Except for when it nipped back to level ground here and there. Cut stone and iron rings framed the narrow tube line. Deep-level lines were smaller than subsurface lines, and they used smaller trains.

The Templar made their way around in the dark easily with their infrared imaging, but Simon couldn't see much. He didn't like having to rely on them to guide him, but he knew using the flash in his pack would give away their position. His imagination kept seeing demons that reached for him out of the darkness all around them.

"Place your hand on my shoulder," Giselle said.

Simon found her after a moment and did as she suggested. He still stumbled over debris and bumped up against train cars that didn't seem to quite be on the tracks.

"What about the electricity through the tracks?" Simon asked.

"All the grids are down inside the city. The power stations were some of the early targets the demons took down."

Simon didn't ask where they were going. He already knew, and he wasn't looking forward to it.

Only a few minutes later, Giselle stopped. Simon felt her shift and knew that she was reaching over her head. A purple light glowed briefly in the palm of her mailed fist.

Then a section of the wall slid away. Simon couldn't actually see it happen in the darkness, but he knew from experience what the terrible grinding noise was. He felt Giselle start forward, so he followed her.

A moment later, Giselle halted. The massive wall section behind them slid shut with a hollow *boom*.

"Speak your name," a mechanical voice challenged.

Simon heard Giselle's helmet flare open in the claustrophobic quiet of the room where they stood. He removed his hand from her shoulder. They were in one of the hidden checkpoints leading to the London Underground—the secret Underground that no one but Templar knew about.

When the city planners had first begun building the Underground as a means of travel under the city after so many of the people moved from the farms and the rural lands, Templar had been inside their organizations. The Templar had sworn to always protect the land and the city because their prophecies had shown that London would one day be in danger.

With their numbers hidden, the Templar had worked on projects throughout the city, establishing beachheads they could use in their eventual war against the demons. Even now, the work continued, as they hollowed out more and more space underneath London.

"I am Giselle Fletcher, Sergeant of the House of Connelly." Her voice was clear and proud.

Sergeant? Simon thought, remembering that Giselle was the same age he was. Then he realized that with all the deaths at St. Paul's Cathedral, field promotions had come rapidly. And there was the possibility that Giselle had made sergeant while he was gone. She'd always been ambitious, her eyes constantly on the prize.

"Welcome home, Sergeant Fletcher. Do you require anything?"

"I've got two wounded. They need treatment."

"Of course. You also have two unauthorized personnel with you."

That hurt Simon a little. He knew when he'd left two years ago that the Templar Underground would be closed off to him. At the time he'd departed, he hadn't cared. He hadn't thought he would ever care again.

But he did. A little. He walled that part of himself off and refused to be vulnerable. Templar were trained to seek out weaknesses in their opponents. At the moment he knew he was going to be viewed as one of their enemy.

"One is Simon Cross," Giselle said.

"We knew that. He's not—"

"He's here as my guest," Giselle said with an edge to her voice that immediately caught Simon's attention. "As is the woman with him. I claim that right."

"You may speak to the proper authorities regarding that matter, Sergeant Fletcher. Please come ahead."

The wall in front of them suddenly parted. High-intensity lights flooded the checkpoint, stabbing into Simon's eyes like daggers. He covered his eyes with one hand, but he kept his other one free—in case he was attacked. He had no reason to believe he was safe.

Giselle started forward and Simon followed automatically. The lights were still bright enough to be blinding. There was nowhere to hide.

TWENTY

"What have you done to Kelli?"

The angry voice woke Warren. He cracked his eyes open and blinked against the light, raising his right hand to ward it off. Someone had moved the curtain over his window.

"Did you hear me, Warren?"

Moving gingerly, Warren rolled over on his side. He was still dressed, almost, in the burned remnants of his clothing. He hadn't wanted to face pulling his clothing off, fearful that so much skin and flesh would come off with it.

George stood at the opening, a cricket bat in his hands. He was tall and athletic, fair-haired and blue-eyed. He belonged to an amateur rugby team and was used to physical violence.

Warren looked at the bat. He didn't want to be hit. George was powerful and the bat was hard. Even if the bat didn't break his bones, it would tear his flesh. He still didn't know if he was healing or merely lingering on the edge of death. He also didn't know if the pain was leaving or if he was growing more accustomed to it.

"Don't . . . hit me," Warren said, sitting up. He focused on George, willing him to listen to him.

A crazed look gleamed in George's eyes. Before the invasion, he'd truly been the fair-haired boy. Where Warren, Dorothy, and Kelli had barely gotten by, George had grown up in a world accustomed to wealth. He'd turned his back on his father, who had wanted to groom him for the family business. George had insisted on a career in art.

As it was, George was usually the one who mishandled his money. He'd never had to manage money, and he didn't feel the same pressure as the rest of them because in the back of his mind he could always go back to his father and his father's money. He wouldn't have to live out on the street.

"Why shouldn't I hit you?" George demanded.

"Because . . . I don't . . . want you to." Despite the fear that quivered through him, Warren met George's gaze.

"I don't *care* what you want." George's nostrils flared. He took a fresh grip on the cricket bat.

He's scared, Warren realized. *Of me.* The feeling that went through him was curious. George had always been disrespectful and standoffish to him. Now George was afraid.

"You can't stop me from hitting you right now," George declared. He took a step forward.

Warren almost dodged back. Only thinking that sudden movement might rip open some of the burns kept him still. "Don't," he said.

"Why not?" George yelled.

Movement at the curtain let Warren know someone was out there. He thought it was probably Dorothy, mousey Dorothy who worked at the bakery and babysat for professional parents. She didn't like confrontations, but Kelli and George sometimes made her ask Warren for extra money for the rent and utilities.

"Because," Warren said softly, nonthreateningly, "I don't want you to." He tried to put more energy into the force he was directing at George.

George hesitated. He looked panicked and confused. "What have you done to Kelli?"

"Nothing."

George cursed. "You're lying, mate."

"I'm not."

"Kelli *never* cared about you, Warren. She *hated* you. She thought you were creepy and disgusting. And she hated the way you looked at her with those calf-eyes."

That announcement hurt Warren. He'd always known he'd never stood a chance with Kelli, and most of the time he wouldn't have wanted to. They had nothing in common. But every now and again, he'd thought she was humorous and attractive. And every now and again she'd treated him like he'd been a real person instead of just a flat mate who had extra money when they needed it.

"Before you got burned," George said, "she wouldn't have given you the time of day. Now she's waiting on you hand and foot. It's hard to get her out of the flat to go scavenge for food. And we *need* food, Warren. Water, too."

Warren hadn't known that. He hadn't been conscious much for—for however long he'd been in bed. The sheets were littered with blood and stray bits of burned flesh that had torn free. The stench was suddenly noticeable too.

"I . . . asked her . . . to watch over me."

"She's acting like she's been possessed. Won't leave the flat." George's eyes hardened. "You did something to her."

"No." Warren's voice sounded firmer and stronger. Some of the pain fell away as he concentrated on George. "She just . . . wants to help."

George shook his head. "Not you, mate."

"You want to help me, too."

For a moment, George hesitated. Then he took a step back and cursed. "Stop."

"What?" Warren tried to sound innocent.

"Just shut up!"

Warren sat still and silent.

"You should have died," George snarled. "Burned up like you were, you should have died. Anybody else would have."

"I didn't. It's not as bad as it looks."

George laughed bitterly. "Yes it is. You're disgusting to look at, you are. A proper fright."

"What do you want?"

"If you'd died, I wouldn't have minded you wasting the water, mate. If it didn't take too long. But it doesn't look like you're going to die any time soon. Now you've done something to Kelli."

"I haven't done anything wrong."

George attacked without warning, swinging the bat off his shoulder straight at Warren's head.

Self-preservation warred within Warren. If he didn't move, he knew George would take his head off with the bat. But he was afraid if he did, he might fall to pieces right there on the bed.

Before he knew it, he reached up with his left hand as he wrapped his right arm over his face to protect himself. He caught the bat and stopped it.

Surprised, Warren looked at the bat. His left hand, still sausage-fingered and burnt black, had curled around the bat. Even though a meaty smack filled the room, there was no pain. There wasn't even any blood.

George tried to yank the bat away. Despite his strongest efforts, he wasn't able to. Not to be deterred, George lifted a big foot and tried to plant it in the center of Warren's chest.

Warren shifted, sliding to the side far more quickly than he would have thought. He caught his attacker's trouser leg, shoving it up and away. At the same time, Warren yanked the bat out of George's hands.

George stumbled backward and got his feet under him again. Warren moved at once, sliding off the bed and getting to his feet. He swung the bat, hitting George on the side of the head.

Without a sound, George sprawled to the floor.

Breathing hard, trembling from fear and physical exhaustion, Warren looked down at his vanquished foe. He couldn't believe what had just happened. Gazing at his left hand wrapped around the haft of the cricket bat, he was surprised to see that his flesh hadn't torn open.

With a scream, Dorothy erupted from the curtained front of the loft and dropped to her knees beside George. She cradled George's head on her lap. Tears poured down her cheeks from behind her cat's-eye glasses.

"You killed him!" Dorothy shrieked.

Even though George had tried to kill him—*And he'll definitely give it another go if he's still alive!*—Warren felt bad about what had happened. He hadn't intended to hurt George. He'd struck before he'd even known he was going to. Before he knew he *could*.

"He's not dead." Kelli came into the room as well. "George is still breathing."

Warren had to admit that Kelli was calmer than she would normally have been. She sat on the other side of George and examined his head.

"Nothing seems broken," Kelli announced.

Dorothy looked up at Warren. "You're a monster! A horrid, horrid monster!"

"And you're a twit," Kelli replied. "Always mooning after George. Like he'd take some notice of you when he has all the other pretty little birds in hand. He shouldn't have come in here and attacked Warren. I told him that."

"He had to." Dorothy brushed long hair from her face. "Don't you see? Food and water are in scarce supply. He couldn't just let Warren keep eating and drinking what little we had without helping us get it."

"I didn't eat," Warren said. But he was hungry now. His stomach growled unhappily. He tossed the cricket bat away. "I didn't even drink much water."

Dorothy just held on to George's hand.

Weary of it, not wanting to face the guilt he felt when looking at Dorothy or wanting to deal with George's predictable anger when he came to his senses, Warren got a fresh change of clothing from his chest of drawers. He headed for the ladder.

"Where are you going?" Kelli asked.

"Out." Warren swung onto the ladder.

Concern etched her features, pulling them tight. "You're not ready to—"

"I think I am," Warren snapped, then missed a rung on the ladder and fell. He dropped twelve feet to the first floor. He landed on his feet, with no more effort than if he'd stepped down from a stair step.

"Warren!" Kelli peered anxiously over the side.

Surprised, Warren looked at his legs. "I'm all right," he whispered, but it was more to reassure himself than her. He stood there, feeling stronger than he had in days. In fact, he didn't know when he'd felt so strong.

He went to the bathroom.

Pulling the rags of his old clothes from his body was the worst. Warren cringed when he first started, but it was less painful than he'd thought it would have been.

The clothing remnants came away in pieces, along with strips of burned flesh. He'd thought that the burn injuries would have been infected or bled. Instead, new skin looked white and wrinkled where the heaviest burns had been.

He was healing.

Disbelief washed over him. He stared at the white skin. Evidently he'd lost the pigmentation in his skin. The new growth wasn't going to come back the same color as his original skin. That bothered him, but he figured that being dead would have been a whole lot more disagreeable.

Kelli brought in snow in buckets, then melted it on the stove. When the water was warm, she poured it into the bathtub.

If the air in London hadn't been so laden with pollutants, the snow would have at least staved off the water problem. As it was, most people were afraid of drinking the melted snow and getting sick.

Warren luxuriated in the bathtub, noticing the care that Kelli showed toward him. George had been right. She had changed.

As he soaked, Warren saw that more of the burned flesh fell away and left the white skin beneath. A lot of debris even floated away from his left hand, leaving his fingers normal-sized again, even though they were dead-white. They were still numb, though.

He remained in the water until it started to cool. Kelli offered to bring more heated water, but by that time questions had filled Warren's mind that he knew he needed to have answered. And there was only one place to get those answers.

He got out of the tub and got dressed.

The fire had ravaged the building where the Cabalists had taken up residence. It stood like a barren crag among the other apartment buildings. The top two stories had exploded outward, leaving jagged teeth of brick and mortar.

Warren stood in the cold winter wind in a long black duster. Black crust still clung to his burns in places, but they were islands in the white skin.

"Is this where it happened?" Kelli asked. She had followed him out of the loft, walking just behind him and never speaking.

Warren had considered telling her to stay at the loft, but he hadn't wanted to be alone. Now, out in the open, he realized how exposed she was to predators, demonic and human.

Neither of them had a weapon.

Footsteps crunched through the snow, closing in from Warren's right. He turned to look, hoping that he and Kelli weren't about to be mugged for whatever food they might have on them.

Six men and women in hooded cloaks approached. The lead man was tall and thin. A single short horn protruded from his tattooed forehead.

Warren turned to face the man.

The man stopped. "I'm Malcolm," he said in a deep, soft voice. "I'm a Seer in the Cabal."

"I'm Warren."

"I know who you are," Malcolm said. "We'd been hoping you would return."

Warren studied the man's features, but they didn't look familiar to him. "Were you here that night?"

The man shook his head. "No. No one who was here that night lived. We lost Jonas and Edith. They were both very important to us. But we found out you'd lived."

"How?"

"I came here," Malcolm said. "To find out what had happened. One of the people in the neighborhood that I talked to mentioned seeing a man who had obviously been burned in a fire. The only fire I knew of was this one." He nodded at the building. "I have a gift for seeing things that have happened in the recent past. I saw your survival. I just didn't know where you'd gone."

"You've been waiting?" Warren was confused. "You couldn't know that I would return."

"It was hoped. I wanted—*we* wanted—to talk to you."

"About what?"

"You've got gifts, Warren. Edith told us about you, just as she told Jonas about you. We didn't believe her. Not until I saw the demon that manifested through the Eye."

"You saw Merihim?"

"Yes."

Fear rattled through Warren. He resisted the impulse to glance around.

"The demon isn't here now," Malcolm said.

Warren relaxed a little.

Malcolm approached, then slowly reached out to touch Warren's face. Warren stepped back.

"I'm sorry," Malcolm said. "I didn't mean to make you uncomfortable."

"I don't like being touched," Warren said. He never had. Growing up in those foster homes had ensured that.

"You were badly hurt." Malcolm studied Warren's face. "When I'd heard how badly you were burned, I have to admit that I'd believed the man I was talking to was exaggerating. Now that I see you, I don't think he knew the extent to which you were injured."

"I'm getting better," Warren said.

"I can see that." Malcolm locked eyes with Warren. "You have a lot of power. I know Edith and Jonas offered to train you to use it and you went to them. I'd like to extend the same offer."

Warren nodded meaningfully at the burned-out husk of the nearby building. "The last time I agreed, things didn't work out so well. For anybody."

"We can handle Merihim."

"Jonas and Edith thought they could too."

Malcolm smiled a little. "The people that I'll be taking you to are much stronger than Jonas and Edith. Also, you'll be in a better-protected area."

"I don't think so," Warren said. He didn't want to be anyone's guinea pig. "I've got enough troubles already, so—"

"The demon has marked you," Malcolm interrupted. "I can see it. Anyone who has eyes can see it. Right now you're living at his largesse. You don't have a life." His words were flat and damning. "You will die whenever you cease to amuse or interest him. Is that what you want?"

Warren looked at the burned-out building, then at his dead-white left hand. He was certain Malcolm was lying to him about something. Even without the gift or curse that he'd been born with, he would have known that. No one could make the promises Malcolm was making.

So what do you do, Warren? he asked himself. He wanted to live. He knew that for certain. After coming so close to dying—*twice* in his life now—he knew he wanted to live. More than that, he believed he truly deserved to live. The question was whether throwing his lot in with the Cabalists would help him stay alive.

In the end, though, he knew he didn't have a choice. He found himself grasping at the unbelievable . . . just like his mother had. The thought shocked and angered him. He hated feeling trapped. He'd grown up that way, then lived that way for years.

"No," he said quietly. "No, that's not what I want." *I want my life back. No matter what it takes.*

TWENTY-ONE

Through his slitted fingers, Simon saw a dozen armed Templar standing before the opening. They held swords and rifles at the ready. Even as a group, they looked worn and haggard.

"Mr. Cross," one of the Templar said, "divest yourself of your weapons. *Carefully.*"

Simon looked at Giselle, but she wouldn't meet his gaze. Being addressed as *Mr.* Cross, like a civilian instead of a Templar, stung. He thought about ignoring the command, but decided against it. *You knew they were going to hate you. You knew that when you chose to come here.* Carefully, he lowered his weapons to the ground at his feet and laced his fingers behind his head.

Leah was forced to do the same.

Simon forced himself to remain calm when two of the men stepped forward with manacles and placed them on his wrists. They secured his hands behind his back, then placed another set around his ankles. They only secured Leah's hands behind her back.

"Who's the woman?" one of the Templar asked.

Simon didn't know the man. The armor gave no evidence of his identity or his rank. If Simon had been wearing his own armor, his HUD would have identified the man at a glance.

"She was with Cross when we found him," Giselle answered.

"I came here to search for my father." Leah looked scared. "I'm not here to hurt anyone."

"You shouldn't have brought her here," the Templar said.

Giselle frowned. "I couldn't very well leave her out there to die. That's not what we're here for."

After a moment, the Templar replied, "We're here to kill the demons, Sergeant Fletcher. Don't forget that." Before Giselle could respond, he wheeled and walked away, giving orders to his men to follow with the prisoners.

Two of the Templar jerked Simon into motion. *Welcome home,* he thought bitterly. He wasn't really surprised about their behavior. But he was surprised he'd thought things might have gone differently.

The Templar Underground was huge compared to what the average Londoner knew about the subterranean transportation routes. Simon didn't know how much bigger it was. All of the various parts worked together, but they were also kept separate so they couldn't all be compromised at once.

Besides residences, medical facilities, and training areas, the Templar Underground supported security posts, generator rooms powered by turbines driven by the River Thames, medical and weapons labs, forges where the armor was made, mausoleums, and the hydroponics farms that were kept ready in case of siege. They were at that point now, Simon supposed.

The guards took him to one of the security posts and left Leah there inside a cell. At least they had the decency to remove her shackles first.

Giselle stayed at Simon's side, and he took some comfort

in that. Until he remembered that she would slit his throat if she believed he was a threat to the Templar. Other Templar passed them in the corridors. None of them would meet Simon's gaze.

Sharp-edged fear moved restlessly in the back of his mind. He kept thinking about ways to escape, and that impulse was kept in check only by the fact he knew the Templar would kill him if they had to.

A short distance farther on, they came to another security checkpoint. After a quick exchange, the Templar guards posted there stepped back while the massive palladium door swung open. It clanged shut behind them after they stepped through.

Several of the doors were air- and water-tight. Sections of the Templar Underground could be shut off and exist independently.

Still, living a subterranean lifestyle hadn't suited Simon. There had never been a time when he hadn't felt the crushing weight of the city above him and longed to be outside.

One of the Templar put a gloved hand on an elevator door in the next hallway. The doors opened and they stepped inside. The elevator went down so fast that Simon felt lightheaded. He swayed and swallowed bile, but remained erect.

Lights flickered as the elevator sank. The deeper the levels, the more important the person was that he was going to see. Simon hated the idea of that, too. His father had occasionally taken him down into the lower reaches of the Templar Underground and Simon hadn't enjoyed it. The deeper someone went, the fewer escape routes there were.

The elevator stopped suddenly. The temporary increase in gravity pulled at Simon, then faded. His escort guided him from the elevator and through another maze of tunnels till they arrived at their destination.

More Templar guards stood before a palladium door. They stepped aside and the doors recessed back into the walls.

Computer equipment filled the room beyond. Men and women sat at workstations. The centerpiece of the room was a tri-dee projector that displayed a section of London. On closer inspection, Simon realized the area was several blocks around the Elephant and Castle station.

A handful of figures ran through the alleys, pursued by demons. As Simon watched, a Blood Angel swooped from a building top and grabbed a fleeing man. Flying high, the demon screamed in triumph, then released its prize. Arms and legs pinwheeling, the tiny figure dropped to the street and lay still.

The other figures tried to fight, but their weapons couldn't hurt the demons. It was a massacre. The pale light from the tri-dee projection limned the hard faces of the men and women around it.

Simon recognized some of the six Templar gathered at the tri-dee, but not all of them. They were all young. The oldest among them was Terrence Booth, now the High Seat of the House of Rorke.

Booth was three inches shorter than Simon now, but he'd been taller when Simon had broken his nose. He had dark hair and wore a goatee, which was new since the last time Simon had seen him. Perhaps Booth thought it made him look older.

Booth shot Simon a mocking glance. "Do you believe in demons now, Simon?" he asked.

Simon started to take a step forward. Giselle interposed herself and kept her back to him. Two guards, both of them there to protect the High Seat of the House of Rorke, stepped forward as well. There was no doubt in Simon's mind that they would cut him down if they felt he was a threat.

"He's come back," Giselle said in a calm voice.

"A pity he didn't come back sooner," Booth said. "He could have joined the others at St. Paul's Cathedral."

Simon took a deep breath and tried to push his anger away. It was easier than he'd imagined, but that was because he felt ashamed to be there among those who had been his peers. All of them knew what he had done to bring disgrace to his father's name. Simon focused on being able to strike back at the demons that had killed his father and the other Templar.

"Do we suddenly have so many warriors," Giselle asked, "that we can afford to turn them away?"

Booth turned his dark eyes on Giselle. "Are you here to fight his battles then?"

"Am I fighting his battles? Or am I correcting your mistakes?"

The blunt honesty aggravated Booth. He waved a hand over the tri-dee, switching views to different parts of the city. The Templar had long ago wired the city with security devices, using the post-9/11 paranoia to cover their tracks. From their inception they'd had independent power sources.

"Your father is dead." Booth stared into the city.

Many of the buildings in the downtown area had fallen and left piles of rubble strung across the narrow streets. Fires still burned within some of them, feeding on ruptured gas lines and combustible materials within those buildings. London had burned before, Simon realized as he looked at all the carnage before him.

"I know," Simon said in an emotion-thick voice.

"You came anyway."

Simon made no reply. His presence was proof enough of his intentions.

"It was a foolish thing to do," Booth stated.

"What should I have done?"

"Stayed in South Africa. Wherever it was you were before you were here."

"That wouldn't have done any good. You know that. The demons have established a foothold here. They're not going to just walk away. Other Hellgates will open soon. If they haven't already."

Booth walked over to face Simon, looking up at him. Simon knew that his height irked the other man as it always had.

"You left us once," Booth said. "Why should I believe you when you say you'll stay this time?"

"I want to see my father avenged."

Booth flashed a cruel grin. "Vengeance isn't enough."

It is for me, Simon thought.

"You were taught that," Booth went on. "Vengeance is a narrow road leading to disastrous consequences."

"I'm not here for revenge. I'm here to do what my father trained me to do. What the Templar trained me to do. If I do that, vengeance for my father will take care of itself."

Booth smiled. "You lie."

Simon tried not to show any emotion but felt certain he failed.

"You're not a very good liar," Booth said.

"It's not something I've cared to practice."

"Pity." Booth started to turn away.

"I came to fight, my lord," Simon declared, hating his attempt to win favor from Booth. "Whether I fight here, with you and the rest of the Templar, or I claim what's mine by my birthright and go out into the streets, I'm going to fight the demons. You can't stop me."

Booth turned to Simon. "No. I can't stop you. But I don't have to help you."

"My lord," one of the other Templars said.

Simon looked at the man, recognizing him as Derek Chipplewhite, a classmate he'd had while growing up.

"I'll vouch for him," Derek said. He was broad and beefy, his body hard from countless hours spent in the training areas. His skin looked black as coal and slightly blue in the darkness. "My word as a knight."

Drawing a slow, quiet breath, Simon waited. A knight's honor was a precious thing. Not accepting it would be tantamount to slapping Derek in the face.

"Very well then," Booth said, looking displeased. "But make certain he lives up to the honor you've shown him."

Derek nodded. "I will."

"Because if you don't, because if he doesn't, I'm going to put him out into the streets."

Simon barely kept from speaking. Booth was pushing the limits of honor.

"Get him out of here." Booth turned away and ignored Simon.

It's just as well, Simon thought. *If he looks at me, I don't trust myself.*

Derek gestured to the warriors. "Remove his cuffs."

The warriors did as they were told.

"Thank you," Simon told Derek.

The other man smiled at him. "Just live up to the trust I have in you. That's all I ask."

"There's a woman here," Simon told Derek. "She arrived with me. Her name is Leah."

"I'll tend to her," Derek said. "But first let's deal with you. If you've come all this way, I know you've got to be hungry."

TWENTY-TWO

You can't fault Booth," Derek said. "He takes that holier-than-thou attitude with people because that's the way he was brought up. His dad was an absolute stickler for the old ways."

Simon nodded and released a pent-up breath. "I know."

"It's because of the office. It's what people expect of him." Derek shrugged. "He's not the only one who acts that way."

They sat at a small corner table in the galley. Simon picked at his food even though it was the first home-cooked meal he'd had in months. The steak came from the ag floors and the potatoes and green beans came from the hydroponics farms. Everything tasted better than he would have expected.

"I don't fault Booth." Simon sipped his tea. "The truth is, I've never liked him and he's never liked me. Before, when he didn't hold office, it really wasn't a problem."

"But it is now," Derek said.

Simon shrugged. "I can work around it. I don't expect to be holed up here for long." He waved his fork. "I want to be out there."

"Out there," Derek told him, "isn't a very good place to be." He sipped his tea. "Out there can only get you killed."

"Maybe."

"Trust me, it would." Derek shook his head, his face

heavy with emotion. "Our numbers are drastically cut. That's what High Lord Sumerisle planned. But we're short of warriors. Everyone we lose out on the battlefield—" His voice came to a stop. "*Everyone* counts, Simon. We can't afford to keep losing trained warriors."

Simon forced himself to work through his food like a machine, stoking the fires in his belly. He sipped water. "I can't stay here," he said finally. "Even if Booth wasn't in charge of this area, we still wouldn't get along."

Derek grinned slightly. "I know. He hates you for breaking his nose and embarrassing him all those years ago."

Once the meal was over, Derek took the lead, twisting through the Underground complex. The Templar Underground occupied several levels, each built so it could be closed off in case of emergency. Most of the tunnels were dim, more twilight than bright of day.

Simon knew the Elephant and Castle station enough to get through it, but not all of the personal levels and quarters. Each section of the Templar Underground was maintained by different houses. House Rorke was located near the Baker Street tube station.

If things had been normal, they would have dressed in street clothes and taken the fifteen-minute trip to the tube station. Instead, they walked.

Armed with a sword and a Spike Bolter, Simon trailed Derek through the dark tunnel. This time, though, Simon wore a compact pair of night-vision goggles that rendered the tube tunnel in various shades of green.

Similarly equipped, Leah trailed after him.

Bodies lay along the tracks. It hurt Simon to look at them. The smell of death was thick.

"Why have you left them here?" Simon asked.

Clad in his armor, Derek glanced around. "We can't do anything with them."

"Why not?"

Derek's faceplate was expressionless, but his irritation at the question showed in his body language. "Think about it. If we start taking the bodies away, what's going to happen?"

The question was enough to point Simon in the right direction. He was embarrassed he hadn't already thought of the answer on his own.

"The demons will know someone is down here," Simon said.

"Yeah."

"So you're just going to leave them here?" Leah sounded like she couldn't believe it.

"We are," Derek said.

"That's . . . that's *inhuman.*"

"That's survival. We're here to fight a war, Miss Creasey." Derek stepped over the body of a woman who'd died protecting a small child that lay within her arms. "It's hard. Every time we pass this way, we're aware that we're stepping away from the softer part of us that keeps us human." He sighed so heavily the audio pickups inside the mask broadcast it. "We do worry about that."

"Do the demons come through the tubes?" Simon asked.

"Yes. Several of them have started using the Underground as a base of operations. And there are humans who have taken up residence in the Underground as well."

"The tubes would be a good ambush site," Simon mused. "Narrow confines. They could only come at you a few at a time."

"We've considered that. But—again—we have to be concerned if they learn we've got dwellings built down here." Derek was silent for a moment as he moved through the darkness. "They're going to figure that out soon enough. Everyone who died at St. Paul's Cathedral bought us some time. We don't know how much. But if the demons think that we're not a threat, maybe we can learn enough about them to be even more of a threat than we are right now. That's what we all hope for."

At the Baker Street station, distinctive because of the Sherlock Holmes wall tiles, Derek continued to the hidden doorway and put his palm against a wall section that only he could see. Simon knew the video circuitry in the helmet allowed Derek to spot the pulse communicator.

He laid his hand across it.

A few seconds later, a deep voice said, "Stand back, Knight Chipplewhite."

Derek stepped back. Simon and Leah followed suit.

Simon felt a little heartened. He'd grown up in the Baker Street tube area, within the hidden walls of the secret Templar base. The fact that it still existed gave him hope, but it also sharpened the pain he had over his father's loss.

The door flared open. Templar knights flared out and brought them into the hidden area. The door closed behind them.

A massive knight squared off in front of Derek. "State your business."

"I'm reporting with Knight Simon Cross," Derek replied.

The Templar inside the security room turned to Simon. The lead warrior opened his face shield. "Simon?"

"Bryan," Simon said, recognizing the younger man. Bryan Hedges hadn't yet been brought into the ranks as a full knight two years ago when Simon had left. Looking at him now, Simon didn't think the young man had even started shaving. He was still smooth-cheeked.

But Bryan was no longer innocent. Simon saw that from the hurt inside the young man's blue eyes. The last few days of the demon infestation had taken their toll.

Bryan hesitated a moment, then held out his mailed hand. "It's good to see you, Simon."

Simon took his hand and shook. "It's good to see you too, Bryan."

Frowning, Bryan asked, "You've heard about your father then?"

Simon nodded. "I have. That's part of why I'm here."

"It's too little and too late," one of the other Templar muttered.

Ignoring the comment, Simon released the younger Templar's hand. "I've come for my armor."

Bryan nodded. "It's with your father's things."

"Where . . ." Simon's voice locked up and he had to try to speak again. "Where's my father?"

Taking a deep breath, Bryan shook his head. "I don't know. Things at St. Paul's Cathedral became extremely complicated. You have heard about the battle there?"

"Yes."

Bryan looked at Derek. "Of course you have," the young man said. "It was confusing . . . afterward. We didn't get a chance to recover the bodies. There were . . . just . . . too *many* of them." Tears glinted in his eyes. "My own father died there as well. We couldn't return for him, either."

"Can you track his armor?" Simon asked.

"Yes. My father's armor is still at St. Paul's."

"Is my father's?"

"No." Bryan looked sympathetic. "The military and police force recovered some of the bodies. They have them in various holding facilities, from what I understand."

"Why?"

"We don't know. Probably to study them."

Simon didn't say anything.

"During the invasion, just as the demons were about to attack and we recognized them for what they were, we took the police and military by surprise," Bryan said. "They've been trying to open up a line of dialogue with us. High Lord Sumerisle has decided not to follow that course of action."

"Why?"

"Because the police and the military haven't been trained to combat the demons as we have. They'll only be cannon fodder in the coming war. Furthermore, they may compromise our own efforts." Bryan frowned. "The sacrifice our fathers made was to dissuade the demons from seeing us as the threat we could be."

"If we'd been more of a threat," Simon said, "we would have beaten the demons."

"We will." Bryan's chin lifted defiantly. "As long as one of us lives, we will strive to find the demons' weakness and use it against them." He studied Simon. "What about you? What are you going to do?"

Simon thought about that and almost said he didn't know, then Derek spoke up. "He'll be with my unit. I've spoken for him."

Bryan nodded and offered a wan smile. "That might be best." He cut his eyes to Derek. "He'll be in your care while you're here?"

"Yes."

Simon tried to hide the hurt and anger that writhed within him. Even though he was certain Bryan hadn't intended the question to be an insult—and had, probably, intended it as a friendly warning—Simon felt as though he'd been slapped.

You're no longer welcome here, he told himself harshly. *You knew that. Don't fight it. You can't win.*

"Take as long as you need," Bryan said. "But remember: the sooner, the better."

Derek nodded.

After a moment, they were waved through.

Derek asked direction as they went. He wasn't overly familiar with the House of Rorke's Underground branch. Simon answered quietly and succinctly. He didn't want to own the hurt and confusion that filled him as he strode through the tunnels he'd grown up in.

They'd been home once, but he knew they never would be again. He knew he'd miss the feeling of belonging somewhere, of having a home.

In South Africa, the loss had seemed far away and negligible.

The attrition of warriors, so evident by the pedestrian traffic in the hallways, brought that loss even more sharply into focus. He had no way of knowing how many had died at St. Paul's Cathedral. Only the High Lord and his inner circle had known the exact number of losses.

And they weren't telling.

Now that he thought about it, Simon also knew he'd never heard how many Templar there had been in the Underground. His whole life had been filled with secrets. He thought he'd known them all.

The truth was they'd been living under siege.

And the monsters were real.

"You lived down here?" Leah asked as they walked.

"Yes." Simon didn't elaborate. He'd been trained from childhood not to talk about his life in the Underground.

"It must have been hard."

"I didn't live down here all the time," Simon said defensively.

"Where else?"

"We took trips through London. Occasionally family trips to France."

"But the rest of the time, you lived here?"

Simon nodded. He'd never talked about his life in the Underground with anyone. Not even with Saundra. He felt uncomfortable talking about it now with Leah. But as out of place as he felt, he knew she had to be feeling even worse.

"It wasn't bad," Simon added.

"Your parents lived down here, too?"

"My father did. My mother died giving birth to me." That had been the beginning of all the guilt he'd felt, knowing he'd taken away so much from his father and never lived up to Thomas Cross's expectations.

"I'm sorry."

"Me too."

Guards stood in front of the armory. The storage space was well away from the Underground living quarters. With all the munitions packed into the armory, no one had wanted to take a chance in case there was an accident.

"Simon Cross," one of the Templar said.

Simon couldn't recognize the growling voice.

The helmet opened a moment later and revealed the craggy features of Miles Graydon. The Templar's hair had turned the color of frost since the last time Simon had seen him. His armor was dark red and black, patterned to disappear in an urban nightscape in case the stealthskin programming failed.

Graydon wore a fierce beard and mustache. His dark eyes regarded Simon for a moment, then crinkled with their customary warmth.

The old Templar stepped forward and embraced Simon. "It's good to see you, lad."

Simon hugged the older man back even though he knew Graydon would never feel it. "It's good to see you, too."

Graydon released Simon and stepped back. "Here for your armor, are you?"

"Yes."

"Well good for you, lad. Your father knew you would be. He left you a letter. You'll find it in your vault."

That surprised Simon and he didn't know what to say.

"Your father knew two things the night that he left for St. Paul's, lad." Graydon ticked them off on his armored fingers. "He knew that he wasn't coming back, and he knew that you'd be here for your armor to do what he'd trained you to do."

Simon swallowed the lump at the back of his throat. "Then he knew more than I did."

Graydon gave Simon a small, sad smile. "He always did. Don't ever forget that, because he knew enough to believe in you." The old Templar nodded at the door. "Open it up and let this young man through."

"I'll wait out here," Derek said.

Leah started to follow Simon inside the weapons storehouse but Graydon stepped in front of her. "Sorry, missy. The only ones who are allowed in here are warriors of the House of Rorke."

"All right."

Simon entered the storage chamber, listening as the power kicked on automatically. Light filled the cavernous space, kicking on in loud waves as it ran the length of the space.

TWENTY-THREE

Vaults filled the sides of the weapons facility. No one else was inside the room, but it made sense that no one else would be. Everyone in the Templar Underground that had stored their armor there while they were off security detail and training would have it with them, either wearing it or keeping it at their personal quarters.

Simon could remember the first time his father had brought him there. Scared and excited at the same time, Simon had peered around with a child's curiosity. He'd seen his father's armor every day, just as he'd seen that of other Templar. But the vault was a revered place. Some said it held the spirits of fallen warriors who would bless those that walked through the doors.

Most of the vaults were empty now. Except for damaged systems that were going to be used for spare parts before being melted down and forged anew.

There was a belief that armor salvaged from a Templar who had fallen in honorable combat was especially powerful. Simon didn't think he believed that. With the temperature the smelters reached, nothing organic would have survived.

Blood's more than an organic thing, Simon, his father had argued the one time that Simon had voiced his doubt. *Blood's also about the magic inherent in being somebody. In-*

dividuals who live life to the fullest and never hold back leave a deeper mark in their armor. That spirit, that bit of arcane strength, is still there for the new forger to make anew.

Even the forgers who worked their armor heavily with technology still believed in that.

Taking a deep breath, listening to his footsteps ring against the floor, Simon walked three-quarters of the length of the floor back to where the Cross family vault was. When he'd been small, the place had seemed so much larger. Now so much of the mystery had been removed.

The sense of invulnerability had gone with it.

The vault was a large ten-foot cube of space built into the wall. Foot-thick walls protected the contents. The slate-gray, featureless carbon-steel door only reflected Simon's shadow. The door didn't look any different than the other doors, but he knew it was the one to his family's vault.

When he'd been younger, the door had seemed impossibly large. Now he couldn't believe something so small could defend so much.

Leaning into the door, Simon put both his palms against the surface. Almost immediately, he felt the metal liquefy a little. Cellular memory, the forgers called it. The doors were programmed to recognize family members through DNA.

"Welcome, Simon Cross," a female voice said.

Simon's father had told him once that he'd considered having the vault coded with his mother's voice. So Thomas Cross wouldn't forget her voice.

Simon couldn't believe his father would forget anything. Thomas Cross had an almost photographic memory. Ultimately his father had decided not to use his mother's voice and had gone with one of the generic ones provided by the security program.

"What do you need?" the voice asked.

"Access," Simon replied. He took a deep breath, knowing

this would be the final proof of his father's trust in him. If Thomas Cross hadn't locked him out, that meant he'd at least had some hope of his son returning.

"Access granted."

The massive door swung open, gliding on a nonorganic, frictionless "liquid" that made it move almost weightlessly. Lights came on inside, reflecting off the dark blue and silver armor standing on one of the armor trees in the room.

Simon stood and stared at the armor for a moment. All of his life, his father had taught him what the armor meant, what he might one day be called on to do.

When he'd been younger, he'd loved the armor for what it had allowed him to do. Suited up, he could run faster, jump higher, survive harsh impacts, and was incredibly strong. The HUD inside the helmet gave him a 360-degree view of the world, as well as access to a range of infrared and thermographic vision.

Even by itself, the armor was a weapon of incredible destruction.

"Is something wrong?" the female voice prompted.

Simon had to speak past the tightness in his throat. "No. Nothing's wrong." He entered the vault and approached the armor.

His father's letter lay on a shelf near the armor. Trembling, Simon opened the letter, knowing the words on the page were the last he would have from his father. He dreaded what he would find.

Instead, his father's gentle words and understanding voice filled his mind and his heart. It was almost too much. For a moment, emotion crippled Simon. He focused, drawing it back into himself and walling it away. *Don't think now. You've got things to do now. There'll be time to think later. Time when you can't do anything but think.*

His father had always coached him to think that way

when he faced battle. When he'd been little, Simon had always imagined being at his father's side, fighting the demons with him.

Only the demons had never come. That dream had gone away when Simon had been a teenager. Simon's need to get out, to do more, had dawned within him then. And his father had tried to tighten the reins.

"Simon Cross," the computer voice asked, "is there anything you require?"

"No. I'm fine." Simon dragged his finger across the seal of one of the pockets inside the armor's breastplate. The pocket opened and he folded the letter inside tenderly.

He stripped to his skin, then dressed in the armor automatically, stepping into the breeches, then sitting on a reinforced bench that would take his weight. The suit was heavy. The designers had realized the need for some extra weight when fighting monsters. Throwing an empty tin can at a target didn't do as much good as throwing one filled with contents.

Fully dressed—because alloy was used, with the thickness of the armor walls, the self-contained environment unit, waste disposal, and the onboard med-system—his weight came in at almost four hundred pounds. For all of that, he felt the microfusion plant and NanoDyne servo-systems made him nearly weightless and move like a circus acrobat, with improved speed and strength.

Once the breeches were locked into place, he slid his feet into the oversized boots. They came with electromagnetic soles that could be charged in a heartbeat to allow him some "friction" on friendly metal surfaces, allowing him to run up walls for a short distance or resist being pushed or even dropped if it came to that. Anchors could be fired from the soles as well, as weapons and to ground him.

He pulled on the breastplate, then the sleeves. They connected to the shoulders of his breastplate at his spoken command. The gloves slid on smoothly, locking into place as well. Already he felt light, stronger, more whole than he had in two years. He couldn't believe how much he'd missed the feeling he now had. Lifting the featureless helmet, he pulled it over his head. It ratcheted into place.

Complete. The thought spun through his thoughts, pulling him into tighter focus.

At first, Simon could only see through the faceplate like it was made of glass. There weren't any special visual adjustments being made.

Simon took a deep breath. "Online."

At once, the suit powered, pulling energy from the solar-charged cells that had been in hibernation. Once powered up, the cells would last for years. Even when the suit was in constant use, the recharge time was minimal. Solar streaming through the microfusion drive proved infinitely better than prior solar batteries.

In addition to the solar cells, most of the armor also ran on arcane energy as a backup. Some, like Derek's armor, operated primarily on arcane energy with the solar cells as backup.

The armor *hardened*. All the seams bonded through electromagnetic or magical means, depending on the nature of the armor. Simon's armor held bonds formed out of both. Liquid poured into the cavities separating his flesh from the form-fitting armor, making everything more solid.

With the liquid in place he wouldn't get jostled or thumped around during impacts or sudden stops. It was even hygienic and therapeutic, capable of cleansing and medicating wounds that weren't life-threatening. If a limb were amputated, the suit was designed to seal, stanch the blood with a tourniquet, and stabilize the wearer with medical drugs.

Simon lifted his arms effortlessly, glorying in the power. He turned and made his selection of weapons. He chose the broadsword he and his father had forged together before they'd made his armor after he'd gotten his full growth. Warriors always grew into their final weapons before they were ready for their armor.

He added a Spike Bolter, holstering the pistol at his side and sheathing the sword down his back. Turning, he looked into the mirror at the end of the vault.

An armored Templar warrior stared back at him. Readouts quickly identified the dark blue and silver image as nonthreatening. He took pride in the look, remembering how he'd first felt when he'd seen himself in armor.

He'd gotten his first real armor at twelve, the age when boys and girls would have been allowed into battle with the demons if they appeared. Thereafter, he'd forged new gear as he'd grown out of what he had. When he'd reached his full growth and had found his best fighting weight, he'd forged the armor he now wore.

The dark blue and silver armor glinted in the light. In bright daylight, without the stealth mode activated, the mirror-bright surfaces could prove blinding.

All that was missing was his father standing behind him.

Simon turned and left the vault. The door swung closed behind him, locking tight with a loud bang.

I hope you can hear me, Dad, Simon thought. *I'm going to be everything you raised me to be. I'm going to make you proud.*

But that was only, Simon knew, if he was given the chance.

Outside the weapons complex, Simon stood for a moment and looked around. Inside the suit now, he felt bigger and more powerful. Leah looked incredibly small.

"Simon?" Leah looked surprised. She took a step back from him.

"Yes." Her voice and his sounded normal to Simon, but he knew his would sound different to her.

She stared at him. "It's just . . . you look a lot different."

"I know." Simon felt different, too. The HUD had him connected to the world in ways he'd forgotten. The sensor relays that had activated once they'd come into contact with the skin over his spinal column gave him a lot of feedback. He could touch and feel, but he had a lot of control over what sensations he experienced. True pain would never touch him as long as the suit's integrity hadn't been breached and the healing wards and drugs remained intact.

"Is that everything?" Derek asked.

"Yes."

"What about personal belongings?"

Simon thought about the other items his father had left in the vault. Images and vid, keepsakes they'd gotten from different places they'd gone to, all of those things were still within the vault.

"Nothing that I want to carry with me," Simon said. If he fell, he wanted those things to remain intact. The Cross family had dwindled over the years. His father had had a younger brother, but the brother—Robert Cross—had died in a tragic accident.

Simon was all that remained of his family.

Derek hesitated. "You might not get to come back for it."

"Yes," Simon said, "I will. If I live, those things are the only inheritance my father left me. I won't be denied what little there is."

Graydon dropped a heavy hand on Simon's shoulder. The old Templar's metal-gloved hand clanked.

"You'll come back and fetch what you need, lad," Graydon said. "Whenever you've a mind. I'll give you my word on that."

Simon took the old man's hand and shook it. "I appreciate that."

"No trouble, lad." Graydon smiled. "You just be careful out there."

Simon said he would, then he followed Derek back out of the House of Rorke Underground.

The trip back from Baker Street tube station was vastly different for Simon than the trip to the area. Even though he'd been wearing night-vision goggles, Simon hadn't been able to truly see.

With the helmet in place, though, the interior of the tube line was lit up as brightly as daylight. Simon walked fearlessly. He was a predator in his natural environment now.

But he was more able to see the carnage that had been left behind by the marauding demons. The HUD was so sophisticated it matched the real colors around him instead of rendering them in green.

He worked so hard on not seeing what he saw that he almost missed the start of the attack. The HUD painted the figures hanging upside down from the tube ceiling green as he turned the corner.

Other twisted and misshapen figures lay in wait behind the overturned cars of the tube train. Once he saw them, though, Simon knew they were Darkspawn.

"Ambush!" one of Derek's men yelled in warning.

Out of habit, Simon reached for his sword and the Spike Bolter. He spotted Leah behind him in the HUD view. Backing into her, he growled, "Get to cover." Then he had the Spike Bolter up in his fist and was firing. A string of detonations ripped away the quietness inside the tube.

The palladium spikes ripped into one of the Darkspawn hanging from the ceiling, pinning the creature to the stone surface. The demon yowled in pain and anger as it tried to rip itself free. Its thin body whipped and twisted, tearing the wounds in its flesh even larger.

Upon closer inspection, Simon saw that the demons had woven a web of cargo netting they'd undoubtedly scavenged from the overturned tube cars, on the ceiling. They'd worked awfully quickly to have set the ambush up on the Templar's return.

A moment later, the Darkspawn Simon had nailed to the ceiling braced its feet and pulled through the spikes. Dark blood ran freely from the wounds. Snarling, the demon landed only a few feet in front of Simon. It lifted a weapon and took aim.

Whirling, Simon dodged out of the way of the deadly beam. The beam struck the wall behind him. Through the HUD, Simon could plainly see that Leah was in hiding beside one of the overturned tube cars.

Simon attacked before the Darkspawn could fire again. He swept the sword cleanly through the demon's neck. The headless corpse stumbled around for a few moments, then collapsed in a broken heap.

Beyond the demon he'd slain, Derek and his men were hard-pressed to keep up. Swords flashed and occasional firearms filled the tube tunnel with bright light and noise. Stepping over the obscene corpse stretched on the ground, Simon moved forward to engage the enemy further.

Four Darkspawn launched themselves at Simon. He lifted his foot and smashed it into the face of the center one. "Spikes," he ordered out of reflex.

Spikes popped out of his boot soles and tore into the demon's face, slicing through two of its eyes and leaving them in ruin as it staggered back.

Firing the Spike Bolter into the face of another Dark-spawn, Simon nailed the creature to the side of an over-turned tube train car. The third creature blocked Simon's immediate sword attack, bringing up a rifle to block the heavy blade.

Shifting, seeing in the HUD that he had plenty of room for such a maneuver, Simon spun to his right, bringing the sword around in a glittering arc. Using all the power that the servo-motors and actuators in his armor gave him, Simon slashed the demon into halves.

The fourth Darkspawn threw itself at Simon's chest and knocked him backward. Other demons fired Grapplers and cluster rifles.

"Warning," the soft feminine voice inside his helmet said. "Incoming."

A bright flare lit up his HUD as he fell. "Rocket!" he warned the others. If they made a reply, he lost it during the conflagration that followed.

TWENTY-FOUR

The rocket slammed into the wall to Simon's left, barely missing two of the Templar entrenched there. The explosion knocked the Templar and the Darkspawn horde to the ground.

Simon heard nothing of the explosion. The armor's automatic dampers cut in, muting all the outside noise. For a moment, his world was total silence, but he was buffeted around by the concussions.

Landing on his back, thrown back across the ground nearly twenty feet, Simon hurtled against an overturned tube car and came to a sudden stop. Slightly disoriented even with the armor's defenses, he looked at his hands, making certain he still had his sword and the Spike Bolter.

When he looked up again, three more Darkspawn were headed for him. Flames clung to two of them. Simon's hearing was already steadily returning as the onboard systems compensated for the auditory onslaught.

"Did anyone see where that rocket came from?" Derek demanded.

"No," Simon answered. He gathered his feet and vaulted over the heads of the Darkspawn. Swiveling to his left, coming around in a tight arc, he pointed the Spike Bolter into a demon's face and squeezed the trigger rapidly. Four spikes knocked the demon back in stuttering steps. It was dead before it hit the ground.

The second Darkspawn managed to lift a sword to block Simon's blow. Shifting, Simon brought his right leg up and down in a heel strike that caved the demon's head in. Another demon hammered Simon's left wrist with a rifle butt, knocking the Spike Bolter free.

Giving ground, desperate because the Darkspawn were coming for him again, Simon gripped the sword hilt in both hands. He swung and parried, feeling the sword once more become a natural extension of himself.

As he fought, he thought of Leah, hiding somewhere in the shadows, defenseless and alone. She wasn't the only one whose life would be like that. He remembered the people who had lost their lives on the coast. They had died only minutes from achieving freedom. He also thought about the people he'd seen hiding in the wreckage of the city, living as best as they were able and turning to preying on strangers.

Simon knew his father had trained all his life to prevent such things from happening. But it had happened anyway.

Breathing hard in spite of the augmentation of the armor, Simon finished the last of the Darkspawn confronting him just as another rocket ripped through the air. The female voice in his helmet warned him again.

This time, though, Simon tracked the rocket back to its source. "Mark target," he told the onboard computer system.

"Target marked. Designation confirmed."

Immediately, crimson crosshairs formed around the demon nearly a hundred yards farther down the tube tunnel.

Unfortunately, the Darkspawn wielding the rocket launcher had a better view this time. The rocket struck one of the Templar and left him lying in a pool of twisted and slagged metal.

Rushing forward, Simon scooped up his fallen Spike

Bolter and sped for his quarry. A knot of Darkspawn blocked his forward progress. Only a few feet in front of them, Simon leaped into the air. Without the armor he could have performed such a maneuver, but with it, the move was even stronger.

Simon sailed a few feet over the heads of the Darkspawn, flipped, and landed on his feet hard enough to crack the cement floor underfoot. Even flipping through the air, the HUD had remained locked on the target and kept Simon oriented.

He ran, feeling the actuators and servos kick in, adding their own response to the sheer, naked strength that drove him. Adrenaline pounded through his system, and he knew better than to let it take over. But he didn't have much choice.

All the years of practice he'd had in the armor hadn't prepared him for how he felt while he was using the full prowess of the armor. Despite the practice he'd had, he couldn't control his body.

He wondered if his father had suffered from the same reactions. Had Thomas Cross suffered from the enthusiastic anticipation that he now felt? Somehow Simon didn't think so. His father was the most competent and complete man he'd ever known.

But he's dead, isn't he? The thought tore through Simon's mind like a palladium spike or a Prayer of Conflagration. He felt his heart accelerate again. He wasn't afraid to die. It was what he'd trained to do his whole life.

And yet . . .

"Accessing stim kit," the armor's onboard entity said. "Standby for anxiety alteration."

"No," Simon said, knowing that he just hadn't acclimated to the suit and the situation. No one could have truly prepared for this. Anxiety, under the circumstances, was understandable. "Override programming." He added the password.

By that time he was closing on the demon with the rocket launcher. The Darkspawn glared at Simon as it struggled to feed another rocket into the breech. A demon stood nearby, this one armed with a flexible curved horn hooked to a blob of reddish-purple moss on its back.

The horn started spewing liquid fire and smoke in Simon's direction. In the next instant, intense fire covered him.

Even with the special armor, Simon knew he couldn't last long. The NanoDyne tech hardwired into the armor as well as the spells weren't inexhaustible. The defense systems dropped on the readout, spiraling downward now.

The HUD automatically switched from light-multiplier mode to thermographic display. The program was so sensitive that Simon could differentiate between tongues of flame that were a few degrees of heat apart.

"Warning," the HUD's feminine voice said, "defenses nearing critical—"

With two more strides, Simon burst free of the flamethrower's superheated blast. He leveled the Spike Bolter at the demon wielding the flamethrower. Instead of aiming at the Darkspawn's face, though, Simon aimed at the fuel reservoir on its back.

He squeezed the trigger twice in rapid succession.

The palladium spikes both embedded in moss, in what he hoped was the fuel reservoir. In the next instant, the mossy blob exploded, creating a fireball that washed over Simon.

"Warning," the HUD called out. "Defenses now approaching critical levels."

Staggered by the concussion, Simon peered through the haze of smoke and distorted vision caused by the HUD's attempt to find focus. He stared in the direction he'd last seen the Darkspawn with the rocket launcher. Heat flooded the armor even as the cooling systems cycled through the liquid cushion. Smoke hung thickly in the tube tunnel. No wind existed to blow it away.

Movement within the depths of the smoke caught Simon's eye. The HUD marked it as well, automatically adjusting to bring the scene into clarity.

The demon swept the readied rocket launcher up. Simon leaped, holstering the Spike Bolter and closing both hands around the sword hilt. Landing near the Darkspawn, Simon whipped the sword down at an angled slashing attack. The blade sparked as it collided with the rocket launcher, then the rocket launcher shattered and the sword's edge bit into the demon's shoulder and sliced through its chest.

Squawling in pain and fury, the Darkspawn fell back. It threw the broken rocket launcher away and reached for the pistols belted at its waist.

Pressing his advantage, Simon thrust his sword before him and followed the point through the demon's heart. His momentum slammed the creature up against the wall behind it and pushed the sword back out. The Darkspawn flailed one large arm at Simon's head. Twisting, Simon caught the arm. According to his training, the Darkspawn were articulated like humans, with elbows and knees structured like hinge joints.

Simon trapped the demon's arm with his own, then jerked. The elbow snapped and bent inward. Bone tore through the flesh. Using his grip to aid him, Simon shoved the sword sideways, shearing through the Darkspawn's chest, hoping to cleave the heart. He felt the spine break, then the demon dropped to the ground.

Breathing hard, knowing he had to find a rhythm to get

his oxygen consumption back under control before he asphyxiated or hyperventilated, Simon placed a foot on the demon's chest and yanked his sword free. Malevolent fires glinted in the Darkspawn's eyes, reflecting the flamethrower fuel still burning on Simon's armor. Then the eyes locked, focusing on some impossible distance.

Another blast of coolness ghosted across Simon's skin as the armor's cooling systems got ahead of the residual heat from the flamethrower blast. He turned and looked back in the direction he'd come.

None of the demons remained alive. Derek and his group stood around two fallen members.

His weapons naked in his hands, Simon walked back to them. He saw at once that the fallen warriors wouldn't be getting back up. The rocket had blasted one's breastplate into pieces, tearing open his chest as well. Blood covered his body, but metal shards stuck out as well. The other had been blown nearly in half, but he still managed to hang on to life for a few desperate moments.

Helmet open, Derek knelt beside the dying Templar. He held the dying man's bloody hand in his own, then softly talked him over to the other side. The man seemed calm, accepting his death without complaint, but Simon knew part of the serenity was due to the drugs that the armor fed into the warrior's systems through slap-patches.

Leah stood nearby. Firelight limned her face. Surprisingly, she showed no emotion.

Simon guessed that she was just overloaded with everything that had happened in the past few days.

Derek kept speaking till the dying warrior could no longer hear him. Then he quieted and sat there on his knees for a time.

One of the other Templar knelt beside Derek and talked

to him briefly. Gently, the other Templar loosened Derek's grip on the dead man's hand.

Standing again, Derek looked at Simon. The Templar's face was haggard and filled with pain. "This is what you came back for," he told Simon. "All the dying, the pain, and the loss. His wife was killed three days ago. Now I've got to tell their children that they've lost their father, too." He took a ragged breath. "Are you certain you're ready for this?"

Simon let out a breath, focusing on hanging on to the calm that he needed as a warrior. They had prepared for this eventuality, of course. But his teachers had colored the loss of warriors carefully in layers of courage, bravery, and self-sacrifice.

Thomas Cross had offered no such illusions. He'd always maintained that dying was hard, frightening business no matter how prepared a person was to end up there.

"No," Simon said. "I don't think anyone can be ready for this. But I'm not going away." He paused, putting everything he felt into words. Not just for Derek, but for himself as well. "You and I both know there's nowhere to go. If the demons are left unchecked, they'll take everything."

Grimly, Derek nodded. "If you're with me, you're going to do what I ask, when I ask. Without question and without fail."

"I will."

"Good." Turning back to the fallen men, Derek frowned. "Let's get these warriors home."

Two of Derek's warriors invaded the tube train and brought back blankets and cargo netting. They placed the dead men on the blankets and rolled them into them. After putting the warriors on the netting, they lifted the bodies from the ground and carried them.

Derek called one of the men forward and instructed him to take the point position. Simon took the man's place on the blanket to help carry one of the dead men. Two other men helped the wounded Templar stagger along.

"You're going to stay here?"

Seated on the bed in the general barracks room that had been assigned to him, Simon gazed up at Leah. "Yes," he answered. He'd been surprised to have been accepted by someone. He'd assumed he would have gotten his armor at best, then been forced out into the city on his own. He would have gone without question.

Derek's willingness to make a spot on his team for him had been surprising. Of course, it looked as though spots were regularly made on the teams.

"What about me?" she asked.

A few of the other Templar listened in to the conversation. A tri-dee at the other end of the room had collected a crowd. There were few new broadcasts from London proper, but the media people seemed determined to fill the channel with old footage and new conjectures.

Simon shifted his helmet in his hands. He'd been working hard for hours to clean the surface. Dirt and grit that clung to the armor made operation of the stealth mode harder. More than anything at the moment, he wanted to finish working on his armor and get some sleep. He was surprised by how tired he felt.

"What do you want to do?" Simon asked.

"I want to find my father."

"We're going out on patrol tomorrow." Simon was amazed at how quickly his thinking had become plural. "If you'll give me the address, I'll discuss it with Derek. Perhaps we'll be able to get by there."

Leah crossed her arms over her chest. "I feel like I should be doing something."

Simon put his helmet aside. "You are doing something. You're surviving."

"It's not enough. I should be out there."

"If you were out there, on your own, you'd be dead in minutes." Simon nodded in the direction of the wounded man a few beds down. "Even armored up, we're taking our chances out there."

"Then why go?"

"Because we were trained for this."

Leah glared at him reproachfully. "You were trained to fight demons." Her tone dared him to make her a believer.

"Yes."

She shook her head. "That isn't something I can believe so easily."

"You've seen them over the last few days. You know the demons are real."

Letting out a quiet breath, Leah said, "Yes, but believing that you were trained to fight these creatures is even harder to accept than believing in demons."

"Now," Simon said gently.

After a moment, she nodded.

"We can hurt them," Simon said. "We can kill them. That's something the London police and the British military haven't been able to do."

"The . . . the demons still outnumber you."

Simon noticed that she still had trouble acknowledging what they were up against even though she'd seen the demons up close on more than one occasion. For most people, one introduction was all that was required.

"Unless there are a lot more of you than I've seen," Leah added.

"There are more demons," Simon replied. "That's why we have to move cautiously. The demons have weaknesses. We've got to discover them."

"But lying here in wait, *hiding*," she said it like it was something obscene, "is only allowing them to terraform more of London."

"We can't stop it. Not yet."

"What if the effects of . . . *whatever* they're doing can't be reversed?"

Simon barely maintained control of the fear that surged within him. Leah was hitting every major fear that he had. He kept himself calm with effort. All his Templar training had been targeted survival and saving people. "You can't think like that."

"Why?" Leah looked more frustrated.

"Because we need to remain hopeful."

"Hope isn't a blessing. It's a curse."

Simon held back his own frustration. The young woman hadn't been brought up as he had. And even he hadn't held to the Templar mind-set.

"Thinking you're just going to get killed," Simon said quietly, "will generally get you that way."

"How did you get trained?" Leah gestured at the barracks. "How did all of this get here? Why are you people so secretive about what you do? Don't you realize that if the police and military had known what you did, that things could have progressed differently?"

Taking a deep breath, Simon gathered his thoughts. "The Templar Orders weren't always secret. And this isn't the first time we've encountered the demons."

Leah calmed a little. "How long have you known?"

"I've been told that since I was born."

"By whom?"

"My father. My grandfather. Everyone I've known here."

"They told you about the demons?"

"Yes."

"Did you believe them?"

That hurt. Simon broke eye contact for a moment, then looked back at her. "No. I didn't. I got tired of living like this. So I left."

"That's what you were doing in South Africa? Hiding?"

"I didn't think of it as hiding," Simon protested. "I wanted my own life. I'd spent twenty-three years down in this place with very little time spent aboveground. I went to South Africa because people there didn't ask too many questions, and I could be away from civilization while I worked as a guide."

"When was the last time you . . . the *Templar* fought the demons?"

"We've never fought them before."

Leah shook her head. "I don't understand."

"Come with me. I'll show you." Simon stood and stripped out of the warm-ups he'd worn down in the barracks. Nude, he started pulling on the armor.

Leah turned away from him.

Realizing that she was embarrassed and knowing he was the reason why, Simon felt bad. Not sorry or modest. "Sorry. You get to where you don't notice nudity down here. We can't wear clothing under the armor."

"It's all right."

Simon wasn't embarrassed. Most of the barracks were co-ed. He finished dressing, then pulled his helmet on. Once the suit had hardened, he opened the helmet and picked up his weapons. They were already clean. Weapons always got cleaned first.

"We don't go anywhere down here without our armor." *Especially not now.* "Let's go." Simon took the lead.

TWENTY-FIVE

Warren sat in the back of a panel van and waited tensely, peering through the darkened window at the bat-winged creature that flew across the face of a three-quarter moon. Snow covered the forested landscape around the vehicle.

"What is that thing?" Kelli asked. She sat beside him in winter wear and under a blanket. When Warren had decided to go with the Cabalists, she'd insisted on going.

He'd thought about telling her to stay with the others, but he hadn't been able to. In his weakened condition, he didn't want to be alone in the company of strangers. Not even ones that seemed sincere about helping him. Kelli wouldn't be much help if there was a problem, but she was familiar.

"It's a Blood Angel," one of the men seated on the floor around them answered. "A hellish thing, it is. Clever and deadly."

"Oh." Kelli pulled the blanket a little tighter.

Warren watched the demon lazily flap its wings. Then it dove and disappeared once more into the forest of tall buildings that made up downtown London. Low clouds and the noxious fog streaming from the Hellgate obscured the view.

"Liam," Malcolm called from the front of the vehicle.

"Yes." Liam was young, his face littered with tattoos and piercings. He dressed all in black and had three horns jutting up from his narrow head. Scabs crusted the horns, showing that they were new additions freshly grafted on.

"Are there any more of them about?"

Liam stared into the distance. Warren felt the energy surrounding the young man and knew that Liam was seeing with something other than his normal vision.

"No," Liam replied. "They've gone from this immediate vicinity. We're safe enough for the moment."

Malcolm gave the driver orders to pull back onto the road. The panel van jerked into motion and pulled out from beneath a tree.

The demon patrols were the heaviest at night, Warren had known. And they targeted vehicular traffic, drawn by the sound as well as the scents given off by the exhaust.

Warren rested, leaning back against the van wall. Malcolm had offered to take him to a Cabalist retreat, so he could be shown what they had to offer him. Knowing that only a fight remained for him to have at his flat, and that he was going to need to learn more in order to survive, Warren had agreed.

But the choice hadn't been an easy one. He didn't like change in his life, but so many things already had. He was afraid he was one of them.

Less than an hour later, they were deep within the Mayfair district, out beyond the reach of the city. Residences out here were separated by vast tracts of land, much of it unimproved. Several of the houses had horse farms.

The twisted, bare limbs of trees stripped by the harsh breath of winter lined the crooked road. Warren guessed by the narrowness of the road that they were on a private lane.

A moment later, the van slowed, then turned and pulled toward the massive wrought-iron gates of an estate. The driver brought the vehicle to a stop.

One of the men in the cargo area got out. He trotted forward and opened the massive gates so the van could pass through.

Looking through the front windshield, Warren stared at the immense snow-covered grounds inside the high stone walls. Surely titled gentry lived here.

"What is this place?" Warren asked.

"The home of one of our benefactors," Malcolm answered. "He's one of the strongest in our group. His name is Hedgar Tulane. You'll be meeting him in a little while."

Warren knew the name. "Tulane? The communications mogul?" From what he remembered, Tulane owned a few communications groups that included television, radio, and newspapers.

"Yes."

"He's a Cabalist?"

"Yes. As was his father and his father's father before him."

That had been a closely guarded secret. Warren knew that if such a thing had gotten out it might very well have meant the end of the man's status, and his business profile.

The van bucked across the trail leading to the main house, a massive four-story structure that almost resembled a palace sitting in the snow. No lights showed in any of the windows.

A moment later, the driver pulled to a stop before the house. The windows remained dark and the door remained closed. Warren had expected a houseman at the very least to greet them. They always did on the vids.

"Doesn't appear to be anyone home," Kelli announced.

"No one aboveground," Malcolm agreed. "Wouldn't do for us to be so exposed, now would it?"

A man opened the cargo door.

Warren got out, stepping into the cold wind. Even inside the van, he'd been warm from the heater and from having the wind blocked from him.

Malcolm took a torch from his coat pocket and led the way. Armed men stood guard over the door, so cloaked in shadows that Warren hadn't seen them until he was almost upon them.

Hooves thudded against the snow-covered earth. The sound was so loud and surprising that Warren truly expected to find himself under attack.

When he looked, though, it wasn't snarling demons that had created the sounds. Instead, five horses stood at a corral fence only a short distance away. Warren had no idea what kind they were. When they breathed out, though, plumes of gray fog flared through their nostrils. They stamped the snow into mud.

"Horses," Kelli said. Her voice held a note of awed pleasure.

"Yes," Malcolm agreed. "As long as they remain alive and there are no attacks by the demons out here, we'll have fresh meat."

"What?" Kelli gasped in disbelief. "You're eating the horses? That's inhuman. They're . . . they're *horses.*"

Warren looked at her, mildly astonished that after all the death and destruction she'd seen inside the city that she could be concerned over the welfare of horses.

"Better we eat the horses than the demons eat them," Malcolm replied. "Horse meat isn't so bad after a while, and if the cook knows how to tenderize the cuts, it's more than palatable." Then he went through the door.

Kelli looked at Warren in disgust. "You didn't say anything about them eating horses," she accused.

Warren didn't bother pointing out that he hadn't known. He turned and followed Malcolm through the door.

Inside the house, Warren was impressed by the size, and the obvious wealth that filled the numerous rooms. His boots echoed against the tiled floor, letting him know how cavernous the rooms were.

They passed through the foyer and Grand Ballroom and walked into a study just off to the right. Books filled shelves. Beautiful exhibits of Asian history filled more shelves. Warren had no doubts that much of it was expensive.

Malcolm walked to the large fireplace that took up most of one full wall. When it was lit and there was a fire burning in the hearth, Warren felt certain the heat would have filled the room easily.

Pressing his hand against a sequence of stones framing the fireplace, Malcolm waved to them to join him inside. Warren and Kelli did so. Standing in the fireplace, though, Warren felt inordinately foolish.

Then the fireplace jerked into motion, spinning around on hidden pivot points. Immediately behind the fireplace was a set of narrow stairs that descended into the earth.

Malcolm took the lead at once, descending into the inky blackness with his torch lighting the way before him. "This way," he urged, standing on the narrow steps that curved down into the darkness.

Warren hesitated. But there wasn't a choice. Going back to the flat might have been possible, but he wasn't ready to deal with what was going on there. He set himself, took a final breath, then followed Malcolm.

"Hedgar Tulane's forebears took advantage of the natural caves under his ancestral home," Malcolm said as they went down the spiral stairs cut from the cave itself. "They had to have a bit of modification done here and there, but for the most part they just made the most of what was already here."

Even with his newly acquired ability to see in the dark, Warren wasn't able to see much. The smooth texture of the cave walls around them spoke of much usage.

"The Tulanes used this place back in World War II, during the raids," Malcolm said. "Of course, the people who were allowed here weren't shown all of the secrets. They've always protected their Cabalists beliefs from unbelievers. But there was some overlap of that during the Second World War. Hitler's minions were after many of the same powerful talismans our organization pursued." He stopped and played his torch over the large pool of water to the left. "Watch your step here. It's actually quite deep. And cold."

As Warren watched, a handful of fish surfaced and kissed the air.

"It's drinking water." Malcolm swung his torch around to show a trail that skirted the pool to the right. "The limestone in the bedrock in this area makes a natural filtration system. It's a bit heavy with minerals, if you ask me, but it can keep a man alive. We filter it a bit more to get out some of the taste."

Warren crossed the damp trail. The rocks felt slippery and his stomach convulsed as he thought about falling into the water. He'd never been a strong swimmer. In his present condition, though he felt stronger, he doubted he'd be able to save himself.

Only a short distance farther on, they entered another passageway that barely allowed Warren to walk through standing upright. Light glimmered in the distance and he thought they were headed there.

Instead, Malcolm halted midway down the passageway

and stood facing the wall. A moment later, the wall opened onto a smaller passageway.

Two armed guards in military riot gear stood post at a small landing. Security vids showed brightly on the wall behind them. Two cameras mounted on the ceiling of the passageway focused on the new arrivals.

Malcolm gave their names and said that they were expected. One of the guards nodded and waved them forward.

Entering the passageway, Warren followed Malcolm to the left. The descent was much steeper than the last passageway, and he felt certain the designers and builders had taken advantage of a natural cave formation to lay in the passageway. The carved stone stair steps followed the striations in the rock.

Near the bottom, Warren spied light. It was weak at first, but grew stronger as they neared. Eventually they emerged into a well-lighted cave filled with computer equipment.

"This is one of the communications centers we keep here," Malcolm said, waving to the computers and the people who manned them.

"Is this where most of the Cabalists are?" Warren asked.

"This cave system?" Malcolm shook his head. "Of course not. There are far more of us than this place can hold. But this is one of the strategic locations for—" He paused. "What you might consider research and development, I suppose."

"Do any Cabalists live within the city? In the Underground?"

Malcolm nodded. "A few. But primarily the larger gatherings of our group are outside the city. At least at the moment. The Cabalists initially moved out of London during the nineteenth century to avoid detection. A few of our constituents started discussing what we knew about magic much too freely. Spirit boxes and séances became all the rage. They were interested in talking to ghosts, though, not contacting the demonic world as we were trying to do. Currently, there is some talk of moving our operations back to London."

"Why?"

Malcolm began leading them to another passageway. "To be closer to the nexus of power, of course."

"What nexus of power?"

"The Hellgate. Surely you've felt the backlash of it lessen as we've come out here."

Warren had felt a decrease in the pressure he'd felt while in London, but he hadn't recognized it for what it was. His mind seemed less clouded, less busy, but at the same time that part of himself that he'd known belonged to his power of suggestion had seemed less strong and less certain.

"Yes," he answered.

"In order to properly study the powers the demons possess, we need to be there. Where the magic and power flows at its most primitive form." Malcolm paused in front of a wall. He put his hand out and looked at Warren. "Can you touch this?"

Warren stretched forth a hand and placed it against the wall. It felt solid and grainy, not as smooth as the other walls.

"Yes," he replied.

Malcolm smiled. "The real question is whether you can pass through." Then he stepped forward and passed through the stone.

Astonished, Warren trailed his fingers across the stone surface. *It's got to be a trick. He can't just have walked through solid stone.*

"Where did he go?" Kelli asked.

"I don't know." Warren pressed both hands against the stone, searching for a trigger or a release of some kind that would reveal an opening. *There can't be an opening. I didn't see one. I would have seen an opening. I was standing right here.*

"You can pass through, Warren," Malcolm encouraged from the other side of the stone. "You just have to align yourself."

Align myself? Warren pressed against the stone and sought to understand what kind of alignment Malcolm might have been referring to. He stared at the stone and tried to see through it the way he'd tried to see through the darkness when he'd gone to the Cabalist meeting.

At first, all he saw was the solid stone. Then, just as he was about to deem the task impossible, he saw configurations that took shape within the stone. The rock wall was made up of several two-dimensional planes that didn't quite touch. In fact, some of them were loose enough that Warren found he could shove them aside. Most of them didn't move easily, though. They moved slowly, and it took a great deal of effort to shift them.

Even as he unlocked the secret of the wall, he also felt the alignment within himself. Pieces of himself seemed to shift as well. Almost unconsciously, drawn by the excitement of this new knowledge, he stepped forward through the wall.

TWENTY-SIX

Moving through the rock was like walking against a strong river current.

Warren thought about what would happen if he didn't make it through the rock, wondering if the shifting patterns could slip beyond his control and rip him apart. The way suddenly seemed much harder. Panic thrummed inside his head.

"Don't think about failure," a man's voice commanded. "You have to assert yourself over what you think of as the natural laws. Only part of how you've perceived the world is true. Many things that you've considered impossible are going to be possible for you. You've just got to master what lies within you."

Concentrating again on the whirling two-dimensional shapes, Warren pushed through. A moment later, he stood inside another cave. This one was more elaborate, more finished. Arcane drawings that glowed with power adorned the walls. Glass cases and shelves held all kinds of objects. A lab stretched out behind Malcolm and another man as they stood and smiled at Warren.

The other man was almost seven feet tall. His body was elongated like an insect's. His head looked massive, broad forehead and long-jawed. Tightly cropped reddish hair covered his head. Tattoos and scars covered every square inch of skin that Warren could see. Two curving horns a foot in length jutted up from his temples and flared into three points. He looked like he was in his late twenties.

The man's appearance immediately put Warren to mind of Cernunnos, the Horned One from Celtic legend. Cernunnos was supposed to represent horned male animals and fertility. The god had been featured in a few of the books Warren's mother had read in her studies of the arcane.

"Ah, you've arrived," the man said.

"I told you he was strong," Malcolm said, looking pleased.

The horned man drew a symbol in the air. Warren saw a ghostly afterimage for just a moment, then it vanished. But he felt a wolf's warm, fetid breath over him. Since he'd never had a wolf breathe on him, though, he wondered how he knew what the sensation was like. But he was convinced that was what it had been.

"I never doubted you." The horned man gazed at Warren in open speculation. "But being able doesn't mean that he will choose to embrace his ability."

"The demons have marked him," Malcolm said. "Look at him."

Warren grew self-conscious of his burns and pulled his cloak more tightly about him. "Who are you?"

"I am Hedgar Tulane," the man answered. "Welcome to my home."

"Warren!"

Hearing Kelli through the stone wall, Warren reached back for her, negotiating the spinning two-dimensional shapes much easier this time. "Take my hand." When he felt her fingers in his, he pulled her through the wall. A moment later Kelli stood inside the cave with him.

Malcolm and Tulane stared at him.

"She's with me," Warren said defensively. "Where I go, she goes."

"Of course," Tulane said. "I'm just surprised that you could pull her through the wall like that. It's one thing to negotiate passage yourself, but I've never seen anyone who could bring another through." He paused, examining Warren more closely. "Working with you, helping you discover your true potential, is going to be exciting."

Warren bristled at that. "I didn't come here to be someone's science project."

"Oh no," Tulane agreed. "You won't be anyone's *science* project. This isn't about science. At least, not about science in the truest sense of the word, which has been rather limited in our experience. This is definitely about the arcane forces in our world."

"There are several groups like this scattered throughout London and England," Tulane said as he headed the procession through the caves. "Throughout the world, in fact. Ever since the human race first came in passing contact with the demon world through visions and voices, there have been those among us who have studied them. We've never accepted that the power the demons wield are out of our reach."

Warren stared into the various rooms they passed. He'd seen dozens of Cabalists during the last few minutes. Several of them were undergoing tattooing or taking part in experimentation.

"Why do you wear tattoos?" Warren asked.

"Me? Or Cabalists in general?"

"The Cabalists."

"Tattooing allows us to focus our powers," Tulane answered. "Writing of any sort—symbols as well as words—has always provided control over arcane energy. Magic is just a colloquial word we use for the energies we harness. Calling our field of study that makes it easier for newcomers to grasp, and it instantly differentiates us from those who choose to view the world through the limited means we term *physical* science." He smiled derisively as they stopped at a cave.

Inside the cave, a young tattooed woman with an eyepatch gestured at a knife lying on a table. The knife levitated, spun on an invisible axis, then flew toward a freestanding wooden target at the other end of the room. When the knife struck the target, it sank up to the hilt, shearing through the wood as if it were water.

In an adjacent cave, a young man reached into a fire and flames danced up his arm without hurting him. Watching the sight was almost unbearable to Warren, bringing memory of pain and the stench of burning flesh. Turning, the young man held his flaming arm up ahead of him. A second later, the flames flew from his arm and struck a wooden target a few feet away, engulfing it at once.

"There have always been instances of people able to wield the demons' energy in our world," Tulane said. "Once they touched our world, as we believe they must have done, the demons opened fissures that were never truly closed. Some of that energy leaked in. Not enough to do the things you're seeing today, things that you've apparently done yourself. Nor on a scale so wide as we're now experiencing."

"That's because of the Hellgate," Warren said.

"We believe so. Since it opened, there has been a sharp increase in both incidence and ability."

"Why was I brought here?"

"To teach you, of course. And to learn from you."

"Learn what?"

"Whatever there is to learn."

"What makes you think there is?"

Tulane looked at him meaningfully. "No one," he said,

"has ever withstood a demon's attack before. Not one of us, at least."

"We don't combat them," Tulane said as he switched on a holo-vid mounted in the table they surrounded. They sat in an expensively appointed study with wooden paneled walls. Only the fact that there were no windows reminded Warren that they were in a cave far belowground instead of in the massive house. "We observe them."

Images of demons battling military tanks and airplanes in the streets of London played in the vid projection. A huge demon slammed his oversized fist onto a tank's main gun. The barrel wilted before the onslaught, then finally snapped off. Another tank fired at almost point-blank range, but the shell burst against the demon's hide without doing any apparent harm. The demon roared and turned to face the tank, gripping the main gun barrel and ripping the turret free of the vehicle's body. He used it as a hammer to flatten the tank and kill the soldiers inside.

"This is Shulgoth, one of the primary demons," Tulane said.

The note of reverence in the man's voice almost made Warren ill. "Do you know him?"

"We know of him." Tulane watched as the battle progressed. "We know that he is a fierce warrior, totally merciless. I would like to know more, but that hasn't proven feasible at this juncture." He cut the vid and focused on Warren. "How long have you known you were different?"

Warren hesitated, wondering how much he should reveal. He didn't want to tell the man anything. *Tell him. It's the only way you're going to survive.*

"I don't know that I am different," Warren answered.

Tulane held his gaze for a moment, then casually tapped

the keyboard mounted in the table. The vid returned, this time bringing with it images of Warren's parents.

"Your stepfather's name was Martin," Tulane said. "But he wasn't your biological father."

A chill sickness blazed through Warren. His father's broad, cruel face had always had that effect on him. His father's skin was so black it held a bluish tint. He shaved his head, but wore a short goatee that framed his blunt chin.

"Your biological father's name was Hakim N'Bush," Tulane said, "but you don't carry his name."

"No. When I was in foster care, I chose my mother's maiden name instead."

"Tamara Schimmer." Tulane punched another key.

The image this time hurt Warren, but it also confused him. His mother was white but showed her Jewish ancestry. Her dark eyes looked soulful and her dark hair hung in ringlets down to her shoulders. She was too thin and too pale. Warren had never known a time when she looked healthy. He hadn't looked at a picture of her in years. Now, though, he was struck by how young she was. No more than a couple years older than he was.

"She was married to Martin DeYoung, who became your stepfather."

A third image materialized on the vid, revealing a sallow-faced white man with wispy blond hair and small eyes. Martin looked feral and rat-like.

"Your stepfather murdered your mother," Tulane said.

Warren felt Kelli's eyes on him. He didn't look at her. She took one of his hands in hers. For a moment, he felt guilty about using his power over her, but he was too afraid and too hurt to be there alone and have to face this.

"Yes," Warren answered in a thick voice.

"Neighbors called in the attack," Tulane said.

A recording of a frantic phone call came from the vid.

"Yes. Police? It's my neighbors! I think he's going to kill her this time!"

The conversation rolled for a moment, including the screaming voices on the other side of the wall or floor or ceiling. Warren had never known who had called in the domestic disturbance.

The memories opened up and swallowed Warren down. For a moment he was no longer in the cave with Tulane. He was back in that flat, listening to the argument between his mother and father. Then the flat cracks of his father's gun punctuated the conversation between the neighbor and the police.

"I've had enough of both of you," Martin DeYoung declared.

In Warren's mind, he could see his stepfather shoot his mother, then turn the pistol on him.

"People are out to kill me now!" his stepfather roared. "And they want to kill me because I've been struggling to make ends meet for the two of you. Your bloody mother just spent whatever she could get her hands on, and you . . . *you* just kept eating and growing and going through clothes like there was no tomorrow!"

That old fear coiled inside Warren again, twisting like a wild animal trying to escape a trap. He felt sweat break out over his brow. Then the burn scabbing and white skin over his left arm and back began to itch furiously.

"But I'll stop that!" Martin declared.

Vaguely, Warren heard Kelli begging Tulane to stop the recording, but Tulane ignored her. He focused on Warren.

The gunshot pealed within the room, and Warren felt the bullet strike him again. The fear was out of control. He remembered how he'd felt, how he'd never wanted to be hurt again.

Then a child's voice, which had been pleading for the

stepfather to stop, suddenly sounded hot and angry. *"I wish you were dead!"*

The words were small in the context of things. They shouldn't have mattered at all.

But Martin DeYoung had stopped cursing and screaming and had blinked at Warren lying on the ground before him. Then he'd put the pistol to his temple and started pleading for his life.

"No! Don't make me do this! No! Stop! *Please!*" Martin had started crying then, shaking with effort to take the pistol away from his temple. But he hadn't been able to. *"Nooooooooooooo—"*

The sharp gunshot ended the scream. Even the conversation between the neighbor and police officer had ended in shocked silence.

Warren's skin itched even more. He was angry at Tulane for dredging up all those old memories, but he didn't know how to react. Warren knew he might as well have been a prisoner.

The vid vanished.

"When the police arrived," Tulane said softly, "they searched the premises, thinking they'd find a third party there. A neighbor or a friend of your mother's. Someone who had overpowered your stepfather, put the pistol to his head, and pulled the trigger. But that isn't what happened, is it?"

Warren hesitated, weighing his options. "No."

"You wished he was dead," Tulane said.

"Yes. But I had for years."

"But never so fiercely as that night."

"No."

"And then what happened?"

"Martin . . . killed himself."

Tulane stared at Warren. "Because you told him to."

"Yes."

Shaking his head in amazement, Tulane said, "Eight years old. And before the Hellgates opened."

Warren didn't know what to say to that.

"Have you ever used your power since then?" Tulane asked.

Warren thought about lying, but he felt certain Tulane would know he was lying. Since he wasn't sure what would happen to him if he was caught in a lie, he told the truth. "Yes."

"How?"

"To influence people."

"The way you influenced the demon to leave you when Edith found you?"

Warren nodded. The itching along his arm and back grew even more powerful.

"And you survived the demon's attack a few days ago."

Warren nodded again.

"Has anything like that ever happened before? Accidents that should have hurt you didn't do much damage?"

"No." Warren scratched his arm under his coat sleeve. His stomach lurched as he realized something was coming away on his hand. When he looked, he saw that it was white and membranous.

Skin!

The thought terrified Warren. Believing he'd ripped his wound open, he slid out of his coat and pulled his shirt off.

Instead of pink and bloody flesh, though, Warren saw greenish-tinted black scales covering his arm. Where he'd torn the white skin away, the itching had stopped. Unable to stop himself, he raked at his back. More skin peeled away. Beneath it, where he could see along his ribs and side, greenish scales gleamed instead of skin, white or black. Not only that, but the whiteness had spread beyond the burn areas, claiming more of his body.

TWENTY-SEVEN

What is it?" Leah asked.

She was referring to the nine-foot-long lizard-looking demon inside the glass display case inside the House of Rorke's museum/teaching center. The creature stood poised on all four heavily padded claws. Teeth filled the wicked-looking snout that was longer than a crocodile's. The tail was thick, corded muscle. Greenish scales covered the demon. Long scars marked it. If it hadn't been so evil-looking, the demon might have looked beautiful.

Even now, years later and him fully gown, Simon still remembered how scared and awed he'd felt when he'd first seen the exhibit. Back then, the demon had seemed even larger, but no less fierce. Even after the fight in the tube tunnel, gazing on the demon—seeing it poised to strike—was unsettling.

"They named it the Ravager," Simon said.

"This is a demon?"

"Yes."

"How long has it been here?"

"The Templar have had it in their possession for hundreds of years."

"Why wasn't this shown to anyone?" Leah asked.

"It was." Simon stared at the creature. That fear from long ago revisited him even though he was clad in his armor. "No one believed it was real."

"No one?"

"No."

"Even with the proof before them?"

"No one. It might have been more convincing if the Templar had found more. But this was the only one. It was so torn up when they found it that the artists had to rebuild sections of it."

"You can't tell."

"I know. That's another reason people found to disbelieve in the existence of demons."

Unconsciously, Leah placed her hands on the glass before Simon could stop her. She immediately yanked her hands back and yelped in surprise.

"What did you feel?" Simon asked.

"Electricity." Leah worked her hands. "Is that from a security system?"

Simon nodded. From the immediate primitive fear in her eyes he knew she'd feared—at least for a moment—that the demon within had had something to do with what she'd felt. "Some of the demons possess dark powers that cling to their bodies even after death. They can cause sickness or even fatality. Touching them, alive or dead, isn't advisable."

"If you knew the display case was electrified to discourage contact, why didn't you tell me not to touch it?"

"I didn't know you were going to touch it. I never wanted to. Most don't. I certainly didn't expect that you would want to." Simon stared at the reptilian horror on the other side of the high-impact-resistant glass. "And not everyone perceives the dissuasion spell the same way."

"*Spell?*"

"Arcane energy," Simon said.

Leah smiled uncertainly at him. "Magic *and* demons. Surely you don't believe in magic?"

"Arcane energy is real. I can let you talk to Templar who are strong in arcane energy. I know some spells, but that's not where my strength lies."

"What kind of spells?" Suspicion knitted Leah's brows. "Good or evil?"

"You can't classify arcane energy as good or evil. It's not that simple." Simon thought back to the classes he'd received. It was harder than he'd imagined to talk to someone who didn't know and didn't believe in those things. Even when that person was surrounded by it. "Arcane energy, the way I understand it, is a force. Elemental, like the wind or the tide or gravity. The way it's used determines whether people call it good or evil."

"That sounds too easy."

"Define good and evil."

Leah looked at him. "That's simple."

"Is it? Tell me, are a soldier's actions killing enemy soldiers good or evil?"

Leah hesitated. "It depends on whether the soldier is fighting for you or against you."

"Is science good or evil? The research that eradicates a plague is also the same research that enables scientists to modify and change that plague."

"Eradicating a plague is a good thing."

"Is it? When you're destroying plague that can reduce a locust infestation that's defoliating a forest?"

Leah didn't say anything.

"And is it evil to manufacture a plague?" Simon asked.

After a brief hesitation while she thought about the ramifications of her answer, Leah said, "Yes."

"Even if it's a plague you intend to use to eliminate an enemy army?"

She sighed. "I guess it depends on the circumstances."

"It does. Electricity can light a house and keep it warm

in the winter, or it can be used to kill a man on death row in the United States." Simon looked back at the display case. "Anyway, the case is protected by a spell."

"Where did they get the Ravager?"

"I don't know. We'd have to talk to Miller. He's the caretaker of this place." Simon turned and walked away. "Come on."

The museum /teaching center was one of the largest rooms in the Underground. Every House had one. Every House even had demons on display behind glass. Altogether, there were fourteen demons, but only six different kinds.

None of those were real, as most of the Ravager was. Instead, their appearances had been gleaned from visions, nightmares, myths, and brief glimpses psychic voyagers had been able to initiate into the demon world. The other demons the Templar had constructed had been built to allow martial arts training and to learn as much as they could about them.

Books lined the shelves, but there were a number of computers on the tables as well. All of them were—or had been—hooked into a strong Internet connection.

"Who uses this place?" Leah asked.

"Everyone. The children are brought here for instruction." Simon remembered all the long hours he'd spent inside the museum. The Templar had taught him everything they'd known about the demons. He'd been bored after a while because the information had become repetitive early on.

He'd gotten in trouble again and again for not paying attention to his lessons. There had been plenty of others who had gotten into trouble as well, but he could still remember the pained disappointment he'd seen in his father's face.

Hurt slammed into Simon for a moment when he realized he'd never have the opportunity to apologize to his father.

Now it seemed that everything he'd learned was far too little.

"Why aren't the children schooled in London?" Leah asked.

"Because the curriculum taught here is a lot different. And because the Templar don't like their names on government documents. The Order was abolished in 1307 by Philip the Fair, partly because the Templar at that time insisted that the Ravager corpse they'd found be studied and the story spread. Philip claimed all the Templar gold and scattered them to the winds with death threats, claiming that they'd created the Ravager to blackmail the crown. Since that time, the Templar have kept to themselves, living off the grid."

His voice echoed in the silence of the museum. This was the quietest he'd ever heard the place. When he was young, it had always been filled with noise. In fact, most of the Templar Underground had been noisy.

Sadness touched him, and he knew that was only the beginning of it.

As they walked back to the barracks, they passed two female Templar in full armor that were headed to the museum. They had five small children with them. Simon knew the Templar were taking the kids to the museum to train them.

"Hello, Simon," one of the female Templar said.

Simon stood and looked at her, not recognizing the armor.

The Templar halted her charges for a moment, then her faceplate flared open. She was beautiful, with a heart-shaped face and deep brown eyes. A few strands of cinnamon-colored hair showed and matched her eyebrows.

"Anne," Simon said, recognizing her. Despite his dark mood and the fatigue he felt, he couldn't help being happy to see her. When he'd left, Anne had still been working on her final armor.

The young woman stepped toward him and embraced him. The metal of their breastplates clanged slightly when they met.

"You're looking good," Simon said as they separated and stepped back.

"Thanks." Anne smiled, more confident than Simon had remembered. When she'd been younger, she'd never appeared outgoing. She'd always been the quiet one of her family. "So are you." She turned to her friend. "Keiko, this is Simon Cross. Simon, Keiko Nagamuchi."

The other Templar's faceplate flared open as well. Her features were Asian, which explained her slight and almost frail build even with the armor. Her almond eyes held a hint of distrust and displeasure.

Keiko nodded. "I've heard of you."

Her voice was flat and uninflected. Her dislike was evident.

Simon tried not to let the female Templar's rejection touch him. He hadn't known Keiko Nagamuchi when he'd lived in the Underground. She'd been three or four years older, and their paths must never have crossed.

"You're with Derek?" Anne asked.

"Yes."

"The units are going to be reorganized soon. Since we trained together, maybe we'll be put together."

"Maybe." After what he'd seen today, though, Simon didn't think he wanted that to happen. Watching Anne die at the talons of some infernal demon wasn't something he wanted to do. Then he checked his ego. He had no guarantees he would live through the next encounter.

"Graydon is still here," Anne said.

"I saw him."

The four children shifted uneasily. If times had been different they would have been protesting the inactivity. Templar children stayed hurried throughout the day.

But these kids looked pensive. They were already carrying the full weight of their heritage. For them, Simon knew, demons had always been real. They'd never had the chance to grow away from it. Now he wondered if they would ever know a time when demons weren't in their world.

"I could drop by your barracks sometime," Anne offered.

"I'd like that." The words were out of Simon's mouth even as he was thinking he didn't want to try to renew old acquaintances with death staring them in the face. Losing fellow warriors was one thing, but losing friends was going to be even harder.

"We're going to be late," Keiko announced. Her faceplate closed with an abrupt *ping* that conveyed annoyance.

Anne looked embarrassed. "I guess I need to be going."

"It was good to see you."

She smiled at him and looked like the quiet girl he'd known while growing up. "I'll be by sometime soon."

"If you're not, maybe I'll look you up."

The smile became a grin. "See that you do."

Keiko snorted, and the noise sounded even more disparaging through the suit's audio system.

Urging the children into motion, the two Templar headed for the museum. Anne glanced back at Simon again, then her faceplate closed.

"Old friend?" Leah asked.

"Yes." Simon started forward again.

"I got the feeling there might be some history there."

"What do you mean?" Simon asked, although he was pretty sure he knew what the young woman was getting at.

"I sensed a romantic tension."

"No."

"I'm not often wrong about things like that."

Simon considered telling Leah no again, or not responding at all. But being here—with the circumstances being what they were, his father dead and not really a friend left to his name—he was surprised to find that he did want to talk about things a little.

"My father had started negotiations for me to have Anne's hand in marriage," Simon said.

"Marriage?"

"Yes."

"You're kidding. An *arranged* marriage?"

Simon looked at her and wondered how much of their conversation the tunnel security systems were picking up. "This isn't the best place to talk about this. Nor the best time."

"I'm not ready to go crawl back into bed. I feel like talking."

Simon felt the same way. Seeing Anne had been a mixed blessing. Anne didn't know about Saundra, and he'd never mentioned his life in London to Saundra.

He wasn't ready to go back to the barracks, either. Maybe Derek had accepted him into the unit, and maybe he'd been blooded with them today, but there were a lot of warriors there who weren't especially pleased to have him among them.

"All right," Simon said.

TWENTY-EIGHT

At a small table in a corner of the almost-empty commissary over two steaming cups of hot tea, Simon said, "Not every marriage here is arranged. Some of the Templar still fall in love with each other, get married, and have kids."

"But why do the Templar have arranged marriages?" Leah acted like the idea was reprehensible.

"It's not as much of an anathema as you're putting on," Simon said.

"It's positively barbaric. What if the woman doesn't want to be married? What if she doesn't want to be a mother?"

"She," Simon said, "doesn't have any more choice than the man does."

"Oh." Leah blinked. "Men don't want to get married?"

"Sometimes less so than the women."

"Then why get married?"

"To have children. The ranks of the Templar have to be maintained."

Leah frowned. "Propagation of the species?"

Simon felt a hint of anger at her words. He considered only briefly ending the conversation. But the alternative would have meant going back to the barracks and sitting by himself. "We have a unique way of life. Not everyone is

meant for it. Forming liaisons with women—or men—
from outside the Templar world is problematic."

"Problematic?"

"In the mid-nineteenth century, two Templar were put
away in sanitariums."

"Why?"

"They told their wives about their roles as Templar.
Their missions."

Leah frowned. "Back during that time, a lot of people
ended up in sanitariums. Family outcasts. Wives that
couldn't be divorced. Children that couldn't be controlled."

Simon nodded. Those times were chronicled in the
Templar histories that were required reading in school.

"What happened to the Templar?" Leah asked.

"They had to be broken out."

"So no one has ever been brought in from the outside?"

"There have been a few. A very few."

"Doesn't say much for love, does it?" Leah smiled
crookedly.

"Marriages are hard anyway. Trying to add secrets to the
mix, or other loyalties, makes them almost impossible to
manage." Simon waved at the commissary. "Even with
arranged marriages, divorce seldom happens here."

"Because it's a captive environment?"

"Because husbands and wives have the same goals in
their lives."

"Then why didn't you settle down with a nice Templar
girl? How did you end up in South Africa?"

Simon took a deep breath. "I wanted more than the
Templar way of life offered. And I didn't believe in the
demons."

"Not even with those museum exhibits?"

"If you hadn't seen the demons outside of this place, do you think you would have believed?"

Sighing, Leah shook her head. "Probably not. So you broke that young woman's heart?"

Simon smiled. At least it hadn't been that hard. "No. Two years ago, Anne was too young to marry. My father wanted grandchildren."

"He might have been looking for another way to anchor you here."

"Perhaps."

"So that's why she was so chatty in the hallway instead of wanting your head on a platter."

"I talked to Anne before I left. I explained what I was feeling. She understood."

"You seemed to enjoy seeing her today. Any regrets?"

A lot, Simon thought, *but none of them about Anne.* "No."

"Do the Templar stay married?"

"Most of the time. More so here than in the outside world."

"But divorce still sometimes happens?"

"Yes. Some people aren't meant to be married. They still have children, though."

"That's what's important, after all." Leah's voice dripped sarcasm. "The rest of the world is getting overpopulated. It's a wonder that you people haven't."

"That's been a concern since the beginning. The population within the Templar Underground is carefully monitored. Occasionally the numbers have grown too quickly. At that time the word goes out that there aren't supposed to be any more births."

"And if Templar do have children?"

"They generally don't."

"People, as a general rule, don't like being told what to do."

"The people that live here," Simon reminded her, "aren't general populace."

"Holier-than-thou much?"

"After everything you've seen even in the short time that you've been here, if you don't see a difference in these people, you never will." Simon's voice had an irritated edge to it that he hadn't intended.

"Point taken." Leah took a breath and a new tack. "What about the people who choose to ignore the high command and decide to have kids anyway?"

Simon kept his voice neutral, getting the feeling that she was testing him for some reason and not knowing what that was. "There are consequences. People get passed over for promotion. Housing needs are met, but wants are ignored. Special privileges are revoked."

" 'Special privileges'?"

"Some of the Templar are permitted to work outside the Underground."

"Why?"

Simon sipped his tea and found it still almost too hot. "To observe."

"Observe what?"

"Politics. Economics. Developments in technology."

"The Templar seem withdrawn from society. And their technology is ahead of anything anyone else seems to have."

"When it comes to weapons, yes. But the Templar know they're too focused when it comes to tech development. Medicine is just as important, but they don't have the resources to follow up on it. The Templar exist separately from the rest of the world, but are not cut off. They're here—*we're* here—to guard the rest of the world against the demons."

Simon had realized how much he'd cut himself off from the Templar and had tried to change that. But it sounded awkward acting like he was one of them as well. That had been the way it had always been.

"Then why aren't the Templar bringing the other survivors in the city here? Why are they leaving them out there to fend for themselves?"

"Because coming here isn't the answer. If we brought them back here, the demons would follow." Simon breathed calmly even though he was angry because she didn't already see the answer to her question. And perhaps he was partly conflicted with memory of those hard-pressed survivors he'd seen while trekking into the city. "The sacrifice those warriors made on All Hallows' Eve will have been in vain. We have rations here, a plan in place that will carry us through the fight with the demons, but we can't afford to take on a lot of untrained personnel."

Leah looked at him. "What happens to me? I'm untrained personnel."

Simon sat back and didn't answer. He honestly didn't know.

"Simon Cross."

Waking immediately, groggy from the lack of sleep and achy from the pounding he'd taken the night they'd been attacked, Simon looked up and spotted Bruce Martindale pulling on his armor next to the bed. Bruce was Derek's second-in-command. He was young and arrogant, everything a Templar should be.

Taking the man's lead, Simon sat up and started pulling armor on. "What's going on?" Simon asked.

"We pulled an assignment." Bruce shrugged into his breastplate. "We're going outside."

"What is it?" Simon stepped into his boots.

"When you need to know," Bruce replied, "you'll be told."

Simon nodded. He hated the abrupt manner the other Templar showed toward him. But there was nothing he could do to change it. He concentrated on the promise he'd made to his father. That was the most important thing. He didn't intend to break it again.

The readout on Simon's HUD showed the time as 3:14 a.m. He'd gotten a little over two hours' sleep after his conversation with Leah had dwindled away to nothing. When he'd returned to the barracks, he hadn't been able to sleep at first. He dampened his audio and yawned, a real jaw-creaker that bordered on painful. It was enough to make his eyes water.

Traces of white snow gleamed on the streets, windowsills, and buildings, and on the wrecked cars, double-decker buses, and military vehicles and tanks mired in the street. Weak moonlight barely chased back the pitch-black shadows draping the urban landscape. There were no lights, no flames or lanterns or candles to light the existence of anyone who still lived in the city.

After two years of guiding clients through the wild outside Cape Town, the city of London looked strange. And dangerous. Gargoyles sat atop some of the buildings, and Simon knew it would be hard to separate them from the demons that might be lurking.

The Chelsea district where they were now was generally thought of as well-to-do. Residential houses in the area were very expensive. Simon had passed through the district with his father.

"There's a house just off King's Road," Derek announced in a quiet voice to the twenty Templar massed in the tube station. "I'm giving you the location now."

A light pulsed on Simon's HUD, signaling the upload of a map. Superimposed on the viewscreen, a street map took shape. King's Road was clearly marked. The Thames was only a short distance away.

"This is our target," Derek said.

A red dot formed on the map half a block off King's Road seventeen long blocks from their present position inside the Sloane Street tube station.

"One of the lads in the research division sniffed out an artifact we're supposed to lay hands to," Derek went on. "A book."

A few of the men shifted tensely. "A book?" one named Waverly asked with a trace of doubt. "They want us to risk our lives for a book?"

"It's rumored to be a memoir," Derek went on. "Supposed to be written by a mad monk that escaped demonic captivity."

"Never heard of the like," Waverly said.

"Neither had I," Derek admitted.

"Brother Cargill," Simon said before he realized he was going to speak.

The Templar's helmets turned toward him.

"That's right," Derek said. "I was given an image of the book."

The image of a large leather-bound book popped onto Simon's viewscreen.

"What do you know of it, Simon?" Derek asked. "I wasn't given any real information. Just that they wanted the book."

"Brother Cargill was the man who discovered the Ravager corpse in a display case in the Rorke Museum." Simon couldn't believe no one else knew the story.

"I remember Brother Cargill," Amanda Peyer said.

Simon vaguely remembered the young woman from school days. She'd been more successful with the sword than with the pen.

"My father told me the story," Simon said. "Brother Cargill was supposed to have traveled with King Richard I in 1189 during the Third Crusade. Cargill maintained that Frederick I, the Holy Roman Emperor, called Barbarossa for his red beard, was murdered by a demon rather than dying by accidental drowning as everyone believed."

"We don't exactly need a history lesson here," someone growled.

"Frederick's untimely death put an end, more or less, to the Third Crusade," Derek said. "Philip II of France decided to leave. After he did, Richard couldn't do anything more. He had to make a truce with Saladin."

"Cargill returned to England with Richard," Simon said. "But he was supposed to have a fabled book that told of Frederick's murder at the hands of the demon."

"If the demons could come through a thousand years ago, why didn't they come through then?"

No one had an answer.

"Cargill said he'd been taken prisoner by the demon," Simon went on. "The way he told it, the demon took him to their world for a time." When his father had mentioned that, he'd had nightmares that night imagining what that must have been like.

"Why did they take him?"

"Cargill didn't know. He made his escape shortly after that when the demon brought him back to our world."

"Can't believe the fiends didn't kill Cargill outright," someone said.

"The Templar reported that Cargill was crazed by his capture," Simon said. "They didn't believe anything Cargill said about being taken to the demon world. They didn't doubt the Ravager corpse because they had it, but the things Cargill had claimed to have seen, a burned and scarred land, was beyond anything anyone wanted to believe."

"Like Hell itself," Bruce said.

"Like what they're doing to London," someone else said.

"On the way back to England," Simon continued, "the Templar joined up with Richard I. They were shipwrecked during a storm and beached in Austria. Duke Leopold, Richard's longtime enemy, captured him and ransomed him to Emperor Henry VI, who had taken over Germany. Cargill finished his memoirs in Austria while they were waiting to be ransomed. But the book went missing there, too."

For a moment no one said anything.

Simon stared out at the long, dark street.

"Well," Derek said, "that book's supposed to have turned up in Chelsea now. At that house on King's Road. And it's up to us to get it. Ferrell, you've got point."

Ferrell moved out at once. The other Templar followed a slight distance behind.

TWENTY-NINE

Feeling suffocated and trapped inside the MRI machine, Warren willed himself to remain calm while the medical people inspected the changes taking place within his body. The itching was almost unbearable, making it even harder to lie still while they moved him around with the aid of the conveyor belt that ran through the machine.

He thought he could actually feel the scales growing and multiplying across his body, sliding under his old skin and locking into place. He knew—*he hoped!*—that wasn't true and that it was only his imagination.

At first he'd thought the scales might be some kind of scab, something that could be removed. In fact, with the aid of a knife that Tulane had lent him, Warren had tried to remove one of the scales. That was when he'd found out the scales were as much a part of him as his skin was.

Had been, he reminded himself.

He'd succeeded in removing the scale, but it had proven incredibly painful. It had bled only for a moment, though, then had sealed off. By the time Tulane had convinced him to come to the medical lab, a white blister had formed over the area where the scale had been. Warren felt certain a new scale was already growing there to replace the one that he'd torn away.

The machinery hummed and buzzed around Warren.

He forced himself to concentrate on his breathing and not act on the panic that filled him.

Then, mercifully, the conveyor belt rolled him back out of the MRI machine.

The physician pointed at the image of Warren lying naked in the air on the tri-dee projector as he spoke. Warren guessed that the man was around forty, old enough to have a lot of experience with medical ailments, but young enough that he was still up on breaking information.

Not only that, but if Warren could even find another trained physician to examine him, that physician wouldn't have been trained in the ways of monsters as Tulane's man was. In the end, there was nowhere else to go for answers. Or help.

Feeling somewhat nauseous, Warren stared at his image. The tri-dee rendered a ghostly image of his body—although on a two-foot scale—that floated naked in midair. He felt embarrassed over that, but the horror and worry about his physical condition outweighed that.

"As you can see," the physician said, "the third-degree burns have obviously replenished lost tissue as well as coating those areas with the scales."

"How do you know tissue has been replenished?" Tulane asked. He stood at the head of the table and looked on with keen interest.

"From the nature of third-degree burns," the physician replied. "Any time a patient suffers one of those, there is tissue damage and loss."

"Doesn't the body normally replenish lost tissue? I've suffered wounds myself that have healed up and filled in."

"Yes. But only to a degree. Burn scarring tends to impede such a recovery. That's why one of the treatments is to strip the dead flesh away and encourage new flesh to grow.

It's not always successful." The physician shook his head. "And never like this. If you look at those burn areas, you'll see that the flesh has filled in, returning Mr. Schimmer's body and features to normal."

"Only with scales."

"Yes." The physician punched keys on the board. The view tightened up on Warren's left arm, focusing on the burn area covered with greenish-black scales. "Interestingly, though, those new patches of flesh—as well as the scales— possess a different DNA from Mr. Warren's."

"A different DNA?"

The physician nodded. More buttons were pressed and two DNA marking charts showed up on the tri-dee. "Here is Mr. Warren's."

The top DNA string glowed.

"And this is the—well, the *other* DNA."

The bottom string of DNA glowed then.

Warren didn't know much about DNA or how it was charted. He remembered from school that there was something about a double strand that coiled around and around that made it unique, but that was all. He sat there feeling helpless, hating every moment of it.

"Have you identified the DNA?" Tulane asked.

"No. But I can tell you what it isn't."

Tulane waited.

The physician licked his lips and raked his hair back with his fingers. "It isn't human, or from any species that is logged in the computer files."

Not human. Warren stared in growing horror at the scales that covered his skin where the burned areas were.

"Warren's DNA is not human?" Tulane asked.

Concentrating, Warren summoned his attention and tried to listen to Tulane and Haggarty, the physician. The two of them had continued talking between themselves, never seeming to notice the mental shape Warren was in.

"Yes," Haggarty replied. "I can't detect anything untoward or different about it."

Warren stared at Tulane, wondering how it was the man might think he wasn't human. Then he realized that growing scales was a good argument that he wasn't.

"Warren's body now has two different DNA signatures?" Tulane asked.

The physician nodded. "That's not impossible even for a normal human. Say for instance that Mr. Schimmer had been a twin within the womb. If a chimeric resolution had come about—that's where one twin literally absorbs the other twin after it died—that could account for the differing DNA."

"But you would have two human DNA signatures," Tulane said.

"Exactly." Haggarty shook his head. "This second DNA *isn't* human."

Warren stared at the scales, wanting nothing more than to get a knife and scrape them away like a fisherman cleaning a fish. Even if he'd been able to stand the pain and didn't mind risking losing the use of his arm, he remembered how hard it had been to get a single scale away from the crust that covered him.

"We have DNA samples from demons that you can do comparisons with," Tulane said.

"I know," Haggarty said. "I did comparisons. The second DNA is close to those samples we have, but they don't match."

"You think they're demonic in nature."

"I do."

Tulane stared at Warren's image. Breathing out slowly, Tulane whispered, "Fascinating."

* * *

Warren looked at the two men, not believing how quietly and calmly, how *thoroughly,* they conducted their business. Then again, they weren't the one who had been infected.

"I don't understand how this happened," Warren whispered.

Glancing over his shoulder at Warren, the physician said, "Nor do I, Mr. Schimmer. I've never seen anything like this." He returned his attention to the image. "But it is my belief that the scales grew there to heal you. Maybe even to protect you."

"Protect him?" Tulane echoed. "Protect him from what?"

Not what, Warren thought anxiously. *Protect me from whom.*

"How much have the scales spread?" Warren asked.

"I believe the original catalyst took root in the burned areas," Haggarty said. He tapped keys and the burned areas on Warren glowed. "Those areas also show the highest concentration of the scales."

Warren let his breath out as he stared at his injuries.

"But the scales are spreading," the physician said. "For the moment they're content to remain subdural, except in the heavily damaged areas. There they've surfaced." He paused. "Maybe they're more protective in those areas."

"As if they recognize a weakness?" Tulane asked.

Haggarty hesitated. "To say something like that would be like calling them an entity."

"Perhaps they are."

"You mean like a parasite?"

"If you will."

The physician didn't offer a comment to that.

The thought sickened Warren even worse. He knew

from Haggarty's silence that the physician had been think-ing along those lines as well.

"Could you—" Warren's voice failed him. He swallowed, cleared his throat, and tried again. "Could you remove the scales?"

"Surgically?"

Warren nodded.

Haggarty was quiet for a moment, regarding Warren's nude figure floating in the air. "The skin is an organ. The largest organ possessed by the human body. If we at-tempted something like that, *if* we were successful, *if* you survived, you'd be in terrible agony for a long time."

"Couldn't you put me out? Drop me into a coma or something?"

"A coma would reduce the healing factor. And it would be risky. We—*you*—have to consider the possibility that if we could remove this new skin, you might never grow any more."

"I'm being invaded by a parasite that's going to kill me," Warren said, trying to keep his voice level but not at all sure he'd managed.

"You don't know that," Tulane said.

Warren glanced at the man.

"Don't panic, Warren," Tulane coaxed. "You don't know that those scales represent anything harmful to you."

"In fact," Haggarty quickly put in, "I would say that scale layer has saved your life. If not for the healing that your new skin has provided, you very probably would have died. I believe they're the only thing that saved your life. There's no other explanation for why you survived those burns. Or why you're not horribly disfigured."

"I have *scales*," Warren croaked.

"But not scars," Haggarty agreed. "You've even main-tained your sensitivity in those areas." He reached over and touched Warren's arm.

Warren felt the physician's warmth through the scales, and the *softness* of Haggarty's flesh. The man was weaker than he was. On some subconscious level that he didn't understand, Warren knew that was true.

"You can feel this," Haggarty said.

Warren said nothing, but removed his hand from Haggarty's touch.

"You're looking at this wrong," Tulane said. "What you've gotten, Warren, it's a gift."

"It's *not* a gift!" Warren shouted. His voice filled the physician's office. "The demons don't give *gifts!* I've seen them. Up close and personal. No one else in that room that night received a *gift.* They were murdered. Horribly and mercilessly."

"*They* were," Tulane said in a soft voice. "But not you. You were—for whatever reason—spared."

Warren's thoughts turned more desperate. "What about arcane energy? Can this be eradicated by a spell?"

Tulane slumped back in the chair. He rubbed his face. "I don't know. But we're learning. More and more every day, Warren. Give us time. If we can help you, we will. But you have to stay with us. Can you do that?"

Warren wanted to tell Tulane no. In fact, he wanted to leave the cave at that precise moment. But he knew he couldn't. He was trapped. More than that, he knew he'd been cursed. He heard Merihim's laughter in the back of his mind and knew that somewhere the demon was mocking him.

THIRTY

The house stood three stories tall, squeezed between two other houses. It was made of brick, with a series of bay windows that thrust out the front. A wrought-iron fence was curled around the corpse of a motorcycle that some*thing* had picked up and launched into the poles. The motorcycle had caught fire and burned as well.

Scanning the front of the house, Simon found that the address matched the one they'd been given.

In quick, terse sentences, Derek placed the Templar in a security perimeter around the house. Simon was one of the men that Derek wanted with him inside the dwelling.

Drawing his sword and Spike Bolter, Simon followed Derek and the four other Templar up the short flight of steps to the door under a low-hanging alcove. Despite the sheltering darkness, Simon felt like someone was watching him. He glanced around, using the telescoping imaging available through the helmet.

Nothing moved on the street or in the shadows.

Someone had already broken into the residence. The door had been closed, but the lock had been shattered.

"Somebody's been here before us," Derek whispered.

"I'll bet it wasn't Goldilocks," Bruce replied. He led the way into the building.

Derek went next, followed almost immediately by

Simon. Using the light-multiplier function built into the HUD, Simon saw that the foyer had been opulent. Shelves had showcased miniature Asian statues and pottery that now lay smashed on the floor. Delicate rice paper watercolors hung crookedly on the wall. Most of them showed fantastic dragons and chimeras.

"Who lived here?" Bruce asked.

"A fantasy writer," Derek replied. "Robert Thornton."

"I read him," Kyle, one of the younger Templar, said. "He writes good stuff."

Blueprints of the house's interior, broken down by floors, ghosted onto Simon's HUD. He oriented himself as they passed along the hall toward the stairs.

"So where's this book supposed to be?" Bruce asked.

"Thornton's study," Derek answered. "Third floor. The information we have is that he's supposed to have a collection of occult books and objects in a vault there. He used them as research for his novels."

"Where's Thornton now?"

"Gone. He was in the United States on a book tour when the demons struck."

"Lucky him."

Simon looked around the large living room. His father had told him that Chelsea had once been Bohemian, home to writers and artists, but that had given way to the families of military officers and wealth.

A large fireplace nearly filled the living room. Broken glass let the cold night air into the room. Snow frosted the floor and the expensive furniture. Home wasn't going to be the same when—and *if*—Thornton ever returned.

The picture above the mantel caught Simon's attention. It showed a man, a woman, and two young children.

"What about Thornton's family?" Simon asked. "Were they in the United States with Thornton?"

"I don't know."

Simon had to pull his gaze from the picture. He hated to think that the woman and her children had fallen prey to the demons. But it was a grim reminder of what he was fighting for.

The second floor contained bedrooms and bathrooms. They found the study on the third floor.

It was a large room filled with bookshelves and a computer center. Framed pictures of the author and some of his books occupied wall space. Models and toys of fantastic monsters paraded across the desk. None of the windows on the third floor were broken.

"Give me a hand." Derek stood beside the bookcases. Simon joined him. "Behind the bookshelves?"

"That's what I was told."

Simon checked the blueprints on his HUD. There was a void behind the bookshelves.

"Trite," Bruce said.

"It only has to be functional," Derek replied.

Simon trailed his fingers along the shelves.

"Gang way!" Bruce called out. "I've found the switch." He stood at the desk with one hand under the edge.

Simon and Derek stepped back.

"There's not any power," Derek said. "We'll be lucky if it operates. Go ahead."

Bruce pressed the button. Nothing happened.

"All right then," Bruce said. "We'll do it the hard way." He reached under the desk and grabbed a fistful of wires. Another tug popped them free of the wall, tearing them free of the Sheetrock and paint that had covered the wires. They peeled out of the wall like the seal on a sardine can.

The wires went up to the ceiling, across the ceiling, and to the bookshelves. Hunkering down, Bruce traced the wires to a release switch. He laid a forefinger against the switch.

"Let's see if I can tickle it open," Bruce said. He loosed a burst of electricity through his armor.

The latch sprung and a section of the wall popped free on silent hinges.

"There we go," Bruce said, standing. He gripped the bookshelves and pulled, revealing the space behind. More books lined shelves, accompanied by artifacts, vials, jars, and objects that Simon couldn't identify in the infrared view he had.

Derek switched on an exterior torch built onto the suit.

Several dozen books occupied the shelves. Most of them were ponderous things, not the uniform size and shape of the novels that filled the shelves in the study.

Bruce squeezed into the space after Derek. Simon remained outside but watched with interest. Bruce reached for an oblong stick with shiny silver metal thread woven into it. Without warning, the stick sprouted legs and scuttled away from Bruce's fingers.

"Now that's interesting," Bruce commented. "Maybe we should consider taking more of this stuff back with us."

Simon studied the stick as it cowered in the corner. Had it been able to move before? Or had the opening of the Hellgate somehow increased the strength of magic in the surrounding areas?

That was a topic of investigation back in the Templar Underground. Those who studied arcane forces more diligently claimed that some arcane energy, particularly in the younger Templar children, had seemed to be on the increase.

"We'll pack what we can." Derek took down a tome from the shelves. "I think this is what we came for." He opened the book and shined the exterior torch onto the pages.

Under the magical light, the creatures illustrated on the page slithered and shied away. Moans echoed inside the hidden space.

"Do you hear that?" Derek stared at the open book.

"Hear what?" Bruce stood next to him.

"Moans," Derek said.

"No."

"I do," Simon said.

Bruce looked at both of them with a puzzled frown, his features barely visible through his faceplate. "I don't hear anything."

A hand snaked out of the book. Simon saw the four fingers and two opposable thumbs, but only realized how large it was when it covered Derek's helm with its palm and curled its fingers behind the Templar's head.

Bright blue energy shimmered from Derek's armor as a defensive magical shield activated. "Look out!" Derek warned.

"What?" Bruce's hand curled around a dagger at his hip. "I don't see anything." He tried to crouch and back away from Derek.

Flailing again, the hand reached for Bruce. A multi-jointed arm shot out after the hand. The palm slapped against Bruce's helmet without incident this time, and the fingers—thick as sausages—wrapped the Templar's head.

"Something's got me!" Bruce yelled, struggling to free himself.

Simon drew the Spike Bolter and tried for a clear shot. It was obvious that Bruce couldn't see what had him. In the next instant, he was yanked from his feet and pulled into the book. Impossibly, Bruce's body *stretched*, thinning just enough to fit through the page of the book.

Through it but not onto it, because when Bruce disappeared from the hidden room he never reappeared on the page among the scuttling things huddled there. The book leaped from Derek's hands and thudded to the floor.

"What's wrong?" one of the other Templar downstairs called up.

"Stay back!" Derek ordered. "Hold your positions!" He drew a Firestarter pistol, small and compact and immediately recognizable by the hand guard. If that hadn't been enough, the stream of liquid fire that gushed from the barrel would have been.

Flames created by an almost-forgotten concoction of Greek Fire splashed across the book. Incredibly, none of the pages caught fire, though soot did collect on the pages. The figures on the page fled, leaving only blank parchment behind them.

Derek cursed.

The book closed, then shook itself like a dog and lay still. The moans returned to fill the hidden room, but this time they were mixed with Bruce's frightened screams.

"No," Derek said hoarsely. He knelt and reached for the book.

The possessed tome flapped open like a huge mouth and the hand darted out again. Bruce's screams sounded louder.

Simon raked his dagger across the back of the demonic hand. Yellow blood wept from the wound and dripped on the wooden floor. Tiny flames and wisps of smoke threaded up from where the blood touched the floor.

"No," Simon ordered. "Don't touch it."

"Bruce is in there." Derek had sprung back against the wall.

"We don't know how to get him out." Simon flipped the book cover closed. Bruce's screams were muted, but this time they stopped as well.

Simon was certain he knew what the sudden silence

meant. He knelt and placed an armored knee on the closed book. It struggled against him for a moment, then lay still.

"Do you have anything to bind it?" Simon asked. "Otherwise we're going to have to leave it."

Derek pulled a long length of small-linked chain from a hidden compartment inside his armor. "I was given this."

Simon took the chain, examining it. The HUD identified it as palladium alloy. His father's teaching told him the intricate knots that formed the links were magical in nature.

"I was told it's been blessed," Derek said.

"Let's hope so." Simon lifted his knee just enough to allow him to slide the chain under the book. When he had the ends around the book, he twisted them together and took them back around the tome like Christmas ribbon, coming in from all four sides. Then he made a simple but sturdy knot. "They just said to tie it?"

"Yes. I was told a blessing would bind whatever evil existed within it."

Derek sounded better now, and Simon took heart in that. But his imagination was already playing with what other horrors the hidden room might hold.

"They didn't say it would . . . would do that," Derek said.

"If they had, would you have come?" Simon asked.

"They didn't know about this. They would have told me about that."

Simon hoped so. Since he was tying his future—however long that might be—to that of the Templar, he wanted to think they would be honest with him.

"And yes," Derek answered. "I would have come, Simon. The Templar are the only way the world is going to rid itself of these demons."

Simon slid his backpack off and opened one of the compartments. He emptied munitions onto the floor and hoped he wouldn't need them on the way back to the Underground.

As he touched the book, it suddenly bloated like a toad, straining at the palladium alloy chain. Then it leaked dark fluid that looked green on the HUD. Simon thought he knew what it was.

"Is that blood?" Derek asked.

Simon steeled himself and shoved the book into the backpack without answering. Neither of them really wanted to know. He thought he felt the book quivering but was willing to admit that it might have been his imagination.

Just then a voice broke in over the HUD. "Demons have found us, lads."

The immediate threat seemed to calm Derek, giving him something to worry about that he could deal with. "Where?" He walked out of the hidden room back into the study.

"All around us."

Simon settled the backpack across his shoulders and hoped his armor could hold off the fiend if it happened to get away from the blessed chain. He freed the Spike Bolter as he stepped out into the study.

Claws rasped across the roof.

A snarling face suddenly peered in through the window. The massive head looked like a gray-white starfish with huge malevolent eyes shoved into the center of it. The maw gaped, filled with serrated teeth between the two eighteen-inch tentacles hanging from its jaws.

"Gremlin scout," Derek said.

Simon had already identified the creature and was lifting the Spike Bolter. Gremlin scouts, even though that might not have been what they called themselves, performed the job the name implied. If the scout knew Templar were in the building, the rest of the pack did, too.

Before Simon could fire, the Gremlin scout hefted a Shockwave pistol up and pressed it against the glass. The sidearm used HARP technology to gather an electrical charge from the air, then release it in a concentrated blast. The blast was limited to a twenty-foot radius, but that distance easily covered the study.

Simon aimed and started to squeeze the trigger on his Spike Bolter when the world detonated in a blinding white-hot flash.

THIRTY-ONE

The electric discharge blew the glass out of the window and knocked Simon from his feet. As he flew backward, he realized he should have locked his boots down. But the force was so strong he didn't know if even that would have helped.

He crashed against the wall. Books tumbled down over him. He thought the book in his backpack squirmed, but he couldn't be sure. His senses reeled and for a moment he thought he might pass out. Even with the boosted power of the armor, his arms felt like lead.

Derek was knocked flat and rolled backward. He lost his Firestarter.

The Gremlin scout clambered through the shattered window. A second one followed. The high-pitched hum of the Shockwave the first one carried filled the study.

Struggling to swallow the nausea that swirled up in him, certain that his brain had turned to jelly, Simon pointed the Spike Bolter and fired without aiming, knowing all he had on his side was his quickness. The projectiles ripped bloody furrows in the Gremlin scout's neck, then tracked up to its huge face and shredded its eyes.

The Gremlin scout roared in rage and staggered back. It fired the Shockwave a second time.

The massive blast hammered Simon back up against the wall again. The true danger of the sonic wave created by the pistol was that it didn't truly have to be aimed. The blast radiated out from the center of the shooter's mass and grew stronger as it went.

This time Simon did black out for a moment. He came to almost immediately. The rusty taste of blood trickled through his mouth.

The first Gremlin scout dropped to its knees. Its face hung in gory tatters. Broken bone showed through. It tried to bring the Shockwave up again but pitched forward on its face.

Shoving himself to his feet, letting the armor do most of the work, Simon stood. His hand was empty when he lifted it. The Spike Bolter lay somewhere under the second wave of falling books.

The second Gremlin scout struggled to its feet and gripped the war axe it carried. Some kind of rifle hung over its shoulder. Falling snow eddied in through the broken window behind it.

Simon drew his sword. Derek lay silent and still near the doorway. Simon didn't know if the Templar was alive or dead.

The Gremlin smiled and growled. Though he didn't know the words, Simon realized a challenge had been issued.

Simon moved forward. The Gremlin brought the axe around in an abbreviated arc. Reacting instantly, knowing the outcome would be decided in seconds, Simon blocked the haft of the axe with his sword blade. Even with the augmented strength given him by the armor, Simon was barely able to stop the axe.

The demon snarled in a guttural voice.

Twisting, Simon drove a side kick into the demon's face that snapped its head back. He followed it with two more kicks, not believing the massive creature was still standing when the armor gave him enough strength to kick down a wall.

Unable to bring any true sword skill into play, Simon headbutted the Gremlin in the face and knocked it back a half-step. He thought he almost brained himself in the attempt. But he ripped the sword away from the axe haft, took a step back, pointed the sword before him, and lunged.

The sword slid through the demon's chest with effort. The sound of splintering bone and ripped scales cracked through Simon's auditory receptors.

The demon dropped its axe and reached for the sword. Shouting harsh, guttural noises, the creature wrapped its hands around the blade. Incredibly, it halted the sword as Simon locked his boots down and put the armor's weight behind his effort.

For a moment, fear touched Simon, almost consuming him in its intensity as the demon fought him to a standstill. He pushed the weakness away and concentrated on his father, on his loss, and all the training and faith his father had put into him.

He shoved.

The sword sawed through the Gremlin's fingers and sank to the hilt. Savagely, Simon twisted the sword hilt and carved through the demon's flesh.

It died on its feet, mouth open in surprise.

Holding fast to the sword hilt, Simon drew up a leg and put his foot against the demon's chest. He forced the demon's body backward at the same time he pulled the sword free.

The Gremlin fell backward through the broken window. Breathing hard but in control, Simon stumbled back over the dead body of the other Gremlin and steadied himself. He caught hold of the window and peered out just in time to see the demon crash down hard enough to crack the sidewalk.

Two other Gremlins started climbing the building's wall.

Simon turned back to Derek. The other Templar was just getting to his feet. Crossing the room quickly, Simon plucked his Spike Bolter from under a pile of books and leathered it. Then he grabbed Derek's arm as the Templar found his Firestarter.

"Are you all right?" Simon asked.

"Yes." Derek sounded winded and disoriented. He stared at the dead Gremlin. "Where is the other one? There were two."

"Gone. Let's go. Others are coming." Simon pulled on his arm and got him moving. Fear drove him. He didn't want to be caught. But he wasn't afraid of dying. He'd accepted his death would come sooner than later. He just didn't want to lose.

Simon pulled Derek down the stairs, bumping into the wall as the other Templar slammed against him again and again, losing his footing several times. He slid his sword over his back again and held the Spike Bolter.

As he turned the last corner that put him out into the second-floor hallway, Simon switched to thermographic display and peered through the walls. Three yellow and red shadows showed in the darkness.

Holding up on the stairs, Simon put the Spike Bolter away and yanked a grenade from his vest. It contained a high explosive made from Greek Fire that burned with a nuclear intensity.

"This is Simon," he said. "Is anyone on the second floor?"

"No. We got outside once we spotted the demons. Do you need help?"

"Negative. I just wanted to make sure you were clear."

Simon pulled the arming ring, then flipped the grenade into the second-story hallway.

The red and yellow shadows shifted in reaction to the noise the grenade made as it hit the floor. If any of them recognized the explosive for what it was, they didn't have time to do anything about it.

The grenade blew up with a deafening report the armor almost blocked out. The floor vibrated beneath Simon's feet and smoke roiled from the room.

Drawing the Spike Bolter, Simon turned the corner. He pointed the pistol in front of him and yanked Derek into motion.

Greek Fire covered the walls and the floor. The house wasn't going to survive the night. As close as the buildings were, Simon felt certain that most of the block would burn by morning. He felt bad about that, but it couldn't be helped.

Another Gremlin emerged from one of the rooms. It carried a strange pistol Simon couldn't identify. Blocky and metallic, the sidearm looked ungainly. Crimson lights flared along the dulled steel-gray finish. The demon fired at once.

Several dozen incandescent flashes streaked from the pistol and slammed against Simon's armor. Most of the bursts bounced and ricocheted from the armor, deflected from the palladium alloy or the protective spells, though Simon wasn't sure which. But his defenses dropped quickly.

He pulled the Spike Bolter up and fired. The Greek Fire coiled up his armored legs, setting off a new set of warnings on his HUD display. More flaming liquid hung from the ceiling and the walls. Some of it dripped down onto Simon and obscured his view for a split second before it slid away.

Behind Simon, Derek was shifting, taking his weight back as he aimed his Firestarter. Streams of fire covered the demon and caused horrific burns immediately. It wiped frantically at the fire.

Weakened by the fire, the ceiling started to buckle. Simon knew it was going to come down. Even the armor might not stand against the maelstrom of fire.

Simon aimed point-blank at the demon and ran toward it, firing the whole way. The palladium needles tore through the Gremlin's flesh and staggered it. As he closed on the monster, Simon lowered a shoulder and caught the demon in the side, propelling it over the second-floor banister.

The demon fell only a short distance, probably not even enough to notice if it had been healthy. But it wasn't healthy. It kicked and tried to get to its feet but couldn't manage the action.

Simon ran down steps that hadn't been built with four-hundred-pound Templar in mind. The steps split and crunched underfoot, leaving pitfalls for Derek.

Instead of taking the stairs, though, Derek simply leaped over the side and made the jump easily. He touched down on a three-point landing and shoved himself back up.

"Come on!" Derek roared.

Simon ran, following close at the other Templar's heels. Just as Derek passed through the doorway, the foyer closet opened and a little girl poked her head out. She wore a frightened expression.

Astonished, Simon recognized the little girl from the photographs of the writer and his family. She was the daughter.

She's still here. The knowledge twisted sickeningly through Simon's stomach. He knew children were caught in the battle with the demons and everything they were doing in London, but he hadn't invaded the houses of any of those.

But he had invaded this little girl's home.

She looked at him, her blond hair highlighted by the house burning behind Simon. Tears ran down her cheeks. Her lips trembled. "Help!" she said. "Please help!"

Simon took her by the hand and started to pull, reminding himself to be gentle or he'd rip her arm from the socket.

"No!" The little girl pulled back against him. "I need someone to help my mother."

Mother! The word cascaded through Simon, leaving sickening greasy tendrils in its wake.

"She's down there." The little girl pointed into the closet.

Peering into the closet, Simon saw that a door had been hidden in the floor. The blueprints hadn't shown anything of a cellar, but that wasn't unusual. Even though the blueprints were supposed to be on record with the police and fire service in case of building collapse, they weren't always listed. There had always been a lot of black market dealing and smuggling in London. That had been part of the life's blood of the poor.

"Simon," Derek called.

"I'm here."

"What are you waiting on? That building's going to come down. Get out of there."

"I can't," Simon said, stepping through the narrow doorway of the closet. It was so tight that he had to force his shoulders through. Wood splintered as he went through. Thankfully the opening in the floor was slightly larger.

Unfortunately, the rickety staircase wasn't built to support a Templar in full armor.

"Simon," Derek called again.

"There are people in here. A little girl. Her mother. Maybe more." There was no way Simon was going to leave them. He couldn't. He knew his father wouldn't have left them, and he wasn't about to.

THIRTY-TWO

In the outer room, the third story started falling down in pieces.

As he shoved his head through the doorway in the flood, and the fire that had dripped in from outside, Simon spotted a middle-aged woman and a boy who was younger than the girl. The woman was inert while the little boy held on to her.

Thankfully the room had a low ceiling. Simon stepped on the staircase and it shattered beneath his weight.

"Simon," Derek said.

Simon approached the woman and the boy, trying to figure out what he was supposed to do. The woman lay under a blanket, but her chest rose and fell. Smoke gathered in the room and she coughed.

"I can't leave them. I'm *not* going to leave them." When his father had read him stories about King Arthur and his knights, when they'd discussed the responsibilities of being a Templar, Thomas Cross had always emphasized the salvation of the weak and helpless. The Templar existed, in his mind, to save humanity as much as to battle the demons. Simon knew he couldn't leave them.

"You're going to get killed."

Simon picked up the boy, who started screaming and fighting to be free. Gently as he could, Simon put the boy out of the cellar and into the closet.

"Get him out of here," Simon told the girl.

Wide-eyed, the little girl stared at him, tears on her cheeks. "My mother—" A fit of coughing stole her voice.

"I'll get her," Simon said. "I promise. Go."

The little girl pulled back from the opening.

Simon grabbed the edges of the opening and ripped it open larger. Returning to the woman, he gathered her easily in his arms and carried her to the opening. He cradled her in his arms and leaped out of the hole.

The jarring woke the woman. She looked up at him with pain-filled eyes. "My children."

"They're out," Simon told her. "We're all getting out." He smashed his shoulder into the closet and tore the frame and part of the wall out, then stepped through the cloud of plaster dust and smoke.

The little girl had the boy by the hand. They stood at the open door. A large shape lurched toward them out of the night.

Simon shifted the woman to his shoulder and drew the Spike Bolter. He took aim just as he saw the Gremlin surging from the shadows. Simon ran forward, firing over the heads of the children. The palladium needles ripped into the Gremlin's head and shoulders.

The little girl screamed and yanked the boy to the side. Simon was surprised she didn't freeze up. He kept firing, staying squared up with the demon and delivering a snap-kick to its face.

The demon flew backward and landed on the ground. Simon kept firing till he was certain the Gremlin was dead. He turned back to the house.

Flames flickered through the windows, greedily consuming the house. The children stood inside the door, backlit by the fire spreading quickly toward the opening, feeding on the oxygen.

"Come on!" Simon yelled.

The little girl yanked the boy into motion and they ran out onto the snow-covered sidewalk. It had evidently started snowing more heavily while they'd been inside because the inches had started to pile up.

The Templar had taken up a position on one side of the street. Their weapons blazed in the night, bright greens and whites mixed with ruby and sapphire.

Simon took up a position on the other side of the street. The woman lay unconscious over his shoulder. The two children stood at his legs. For the first time he realized how far it was back to the Sloane Street tube station.

Lights suddenly flared to life in a nearby alley. A van sped out onto the street, skidding across the new-fallen snow and aiming straight at Simon. It fishtailed for a moment and struck an overturned compact car, setting the vehicle spinning like a turtle.

Vision enhanced by the HUD, Simon saw the frightened man behind the wheel. He looked like he was in his sixties, bundled up tight against the inclement weather. The man locked his brakes and attempted to bring the van to a stop.

Knowing the vehicle wasn't going to be able to halt on the snow, Simon locked his boots down and leaned forward with a hand out. He hoped he didn't destroy the vehicle.

The front of the van collapsed several inches with a sharp *crunch*. The spikes on Simon's boots raked foot-long tears across the pavement. But the van stopped.

The man leaned across the passenger seat and threw the door open. "Get her inside!"

Simon pulled the cargo door open and placed the woman inside. He helped the two children inside as well.

"Where am I supposed to take them?" the man asked.

The question caught Simon off-guard. He hadn't been thinking that far ahead. "Sloane Street tube station."

Weapons fire blasted wrecked cars and buses. Mortar fell from damaged buildings.

The man nodded. "Hurry. When these things find somebody out in the open, they don't give up the scent."

Another blast opened a crater in the street only a few feet away.

"Go," Simon ordered.

The van sped away, careening between wrecks.

Crouching down, Simon pointed the Spike Bolter at a Blood Angel skimming along the street in pursuit of the van. Locked on, Simon squeezed the trigger and rode out the recoil, hoping that the barrels didn't melt down.

The palladium spikes tracked the Blood Angel, slamming into the buildings behind it for a moment, then quickly overtaking it and ripping into the demon. Perforations opened in the wide-spread wings. Other rounds from other Templar weapons drenched it in flames and blew it to pieces. Flaming chunks mixed with the falling snow and plopped onto the street.

The Templar had managed an uneven skirmish line, but they were holding their own against the demons. Three Templar lay dead in the street. One of them had been torn to bits and the other was in flames.

One of the Templar fired a Constrictor pistol at an attacking Blood Angel. A tangled net of palladium alloy wire unfurled in the air, boosted by the SqueezFast memoryware programmed into the metal.

The net flared wide, then wrapped around the Blood Angel as tightly as a lover. The memoryware cranked even tighter, pulling the demon's wings against its body. The creature dropped from the sky, screaming shrilly. It thudded against one of the nearby buildings and thudded to a stop against an overturned MGB.

Simon leaped the car and landed on the pavement. He shoved the Spike Bolter forward from less than a yard away, aiming point-blank at the thing's face. It howled at him in caustic denial. Rage, not fear, twisted its features. A clawed hand sliced through the palladium strands of memoryware that bound it. Arcane energy flared purple as the spell woven into the net repulsed the demon's efforts.

Squeezing the trigger, Simon aimed at the center of the Blood Angel's chest and rode the recoil up to the bottom of its chin. The spikes blew the creature's chest apart. Gore spattered his faceplate.

"Down, Simon!" Derek shouted.

Reacting automatically, Simon dropped facedown and hugged the street. A wave of fire blew over his head and ignited a large section of the nearby building and the street.

"Move!"

Simon pushed up one-handed and stayed low. Inside the armor he moved effortlessly. He almost smiled, knowing that the fear and anxiety that had plagued him for the last few days had passed. He was in his element, right where he belonged.

He fired the Spike Bolter at the wave of Gremlins that darted out from the shadows less than thirty feet away. Laser and electrical shocks from the demons slammed into him in a wild display of energy and color. His armor's defenses dropped, but he knew that running wasn't an option. They'd only leave their flank open to attack.

This was where the Templar had determined to live, fighting foes face-to-face over inches of ground, holding a line where evil and darkness stopped. Simon's heart sang and he knew he was riding an adrenaline high like none he'd ever before experienced.

Freeing his sword, seeing that the other Templar were doing the same thing, preparing to engage the surviving Gremlins, Simon holstered the Spike Bolter, took a two-handed grip on the sword, and charged. He met the first demon with a powerful downward swipe, letting the sword's weight add to the blow.

The palladium alloy sword blazed bright blue with the arcane energy his father had helped him weave into it. The blade slid through the demon flesh, cutting his foe in halves. Before the Gremlin could fall to pieces, Simon stepped around it and engaged another. The demon thrust a spear at Simon's face.

The sharp point skidded across the smooth surface of his faceplate, but the impact was enough to stagger him and nearly drive him to his knees. Then he dropped below the line of the spear and threw his shoulder into the demon's midriff, straining to lift it from its feet.

Torn free of the pavement, the demon went back and down. It landed flat on its back, the breath knocked from it. Dropping with his knees on its shoulders, Simon pinned the demon to the ground, then reversed his sword and thrust the point through the center of its head. The sword didn't stop until it met the pavement on the other side of its skull. Simon twisted ruthlessly and exploded the skull. Beneath him, the Gremlin bucked out its life.

Spotting a dropped Constrictor only inches from the outstretched hand of a Templar who was dead or unconscious, Simon dove for the weapon, scraped it up in his left hand, and rolled to his knees.

Derek battled two Gremlins, managing to put up a lightning-fast defense to parry the sword and axe his opponents wielded. Despite his skill, though, Derek was being forced back.

Taking quick aim, Simon fired the Constrictor at the nearest Gremlin. The net sprang out and wrapped around the Gremlin, cutting into its flesh and binding it.

The demon stumbled and started to fall. Derek caught it in one hand and used it for a shield. He performed a quick parry on one side of the bound demon, then whirled around it and slashed at the other demon. The sword blade met the demon's neck cleanly, taking its head off before it knew he'd even changed places.

"Thanks," Derek said.

"No problem," Simon replied. He dodged an attacking Blood Angel, then turned to fire the Constrictor. Before he could squeeze the trigger, the demon turned her head and screamed at him. The crimson runes carved into her skin glowed brightly as she threw out a hand.

Simon thought he saw a vague shimmering in the air before him, but before he could move an incredible force battered him, lifting him from his feet and throwing him backward forty or more feet. He hit the ground and rolled as he'd been taught, immediately coming to his feet and moving sideways to cover.

The Blood Angel pursued, flapping its wings and powering toward him.

Aiming the Constrictor, Simon fired twice. The first net missed the target and spread out in a metal rectangle against the black sky before disappearing. The second wrapped and trapped the Blood Angel, but not before the runes in her skin glowed again.

Another wave of force hammered Simon backward.

"Defense critical," the calm voice advised him.

Standing, slightly disoriented, Simon looked for the Blood Angel and spotted her lying in the street sixty feet away. He took out a grenade and armed it, then tossed it at her. She tried to roll away, but the grenade went off and enveloped her in flame, killing her in shrieking agony.

There were a few other skirmishes, but when they were done not a Gremlin remained alive in the street. They'd lost five men, not counting Bruce.

No one spoke after Derek gave the order for them to gather their dead and leave. Simon helped pick up one of the dead men, settling him across his shoulders. Then they ran back to the Sloane Street tube station.

THIRTY-THREE

"What you have is extraordinary." The woman trailed her fingers along Warren's left arm, delicately pulling at the small scales with her fingernails. The effect and her voice were almost sensual.

A prickling sensation crawled under the scales, then spread along Warren's arm and concentrated at the back of his scalp. He wanted to pull his limb back from the woman's grasp, but he didn't. Tulane had told him that Naomi was the most sensitive and skilled among the Cabalists there in the caves.

She was perhaps a couple years older than him, he guessed. Surely no more than four. She would have been pretty if not for all the tattoos and piercings that adorned her flesh. There was also the matter of the two short, curved horns that thrust up from her forehead and made her look positively wicked. She was petite and full-figured, dressed in a low-cut black blouse, black leather pants, and calf-high boots with silver chains.

It was a look, Kelli would have said sarcastically. If Kelli was still in a sarcastic frame of mind. Instead, Kelli sat across the room on the floor and obediently waited for Warren.

Warren felt bad about Kelli's behavior. Even though she'd been mean-spirited and—at times—cruel to him, he hadn't known how much effect he'd had on her life until these past few hours. Before that he'd been too sick, in too much pain, to notice.

Still he felt more afraid of being alone in the midst of strangers than guilty about his control over her. So he continued to wish her to sit and wait for him.

"I don't think it's extraordinary," Warren replied.

The woman looked up at him, then over to Tulane, who stood nearby. They were in another room, this one filled with old books in dozens of languages. Plastic cases contained different herbs and powders.

"That's because you haven't been properly trained to appreciate what you have," the woman said. She continued to stroke his arm as if it were some kind of pet.

The prickling increased intensity.

Naomi looked into Warren's eyes. "You know the demon that did this to you, don't you?"

That caught Tulane's interest. Neither of them had mentioned Merihim's name to the woman. Warren was too surprised to speak.

"You know his name, don't you?" Naomi repeated.

"Merihim," Warren said.

Naomi smiled a little and released his arm. She pushed up from her chair and crossed the small room to the overstocked bookshelf. After a moment's consideration, she chose a thick book with ornate leather covers and returned.

"He is one of the Greater Demons Cabalists have seen in their visions," Naomi said. "One of those who have been Named."

"*Named?*" Warren repeated.

"Not all of the demons have Names," Naomi said. "Most of them are just things. Powerful things, yes, but they're little more than tools. They have to claim Names for themselves, and they only do that by fighting their way to the top of the hierarchy." She looked at Tulane with some confusion. "He doesn't know about the demons?"

"He hasn't been formally trained," Tulane replied.

Naomi searched Warren with her gaze. "What," she asked, "made you so special in the eyes of a demon like Merihim?"

Warren didn't have an answer and didn't try to give one.

"What do you know about Merihim?" Naomi asked.

"He called himself the Bringer of Pestilence."

Naomi nodded and opened the book. She laid it on the table between them. There, on the page, the demon stood revealed in all his dark glory. His blue-green armor shimmered and his green trident gleamed. Dismembered corpses lay in disarray around him.

"He has been to this world before," Naomi said, "but it has been a long time. Back in the Middle Ages, a select few of the demons visited our world, studying it to see what they would encounter here. Merihim brought death and disease to the people in Europe. Thousands, hundreds of thousands, died with him. Some say that he journeyed with Christopher Columbus to the New World and was responsible for the deaths of so many Native Americans there. The Spaniards claimed that demons were the cause of so many deaths there."

Warren barely remembered the stories of Columbus and his voyages along the New World. He did recall the stories of the deaths, the fact that millions of Native Americans had died as a result of contact with the Europeans. Smallpox and other diseases had ravaged them.

"Some say the Native Americans knew Merihim for what he truly was," Naomi went on. "The Native Americans were more in touch with their world. Some say they see the demons more easily than others. That's where their legends of the Wendigo come from."

Warren knew the Wendigo legend. The Native Americans claimed that evil "spirits" sometimes took over warriors and gave them a taste for human flesh. The cannibals and the spirits were both called Wendigo.

"The Native Americans tried to fight Merihim and bind him. He stayed in that world for over a hundred years before he was finally bound by a group in Roanoke, Virginia. The cost there was high, though. When they banished him from this world, it was at the cost of every man, woman, and child that had lived in that town."

"What happened to them?" Warren asked.

"It's believed that they were pulled into the demons' world. That sometimes happens even when someone banishes them."

"Banishment isn't the answer," Tulane said. "Control is. We need to find a way to control the demons, then we'll have nothing to fear from them."

Warren gazed at the greenish-black scales that had taken the place of his skin along his left arm. Control wasn't going to be easy. He looked back into Naomi's dark eyes.

"What would Merihim want with someone like me?" he asked.

"He let you live," Naomi said. "I would guess that he wants to claim you for his own."

"For what reason?"

Naomi shook her head. "I don't know. But we can attempt to find out. If you're willing. The way will be hard and dangerous."

Warren considered that only for a moment. The prickling under the scales on his arm and at the back of his head continued. The way was already hard and dangerous.

"Okay," he agreed.

Warren lay on his back on a small pad at the center of the room. Naomi was on her hands and knees nearby, drawing intricate symbols on the smooth stone floor with a piece of blue chalk. Yellow-green flames danced atop blue candles that surrounded them.

"Will Merihim know you're there?" Tulane asked. He stood outside the circle Naomi had drawn.

"I will try my best not to let him." Naomi put the chalk back into a wooden case covered with carved symbols.

"But if the demon does know you're there, can he use the connection to come through?"

When Tulane had first heard the idea of spying on the demon, he'd been immediately interested. Now that he'd figured out that Merihim could use that contact as his own, he didn't seem quite so anxious to get on with things. Warren wasn't, either.

Naomi sat with crossed legs, her palms resting on her knees. "You know yourself, Lord Tulane, that we don't understand everything the demons can do. And I've never successfully spied on one as powerful as Merihim."

"You spied on Shulgoth during the invasion after he arrived here. You said it was easier to watch them with your gift while they were here."

"Only because Shulgoth didn't try to stop us from seeing all that he was capable of," Naomi said. "He also remains far beyond our control."

Fear ran rampant through Warren as he lay on the pad. The smell of cooking flesh—his own, that of the Cabalists in the room that night, and his stepfather's own scorched flesh—intermingled in his mind.

"This could be a trap," Warren said before he knew he was going to speak.

Tulane stared at him.

"What if Merihim only changed me like this so he could come here?" Warren asked. "What if his target all along was the Cabalist network?"

A heavy silence fell over the room, letting him know that Tulane and Naomi hadn't considered that.

"He killed Edith and Jonas effortlessly," Warren said, "and he reclaimed the Eye of Raatalukkyn that night. It's possible that he set me free only so that I would come in contact with more of you."

"I'll be careful," Naomi said. "I mean no disrespect to the dead, but I'm far more capable of what we're about to do than Edith and Jonas were. This is my area of expertise." She placed her hand on Warren's forehead. "Rest. Just close your eyes and I'll guide you through the rest of it."

Despite his heart hammering and flooding his body with adrenaline, Warren felt the warm lassitude spread throughout his body. Tension drained from him.

"Close your eyes." Naomi leaned over toward him and pressed her fingertips against his eyelids, keeping his eyes shut.

Momentary panic spurted through Warren. He had to fight the urge to sit up and knock her hand away. In his mind, he could see shadows uncoiling from the wall and coming toward him.

"Relax," Naomi said. "Breathe."

Warren did, opening his lungs and filling them with effort.

"There's a connection between you and the demon," Naomi said. "He built it for his own reasons, but we can use it."

The pull of that connection grew stronger inside Warren. The more it pulled, the more he became afraid. He withdrew from it and tried to find some way of building a wall between him and that dark force.

"Don't fight it," Naomi whispered. "Go with it."

"I can't," Warren gasped. "I'm afraid."

"Fear is good. It can give us more strength than we can achieve on our own. Embrace your fear and use it, but don't give in to it. Breathe." Naomi paused to let him. "Again."

Warren drew in his breath at her command, and let it out as well.

"Good. You're doing good."

Finding the rhythm she wanted, Warren relaxed a little more. Then the blackness trapped inside his mind seemed to open up and swallow him whole.

Warren stared down at the dark expanse of the River Thames. He stood at the middle of a bridge. Gazing around, he realized that he was on London Bridge.

Scores of stalled cars filled the bridges. Some of them were overturned and more were charred ruins. Bits of wreckage from an army helicopter lay scattered nearby, creaking as the wind moved it. A dead man hung from a safety harness halfway out the door. Another was embedded in the Plexiglas nose.

Sensing movement to his right, Warren faced in that direction. At least twenty demons milled there. They were frightful creatures with guttural voices.

Cautiously, staying within the shadows as much as he could, Warren turned to look for Naomi, only to find that she wasn't there. Feeling his heart slamming inside his chest, he looked for an escape route.

I'm not here, he told himself. *All I have to do is open my eyes and wake up. I'll be back in the caves. I've just got to wake up.*

But he didn't wake up. He remained trapped in the dream. Gazing over the side of the bridge, he wondered what his chances of surviving a leap into the river would be.

You don't need to jump, a powerful voice told Warren. The words exploded in his mind and he knew at once who was talking to him. *They won't see you as long as I don't want them to.*

THIRTY-FOUR

Warren looked behind him, finding Merihim there this time when he hadn't been there only a moment ago. The demon towered over him, full of threat and arrogance.

Don't be afraid, Merihim told him. A grim smile pulled at the scaled face. *I didn't allow you to live just so these insects could have you.* He gestured at the demons moving restlessly through the stalled vehicles. None of them even looked in Warren's direction. *I have far grander plans for you than that.*

Warren felt certain those plans included torture and dismemberment at some point. But if he could forestall that moment, he had time to think and plan.

Laughter rumbled from Merihim. *No. Death and dismemberment would be . . . diverting. But I want you for another use. I can make you a leader within my own army. You know the people we hunt, and you know this place. Either of those things could be invaluable.*

Warren tried desperately to wake up, but couldn't.

"Wait." Naomi's soft voice reached him from a distance. "He can't hurt you in this place. I can protect you here."

Uneasily, and only because he had no other choice, Warren stood his ground. If both Merihim and Naomi told him they could protect him, someone was lying—

"Demons lie," Naomi told him.

—but Warren didn't know who it was. He guessed that both of them would lie to him for their own reasons.

The demon's gaze fell onto Warren's arm. Dressed in a black t-shirt, the arm was in plain view. The reptilian scales seemed to reflect a glow that came from the demon himself.

I see my gift has taken root. What do you think of it? I was very generous.

"Why did you do this to me?" Warren asked.

You were too weak as you were. You would never have stood the rigors of this world on your own. The burns that you suffered alone were enough to have killed you if I hadn't aided you. Merihim rolled Warren's head from side to side with the trident. The metal was so cold it burned. *You've come far, but you've farther yet to go.*

"I didn't ask for this." The anger, for a moment, surmounted the fear that cascaded inside Warren.

I'm not in the habit of granting wishes, the demon replied. *If you'd asked for anything, I would have killed you on the spot.*

The anger inside Warren melted and left only the fear. For a moment, though, he wondered if dying would have been easier.

Merihim cocked his head and looked at Warren. *Would you have rather died? There are others out there who would preserve their lives and serve me.*

The need for self-preservation pushed away Warren's fear and indecision. "No."

That's right. You wanted to live. You still do. A smile twisted Merihim's lips. *Tell me, then. Tell me that you're glad you're still alive.*

Warren suddenly loathed himself more than he ever had. He remembered how he'd felt when he'd seen his mother killed in front of him, and had commanded his stepfather to take his own life, knowing with certainty that his stepfather had no choice, and knowing that he could have stopped the suicide before it happened by simply telling his stepfather to sleep instead of die.

For weeks after the deaths of his mother and stepfather, Warren had blamed himself. Not just for his stepfather's death, but for his mother's as well. He'd always come up in their arguments, and he'd always been a source of friction between them. He didn't know exactly how it was his fault that they were dead, but he was certain it was. Back then when he'd been in the hospital recovering from the gunshot wound, he'd often thought that it would have been better if he would have died, too.

Then, when no one had ever adopted him after they'd discovered his personal tragedy, Warren had blamed himself again. He'd been worthless, a cursed child, and everyone that had come through the orphanage had seen that in him.

You were *worthless,* Merihim said. *I have changed that. I have changed you. You have value now. I elevated you. Do you think that your new friends would be so interested in you if I hadn't taken care of you?*

Warren knew that was true. The Cabalists wouldn't have been looking for him if he hadn't survived that fire.

"We were already looking for you," Naomi reminded him, "before the fire that night."

The truth of that helped a little, but then Warren realized that Merihim knew that he was among the Cabalists.

Children playing with shadows of things they've never seen, Merihim scoffed. *Misled to visions of grandeur by the paltry bit they've been able to ferret out.*

Arrogance? Warren wondered. *Or truth?* He didn't know.

"Steady," Naomi said. "Every moment you have the demon's attention, we're learning something."

Merihim's gaze erupted in baleful black fire that

streamed from his eyes. *Tell me now that you're glad to be alive or I will kill you where you stand.*

"Warren." Naomi's voice was tense and anxious. "Do what he says. Do what he says or he's going to kill you."

Warren had never felt so helpless in all his life. No matter what he said, no matter what he did, he was doomed. There was no escape.

"You don't know that. We can help you. But you have to save yourself till we can."

"I'm glad to be alive," Warren breathed out in a ragged sob. Hot tears cooled on his cheeks, and they felt like so many he'd shed while in foster care. He knew he was telling the truth, and he knew that if Merihim had sensed he was lying the demon would have slain him before he could take his next breath.

"Good. Everything's going to be okay."

Warren didn't say anything, but he didn't feel like anything was going to be okay. He just wanted off the bridge and away from the demon.

Merihim smiled and preened. Then he regarded Warren. *How did you find me?*

"I don't know," Warren replied. Since he didn't know how Naomi had sent him on his journey or how she had traced his link back to the demon, Warren hoped that was close enough to the truth. "I went to sleep and you were there."

Merihim considered that. *Perhaps the bond between us is stronger than I thought.*

Warren wondered if that made the demon somehow more vulnerable. Or if Merihim thought it did. Either case could prove disastrous for him.

And why did you come to me?

"I didn't want to." That was *definitely* the truth.

Yet here you are.

"Hold on to him. Let me see what I can find out."

Warren wanted to tell her no, that he was going to be the one who paid the price for the chances she took.

Merihim stepped closer to Warren, dwarfing him immediately. The heat from the demon's body soaked into Warren and took away the chill of standing atop the bridge in the winter wind.

I can use you, though, so it's good that you showed up.

Fear rose in Warren again. He cursed himself for going with the Cabalists. If he wasn't there with them now, he wouldn't be here.

I want you to locate something for me, the demon stated.

"What?"

Merihim grinned mirthlessly. *You don't need to know. You only need to know that if you don't find it for me, I'll crush you.*

Warren felt Naomi's power coursing through him, and he worried that if he could feel it surely the demon could, too. But Merihim gave no indication that he was aware of anything.

"I told you I was good at what I do." A trace of pride accompanied Naomi's words as they bounced inside Warren's skull.

Merihim hefted his trident and placed the tines across Warren's brow. *You'll be my warhound in this matter. You'll run what I seek to ground. The humans are pursuing it as well, and I don't want them to succeed. The prize is mine, and mine alone. Find the thing that I desire and let me know when you do.*

"How?"

You will be given the way.

"How will I know what it is?"

Because you will know.

Dark energy blazed through Warren's brain from the trident. He heard Naomi scream deep within his mind, then he didn't feel her anymore.

Go, Merihim commanded. *Don't trouble me any further. Complete your assignment as quickly as you can. I would have my prize before the next day breaks.*

An incredible force slammed into Warren, knocking him over the side of the bridge hard enough to drive the wind from his lungs. He flew backward at least a hundred feet and—for a flicker of a moment—hung out over the long drop.

He fell toward the dark river where demons capered aboard burning boats and ships. Stretching out his hand to try to turn his fall into a dive, he felt certain that he was about to be knocked senseless from the plummet.

Too late he saw that he wasn't going to hit the water at all. He fell directly toward a burning tanker ship that suddenly exploded. Flames reached up for him and he cried out in fear. He crossed his arms in front of his face as the heat rushed out to consume him—

—and woke on the thin pad in Naomi's office gasping for air.

Hedgar Tulane stood just outside the circle. Concern tightened his features, but he wasn't looking at Warren. Instead, his gaze was locked on Naomi, who lay curled in a fetal position.

"What happened to her?" Tulane demanded.

Trying to push through the fog that filled his head, only then noticing the pounding at his temples, Warren ignored the question. Out of breath and dizzy, feeling changed somehow, he pushed himself into a seated position and reached for Naomi.

"Hey," he called. "Hey. Wake up."

Gradually, she awakened. Pain etched hard lines on her face. She tried to sit up, then got sick immediately. She waved an arm and the candles all extinguished.

Tulane stepped across the circle then and helped her to her feet. He sent for assistance while Warren sat with his back to one of the walls, too weak to help.

Kelli stood across the room, staring at them. For a moment she looked afraid.

Don't be afraid, Warren thought.

Kelli took a deep slow breath and the fear inside her dwindled. No emotion showed on her face.

Help me.

Like an automaton, Kelli joined Warren. She looked less like herself than ever. Warren knew he should feel guilty, but the fear inside him outweighed whatever remorse he might have felt. Her hand was cold in his, but he didn't care about that, either. He just didn't want to be alone.

By the time the physician arrived and examined Naomi, she was feeling better. She waved Tulane's attentions away and walked unsteadily over to Warren.

"Your ties to the demon are stronger than I'd believed," she said.

"I know." Warren stood in front of her on trembling knees. He still didn't feel right. His stomach rolled threateningly.

Naomi gazed at him as if she could see through him. "Do you know what Merihim wants?"

"No."

"Didn't he tell you?"

Warren felt anger within him and concentrated on seizing it instead of giving in to the fear that rattled through his bones. "You were there. Did you hear him say anything?"

Naomi reached up suddenly and laid her palm against his temple. Warren shifted, intending to knock her hand from his flesh, but then a blinding electrical pain surged through his brain and everything went black.

THIRTY-FIVE

What were you thinking?" Terrence Booth demanded. The High Seat's face was beet-red with emotion. He paced back and forth in the debriefing room.

Simon stood in Booth's office with his helmet under one arm. Bruised and bloodied from the battle, he stared at Booth in disbelief. "I was thinking I was saving those people."

"Those people made their choice to stay in that house!" Booth roared. "They weren't our bloody problem!"

Simon barely kept his mouth shut. *You weren't there. You didn't see the look on that little girl's face.*

"When Sergeant Chipplewhite decided to stay to try to save you, he put his team at risk," Booth continued. "I've got six more dead Templar than I had last night."

Simon didn't point out that Bruce's death was due to the book they'd been sent after, not the encounter with the Gremlins.

"In all fairness, sir," Derek spoke up from where he stood slightly behind Simon awaiting his turn for Booth's wrath, "the situation wasn't—"

"Wasn't for Simon Cross to muck about with," Booth interrupted, swinging his baleful gaze to Derek. "Nor was it yours. Do you consider trading the lives of six warriors for one a good trade, sergeant? Because if you do, I've seriously got to rethink your position as a leader."

Derek closed his mouth and put up no further protest.

Booth stared hard at Simon, like the effort was going to wound him in some manner.

The old resentment rose in Simon. For a moment he felt like they were back at school when Booth had thought he could bully a smaller and younger classmate. Everything in him cried out to prove that wasn't about to happen now any more than it had then.

Don't go there, he told himself. *You won't win the political battle involved in this encounter.* Still, he hated to acknowledge that even to himself.

"You had your assignment when you went there," Booth continued. "You were to get that book and get out of that house. It should have been easy. No muss, no fuss." He paused. "And no loss of life. Not of my warriors."

"That little girl," Simon said in a tight voice, "those people, needed help. If they'd stayed in that house, they would be dead now."

"That's not *my* problem," Booth said. "That's not *your* problem." He cursed. "There are a lot of people dead out there. I've seen their bodies. And I've got a vidburst for you, Cross: there are going to be a lot more of dead people before this is finished."

Simon breathed out, concentrating on controlling his reaction. He didn't have to get mad. That was a luxury he couldn't afford at the moment.

"And to make matters even worse, you brought them *here*. This base is supposed to remain *secret!*"

"There was nowhere else to take—"

"Those people are *not* our responsibility! We're here to save a world. Not a handful of people. We can only do that by defeating the demons. Not offering sanctuary. When that woman and her children choose to leave here, if they choose to do that—and if they don't then you've served only to increase the burden here—they could tell others about the secret areas we have in the Underground. It won't be long before the demons learn where we are."

Simon hadn't thought about that until he'd returned to the Underground himself. He'd concentrated solely on getting the family out of the burning house and to someplace safe. Saving them had come first.

"We're not here to save *people*," Booth said. "That's not what all those Templar intended when they died at St. Paul's Cathedral. That's not what your father intended when he died so that we could have a chance to carry on this war."

You don't know what my father intended, Simon thought angrily. Then guilt assailed him. He didn't know what his father intended either because he hadn't been there with him at the end.

"We're here to win the war against the demons," Booth continued. "Not to lose it slowly."

Simon concentrated on his breathing. Whatever Booth said wasn't going to matter. He'd learned something tonight that had felt good. Saving that girl and her family had felt good.

"Are you listening to me?" Booth demanded.

"Yes, sir."

"Those people," Booth spoke carefully, "are part of generations that stepped away from everything the Templar tried to teach them about the demons. They didn't want to see the demons. They didn't want to heed the warnings the Templar had that the demons existed. Those people watched as King Philip IV broke the ranks of the Templar in 1307. None of them believed in demons. They didn't want to. No one wanted to admit beings of such immense power existed because it might lessen the place they believed they had in the world. So they lived their lives in denial while the Templar went underground and worked to rebuild their lost fortunes so they could continue that war. That's not going to change just because you want it to."

Simon breathed out.

"We need warriors," Booth said. "Not heroes. The heroes all died at St. Paul's Cathedral. We don't have that luxury."

Simon almost said something. He thought Derek had to hold back a comment as well, but he couldn't be sure.

"We can only win this war if we manage to keep enough Templar alive long enough to figure out the weaknesses of the demons and get the job done. They're not going to do that by trying to play the *hero*." Booth spat the word as if it were a vile thing.

Keeping a tight rein on his emotions, Simon remained silent.

"If you want to be such a bloody hero," Booth said, "figure out how to defeat the demons. I'll mark you in the Book of Champions myself." He snorted in disgust. "The only reason I'm allowing you to stay at this point is because we need every able-bodied warrior. But if you screw up again, if you risk my Templar by inciting them to act foolishly, you'll be gone. And I mean forever banished from our ranks. Do you understand?"

"Yes." Simon's voice was low and tight.

"Good. Now get out of my sight."

Simon turned on his heel and marched out of the room. He resented Booth's heavy-handedness and wanted to retaliate, but he knew it wouldn't do any good. He had to walk a narrow path inside the Order.

Simon went to the hospital ward even though he was tired. When he'd arrived at the Underground, Booth had sent for him at once. The children's mother, Emily, hadn't been in good shape. He wanted to know if events had conspired to make orphans of the girl and her brother.

A few minutes later, he'd found his way through the tunnels to the med center.

A pretty woman, Simon thought her name was Kaye, stood in lavender scrubs at the triage center. She looked up at his approach.

"Cross, isn't it?" Her voice was open and honest. She looked tired.

"Yes." Simon stood at the desk. "I brought in a woman and—"

"—and two children." Kaye smiled. "Quite outgoing children actually."

"I wanted to find out how they were doing."

"The kids are fine. The mother is going to need a bit of recovery. Apparently she's a diabetic and had run out of medication. She'd lapsed into a coma. If you hadn't found her when you did, she would have been dead within a matter of hours."

"But she's going to be all right?"

"She is. She's resting naturally now."

Simon breathed a sigh of relief. After everything the night had turned into, that was a welcome bit of news.

"Would you like to see them?"

Simon shook his head. The last thing he needed was for Booth to find out he'd stopped by the infirmary to check on the people he wasn't supposed to have saved. "No. I've got to—"

Kaye smiled and looked over Simon's shoulder. "Too late."

Turning, Simon discovered the boy and girl were in a doorway behind him. Both of them had on new clothing and a few bandages. They stared at him shyly. The boy kept dropping his eyes and looking away.

"Are they all right?" Simon asked.

"Other than a few bumps and bruises, they're fine." Kaye walked around the desk and over to the children. "Come on. I'll introduce you."

"I really don't think—"

"They've been waiting on you. They've been begging me to send for you, actually."

Reluctantly, Simon followed Kaye. The young woman kneeled down by the kids.

"This is Emma," Kaye said, "and this is Stephen."

Emma stuck her hand out, then elbowed the boy to get him to do the same.

"Hi." Simon shifted his helm which he carried under his arm, and pulled the glove from his right hand. He shook hands briefly.

"You're the one who saved us," the little girl said.

Simon didn't know what to say to that.

"Yes," Kaye said. "He is." She looked at Simon. "From what I hear, what he did was a very brave thing."

Feeling embarrassed and uneasy, Simon wanted more than anything to escape the encounter. Nothing good could come of this if Booth heard about it. He started to make his departure.

"Thanks for saving my mom," the little girl said. "I was really scared that the monsters were going to find us before Daddy came home."

Simon was surprised at how strongly emotion moved within him. After learning of his father's death, after seeing how many deaths had happened in London, the child's simple thank-you touched him more than anything had in a long time.

"You're welcome," Simon said. "But it wasn't just me. There were others."

"I know. But you're the one who came in after us."

Simon smiled. "I couldn't leave you."

"You could have," Emma said. "Others did. When Mom got sick and we couldn't wake her up, I went to some of the neighbors that lived around us and tried to get them to help us. No one wanted to come out of their houses."

Thinking about the little girl running through the streets knocking on doors, easy prey for the demons, almost made Simon sick.

"Well then," Simon said, "I'm glad you asked me." He squatted down to look her in the eye. "You did a very brave thing coming out to stop me."

The little girl smiled a little bigger. "I knew you would save us. You had to. You're a knight in shining armor."

Simon knew his armor didn't shine. It was covered in soot and debris from the battle. Blood: his own and that of demons and other Templar. "I'm not—"

"You are," Kaye interrupted, smiling, too. "We've all got to have something to believe in these days, don't we?"

"Do you know King Arthur?" Stephen asked. "Have you gotten to meet him?"

"No."

"Oh." The little boy seemed disappointed. "Mom reads King Arthur to us a lot. King Arthur is my favorite hero. The legends say that Arthur will return when Britain needs him most."

Simon grinned, remembering the times his father had read some of the classics to him when he was small. It had been apparent that his father had loved those stories, and even seen what the Templar were doing as noble and heroic. Simon had never bought into that, but he'd never before felt the way he did now.

"I always liked Sir Gawain," Simon said.

Emma took a strip of blue cloth from her pocket. Without a word, she approached Simon and wrapped the strip

around the armor at his biceps. She tied it into a bow and
stepped back.

"It's a favor," Emma said.

Touched, Simon nodded. "I know."

"I hope it brings you luck."

"Thank you."

"All right then," Kaye said, standing again. "I think we'd
better let Simon go rest. He's been up for a long time."

The children said a final good-bye and returned to their
mother's room.

"I've put cots in there for them," Kaye said.

"If they need anything," Simon said.

"We'll take care of them. Don't you worry about that.
But you do need to rest. You look as though you're ready to
keel over."

Simon felt like it, too. He'd been on his guard around
Booth, but the fatigue was kicking in again. He told her
thanks and good-bye, then headed back to the barracks.

The barracks were quiet when Simon returned. Only a
few Templar were there, telling him without looking that
it was daylight. The Underground tried to maintain a
day/night rotation that matched the outside world. Even
with the chaos that had consumed London, evidently the
effort was still being made.

He stripped out of the armor, exchanging a few com-
ments with some of the other men from Derek's unit before heading to the showers with a towel and a pair of sweat
pants.

Standing under the shower, he felt guilty about resting
while other Templar might even now be out in the streets
fighting for their lives while he was preparing for bed. The
hot spray broke stinging needles against his skin.

You can't be everywhere at once, Simon, his father had

told him. *When it comes to fighting, you'll get more than your share of it. But when the demons come, it won't be one encounter or one day. They'll come in strength. The Templar taught them they would have to do that when we fought during the Crusades. When they come, you'll fight until you're sick of it. So when your mates step into the fray to carry the burden of it for a time, do yourself and them a favor by letting them.*

Images of the battle played through Simon's mind again. Most prominent in his thoughts, though, was the helplessness in the girl's face when she'd come to him.

Would another Templar have helped her? Would he or she have gone against Booth's wishes and simply stuck to the mission?

Or would that Templar have left her there to die?

Simon couldn't believe they would have been asked to do something like that. Not all of the Templar Houses could possibly feel that way. There were a lot of people still trapped in London. He'd seen their campfires.

When the Dark Times come, Simon, we'll have to be the light that leads humanity out of the night. We can do that. It's our destiny.

Some destiny, Simon thought sourly. *I ran off and wasn't here when you needed me, and High Seat Booth wants us to sit back and watch innocents die. That's not what I expected from the Templar, not what I want to be part of.*

No longer able to take the heat, Simon turned the shower to full cold for fifteen shivering seconds, then stepped out, dried himself, and pulled on the sweat pants.

When he stepped to the door, he was confronted by a tall, powerfully built woman with short-cropped red hair. She wore a cropped t-shirt, sweat pants, and sneakers.

"Simon Cross," she snarled. "You got my sister killed tonight!"

Before Simon could think of anything to say, the red-head doubled her fist and slammed it into his jaw. She put enough muscle and weight behind the blow to knock him backward. His feet slipped on the wet tiles and he went down. In the next instant, the woman straddled him and curled both hands into fists. She attacked without hesitation, driving blows into his face.

THIRTY-SIX

"T emperance! Temperance, get off of him!"

The woman scored hit after hit, bruising Simon's face with punishing force. Someone pulled at her from behind, but she locked her legs around Simon's midsection even tighter. With her seated on his chest and squeezing him in the middle, he had a hard time catching his breath.

Bucking his hips up, Simon lifted himself and the woman from the floor. Then he reached across his body with his right arm and slammed his hand against the inside of the woman's right elbow, trapping her right wrist in his left hand. Using the leverage provided by the grip, he pulled her weight to the side, dumped her off of him, and stood.

He'd no more than got to his feet when someone else delivered a roundhouse kick to his face. Simon barely got his hands up in time, palms turned out and open to cushion the blow across the meaty parts of his forearms. Grabbing the leg with one hand as the new attacker tried to pull it back, Simon shifted and uncoiled a side kick to the center of the man's chest and knocked him back against the tiled wall. The man hit the wall hard enough to knock tile from the wall.

Breathing hard, vision blurred by pain and tears, one eye already swelling closed, Simon turned to the redhead as she scrambled up. She attacked at once, throwing a series of punches and kicks.

Simon blocked the attempts as quickly as the woman threw them. She was good, though, and several of them connected with his face and stomach. He knew he was in trouble if he tried to fight defensively. He was taller and heavier, and had more reach. But the cramped quarters of the showers took away all those natural advantages. He was easily inside her reach, and his larger size made him easier to hit and impeded his own efforts.

Avoiding the woman, Simon wrapped his arms around her from behind, pinning her arms against her sides. She headbutted him in the mouth, sending comets erupting into his vision. Then she lifted her arms like she was going to perform a jumping jack while bending her knees and dropping slightly. She slid right out of his grasp and delivered a spinning side kick to his temple.

Knowing he could no longer fight defensively, Simon caught the woman's foot before she could draw it back. He swept her other foot from beneath her with his own and tripped her to the ground.

Another man threw a punch at Simon's throat. Simon dodged to the side, flung his own arm up and locked it inside his attacker's, then stepped behind the man and yanked. The attacker left his feet in a rush and went flying, rebounding from one of the bathroom stalls with a harsh clang.

The woman scrambled to her feet, looking more intent than ever.

"Enough!" The harsh voice rang out inside the small enclosure.

Hands open at the sides of his face to defend himself, Simon stepped back.

A grizzled sergeant stepped into the room. "Attention!

Every one of you! Right now, or I'll have you up on charges and in a conditioning room running laps for the next twenty-four hours."

The Templar came to attention in a heartbeat. They weren't rested and weren't getting much sleep. No one wanted to give up what little time they had for relaxation and sleep.

Even Temperance stood at attention.

"What's going on?" the sergeant demanded.

"It's my fault, sergeant," Temperance said. "I came here to see Cross, to tell him what I thought of him getting my sister killed over noncombatants too stupid to leave London. Things got out of hand."

"Those people aren't too stupid to leave," another Templar said. "They can't leave. A lot of people are stuck in their homes because they lack the wherewithal to get out of the city. You've got invalids and children that would never survive the trip. If they ever made it out of the city."

"I said, that's enough," the sergeant roared. "Get back to your bunks. Every last one of you. Another word, another blow, and I'll make sure you regret it."

For a moment, the tension in the room held. Then Temperance turned away from Simon and walked back through the door. Those who had come with her followed.

Simon let out a tense breath.

The sergeant turned to him, then walked over and took his face in his hands. He was rough, but gentle and thorough. "You've got a cut over that eye that needs tending."

Simon pulled his head back. He felt blood running down the side of his face. "I'll be fine."

"That won't close on its own. Either we close it or you go to the infirmary."

"I don't want to go to the infirmary," Simon said.

"Fine." The sergeant snapped an order over his shoulder, sending one of the men with him scurrying for a med-kit.

"This is going to sting."

Simon sat on the floor in the bathroom as the sergeant had directed him. He had his hands crossed over his chest. He didn't think a sting was going to be any worse than the pain already throbbing in his face.

The sergeant's name turned out to be Brewster. He was taciturn but opinionated when he decided to let his thoughts be known. He flicked on the portable Nu-Skin cauterizer. The device powered up with an insect-like whine.

"One of the med-techs in the infirmary would do a better job of it," Brewster said.

"I want to get to bed," Simon said. "Getting to the infirmary and back, and waiting, will take too long." Plus, he wasn't sure if he'd make it under his own power.

"They'd also have some slap-patches for pain."

"I don't think a really deep sleep would be safe," Simon replied.

Brewster grinned sympathetically. "Prolly not. Temperance Caine isn't known for her forgiving ways. But she went easy on you."

"You could have fooled me."

"If she'd have wanted you dead, you'd have been dead before you ever saw it coming." Brewster leaned in. "Now hold still."

The cauterizer hissed as it made contact with Simon's flesh. Pain bit into his head just above his eye. He forced himself to keep breathing through it, and he tried to push it away from himself, denying the pain and its hold over him. He almost succeeded.

"Nearly done," Brewster advised.

"All right." Simon smelled cooked meat. The cauterizer was quick and efficient, pulling a cut together, then bonding it with searing heat and a line of Nu-Skin, a hypoallergenic layer of protein-sub that gradually broke down as a wound finished healing.

True to his word, Brewster finished in just seconds. He stood and put the cauterizer back into the med-kit and handed it off to the Templar that had gotten it for him.

"How do you feel?" Brewster asked.

"It hurts."

The Templar laughed a little. "Give it a few hours. It'll feel better."

Simon forced himself to his feet. His head protested, flipping woozily. For a second, the room spun.

Brewster grabbed his arm and helped steady him.

"I've got it." Simon pulled his arm away, resenting the fact that the others could see the weakness in him.

"Sure you do." Brewster stood back, though.

Crossing to the sink, Simon peered into one of the mirrors. The line of Nu-Skin looked slightly pinker than the rest of his forehead. His face was the real proof of the pudding, though. Bruises decorated his cheeks, chin, and forehead.

"Temperance did a good job," Brewster said. "You have to give her that."

"Yeah." Simon dipped up a double handful of water and washed his face. "Her sister was one of those who died tonight?"

Brewster's face grew more solemn. "Charity. Yes. They were close. They were the last family either of them had. Both their parents died at St. Paul's."

Simon felt bad for the young woman.

"What you did tonight," Brewster said, "saving that woman and those two kids?"

"I know," Simon said. "I screwed up."

"Will it happen again?" Brewster's face showed keen interest.

Simon thought about how best to answer the question. He didn't know. Not without a shadow of a doubt. "Probably. If I see someone who needs help and I think I can help them." He took in a deep breath, thinking he'd just successfully killed his career and would be put out on the street.

"Good," Brewster said, smiling. "When I became a man and made the decision to join the Templar, I did it because I wanted to help people. I know that High Seat Booth is presenting a case against it, and he's got good reasons in light of everything, but there are a lot of people out there who feel the way I do."

Simon stared at the man's reflection in the mirror.

"What you did tonight, saving that woman and those kids," Brewster said softly, "that took courage. Despite Booth's threats, there are a lot of us who respect what you did. When Temperance calms down, I think you're going to find she respects you, too. After all, her sister stuck it out with you."

Simon blotted his face dry, careful of the Nu-Skin.

"If you want," Brewster offered, "I'll post a guard over this barracks. Make sure you get a good night's sleep."

"No, but thanks anyway."

"Suit yourself. If you need anything, give me a call."

Simon said that he would. In the mirror, he watched the sergeant and his men leave. Simon remained there a little longer, waiting for the pain to subside. But it didn't. Not then.

He retreated to his rack and tried to sleep. It was hard because he could feel the stares of the others in the room. Finally, fatigue pulled him down into the darkness, but it was infested with demons that kept rising from the dead no matter how many times he killed them.

Hours later, still in some pain and aches, Simon stood in front of the dorm where Leah was staying. He wore his armor but carried his helm under his left arm. He knocked.

A young woman with long brown hair and milk chocolate skin answered the door, peering up at him. "Simon Cross," she said. Her dark eyes glittered.

Simon didn't know her, so he had to assume that the Templar were talking about him. "Sorry. I must have the wrong dorm. I was looking for Leah Creasey."

"You have the right dorm." The young woman leaned back against the door frame and crossed her arms over her chest. "She was here."

"*Was?*"

"She left."

That threw Simon for a moment. "Where did she go?"

"I don't know. I was rooming with her. When I came back from rotation this afternoon, she was gone."

"Maybe she's just out getting something to eat." Simon doubted that, though. He'd checked the commissary before coming to Leah's assigned quarters.

"All of her things are gone," the young Templar said. "And a spare Spike Bolter from the weapons cache I keep with me these days."

Why would she take that? Even if she didn't feel safe in the Underground, she knows better than to try to go around armed here. I should have talked to her after I got back last night.

There was every possibility that Leah had heard what happened and figured that whatever protection Simon was able to provide for her might be gone. He'd slept almost eleven hours. That was unusual for him. Even more unusual, Derek had given orders not to disturb him.

Of course, there's always the possibility that Booth made her leave.

Except for the matter of the missing Spike Bolter.

"She was here this morning?" Simon peered into the room.

The dorm was small, barely enough room for two people. They were usually reserved for married couples who didn't have children.

"She was here when I left," the Templar replied. "I haven't told anyone she's gone yet."

"Why not?"

"Because I'll be reassigned to barracks and I've enjoyed having the semi-privacy of the room. Leah was easy to be around. Except for all the questions."

"Questions?"

"She asked a lot of questions."

"About what?"

The Templar shrugged. "About everything, I suppose. The Templars primarily. Seeing as how she was dragged down into the Underground, I figured that was natural."

Simon thought it was too. But Leah's disappearance—with a Spike Bolter—didn't seem natural. "Did she say anything about leaving?"

"This morning?"

"At any time."

The Templar shook her head. "She talked about her father a lot. Wanting to know what happened to him. If he was all right. I didn't blame her."

"Did she leave a note?"

"No." She stepped back. "You're welcome to come in and look around if you want to, but there's nothing here."

"That's all right. I've got to get back to my unit. We're going out tonight."

The woman frowned at him and trailed fingers over his

face. Even the slight contact hurt. "You don't look as though you're up to it."

"I'm fine."

She pulled her hand back. "If you say so."

"Leah may come back," Simon said, even though he doubted it. "If she does, could you tell her that I'd like to talk to her?"

"Sure. But since she took my Spike Bolter, I don't think she's coming back. That's not something you can just say, 'Oops, didn't mean to take that,' you know?"

Simon knew that. "If she comes back."

The woman nodded. "I'll tell her."

Simon turned and walked away. He felt the woman staring after him.

"Hey, Cross," she called.

Simon stopped and looked back at her.

"Be safe out there," she said in a softer voice. "What you did last night was really cool, but not everybody thinks so. You may find that your mates no longer have your back as well as they might have."

Simon already knew that. "Thanks."

"My name's Vivian." The Templar shrugged. "I don't always agree with the High Seat's rules of engagement, either. If you need a friend, I'm here." She frowned. "At least until they reassign me."

Simon nodded. "Thanks." Then he turned and got back under way. If he hurried, he had time to check with security before he had to join the unit.

The security detail over the operations center weren't enamored of Simon. He knew that from the cold reception he got. But they were willing to show him the vid footage of Leah Creasey leaving the Underground at the Baker Street tube station.

Equipment filled the security center. Lights flashed and some of the units hummed. Dozens of viewscreens opened windows on different parts of the Underground, the city, and the tube lines. The demons were present aboveground and in the tube lines.

Simon stood silent and watchful as they brought up the vid showing Leah's departure. The time/date stamp showed that she'd left early that morning, roughly about the time Simon was having his face cauterized.

She'd gone by herself, a backpack slung across her shoulders. Her expression was grim and resolute. The security vid kept her in sight until she stepped out of the tube station. She never looked back. Then she was gone.

"Why didn't someone stop her?" Simon asked. He felt guilty that he hadn't been there for her, but there'd been no way. Only his compliance with his assignments had allowed them to stay there.

"No one was told to," the young security officer said. The instrument panels limned his face green and blue in the semidarkness. "She was your *guest*. Your responsibility if you wanted her to stay."

"She's out there alone," Simon said before he could stop himself.

"There are a lot of people out there alone, Cross," the sergeant said. "At least that one had a choice about staying here where it was safe."

"Safe until we rile the demons up and bring them back to us," someone in the back said in a low voice.

"Is there anything else?" the sergeant asked, ignoring the comment from the back.

"No." Simon thanked him and left, feeling confused. It didn't make sense for Leah to leave. She was safe in the Templar Underground.

Her father's out there, he reminded himself. Then just as

quickly he told himself that Leah would realize that the chances of her father still being alive were incredibly small.

He tried to remember if she'd ever given him her father's address. They'd talked about it. He could remember that. But he'd never written an address down. Nor could he remember if she'd ever told him. It was possible that he had forgotten she had.

Frustrated and impatient, conscious of the stares of Templar he passed in the corridor, Simon pulled his helmet on. It sealed and the HUD came online. He had four minutes to make his rendezvous with his team. He tried to focus, knowing that he was about to put his life on the line again.

THIRTY-SEVEN

A mournful howl woke Warren from the cold dead blackness that cocooned him. He'd expected to wake up in the Cabalist infirmary. After all the pain Naomi had sent into his mind, he couldn't imagine waking up anywhere else.

Instead, he found himself in a room made of burnt orange glass. Or maybe it was crystal. Warren wasn't sure. He was sure he had never seen anything like it.

The material was translucent. The walls were thin enough that he had a sense of the world beyond them. Other buildings cascaded across a broken skyline, orderly, yet somehow jarring, as if something were missing.

The floor was evidently much thicker, because a few inches in, it turned ink-black. He knew he wasn't at ground level because the view through the walls showed that he was quite some distance up.

Symbols adorned the walls. The light source was a ball filled with glowing spiders, each about as big as his fist. They crawled over each other and, though they never created any shadows, the light's intensity wavered.

Warren was surprised to find he was standing, but he was. The golden light from the spider ball gleamed against the greenish black scales showing on his left arm. He turned, looking around the room and wondering what he was doing there.

Did Naomi send me here, or is this just a dream? For a moment, it crossed his mind that he might be dead and this was someplace beyond the life that he had known. But he rejected that. If he was dead, he was sure he would know.

"Welcome, Devourer," a loud voice boomed.

Instinctively, Warren stepped back toward the nearest wall, wanting to limit an attacker's choice of approach. The room remained empty and he didn't know where the voice had come from. The burnt orange glass or crystal, or whatever it was, of the wall behind him felt warm to the touch.

"What would you have?" the voice asked.

Hesitant, but not feeling anyone else in the room, having no place to hide, Warren said, "I don't understand."

"I can explain. You have but to ask."

"Ask what?" Warren listened but there was no telltale echo to let him know the voice was coming from any other room than the one he was in.

"Whatever you wish to know."

"Why am I here?" Warren pushed himself free of the wall and stepped toward the back of the room. There, barely revealed in the light, was a rectangular shadow in the burnt orange that might be a doorway. As he neared it, he saw that it was a door that sat at an angle to him and was hard to see.

"You are here because you wish to be here."

"No. I didn't come here on my own. I didn't know about this place, so there was no way I could wish to be here."

"Merihim the Bringer of Pestilence opened your way to this place."

Cautiously, Warren stepped through the door. It opened onto another room, this one as empty as the first. "Where am I?"

"This is the Hall of Weapons," the voice said. Now it

appeared to be coming from the center of the next room.

Warren considered the information. "Why would Merihim open this place to me?"

"So you may learn more about that which you must seek."

"What am I supposed to seek?"

"The Hammer of Balekor."

Confusion twisted tightly inside Warren, but he was intrigued as well. "What is that?"

"A magnificent weapon. It was lost to the human world hundreds of years ago."

"What does it do?"

"It kills. It destroys. The hammer is one of the most powerful weapons ever created by Vegalok."

"Who was Vegalok?"

"A smith of the Dark Forge," the voice replied. "It was his strong right arm that smithed many of the personal weapons of the Dark Wills."

Warren wanted to ask what the Dark Wills were, but he was afraid to. "Tell me more about the Hammer of Balekor."

"What do you wish to know?"

That stumped Warren for a moment. He hadn't expected to be asked that question. It stood to reason that if the voice knew how he came to be there, it would also know why.

"Tell me about the hammer's history."

"After Vegalok made it, he presented it to Passapar, the Bringer of Flashing Ruin."

A demon, Warren thought. "Why was it made?"

"As a weapon of war."

"Against whom?"

"Whomever Passapar wished to wage war on."

"Where is Passapar?"

"Dead. Not yet resurrected."

Not yet resurrected? The announcement chilled Warren. Even if the demons could be killed, they could be resurrected? He hadn't guessed that. Fighting them was futile then.

"Where is the hammer?" Warren asked. He had to survive, and if Merihim had staked his survival on finding the hammer, Warren intended to find it.

"It was lost in the human world centuries ago," the voice continued.

"If the hammer isn't here, then why am I?"

"Because you came."

Warren chose not to argue the point. He walked to the nearest wall and peered out at the jagged skyline of the city. "Is this the world of the demons?"

The voice didn't answer for a moment. "I will accept your designation of those who live here as 'demons.' The term has been used before."

"Is there another name?"

"There are many other names. You may give them another if you wish."

"No." Evil grew as it got more names. Warren remembered that from the books his mother had read. "You said this was a place of the Dark Wills."

"Yes."

"What is a Dark Will?"

"A ranking within the demon hierarchy. A demon warrior must kill billions to achieve this designation."

"Is Merihim a Dark Will?"

"Not yet. But he aspires to be."

"Will getting the Hammer of Balekor help Merihim achieve that designation?"

"Yes."

Then I'm going to be helping him, Warren realized.

"You will be helping him," the voice said. "You should rejoice."

"Why?"

"Because Merihim might choose to be generous."

"And if he chooses not to be generous?"

"Then he will destroy you."

Nausea twisted through Warren's stomach, but he managed to keep control of himself. He didn't know what would happen if he got sick inside the tower.

"What does the hammer do?" he whispered.

"It controls the darkness," the voice replied. "It casts withering black fire, controls the elements, and opens gateways in Shadow."

"Shadow?"

"The places that lie between the worlds. The possessor of the Hammer of Balekor can draw up the dead to fight at his side."

The announcement, delivered so matter-of-factly, left Warren chilled. He was being asked to be part of that? *Not being asked*, he reminded himself. *Being commanded. That's different. And if you don't do it, Merihim will kill you and find someone else to do his dirty work.*

Fleetingly, he wondered if Tulane and the Cabalists could save him from the demon if it came down to it. Once the question was posed, though, he immediately doubted it.

"Your time here grows short," the voice said. "Even with the way made open to you by Merihim, even he can't keep the way open for long. You must finish your task."

"How?"

"Come." One of the room's sides suddenly glowed brighter than the rest.

Feeling hypnotized, Warren crossed the room and stood in front of the wall.

An image took shape in the air before him, like a tri-dee coming to life. He recognized the war hammer from books he'd read while growing up. It looked like a Norse weapon, but the head was massive—over two feet in length and a foot wide and thick. It had to weigh a couple of hundred pounds. The black metal had crimson threads that ran through it. Most Viking hammers were four or five feet in length, but the handle on Balekor's weapon was at least eight. It might be unwieldy even for Merihim.

Before he knew what he was doing, Warren reached for the hammer. A green electrical shock leaped from the haft just before he touched it. Reeling, his hand spasmed and closed around the haft, passing through it without touching anything substantial.

"You're linked with the hammer, Devourer," the voice boomed. "Now find it for your master."

The blackness returned and pulled Warren down into it. He fought against it, trying to stave it off. The effort was pure reflex, though, because as he thought about it, he didn't want to stay in the tower, either. He just wanted some kind of control over his life. But he wasn't strong enough to stop the blackness from washing over him.

When Warren woke, he was freezing. He pulled weakly at the covers that lay across him and tried desperately to find more warmth. His thoughts spun dizzyingly, shattering against each other.

"Get me another blanket," a woman's voice said. "He's burning up with fever."

The rustling noises reached Warren, but he couldn't open his eyes even though he tried his hardest. He felt increased pressure over his body as another blanket was added. He clung to it gratefully.

"Were you able to stay with him?" a man's voice asked.

With the echoing in the room, or in his hearing, Warren barely recognized the voice as Tulane's.

"No." That was Naomi. "There was a barrier. I couldn't get around it."

"Do you think he managed to get there?"

"I don't know."

Warren's teeth chattered. His back and legs ached from shaking.

"His fever's nearly reached a hundred and five," another male voice said. Warren thought that one belonged to the doctor he'd met earlier. "We've got to get him into an alcohol bath before we lose him."

"He's going to be all right," Tulane said.

"You don't know that," the doctor argued.

"Merihim didn't contact him just to kill him."

"The demons have killed countless numbers of people. One more isn't going to make a difference."

"He's going to be all right."

Something touched Warren's head. It felt ice-cold.

"He's at a hundred and six," the doctor said. "If you don't let me treat him, he's going to die within minutes. He may be brain-damaged already."

Warren didn't know what would happen if his brain overheated. He'd heard about the danger of high fevers, but he didn't know what they actually did to the brain. Did it cook like an egg? Or did it melt like candle wax? He wasn't sure.

Tulane answered reluctantly. "All right. Treat the fever."

Immediately, several pairs of hands grabbed Warren and yanked him from the bed. He tried to fight against them, but he was too weak. They stripped his clothes from him, carried him across the brightly lit room, and lowered him into a waiting bath of freezing liquid. A fresh wave of nausea swirled through him.

"We shouldn't have let him go to the demon world," Naomi said.

"He didn't go," Tulane argued. "He remained here."

"His body didn't leave, but I felt his mind go. I couldn't keep up. Getting glimpses of the demon world is dangerous enough. Everyone who's ever been there has always come back insane or mentally damaged. We shouldn't have let him go."

"Naomi," Tulane said in a softer voice, "he's compelled by the demons. He's in thrall to Merihim. I don't think you could have stopped Warren from going even if you'd tried."

"I should have tried. What's happened to him . . . it's more than anyone has ever dealt with."

"We're all dealing with harsh times."

"We've been trained for this. We knew it was out there. Warren didn't."

For a moment, Warren felt good about the fact that Naomi cared enough to argue over him. But the sobering realization was that he'd probably never get to thank her because he was about to die.

Enough, Merihim said. *You're not this weak.*

The demon's voice speared agony through Warren's head. He jerked in the grasp of those who held him, almost exploding out of the tub. Startled shouts and curses rang out around him.

"He's convulsing!" the doctor shouted. "Hold him down or we're going to lose him!"

Warren fought, but he was pressed back down into the cold liquid.

You will not be held, Merihim commanded. *You are stronger than they are. Get free. Go find Balekor's Hammer before it falls into Templar hands.*

Unable to resist the order, Warren renewed his struggles. This time he felt the fever die inside his mind. Strength like he'd never known flooded through him. He pushed up from the tub, then swept a hand out, knocking the doctor and the medical attendants away from him, sprawling them across the room and the floor.

"Stop him!" Tulane cried.

Naomi darted forward, her hand raised.

Moving more quickly than he thought he could, Warren caught the woman's hand. "No," he said.

She stared into his eyes, then he felt the power surge from her. The last time, it had knocked him out. But this time he short-circuited it, never letting it leave her flesh.

"No," he repeated, more gently this time. He released her hand and allowed her to step back from him. Another feeling dawned within him, a siren's call that urged him into motion. "I have to go."

"Why?" Tulane demanded.

"Where are my clothes?" Warren stepped from the tub and looked around the room. He didn't see his clothes anywhere. He didn't see Kelli, either. "Where's Kelli?"

"You're not leaving," Tulane said.

"We sedated Kelli," Naomi said. "When you started convulsing, she began screaming like she was in pain."

Warren continued the search for his clothing. "Is she all right?"

"I don't know."

What if she isn't? If something happened to her, it's your fault. Warren struggled with the guilt he suddenly felt, then pushed it away and concentrated on finding his clothes. They had to be somewhere in the room.

"I said, you're not leaving." Tulane stepped in front of Warren.

Angry and feeling trapped, Warren turned on the man. "I am leaving, and I'm leaving now."

"We'll see about that." Tulane barked orders.

Instantly the room filled with armed Cabalists in security gear.

Do not let them stop you, Merihim commanded.

Unconsciously, Warren squatted and slapped his left hand—the one that was covered in the greenish-black scales—against the floor. He operated on instinct, unleashing the power inside him.

Immediately, pale violet electrical bolts sped through the floor and reached the men. When it touched them, they were blown into the air and fell down, unconscious to a man.

Standing again, Warren spun around and grabbed Tulane with his left hand, bunching the man's shirt and coat in his left fist. He lifted Tulane almost effortlessly from the floor, realizing that he could just as easily have thrown the man from the room.

"I'm leaving," Warren said. "You can't stop me. You *won't* stop me." He used some of his old power, the one that he had grown up with and was most familiar with. "Do you understand?"

Tulane fought against the persuasion. Sweat blossomed on his brow and his face knotted up.

"It's the demon." Naomi came around the side, stepping into Warren's view but addressing Tulane. "The demon is siphoning power into him. I can't do anything."

"All right," Tulane said. "You can leave. But let us come with you. There's so much we can learn."

No, Merihim said.

Warren fought against the demon's wishes, but it was hard. Still, there was a part of him that wanted to be in control.

"I can help you," Tulane said. Despite his effort at appearing calm, Warren could smell the stink of fear on the man. "What are you going to do? Leave here on foot? I can put vehicles at your disposal."

You will not let him come, Merihim said.

Releasing his hold, Warren dropped Tulane. The man slid bonelessly to the floor. "Do whatever you want," Warren said. "Bring me my clothes."

A few minutes later, dressed and still feeling strong, Warren stepped from the Cabalists' house and into the large landscaped yard. Tulane already had the panel truck waiting.

You won't defy me, human, Merihim said. *I can kill you where you stand.*

Warren closed his eyes and shut out the demon's voice for a moment. He concentrated on the urging that filled him. Almost immediately, an image popped into his head.

It was somewhere down on the River Thames. The building was a large, rambling affair, dark now because the city's power was off. He struggled to read the faded name painted across the building's brick walls.

HOLDSTOCK GLASSWORKS MANUFACTURING.

"I can get you what you want," Warren whispered to the demon. And he knew that he would. He was too afraid of Merihim not to. "But I can't do it alone. I need their help."

When there was no further argument from the demon, Warren joined Tulane and Naomi in the panel truck. The vehicle was packed. Another followed behind them as they pulled through the gates and sped out onto the road.

"Do you know where we're going?" Naomi asked.

"Yes." Warren ignored Tulane's baleful stare. The Cabalist leader was less of a threat than the demon, and at the moment Warren knew that he had enough power to save himself from Tulane. Even if he was doing the demon's bidding, it was enough that he knew he had enough power to save himself. The realization was comforting.

"Where?" she asked.

Warren ignored the question and looked through the

front windshield. London's tall buildings could be seen in the distance.

"Warren," Naomi tried again.

"No," he told her. "You'll know when you need to."

"What about the other demons?" Tulane asked. "Will we be protected from them?"

"No."

"Then this is foolish."

"You can leave if you want."

For a moment, Tulane glared at him, then broke eye contact and looked away.

Warren didn't let the other man's animosity bother him. He was more worried about surviving the coming encounter. Part of whatever the arcane spell was that tied him to Balekor's Hammer also told him others were searching for it as well. He didn't know if he would live to see morning, but he was going to do everything within his power to see that he did.

THIRTY-EIGHT

The deadest light of the day came at dusk. Light drained from the sky, leaving the world monochromatic gray and black, the two colors blending into each other effortlessly. Mornings came with some color that intensified, but evenings only got darker until it was night.

Dusk was also the most dangerous time of day. Many predators naturally came out at that time to hunt, staking out water holes and game trails. They went where prey gathered.

As it turned out, many of the demons held that same predatory inclination. And much of their prey gathered inside buildings, hunkered around fires too small to stave off the bitter winter cold.

Crouched in the shadows of a manufacturing plant not far from Queen Anne's Docks, Simon watched as Darkspawn and Gremlins hunted through the streets. He'd seen only the bodies of humans, and some of those had been freshly killed. Sickness twisted in his stomach and he barely kept it at bay.

Gazing out along the Thames, Simon spotted more demons along the London Bridge. Cars littered the bridge, many of them burned-out hulks. Several boats and ships floated out on the river as well, creating a mire of vessels that would make navigation through them almost impossible. Dense fog eddied at the river's edge, thicker than was normal at this time of year. Light snow fell in tight, dry flakes no bigger than shirt buttons.

Blood Angels circled over the river, occasionally dropping down to the ships. They rose again almost immediately, clutching corpses in their claws.

"What are they doing with the bodies?" someone asked.

"Prolly eating them," another said.

As a Blood Angel descended toward a boat, the vessel suddenly powered up and sped away. The demon changed directions in mid-descent and took off in pursuit. It screamed, and the piercing shriek could be heard plainly where Simon was concealed.

Three other Blood Angels leaped from London Bridge and shot toward the fleeing boat as well. They closed rapidly, wings drumming fiercely.

Simon increased the magnification on the HUD, locking onto the frantic figures taking up defensive positions onboard the boat. The crew raised their weapons, but they were standard military arms, light machine guns and machine pistols that did nothing to the demons. The tracer rounds stopped dead against the demons' hides.

Ignoring the gunfire, the Blood Angels swooped to the deck and began rending the crew. Claws flashed and the dead dropped to the ground.

The boat's pilot abandoned his post and leaped over the side. He hit the water and went under just before the boat slammed into a cargo ship and exploded into a ball of flame. The sound of the explosion reached Simon after the flaming debris started descending into the river.

The pilot surfaced several yards away, coming up long enough for a breath of air, then diving back under to swim some more. A Blood Angel skimmed the water toward his last position. When the man surfaced again, the demon was there. She grasped him by the head and one shoulder, claws digging in cruelly. The man kicked and fought but to no avail. Almost effortlessly, the Blood Angel carried her prize into the dark sky.

The remains of the boat burned for a time before sinking below the river's surface. Flames clung to the side of the cargo ship, but the metal sides quickly burned clean. Within minutes, the Thames was once more dark.

None of the Templar spoke. And the demons kept taking corpses.

"The river level's dropping," Wertham said. "It's five, maybe six feet lower than it was before the Hellgate opened."

Accompanied by a small group of Templar, Simon surveyed the Thames. Their objective lay close to the river's edge and they were currently only twenty yards distant. He couldn't tell any difference in the river.

"Are you sure?" Naughton asked.

"I am," Wertham replied. "I fished this river every day for the last thirty years. I didn't spend all my time in the Underground the way some did. I had my fishing business. And I'm telling you the river is lower than it's ever been. It must have something to do with what the demons are doing."

Reports had continued to come in concerning the changes being made in the landscape around St. Paul's Cathedral. The Burn—which was what the Templar had taken to calling the manifestation—was growing larger every day, consuming everything in its path. Part of it had overlapped the Thames.

"You think the demons are behind this?" Naughton asked.

"I can't think of another reason," Wertham answered.

"That's impossible. Even if the Burn was capable of affecting the river, the Thames feeds into the North Sea. They can't be draining an ocean."

Simon heard the nervousness in the man's voice. None of them knew for certain what the demons were capable of.

"Could be they're draining the water from the locks," Wertham said. "There are forty-five locks along the Thames. If the locks were closed, they could drain the river."

"They wouldn't close the locks," Cedric Southard said. Like Simon, Cedric was young, but he was black and intense, normally quiet.

"And why not?" Naughton asked.

"Because that would shut off people's escape routes," Cedric replied. His dark red and gold-trimmed armor glimmered slightly in the shadows. "The river's still the fastest way out of London and the interior of England."

Simon knew that was true. But if the locks weren't closed, they had to accept that not only could the demons drain the River Thames, but they were capable of draining the oceans of the world, too.

"And if they drain the river," Cedric said, "that's going to pull the sea in. Instead of fresh water here, we'll have brackish, with the salt mixing with the fresh. They already got that problem in the lowlands."

That thought was too horrible to contemplate. The environmental changes alone would cripple humanity's efforts to survive. A lot of food came from the sea, and without the sea to provide airborne moisture in the form of rain, crops on land wouldn't receive the necessary irrigations. Crops, livestock, and wild game would die out. But fresh water was the key to all of it.

After a few more minutes of sober silence, Derek's scouts returned, informing them that there was a problem.

* * *

"We found the private museum where we were told it would be," Mercer said. He was short and wiry, a perfect scout. "But someone got there before us."

"Who?" Derek asked.

The Templar's disgust tightened his voice. "A group of those demon-worshipping Cabalists."

"They don't worship the demons. They study them."

"The Cabalists want to leave the demons alive," Mercer growled. "For me, that's enough to put the Cabalists in the enemy camp. I don't trust them."

"They helped Lord Sumerisle gather the information he needed to stage the attack on St. Paul's Cathedral."

Mercer cursed. "By morning, whose blood was it that soaked into the battlefield there?"

Derek didn't say anything.

"The Cabalists didn't fight and die with us," Mercer went on. "That tells you something. They're more interested in saving their own necks."

Simon had yet to see the Cabalists, though he had heard about them. He didn't know how he felt about them, either. Anyone that wanted to study the demons was suspect in his book.

"They're making themselves look like the demons," Mercer went on. "They wear demon armor and are covered with tattoos. Some of these I saw had horns. Not horns that you wear, but ones growing right out of their heads. Some of them look like they're wearing lizard skins, only it's their flesh and not some kind of garment."

"Could be they're trying to pass as demons," someone offered. "As a disguise, maybe."

"And maybe they're trying to worship the demons," Mercer snarled. He spat. "I'd just as soon kill 'em all."

"What are the Cabalists doing at the museum?" Derek asked.

"I don't know. There's a manufacturing plant there. Used to be Holdstock Glassworks before they closed it down a few years back."

Simon knew why the Cabalists' presence there troubled Derek so much. Even though the Cabalists had remained separate—for the most part—from the Templar, they still apparently knew a great many things from their own studies of the demons.

"Well then," Derek said, "let's go see what's brought the Cabalists out."

The Templar stayed in the shadows of the back alleys and skirted the riverfront. The dead littered the way. Some of them had been there since the demons had arrived, but others looked fresh.

Tense minutes later, Simon fell into position with his group and scanned the museum with the thermographic display capabilities of the HUD.

Located next to the manufacturing plant that had closed nearly thirty years ago but hadn't yet been revitalized, the Turnbull Museum was a privately owned collection that extended visitation privileges to only a few. From what Derek had told them earlier, Geoffrey Turnbull had been something of an adventurer and had journeyed to the far corners of the earth gathering artifacts. His taste, and his collection, had been eclectic. An invited guest might find a shrunken head from the wilds of Borneo as easily as he could find Ashanti pottery or Mongolian trade coins.

However, what no one had known until lately, was that Geoffrey Turnbull also had a taste for the arcane. This information the Templar had ferreted out from the same document they'd gotten their hands on that had told them of Robert Thornton's cursed book. When they'd learned that, the Templar team hadn't exactly been excited about the prospect. The story about the book devouring Bruce was still fresh in their minds.

What the Templar were there to find was a hammer that was supposedly forged by a demon blacksmith. The entry regarding the weapon called it Balekor's Hammer. It was supposed to have the power to open gateways into the demon world.

The Templar hoped to use that power to their advantage. But, failing that, they wanted it safely locked away so the demons couldn't use it.

The museum occupied the bottom two floors of a six-story building. The upper four floors held small business offices and storage areas. If the information they'd received was correct, Turnbull had another museum holding even more exotic items secretly hidden in a sub-basement level no one but the builders had known about. Wealth had its privileges, and the wealthy enjoyed their secrets.

Across the alley, the Cabalists entered the manufacturing plant.

Simon used the magnification application in the HUD to take a closer look at them. Their appearance, most of them looking like demons themselves with their grafted-on horns and demon-hide armor, put him off at once. He couldn't muster much sympathy for them.

The sight of the two women in the ranks of the Cabalists reminded Simon of Leah Creasey. He wondered why the young woman had left the Templar Underground, but realized that she might have been just as put off by the Templar as he was by the Cabalists.

Derek called for the scouts, then got them moving once again. They froze against the alley wall as a Blood Angel flew by overhead. Then they resumed their approach to the museum.

* * *

A thick chain secured the museum's main doors. The broken windows overhead offered mute testimony that someone had broken into the building, though. The occasional scream sounded somewhere out on the river.

Simon couldn't help thinking about the people seeking refuge from the demons. None of them had been trained to fight the demons. *Or to survive in winter conditions when power to the city was nonexistent,* he added. Even if some of them managed to avoid getting killed by the demons, they wouldn't make it through the winter months.

Some of them would be children like the two he'd rescued. That didn't sit easily in his mind.

"Everybody go easy inside," Derek advised. "We may have innocents lurking."

The Templar acknowledged that, then Mercer gripped the chain in his mailed fists, pulled, and shattered a link. He stripped the chain from the doors and pushed them open.

THIRTY-NINE

Warren stepped into the darkness that filled the manufacturing plant. His physical senses relayed images of detritus and abandoned equipment, the sounds of the wind outside the building and the cries of the demons and their prey, the smell of must, and the biting cold that permeated the warehouse.

But it was other senses, ones that had grown steadily stronger since they'd left the Cabalist redoubt, that conveyed more to him than he'd ever believed possible. The new senses overlapped his accustomed ones, though, creating some confusion.

From the corner of his eye, he saw shadows of work and workers that had once filled the plant. The heavy steel pots that had carried molten glass in the past glowed cherry-red but held only shadows. The large furnaces were empty and blazing at the same time. Warren heard the whisper of voices, jokes, and curses, intermingled in the heavy silence enhanced by the layer of snow on the building. Heat mixed in with the cold, so hot and fierce that Warren wanted to take his coat off.

The past and the present were coming alive around him, intermingling so tightly that Warren had to work to focus on what was real. The problem was that it was all real. It just wasn't all right *now*.

"Is something wrong?" Naomi asked.

Warren forced himself to concentrate on the present, on the winter and the abandoned premises. "No. I'm just making sure."

"Do you know where the Hammer is?" Tulane asked.

Warren did. The feeling that had brought him here wasn't lost in the confusion of present and past. "Below us." He pointed toward the east wall, the one closest to the six-story building across the alley.

"Below?" Tulane gestured at his security men.

The guards spread out at once, searching the premises with infrared goggles instead of using the night sight Warren had learned. Most of Tulane's guards were unskilled in the ways of the Cabalist. They were selected because of their guard experience and weapons proficiency. Still, some of them were progressing in the Cabalist teachings.

Warren closed his eyes. Immediately an image of the warehouse mapped inside his head. He saw the floor plan as though from the side. A glowing purple tendril sprang from him and tracked directly north, away from the pull that he was certain revealed the presence of Balekor's Hammer. He watched as the tendril moved through a door, down a flight of steps, and to a wall in the basement.

There was no door, but Warren saw the hammer in a room-sized safe built into an adjoining room.

Opening his eyes, Warren said, "Wait. We're in the wrong building."

Tulane glared at him. "You said the Hammer was in here."

"I was wrong," Warren said, but at the same time he didn't know how he could be wrong.

Several of the Cabalists exchanged worried glances. None of them had been happy about returning to the city, much less the downtown area where the demon activity was still so prevalent.

"Which building is the right one?" Exasperation sounded in Tulane's demand.

"Next door," Warren said. "The Hammer is in—" Pain lanced through his head, so intense it temporarily made him blind.

Stop! Merihim's voice thundered inside Warren's head.

Dropping to his knees, unable to keep his balance, Warren threw up. Head pounding, stomach wracked, he noticed that no one tried to help him. The Cabalists all stepped back as if he were going to blow up. Considering the pressure inside his head, he thought that was entirely possible.

One of the security guards returned to Tulane and told him that the basement was practically empty and that there was no sign of a hammer or any other tool in the room.

"Not this building," Tulane said. "It's next door."

"The museum?" The guard sounded confused.

Naomi continued to watch Warren. He felt her eyes on him.

You can't enter the museum, Merihim said. *That way is protected from me. And—now—from you.*

Tulane and the guards started to leave.

Stop them!

The pain snapped Warren to his feet before he knew it. He threw out his left arm, the one mottled with all the demon scales, and cast the power from him. Flames blossomed in front of the door, drawing Tulane and the guards up short.

"No," Warren commanded hoarsely, and he knew it was Merihim's voice as much as his own.

The security guards yanked their weapons to shoulder and prepared to fire. One word from Tulane, and Warren knew that was exactly what they were going to do.

"You can't go that way," Warren said. "It's protected."

Tulane studied Warren, and Warren could almost read

the man's thoughts. Tulane was considering telling his guards to shoot.

"If they do," Warren whispered menacingly, "you won't live to see if they succeed."

Tulane frowned. But he didn't give the order to fire.

"We can get to the Hammer from here," Warren said.

"How?"

"Through the basement. That way isn't protected." Head throbbing, feeling Merihim's power bubbling inside him, Warren turned toward the door leading to the basement. For a moment he thought Tulane might have him killed then, but he heard their footsteps fall in behind him.

The basement steps spiraled down into a room almost as large as the one overhead. The stink of must and disuse grew stronger.

More sure-footed now, Warren walked toward the wall. It was featureless except for a few cracks. A huge furnace filled the opposite wall, but it was cold and dark with disuse.

You must hurry, Merihim said. *There are others who search for this prize as well.*

"Who?" Warren asked.

Don't concern yourself with them. Concentrate on your task here.

Surveying the huge wall, Warren couldn't see an entrance or a secret door. He pressed his palms against the rock and mortar. He could feel the Hammer on the other side of the wall even though he didn't know how he could do that.

"You're certain the Hammer is there?" Tulane asked.

"Yes."

Tulane barked a command to the security men. Half of them shouldered their weapons and approached the wall with knives, but it was quickly apparent they weren't going to be able to get through the wall quickly.

Kelli came to stand at Warren's side. She hadn't uttered a word in hours. No emotion showed on her face. Not even a flicker of interest at what they were doing. Warren took her hand and held it, drawing the warmth from her.

"Do you know what you're doing to her?" Naomi asked quietly.

Feeling defensive, Warren said, "I'm not doing anything to her."

Naomi's dark eyes studied him. "If not for you and your control over her, she wouldn't be here."

"If not for Malcolm, I wouldn't have met you," Warren said. Sometime during the testing phase, Malcolm had left the house. Warren presumed the man had gone back to London, or had other duties at the house. "If not for you and Tulane, I wouldn't be here."

"You'd be here," Naomi said. "The demon wanted you here."

One of the security team leaders told part of the team to go back upstairs and search for hammers and chisels, anything they could use to chop through the wall.

"The demon could have had me come here without ever meeting you," Warren pointed out.

"You came to us for other reasons."

"What reasons?" Warren felt frustrated. All of his life had been dictated to him by someone. First it had been his parents. Then it had been foster care. Lately it had been his flat mates, with their needs and disregard for him.

Naomi shook her head. "I don't know." She paused. "Do you hear Merihim?"

Warren hesitated.

"You do, don't you? You hear his voice."

"And what if I do?"

"I don't know. I've never met anyone who could talk to demons."

Warren laughed bitterly at that. "But all you people want to do is talk to them."

"That's not true. We want to learn their secrets, that's true. But talking to a demon, listening to it without the proper safeguards, is dangerous. In all my studies, that's been one of the constants. Our literature and culture are filled with tales of men and women who have sold their souls to demons. Do you think that's all fiction?"

Uneasiness flickered through Warren. "I haven't made any trades, deals, or bargains."

"Are you sure?" Naomi gazed quietly at him. "When you were burning, when you were falling, don't you think it's possible you did?"

Warren couldn't remember those incidents. Everything had happened too fast and been too filled with pain.

"Somewhere in all that confusion and agony," Naomi said, "are you sure you didn't reach out to *something* to save you?"

"I didn't. I would have remembered something like that."

"Would you have?" Naomi took a breath. "Demons are filled with trickery, Warren. That's their nature."

"And you want to be like them," he accused.

"No. I want to understand how they use the power they do. I can do a lot of good with it."

Warren sneered at her. "Is that why you're here? To do *good?*" He shook his head. "Everybody is out for whatever they can get. It's not about power. It's about power over others. That's what Tulane wants."

If Tulane heard the accusation, he gave no sign of it. The security men who'd gone upstairs returned with a few hammers and crowbars. They attacked the wall again, pulling out rocks they chopped free.

"You don't have to face this alone," Naomi said.

Warren tightened his grip on Kelli's hand. "I'm not alone."

"She wouldn't be here if you weren't controlling her mind."

"I'm not controlling her." Warren looked into Kelli's vacuous gaze and saw that she looked right through him. George's words screamed into his mind again.

"You are," Naomi replied. "And you may kill her."

She's dead anyway, Warren told himself. *She'll never make it out of the city. She's too weak.* He felt guilty at once for his thoughts. But he didn't feel guilty for having her with him. He'd been alone all his life. Now that he had the power to change that, he didn't see why he shouldn't use it.

"Do you want to kill her?" Naomi asked.

Warren looked away from her, staring into the cloud of mortar dust that had formed in front of the wall. He held Kelli's hand in his, afraid to let her go.

"You're afraid," Naomi said.

Warren ignored her.

"I can see it in you," she continued.

Looking at her then, Warren demanded, "Are you going to tell me you're not afraid?"

"No, I'm not going to tell you that. The truth is, I am afraid. But part of me is starting to be afraid of you."

Warren felt a surge of savage joy crest inside him at that unexpected announcement. But it died the moment one of the security guards poked his head into the hole that had been made in the wall.

"We're through," the man said. "There's a room over there. Filled with a lot of stuff."

Excitement flared within Warren. He released Kelli's hand and started forward. He felt Balekor's Hammer on the other side of the wall. It felt powerful, almost overwhelming.

Tulane was there first. The Cabalist reached into a pocket and removed a flash. Switching the beam on, he peered into the room. Then he stepped back, nodding at the security guard commander.

"Make the hole bigger."

Scratching noises drew Warren's attention. For a moment he thought it was coming from inside the room on the other side of the wall. Then he realized that it was a trick, an echo created by the size of the room. He turned back toward the furnace.

The scratching grew in intensity, coming from the hollow depths of the furnace. Several of the security guards faced the furnace as well and drew their weapons.

Light suddenly streamed from behind Warren. He turned back to the hole and the room on the other side of the wall, spotting a rectangular opening and a metallic figure that stepped into the room.

Then horrendous cries rose up from inhuman throats.

Spinning back around to the furnace, Warren watched as demons invaded the basement through the furnace's chimney. Looking like insects, they poured from the furnace in flailing masses and formed a skirmish line.

Get the Hammer, Merihim commanded.

Driven by pain, Warren turned back to the hole in the wall and instinctively put his hand out before him. He *pushed,* and he sensed more than glimpsed the waves of nearly invisible force that leaped from his hand.

The wall exploded, caving inward in a rush of mortar and stone. The armored figure inside the room was thrown backward.

Warren went forward as the demons rushed the Cabalists.

FORTY

From the darkness of the Turnbull Museum, frightened eyes studied Simon. He stared back at them over the Spike Bolter, adrenaline surging through his system. All of the Templar stood ready to fight.

"Don't fire!" Derek shouted. "Don't fire! These are non-combatants!"

Simon lowered his weapon, looking out over the museum. With the moonlight slivered through the swirling snow and the dusty windows, the fugitives hiding in the building would have been barely visible. Except for the night-vision capability of the HUD. But he was willing to bet that the people inside the building could barely see each other. He didn't know what the people must have thought of them as they came through the door.

The snow swirled in through the open door, white against the darkness, then disappeared on the floor as it melted almost at once. The cold came as well, more active and biting than it had been with the door closed. Several of the people taking shelter inside the museum pulled their coats and blankets more tightly around them. There were at least three dozen of them that Simon could see, but he felt certain there would be others scattered throughout the building.

Derek held his hand up, freezing the Templar into position. Then he cursed, frustrated by the turn of events that had put innocents in harm's way.

"What are these people doing here?" someone asked.
"Taking shelter," someone else answered.

Derek stepped forward, dropping his hand. His voice broadcast through the armor. "You people can't stay here," he said.

Simon knew Derek was remembering what had happened at the Thornton house with the book. The hammer they were after was known to have powers. All of the people inside the building would be in danger if they stayed.

A thin man in his fifties, gray and bent with age, stood to face them. "We can't go out there. This is the only safe place we've found. The demons don't come in here."

Looking around, Simon noticed there were no dead bodies like there were outside the building. Nor did the museum show signs of violence or combat. Most of the exhibits were long gone, leaving only empty shelves and floor displays, but they were largely undisturbed. Maybe thieves had come in over the years to pick over what had been left, but not demons. There was plenty of room for the makeshift beds that littered the floor.

"The museum must be warded," Derek said over the armor's privacy channel. "Someone laid a spell over this place and invoked some kind of sanctuary."

"Are you the knights?" the man asked quietly. He held a long kitchen knife in one hand, but he must have known it wouldn't have done any good against armor or the demons. "Are you Arthur's Knights of the Round Table? Come to help us in our time of need?"

Derek didn't say anything, but he remembered the boy asking the same question. Those stories, though forgotten to some degree, had resurfaced now. He was surprised at that.

"I was always told that Arthur Pendragon would return some day," the man went on hopefully. "That when England was in her greatest need, he would once again take up Excalibur." He looked at the Templar. "Are you here to help us?"

Derek hesitated, then said, "That's just a story. We're not part of that."

"I see." The man's shoulders rounded and he pulled a frayed blanket around his shoulders.

Demons screamed outside the door. Simon stepped back long enough to close the door and preserve what little heat remained within the museum. The people all looked so vulnerable.

"Do you have any food?" a woman asked. "Food is always hard to come by." Tears ran down her cheeks. "I'm not asking for myself, but for my boys." She moved the blanket and revealed two small boys hidden there. Both the boys looked frightened near to death. "I hate watching them go hungry, and we've all gone hungry for days now."

Simon sheathed the Spike Bolter and reached for the rations they carried out into the field in ammo compartments of the armor. They were primarily energy bars and soy-sub. The Templar only carried self-heats outside the city.

"It's not much," he apologized. He added the water containers that fed through the suit's drinking tube as well.

The woman smiled her thanks at him, then quickly started sharing the meager amount with other parents with children. The rations went quickly.

Other Templar came forward and handed their rations over as well.

"You're a bunch of fools," Mercer snapped. "If we get pinned down somewhere and can't make it back for a few days, you're going to go hungry."

"I can miss a meal or two," Wertham said. "I'll not knowingly leave children to go hungry." Raw emotion twisted his words. "That's not something I'll do. And it's not something I thought I would ever be asked to do."

A few more Templar, shamed by the words, stepped forward and gave up their supplies as well. Derek put his in as well. Only Mercer and three others didn't volunteer theirs.

"You'd better hope High Seat Booth doesn't hear about this," Mercer threatened.

Derek turned to Mercer. "If the High Seat does, we'll know who told him."

Mercer held his commander's gaze for an insolent moment, then turned away.

"Can you take us out of here?" the man asked.

"Where would you go?" Derek asked.

"I don't know. Isn't there somewhere safe?"

"Not in the city."

"We can't stay here," one of the women said. "The demons can't enter this place, but it doesn't stop them from waiting for us outside. When we go out to try to find food, they hunt us. Staying here is just a slow death."

"The coast," Derek said. "There are still ships that take refugees to France."

The man shook his head. "We'd never make it. Not as poorly equipped as we are for the winter, or in the shape we're in. We're too weak."

Simon looked at all the people and felt torn. All of the people in the museum were doomed, trapped by their vulnerability and needs. Staying in the museum was going to be a slow, horror-filled death, and none of them would escape.

Unless they die in the next few minutes, he couldn't help thinking.

"I'm sorry," Derek said. "I wish we could assist you. But we can't. We've got our orders."

"Are you part of the military?"

"No." Derek paused, looking away from the man and the other unfortunates. "It would be better if you leave now. Safer."

"We can't. You can't ask us to do that. We've got old people and children among us."

"I'm sorry." Derek started forward then, aiming for the back of the museum. The schematic they had of the building showed the entrance to the basement there.

Trying not to think about the people barely living through the freezing cold around him and the fact that they were about to possibly endanger them all, Simon followed. He wondered what his father would have done, then wished that he'd have been able to ask him.

"Do you think this place is warded?" Wertham asked as they descended the steps leading to the basement.

"I don't know," Corrigan told him. "I've heard of such things, but I don't know if that's possible."

Simon didn't either, and he wondered if that was part of the protection hiding the Templar Underground from the demons.

"Warding doesn't matter," Mercer growled. "Demons have ways of getting past wards. None that have ever been put up have remained effective."

Trying not to think about that, Simon kept watch. The basement was large, stuffed with boxes and crates that contained remnants of exhibits that had once filled the museum. A few more of the displaced Londoners squatted there as well, but they quickly gathered their belongings and headed up the steps when the Templar arrived.

They don't trust us, either, Simon realized. That troubled him more than he thought it would.

Derek spent some time at the west wall. "There's supposed to be a trigger. Ah, there it is." He pressed on a section of the wall.

With slow, easy grace, a ten-foot section of the wall pivoted to a ninety-degree angle, basically becoming two doorways leading into the darkened room beyond. The Templar followed a spiral staircase around and down, reaching the other door in short order.

The new door was filled with symbols. Even with his meager magical ability, Simon sensed the power locked into the door.

It's probably throughout that room, he told himself.

Derek tried the door but it was locked. He stepped back and called to Wertham. "These are supposed to be your specialty."

"They can be," Wertham agreed. He took his gloves off and placed his bare hands on the metal door, then started chanting. As he spoke, the symbols lit up. Less than a minute later, the bolts holding the door closed shot back with metallic *snicks.*

Wertham seized the door and opened it, then stepped back out of the way. Shelves of artifacts stood barely revealed. Simon made out weapons and works of art, models, vases, and other fragile things the museum owner had put together after so much work and dedication. The man had obviously cared about what he was doing.

Almost immediately, Simon saw the movement taking shape in the shadows. He shifted from the light-multiplier application to a true infrared, spotting the hole in the back of the room because it stood out in sharper relief, glowing a little from heat.

Demonic roars came through the opening. Magnifying and enhancing the images, Simon saw dozens of demons bearing down on a group of Cabalists, who were just then starting to run for their lives.

"Look out!" Mercer cried, drawing his sword. He stepped into the room after Derek, who had gone at once toward the Hammer in a special case on the wall.

Balekor's Hammer gleamed a rich dark purple, like it had been roused from slumber.

The other Templar drew their weapons as well. They didn't even have time to get set. Through the hole, Simon saw a young black man charging toward them. He was dressed all in black, but he didn't wear the horns and tattoos of the other Cabalists he was with.

Before any of them could get set, the young black man threw out a hand. Simon saw a vague rippling take shape in the air before him, then an incredible force blasted the wall into pieces.

FORTY-ONE

Rock and mortar pelted Simon as he was blown off his feet and driven backward. He flailed as he flew backward into another Templar. Both of them went down, buffeted by the waves of force that slammed through the vault.

"Get back!" Derek shouted. "Back up the stairs or we're going to be trapped!"

Shoving himself to his feet, Simon took a firm grip on his sword and peered through the gaping hole in the wall. The vault had evidently butted up against the basement of the building across the alley, crossing under the alley. The wall on that side of the room had shattered and been strewn across the floor.

The Cabalists rushed into the vault, adding confusion to the threat of sudden death. Several of the Templar aimed their hand weapons at the new arrivals and backed them off, not certain if they were attacking with the demons or merely under attack themselves. The answer came quickly enough when the demons fired and two of the security people with the Cabalists went down. The security guards took cover at the edge of the wall and returned fire, but the effort didn't slow the rampaging demons.

Simon had his Spike Bolter up, aiming it at the black-clad man that had blown the wall apart. The man was younger than Simon had at first believed. Then Simon saw the scaled fist that thrust through the man's coat sleeve. It looked like his skin had been removed and lizard's hide transplanted there.

"Help us," a tall Cabalist cried out as he took cover. "We were ambushed by the demons."

"Let them through," Derek commanded.

Grumbling and cursing, the Templar pushed the Cabalists behind them and took up arms against the demons. They stood with the security people. And the demons continued their assault.

"Mercer," Derek yelled, "get these people out of here. All of you fall back. We can't fight them here."

Mercer fled up the stairs.

Derek had Balekor's Hammer in both hands as he sprinted back toward the exit. He pushed into his men, urging them onward as the demon hordes pressed in from behind.

Weapons fire from the demons struck within the vault. Sparks erupted from Simon's helmet as some kind of beam splashed against him. The force rocked him on his heels but he stood his ground.

"Derek!" Mercer yelled from the top of the stairs. "The door has closed! It's jammed and I can't get it open! We can't get out!"

Simon wondered if the door had been blocked by the people they'd told to leave the premises. He wouldn't have blamed them.

"Get the door open!" Derek shouted back.

"Wertham's trying!"

Simon pushed himself forward through the advancing wave of Cabalists. The man in black who had caused the wall to explode brushed past him, obviously looking for the fastest way out.

"Derek," Simon said as he watched the demons approach. He stood in front of the Cabalists, drawing weapons fire and providing the protective wall of his armor. "We can't run. There's no time. If the demons bottle us in here, they're going to pick us off. We can't get trapped in here."

Derek stood beside Simon.

"It's time we fought back," Simon said. He held his sword and the Spike Bolter. "Live or die, we can't run from this fight."

"Here!" Derek shouted. "Form a skirmish line! We're going to take the fight to them!"

Scared and pumped up on adrenaline, Simon reached for the anger that fired through him. Maybe these weren't the demons who had slain his father, but it had been demons like them. He stood ready.

Derek flashed him on a private band through the HUD. "We can't let the hammer slip out of our hands. No matter what happens."

Simon nodded grimly, rocked by another salvo of beams that sliced through the blown-out wall. "We can't stay here, either."

"I know." Derek slung the Hammer over his shoulder and freed his sword. "Charge!"

As one man, the Templar boiled out of the vault, racing over the bodies of the dead and injured Cabalists bleeding on the ground. War cries, amplified by the HUD's audio enhancers, pealed from the walls of the rooms. They met the demon horde less than ten feet from the opening in the wall.

A solid wave of Templar met the ragged line of demons. For a moment, the demons held their ground, then they were knocked aside and down as the powered suits got the upper hand.

Simon thrust the Spike Bolter into a demon's face and

squeezed the trigger. The demon's head blew into pieces, scattering gore all over Simon. Setting himself, Simon swung his sword and cut deeply into another demon's body.

There are too many, his mind screamed at him. *But there are already two less than there were,* he told that scared part of himself. They were also packed so solidly in front of him that he couldn't miss. All he had to do was keep fighting.

Metal ground against metal as the Templar blades and armor met the armor the demons were wearing and the weapons they carried. Already several of the demons were down, some of them dead and others mortally wounded and crying out in fear. The Templar killed them without mercy, just as the demons did to the fallen Templar. The din was horrendous, like a scene cut from the deepest pits of Hell.

Simon kept moving, using the HUD to keep track of the other Templar. They tried to stay in a group, but it was impossible with all the close-in fighting that was going on. Reaching across his body, his sword raised to block an axe blow, he pushed the Spike Bolter against the back of a demon's head that was attacking a fallen Templar and pulled the trigger.

The demon's head went to pieces, but as the creature slumped, Simon saw that he'd acted too late. The demon had already succeeded in shoving a spear through the fallen Templar's chest. Electricity and arcane forces fired at the breach in the armor, but blood was there, too. The falling demon draped the Templar.

Lifting his foot, Simon drove his other attacker backward with a kick. Simon reached down for the fallen Templar, just enough to make suit contact so he could read the other man's vital statistics.

All his suit received was a series of flat lines that confirmed what he'd feared. There was no pulse. No respiration. The man was dead.

"Simon! Look out!" Derek chopped with his sword, turning aside a spear that had been aimed at Simon's heart. The demon behind the spear thrust was a brutish beast almost twice as large as Simon.

The demon swept a massive fist back, striking Derek full in the face. If he hadn't been in armor, the blow would have killed him. As it was, Derek crumpled against a wall nearly twenty feet away, his senses wavered, and for a moment he thought he was going to drop. He took a deep breath and shook off the effects of the blow.

Simon waded into the fray again. With all the limbs and weapons waved around, with beams tracking scorch marks on the floors, walls, and ceiling, it was impossible to know which way the battle was turning.

Swinging his sword, Simon buried the blade in the thick corded muscle of a Darkspawn's neck and chest. The sword lodged, trapped there as the demon fought with its last breath to stick him with the sword it carried. Simon kicked at it, trying to free the dying creature from his sword.

Before he succeeded, another Darkspawn shouldered its wounded comrade aside and aimed a pistol at Simon's face. Simon attempted to duck but couldn't get out of the way in time. Bilious green liquid splashed against his helm, followed immediately by a cloud of white smoke that partially obscured his vision.

Abandoning his hold on the sword for the moment, Simon fisted his right hand, twisted his hips to get everything he could into the effort, and punched the Darkspawn in the throat. Bone snapped and gave way before the blow.

The demon *hu-urked* twice, stepping back as it struggled to breathe. Simon hit his opponent twice more, tearing the leathery hide and flesh from its face and crumpling the skull bones.

Spotting the demon that still had his sword in it, Simon stepped over to it, placed a foot on its chest, and yanked. The sword tore free. In that moment, he spotted the pitting left by the liquid the demon had shot him with.

"Armor integrity," Simon said, moving toward the closest demon.

"Armor integrity is at 83 percent," the HUD computer answered.

"Identify substance coating armor." Simon thrust his sword into a demon's back, hoping the heart was close by. Demon physiology was different and they weren't necessarily all the same.

"Substance: unknown. Never before encountered."

New weapons or old ones we haven't seen before? Simon wondered. The demon he attacked tried to whip around. Using his left arm to block the creature's attempt to point a pistol at him, Simon yanked hard on the sword with his right. The spinal cord separated with a loud *crunch*. Lower body paralyzed, the demon sank to the ground. Simon blasted it in the face, killing it.

"More of them are coming!" someone shouted.

Simon threw himself at a pair of Gremlins that had pinned a Templar against the shattered wall. One of them had hold of the Templar's sword, trapping it in a swordbreaker. The other fired fiery bolts from a pistol that left ghostly images on Simon's HUD.

Wrapping his arms around the head of one Gremlin, Simon managed to get a shoulder into the next and knock all of them to the ground. One of the Gremlins recovered almost at once and was on top of Simon in a heartbeat. It slammed a razor-sharp blade into his faceplate twice before Simon shoved the Spike Bolter up under the Gremlin's chin and pulled the trigger. The palladium spikes chased the last fleeting thoughts from the demon's head.

Simon pushed himself from beneath the dead weight just in time to get slammed with a huge hammer that caught him in the center of the chest. The impact knocked the breath from his lungs. For one brief moment he panicked that the blow had smashed in the breastplate to the point it was going to suffocate him. Then he managed a breath, realized that the breastplate had only transferred the hydrostatic shock it hadn't been able to transfer throughout the suit, and caught another blow on the shoulder that spun him over.

Dazed, Simon pushed himself away and scrambled across the bodies of Cabalist security men, demons, and a fallen Templar. The brief contact with the Templar let him know that the man was dead.

He shoved himself around, swinging his legs to take out the legs of the Gremlin that had hit him. When the creature fell, Simon rolled to straddle it, then slammed his sword through its chest and twisted. The Gremlin bucked through its death throes.

On his feet again, Simon swept the battlefield. More demons were coming through the chimney at the other end of the basement.

This was a trap, Simon realized. *They knew we were coming.* Then he remembered the Cabalists and amended that. The demons had known that someone was coming.

There were too many to fight through. Nearly a third of the Templar had fallen, most of them dead. It wouldn't be long before they all fell because the demons didn't seem to worry about dying.

FORTY-TWO

Simon thought desperately, looking for a way out. He parried the blade of another Gremlin, then rolled behind an attacking Darkspawn that lunged at him. He thought about the tunnels that ran under London. The city was honeycombed with them. Tunnels allowed pedestrians to cross under the Thames. They carried waste in huge sewers. And they were used to transport cargo.

"Bring up building schematic," Simon told the computer. "Visual overlay. Mark my position."

"Complying," the computer responded.

Simon shot the Darkspawn in the back of the head before it could turn to face him. As the demon fell, Simon put a shoulder into its back and propelled the dead weight into the Gremlin. Both demons went down in a tangle of arms and legs. Crossing to them, Simon pierced the Gremlin's chest with his sword before it could get up, then kicked it in the face hard enough to snap its neck.

"Schematic processing," the computer said.

Almost instantly, a fine gold three-dimensional blueprint overlaid the HUD. A gold dot marked Simon's position.

"Are there any tunnels beneath this room?" Simon asked. He stumbled back as a beam hit him and chipped his armor. Turning, he moved in behind a Darkspawn for cover and watched as the next beam hit the demon instead of him.

"Affirmative," the computer responded.

Immediately, a wide tunnel showed up in silver on the HUD.

"What is it?" Simon asked.

"A private cargo tunnel from the docks. It was used by Holdstock Glassworks until the business closed."

"Is it still viable?"

"Unknown."

"Mark it on the blueprint," Simon ordered. He slashed with his sword as the demon turned to face him. One side was a smoking, charred ruin from the flames shot by another demon. Simon's sword blow opened the demon's abdomen and he dodged away as it fell apart. "Derek."

"What?" Desperation tightened Derek's response.

"There's a tunnel under the floor." Simon spotted the demon with the pistol, pulled up the Spike Bolter, and opened fire.

The palladium needles drove the demon backward in stumbling steps.

"If we can use a shaped charge and blow through the floor, we might be able to escape."

Blood and other matter covered the concrete floor. Footing was treacherous. Still, the Templar had managed to press out from the vault where they'd been trapped. There wasn't much in the way of cover, a few support pillars and discarded equipment the size of cars all the way down to small crates.

"I've got a map," Simon said.

"Send it," Derek replied.

Simon did, continuing to fight for his life. He couldn't tell if the demons were still coming through the chimney, but there were more than enough on hand already to do the job.

"Higgins," Derek called.

"Yes," the man replied.

"I need a shaped charge. Place it where the map is marked."

Even as Simon fired his Spike Bolter, he took note of Derek's choice. The spot was behind their present position, midway to the vault room they'd vacated.

"When we get into the tunnel," Simon said, "we're going south. To the river. There should be a door."

"If it hasn't been mortared closed," Mercer replied. "If a new dock hasn't been built over it. If a ship's not sitting on it."

"Either way," Wertham said, "we're going to die. At least this gives us a chance."

"You were supposed to be working on the door," Mercer yelled.

"The door's jammed," Wertham said. "I think those people upstairs had had enough of us and locked us in. The door didn't get opened under power. It's a system of counterweights. It wouldn't have taken much to sabotage it."

"You shouldn't have stopped trying," Mercer yelled.

"I came down here to fight with my mates," Wertham said.

"Shut up and hold the perimeter," Derek said. "Get grenades ready."

Simon looked around the room. They'd made a wall of dead demons, creating harsh ground to cross if the demons wanted to continue the fight. For the moment, the demons had backed off and were continuing to fire from a distance. The Templars proved their superior marksmanship, though, and it was evident that the demons' only real edge lay in numbers.

"They're massing to attack again," Wertham said.

"Steady," Derek said. "Hold the grenades till I tell you different, then we throw toward the mass of them."

"What about the Cabalists?" Mercer growled.

Simon checked his HUD and saw that the Cabalists remained within the vault. The black man with the lizard-scale arm stood near the doorway. The woman stood at his side. The tall man hunkered on the other side of the opening. Few of them were left.

Something about the black man's gaze bothered Simon, but there wasn't time to think about it. The demons were massing and readying for another charge.

"Wertham?" Derek asked.

"I'm ready." Wertham grabbed the body of a nearby dead demon and used it to smother the shaped charge. Two more bodies were quickly added. "Just to make sure the explosion heads in the right direction."

"Grenades!" Derek yelled.

As one, the Templar threw the grenades, lobbing them into the mass of demons. Most of the creatures were too dull-witted or inexperienced to know what the grenades were, but there were some that dove for cover.

Simon threw himself flat, hugging the blood-covered floor. His heart pounded and he knew he needed to get himself in hand before the armor kicked in and controlled his fear for him.

"Wertham!" Derek shouted over the blasts. "*Now!*"

The grenades went off first, shooting out fierce blue light from the Greek Fire contained inside. Traditional grenades wouldn't have done much, but the deadly concoction of chemicals in the Templar munitions did a great deal of damage.

Simon glanced up, his HUD automatically filtering the bright light. The detonations broke the demons' ranks and hurled them in all directions. But several of them were on fire now, covered in a nimbus of blue-white flames that ate their flesh and cracked their bones. A

Blood Angel went down like a blazing comet and didn't move.

Then the shaped charge went off, blowing the bodies of the demons that Wertham had stacked atop it up against the ceiling. Simon felt the seismic reaction even through the armor. The floor *shifted* beneath him.

Checking the HUD, looking back without turning his head, Simon saw that a large hole had opened up in the floor. Smoke poured from the opening as pieces of demon dropped from the ceiling.

"We're through," Wertham said. "There's a tunnel below."

"Go!" Derek ordered. "Wertham, you've got point. Move!"

The demons gathered themselves and charged, obviously sensing that something had changed.

"Pistols," Derek shouted. "Hold them off till we get clear. Fall back and withdraw."

On his feet and firing, Simon noticed the gaping hole in the floor. The cargo tunnel was eight feet in diameter, providing plenty of room for a forklift to handle shipments leaving the factory for the warehouses. It was black as night inside, but night vision ripped the darkness away.

One by one, in quick succession, the Templar dropped down into the hole.

Derek turned to the Cabalists. "If you want out of here, now's the time."

The Cabalists fled. Two of the security men went down from the demons' weapons, one hit by what looked like a bolt of lightning and the other engulfed in flames that left only his blackened shadow on the wall.

A female Templar next to Simon went down, part of the armor blown from her right leg. He helped her up and got her moving toward the hole.

* * *

Seize Balekor's Hammer! Merihim's voice thundered inside Warren's head. *Get it now!*

Warren couldn't believe the demon was demanding that now, when the other demons were rushing their position and escape was so close to hand. The Templar were trying to help save the Cabalists. Trying to get Balekor's Hammer, even if he failed and he honestly didn't know how he was going to succeed, was only going to turn the Templar against them.

Now! Merihim roared. *Just lay your hand on the Hammer and I'll do the rest. If you don't you'll never leave this place alive.*

Pain smashed through Warren's head, almost causing him to black out. He stumbled but managed to go forward. Naomi offered to help, but he brushed her away. Even that fleeting contact, though, must have hinted to her what he was about to attempt.

"No, Warren," Naomi said. "You can't—"

Then Warren was by her, charging toward the Templar with Balekor's Hammer strapped over his back. The Templar must have sensed him coming, because he tried to turn around. Warren was quick, though, and he reached for the Hammer's haft.

He closed his right hand around it and the contact was electric and powerful. Immediately the Hammer glowed with a phosphorus-bright intensity. Then a wave of force exploded from it, blowing the Templar away and leaving Warren standing there with the Hammer in hand.

Weapons fire from the demon guns hit all around him. He knew with the hammer in his hand and lit up by the glow that he was an immediate target. Before he could move, and he wasn't sure if he could move, three bullets suddenly stopped in midair only inches from his chest. If they'd hit him, he had no doubt that they would have punched through his heart.

Warren gazed in wonder at the bullets, wondering if he had somehow stopped them. He hadn't known he could blow the wall apart with a gesture either. The encounter with Merihim had changed him.

You didn't do that, Merihim told him derisively. *I saved you. And if you listen to me, I'll always save you. I have marked you, Warren Schimmer, and you are mine.*

The demon's threat chilled Warren, but he felt comforted by it. The demon had claimed him. For all of his life, no one had ever told him they wanted him. No one had ever protected him.

He stared at the bullets as four more joined them. He was protected now.

Call my name, Merihim urged. *Call my name so that I can come to you.*

Holding the Hammer with both hands, Warren could "feel" the demon. Merihim was already getting closer. He could sense the demon's proximity.

Call my name!

Lifting the Hammer, following the urge that squirmed through him, Warren shouted, *"Merihim!"*

Instantly, a purple, two-dimensional disc irised open in midair almost in front of him. Lightning stirred within the disc, occasionally erupting from it. The static electricity caused Naomi's and Kelli's hair to lift. Sonic booms cracked within and pealed out over the basement.

Warren felt like ants were crawling over his body. *"Merihim!"*

Incredibly, the demon started to crawl from within the disc.

FORTY-THREE

Simon pushed himself up. His senses still swam from the explosion that had occurred after the man had grabbed the hammer from Derek's back. Despite the armor's protection, he tasted blood in his mouth. His eyes focused on the shimmering purple disc as the demon began to crawl from it. The bullets frozen in midair before the man—*His name is Warren*. Simon remembered the woman Cabalist calling out his name just before Warren had lunged for the Hammer.

"Stop him!" Derek said. "Take the Hammer!"

There was something about the monstrous form of the demon that touched a well of fear inside Simon. The feeling was like nothing he'd ever known before. It was primitive and unstoppable, and it ran rampant through Simon. The last thing he wanted to do was approach the demon.

But only he and Derek were left aboveground. And Derek was struggling to get to his feet. His breathing sounded labored. As Derek forced himself up, Simon saw the broken shard of a demon's spear that had been thrust into his stomach.

"Simon!"

Derek's voice broke whatever spell was on Simon. He moved forward at once, but felt pressure immediately shoving him back. Now he understood why the bullets hung in the air. Arcane energies protected Warren.

Still pushing forward, Simon summoned his own arcane energy, aiming it like a weapon at Warren. When he had it strong enough, he fired it at Warren. Something rippled in the air between them.

Warren staggered back, his concentration shattered. The disc held its form, though, as the demon pushed through and into the basement.

When the pressure went away, Simon swung his sword, intending to knock the Hammer from Warren's grip. Instead, Warren shifted. The blade caught him on the right wrist and sliced through.

Warren's hand fell away from his wrist. Blood gushed from the horrible wound. Crying out shrilly, he dropped the Hammer and closed his other hand over the end of his maimed arm.

Simon felt bad about the turn of events, but he closed on the Hammer and lifted it from the floor. The bullets resumed their course and at least one of them struck Warren as he fell.

The disc imploded, but the arcane forces shot the demon from it like an inhuman cannonball. Before the demon went far, however, it stopped in midair and sank to its knees, obviously stunned. Its voice rose in ire and pain, and Simon knew he didn't want to be there when it recovered.

The two women ran to Warren. The dark-haired one tended to his amputated wrist while the other one stood by him and held him with a wooden smile on her face.

Knowing the Cabalists weren't friendly or even neutral, Simon abandoned them, following Derek down into the hole in the floor.

"Can you make it?" Simon asked when he landed on the floor beside Derek.

"I have to." Derek straightened with effort. Blood ran down the front of his armor. "Give me the Hammer."

Simon did, then accepted the explosives Derek handed him.

"Mine the tunnel," Derek said, glancing back up at the hole. "The demons will be down on top of us as soon as they've finished with those people up there."

Simon nodded and slung the explosives over his shoulder. They ran.

Only a short distance ahead, the tunnel curved, heading toward the river according to the map on Simon's HUD. He stopped, inserted a detonator into one of the explosive blocks, and dropped the pack of explosives to the ground around the corner, hoping the curve would deflect some of the concussion.

Farther back up the tunnel, the first of the demons had started coming through the hole, dropping to all fours. They barked and growled, then lifted their weapons and started firing.

Dodging around the corner, Simon checked to make certain Derek was still moving under his own speed. "Wertham."

"Yes?"

"Have you reached the other end of the tunnel? Is the way open?" Simon didn't relish the idea of blasting the tunnel closed and effectively creating their own tomb. It was possible that they could somehow dig their way out, but he didn't want to risk it.

"Give me a minute. Almost there."

"Simon," Derek called, "blow the tunnel."

Footsteps, picked up by the armor's enhancements, sounded in the tunnel around the corner. They were rapidly growing closer.

If the tunnel's blocked, even if the tunnel's not blown up and closed, we can't get past the demons. They'll kill us all. I'll only be delaying—

"It's here!" Wertham shouted. "We can get out!"

"Simon, blow—"

Using the armor's systems, Simon detonated the explosives as the footsteps sounded right around the corner and he hurled himself forward. The concussion shivered through the tunnel, causing the floor to vibrate under Simon's feet. Then it overtook him and blew him forward, enveloping him in a coil of yellow and orange flames.

He cut off my hand! Even as he stared at the bloody stump that truncated his arm, Warren couldn't believe it. He'd been watching Merihim push out of the disc and hadn't even seen the armored figure until it was too late.

There wasn't as much pain as he thought there should be. In fact, there was hardly any pain at all. Merihim screaming inside his brain was worse. The demon was angry and hurting, roaring with rage as it got to its feet.

Naomi leaned over him, holding him down with her weight as she fought to wrap his wrist with the bootlace she'd taken from his boot. "Lie still! You're going to bleed to death! Lie still!"

Warren didn't care. Another horrible thing had happened to him because he couldn't defend himself. Because no one cared enough about him to protect him. Chill weakness passed through him, stealing his strength and fading his vision. He continued to struggle, but he was too weak to fight against Naomi.

She got the bootlace tied around his wrist and somehow managed to stop the bleeding.

"Don't," he whispered. "Please, don't." He was ready to die. She didn't know that, but he was. He was prepared now, while he was still in shock. He wasn't afraid. Death could come for him now and he wouldn't fight. He fumbled for the bootlace with his other hand, wanting to untie it and bleed out.

Naomi captured his hand. "Stop," she said. "Please stop, Warren."

"*He cut my hand off!*" Warren's voice sounded weak in his ears.

"I know," Naomi said. "I know. It's going to be all right."

"*I'm a cripple!*"

"You're alive."

Hot tears flooded Warren's eyes. He didn't want to be alive. He wanted to be dead. And he wanted the man who had crippled him to be dead too.

"Look out," Tulane said. "Here they come."

Warren barely noticed the approaching demons. Some of them had slipped down into the hole the armored men had blown through the floor. But the others closed on the Cabalists. There was no doubt what they had in mind.

One of the Darkspawn picked up Warren's severed hand and grinned.

A Fetid Hulk, a great green demon that towered above the others and looked vaguely like an unfinished clay model of a human, snorted and slavered behind the Darkspawn. Smooth scales covered it. Its head was huge and monstrous, smooth and earless, showing off a large maw filled with sharp teeth.

Still grinning, the Darkspawn tossed Warren's hand into the air. The Fetid Hulk's head whipped forward on its elongated neck and caught the hand in its mouth.

"No!" Warren shouted, trying to get up again.

The Fetid Hulk chewed a couple of times, crunching through the bones, then swallowed. It gazed at Warren again, as if speculating where to start next.

The demons started forward, baring blades, obviously intending to make their kills on unprotected prey as personal as possible.

Merihim stepped between them. *No,* the demon said. *These are mine. I claim them.*

The demons grimaced and growled unhappily. Three of them started forward.

Merihim gestured at one of them with his great trident. The Gremlin started screaming and slapping at its head. In the next instant, the demon's head burst like a blood-filled balloon.

The other demons drew back.

Go, Merihim told them. *Pursue the others if you will, but leave these alone.*

Reluctantly, the demons backed off.

Yes, Merihim said a moment later, *the dead ones you can have.*

The demons pounced on the corpses in a frantic scramble. The room filled with the smacking and crunching of their feeding.

Merihim turned to Warren. *You let them take Balekor's Hammer.*

Warren didn't reply. He only hoped that death would claim him quickly.

You're not going to die, Merihim said. *I still have use for you.*

I can die if I want to, Warren thought. *There's nothing you can do.* He could already feel his heart slowing and see that his vision was graying around the edges.

Merihim walked over to him.

Warren felt Naomi's grip tighten on his arm and knew that she was afraid. He didn't care. He didn't care about anything.

Then the demon leaned down and placed his hand across Warren's chest. *Live,* he commanded.

Without warning, electricity surged through Warren's body. Only it wasn't electricity. It was something else. Something more powerful and more ethereal. His heartbeat sped up again.

And pain returned to him in a huge wave that splintered all hope of dying. No one who was going to die could be in that much agony.

"My hand!" Warren yelled. Because everything he'd missed feeling earlier, he felt now.

Merihim picked up a nearby axe. *I'm going to give you a gift. I expect you to use it well.*

Barely holding on to his consciousness, Warren watched in horror as Merihim placed his own arm on the stone floor and chopped off his hand at the wrist. Blood stopped flowing almost immediately.

The demon never uttered a word. He tossed the axe aside and picked up the severed hand with his remaining one. Then he spoke in English, addressing Naomi. "Give him this or you will know my wrath." He tossed the hand to her.

Naomi tried to grab the hand, but missed. Before it could fall, though, the fingers closed around her wrist and held on. She barely muffled a scream.

Merihim laughed and held up his stump. Black tendrils shot up from his wrist and twisted together. In seconds he'd grown another hand.

Sleep. Heal. I'll have need of you again.

Warren crashed into the darkness, fearing that he wasn't going to die, that he was going to live. And if he had to live, he meant to see that the armored man that had cut his hand off was going to pay.

Dazed by the blast, Simon rolled to his feet, somehow managing to hang on to his sword. The armor's audio dampers saved his hearing and the HUD compensated for the bright lights, then the tunnel filled with dust. The armor filtered the dust out and kept his air supply clean.

He drew the Spike Bolter and examined the blockage that had filled the tunnel. Rock and debris had tumbled down from above, opening into another room of another building. The debris hadn't quite filled the tunnel. A gap no more than a few inches existed at the top, but nothing moved there.

Turning, Simon ran the other way, quickly overtaking Derek. He gathered Derek's arm across his shoulders and helped him increase his pace. Together they headed for the other end of the tunnel.

A few minutes later, Simon stood outside the tunnel only a few feet from the River Thames. The mud that stretched out from the bank testified that the river was indeed dwindling. Several boats and ships sat mired in mud as well, even the ones that were broken.

Blood Angels flew silently overhead, staring down for prey. Other demons worked the buildings and boats.

Standing there with Derek's arm across his shoulders, Simon thought of the men, women, and children they'd left behind in the museum. He didn't know if the fight down in the vault had disrupted the wards that protected the place or not. He hoped it hadn't. The thought of those people becoming victims during the night made him sick.

Quietly, the Templar moved out, staying within the shadows. Lisa, one of the female Templar, came back to help Simon with Derek, who faded in and out of consciousness. Evidently the injury was too much for the armor to slap-patch him through.

"Look," Wertham said, pointing downriver.

Using the magnification application on the HUD,

Simon picked the figures out of the darkness. He identified the Cabalists as they made their way out of the glassworks building. They carried someone on a makeshift stretcher, what looked to be a section of carpet cut up from some office floor.

"They're in league with the demons," Mercer said. "Just goes to show that you can't trust them." He cursed. "We oughta kill them all and be done with it."

Simon didn't say anything, but he didn't think the Cabalists were in with the demons. When they'd found them, they'd been fleeing for their lives. He had no doubts about that.

But he couldn't explain the Cabalist—*Warren*—trying to take Balekor's Hammer from Derek and somehow using it to call forth a demon. Were they using the demon? Or was the demon using them?

He tried to push the matter from his thoughts. He had other things to think about. Provided they made it safely back to the Underground, he was going to make some changes in his life. Sitting back and going on missions for the High Seat wasn't what he wanted to do. It wasn't what his father had trained him to do.

FORTY-FOUR

Y ou're a fool to go out there like this, you know."
Simon ignored High Seat Booth's comment and
kept packing, throwing a few clothes and rations
into the duffel bag on his bunk. There wasn't much room
in the bag, and the way he planned on living was even
harder than when he'd been in the South African bush. He
was acutely aware of the other Templar in the barracks who
were watching him.

"You won't last a day on your own," Booth warned. "If
not anything else, you should have learned that since
you've been back."

Simon rolled the duffel and hoisted it over his shoulder.
He turned, but Booth stepped into his path.

"Are you listening to me?" Booth demanded.

Looking down, Simon locked gazes with the man.
Booth's arrogance was palpable. "I hear you," Simon said,
"but that's not stopping me from going."

"Then why are you going?"

"There are people out there—"

"I know there are people out there," Booth interrupted
irritably. "I'm not an idiot."

"They need help getting out of the city," Simon replied.
"Before the demons kill them, or the Burn. Or even winter."

"The smart ones will figure that out on their own,"
Booth insisted. "They'll abandon the city."

"They're not strong enough to do it." Simon knew that the other Templar were listening in, and some of them looked sympathetic. "And they're not strong enough to survive the attempt without help."

"So what are you going to do?" Booth put his hands on his hips and glared at Simon.

Simon was tired of dealing with Booth. It was primary school all over again. Booth was loud and he was a bully. He still didn't like it when things didn't go his way.

For the last two days, Simon had recuperated and made his plans. And he did have plans, despite Booth's doubts. Maybe they weren't as well thought out as Simon had hoped they would be before he left, but he knew what he wanted to do. He'd also figured out where he could get what he needed to pull it off—maybe.

Derek was still in the hospital, but he was doing well. The doctors expected a full recovery in a relatively short time. They'd mourned their dead. Recovery teams had gone back out the next day in an attempt to bring back the bodies and armor. Simon had gone with them, part of the final duty he figured he owed to the Templar. In the end, they'd brought most of them back, but none of them had been whole.

Only an hour ago, Simon had sent a message up through channels that he was leaving the Underground. He had expected some resistance because Booth didn't like having his orders disobeyed, but he hadn't expected the High Seat to come himself. But there was the matter of the long-standing feud between them.

"I'm going to get as many of them as I can out of London," Simon said.

"Do you plan on carrying them out of here on your back?"

"If I have to."

"You're not going to save many of them that way."

"If I save even one of them, it'll be worth it. And I plan on saving more than one."

"You haven't changed," Booth declared. "You've got the same bleeding heart you've always had. Just as full of yourself."

Simon tried to step around Booth. The High Seat stepped in front of him. Simon took a breath. "Get out of my way."

"No," Booth said. "You're under my command."

"Not anymore."

"I'll have you locked up for disobeying my orders." Booth had come accompanied by eight members of his personal guard. "I am the High Seat. I outrank you."

"You only outrank me if I choose to stay here," Simon promised. "I don't. And I guarantee that locking me up isn't going to be easy."

"It'll be done."

Taking a breath, Simon focused totally on Booth. "If you want to give orders, then give ones I can respect. Give me orders to defend those poor people starving and freezing to death out there in the rotting corpse that this city has become. Give me orders to get those people out of here. Give me orders to feed them and clothe them and protect them until I can get them out of here." He let out his breath. "Those are the orders you and the other High Seats *should* be giving. Not telling us to hide in shadows and bring back whatever you send us out there for while they die scared and alone, hungry and in pain every day."

For a moment the barracks were silent. Simon grew self-conscious. Naked and out in the open like that, his words sounded hollow. That was why he hadn't talked to anyone about what he was going to do.

"The missions we assign are important," Booth argued.

"Recovering the artifacts we send you out for is crucial to our chances of beating the demons. The things we've known about but have never been able to act on, the secrets we've learned and kept over the years, all of those things can tilt the balance against the demons. We know what we're doing."

"Fine, but if you manage to save the world and there's no one to live in it, what have you accomplished?"

"We're here," Booth said. "The Templar will live in it."

"We're not the only people here."

"We—"

"Shut up!" Simon exploded, taking a step toward Booth. The man closed his mouth at once and stepped back. "For all my life, I trained to be a Templar, as did my father before me and his father before him. I trained to fight the demons, and to protect those who couldn't protect themselves. And the ones who denied the existence of demons."

Booth scowled.

"My father raised me up to be a Templar *knight*," Simon stated. "Not an armored errand boy. He taught me to be chivalrous and generous, to be modest and intelligent. And to always know that I was supposed to protect those that couldn't protect themselves." He took a breath. "That's what I learned to believe in, and that's what I wanted to grow up to be like."

The silence in the room was deafening.

"I walked away from this life—"

"Just like you're trying to walk away again," Booth sneered.

"No!" Simon shouted. "This time it's different. The last time, I left because I didn't see the need for me to give up my life, for me to turn away from the things I wanted to see and do, just to sit around and do nothing with the training I'd been given. I lost faith. But now—*now* the demons are *here.* They've come to our world and they mean to make it over as they see fit. They killed people—*thousands* of innocent men, women, and children—with impunity. I intend to use the training my father invested in me and save as many of those people out there that I can. Because—to me—that's what a Templar does."

Someone in the barracks started clapping, slowly at first, then gaining momentum. Other Templar quickly joined in.

Simon felt embarrassed. He couldn't see Booth's face behind the helm, but he felt certain the man was livid with anger. He tried to step around the High Seat again.

Booth drew the Surgecaster from the holster at his side. The pistol was solid and heavy, capable of shooting out balls of electrical energy.

"You're going to be taken into custody," Booth said. "And you won't—"

Simon grabbed Booth's wrist and twisted. The bolt from the Surgecaster whizzed across the room and struck the wall. Simon's HUD had shown him that no one was there, and the rooms were built to be self-contained and resistant to bombing.

The secondary detonation went off as Simon twisted the pistol from Booth's grip. A swirling ball of fire ignited and climbed the wall. Klaxons shrilled, sounding the alarm.

Simon drove his fist into Booth's helm, striking sparks from it as metal grated against metal. Booth tried to get away, but Simon grabbed him by the shoulder and hit him again, using everything he had. Booth flew helplessly across the room, sending Templar diving for cover, and rebounded from the wall.

By the time the High Seat crawled to his knees, Simon was on him. Anger boiled out of Simon, uncontrollable, dark, and terrible. He kicked Booth in the head and sent him back down to the floor. Simon lifted his foot and smashed it onto Booth's helm again and again, shattering the armor but not yet breaking through.

Someone grabbed him from behind and pulled him back. Simon turned to defend himself, then recognized Wertham's armor.

"Stop," the old Templar said. "Stop it now. Before you kill him." Wertham allowed his helm to become transparent enough for Simon to see his features. He maintained his hold on Simon's arms. "Do you hear me?"

Breathing hard, Simon couldn't answer at first. He nodded, then said, "Yes."

"Kill Booth and they'll never let you leave this place," Wertham said.

Simon knew that. He looked beyond the Templar and saw that Booth's personal guards stood ready, but some of the Templar had interposed themselves between them and Simon.

"Kill him!" Booth yelled. "Kill him!"

"No," Wertham said. "There will not be any killing done here today."

"If you support him, I'll have you locked up in the same detainment center with him," Booth threatened.

"Try to stop Simon from leaving," Wertham replied in a calm voice, "and you'll have to put more than just me in that detainment center."

Booth swayed, cursing loudly.

"The Templar have never recognized masters," Wertham said. "Only leaders. Each Templar chooses his own way. You know that, High Seat, and even under these times that must be upheld."

Simon stood, not knowing what to do. He hadn't intended to snowball this into a big problem. *I should have just left.* He could have simply stepped out into one of the tube tunnels and never come back.

But he knew he hadn't wanted to go that easily. There was something in him that hadn't relished the idea of walking away without telling Booth what he thought of the way he was running things.

"We're not supposed to be guerrilla fighters," Simon said. "We're supposed to be champions. Warriors that fight the demons and preserve life. *All* life. Not just our own. By hiding in the shadows and picking and choosing your precious *missions*, you're just as guilty of walking away from everything the Templar stand for as when I left." He paused. "I'm not going to dishonor my father's memory. I'm going out there and I'm going to do what I can to help those people trapped in this city. You're going to have to kill me to stop me."

Booth walked over to Simon. The High Seat moved unsteadily and with effort.

Wertham slid between the two.

Booth's helm popped open, revealing his bloodied face. One of his eyes was swelling shut. "Go then. But don't you *ever* try to come back here." He spat saliva and blood onto Simon's faceshield. Then Booth stepped back and raised his voice. "Let him go. Let the demons have him."

Without a word, Simon shouldered his duffel again, turned, and walked away. Fear trickled through the anger that he still felt, breaking some of his conviction, but he remained convinced that he was doing what he had to do.

Booth's private guards and some of the Templar followed Simon all the way to the exit that let out into the tube. They passed him through the security doors and he stepped out into the darkness where the monsters lay in wait.

His footsteps sounded hollow in the tube. They also sounded vulnerable.

A moment later, Wertham and three other Templar stepped out into the tube. Each of them had duffels over their shoulders.

Simon stopped and looked back at them. "What are you doing?"

"Coming with you," Wertham said. He made his faceshield translucent, revealing his wide grin. "What you said back there reminds me of why I took pride in being a Templar. Over the years, I've had my own doubts about all the training I went through and the secrets I had. I can't fault you for those. But I'm not going to sit idly by while you go off on your own to try to do what I think we should be doing."

Simon stared at the older man. "If you come with me, you're probably going to get killed."

Wertham grinned. "Maybe you've got some doubts, but I don't think they've made the demon tough enough to take me." His grin grew wider. "Or, at least, that demon hasn't caught up with me yet."

"Booth won't let you back," Simon said.

"Regular meals and a bed to sleep in are overrated, if you ask me." Wertham sobered. "Those people we left back in the museum . . . I didn't like doing that. Just walking away from them and leaving them there."

"I know."

"I suppose we'll be checking in on them? After you've figured out how we're going to get them out of London?"

"I have a plan," Simon said.

"Well, now's the time to hear it," one of the other Templar muttered.

"How much do you know about trains?" Simon asked.

FORTY-FIVE

Warren woke in an anesthesia-induced fog. He remembered the feeling from when he'd been a child, after his stepfather had shot him and he'd spent days recuperating in the hospital.

He lacked the strength to sit up or pull the plastic mask from his mouth and nose. It was everything he could do to roll his head to the side. An IV ran a drip into his left arm, taped to his scaled skin, but the blue tinted liquid with small fishy-looking creatures didn't resemble anything he'd ever been given in the hospital before.

One of the creatures pressed its flat face against the plastic bag and ballooned its mouth. An inky substance jetted from its mouth, then dissipated in the liquid, turning the blue slightly more blue. Almost immediately Warren's head felt thicker, more distant from the rest of his body. Whatever the fish creature secreted had something to do with the disorientation he felt.

Seeing his left hand reminded him of his right. His wrist *hurt*. He rolled his head back over the other way.

Tubes ran into and out of the demon's hand that had been grafted to the stump of wrist. A circular affair of wires held the grotesque hand palm down and fingers spread like it was a piece of art. An ill-smelling poultice wrapped the sewn ends of flesh, but it was made of a clear jelly material that allowed him to see. The thread didn't look like thread, but more like the sinew he'd seen when his biology class had dissected a cat in lab. The flesh, his own and the demon's, were reddened from inflammation.

The Cabalists had done it. They'd reconnected Merihim's hand to him.

"No," Warren whispered hoarsely. The events in the building came back to him in a maelstrom of fear, pain, and loss. He could still feel the cold, cruel bite of the armored man's sword cutting through his arm and feel the solid thump of the demon's hand dropping onto his chest.

"Warren." Naomi rose from the wingback chair she'd been sitting in beside the bed. She looked exhausted and concerned about him.

Kelli sat in another chair at the foot of the bed. Her eyes stared at him, but they were dark and listless, like nothing was going on behind them.

"What have you done?" Warren tried to lift his right arm but restraints held it down.

"It's going to be all right," Naomi said soothingly. "The doctor who reattached your hand said the surgery went well."

"*My* hand!" Warren croaked. "That's not my hand." He remembered the Fetid Hulk eating his hand.

"It is now." Naomi touched the back of the hand almost reverently.

Astonished, Warren realized he *felt* her soft fingers against the back of the demon's hand. "Don't. Don't touch me."

Naomi gazed at him curiously. "You felt that?"

Warren refused to answer.

Naomi pinched the back of his . . . *the* hand. The skin tone lightened, then resumed its natural color. But she'd pinched hard enough to hurt.

"Ouch," Warren protested.

"You *did* feel that." Despite her exhaustion, excitement

filled Naomi's features. "The physicians didn't reattach any of the nerves. They were in surgery with you for almost eighteen hours connecting arteries and veins. They had to map a whole new way through the hand. I watched the procedure. I've never seen anything like that before. They figured they would reconnect the nerves if the hand survived transplantation."

"They shouldn't have done this," Warren said. He tried to reach for the offensive hand but discovered that his left hand had been secured to the bed as well. "Let me go."

Sorrow showed in Naomi's eyes. "I can't."

"Let me go!"

Wordlessly, she shook her head.

Fighting back tears of frustration, Warren cursed loud and long. When he ran out of breath and strength, he stopped. He sucked in oxygen from the mask, getting a sudden rush that was akin to intoxication. He lay back on the bed, no longer able to strain against the bonds that held him.

"You had no right," Warren whispered.

"Hedgar Tulane felt we had no choice. Merihim ordered us to do it."

Merihim. Warren noticed how easily she acted as though she were on a first-name basis with the demon.

"He gave you a gift, Warren. Without his help, you had no hand."

"That would have been better." Warren closed his eyes and lay back, exhausted. In a matter of seconds, sleep claimed him.

Four days passed. During that time, Warren's health improved. So did the health of the demon's hand at the end of his arm. The physicians Tulane had brought into the manor house seemed satisfied and even surprised by his progress.

Truthfully, so far, Warren had been surprised and re-pulsed by the hand. But he'd been equally sickened by the way he'd been treated. The methods they'd used had been a combination of traditional medical efforts and Cabalist homeopathic remedies they had been using.

The "fish" in the IV bag hadn't been fish at all, but a small species of demon now present in the River Thames. Some of the Cabalists believed that the snow had turned toxic from the Burn, and that new flora and fauna and life forms were showing up in the affected areas.

Experimentation with the secretions from the Nester demons, as they'd been termed so far, had revealed that the liquid they released held natural anesthetic as well as a healing effect.

Warren hadn't believed that there were any demons that would be helpful to humans.

"They aren't helpful," Naomi said. "The Nester demons produce anesthetic to sedate their prey. Then they burrow into them and eat them from the inside out, starting with fats and unnecessary muscle tissue. They save the heart, lungs, and other vital organs for last. Their secretions also help their host bodies live while they're being eaten, sealing off wounds and keeping the rest of the body healthy."

One of the most horrific sights Warren had ever seen had come yesterday, when he'd finally been allowed up from his bed to walk around. Naomi had guided him down to the labs where they were working with the Nester demons because he'd wanted to know more.

There, suspended in a glass box in the middle of a large cave filled with strange-looking equipment that was an ag-gregation of cutting-edge tech and something from the nineteenth century, and attended to by a handful of lab as-sistants, a middle-aged man floated in water. X-ray machines showed the pockets of Nester demons inside him. His skin hung loosely on him, showing that all the fat had been eaten away. Most of the muscle tissue had disappeared from his legs.

"They're not going to save him?" Warren asked.

"No," Naomi replied. "They'll learn more from him by observation."

"He's going to die."

"If a research team hadn't found him, he would have died anyway. And they haven't been able to separate the Nester demons from the host without killing the host yet. Maybe before this man dies, they will."

"And if they don't?"

"There are other victims. They'll observe them."

Warren contemplated the man. Although the man's eyes were open, they appeared to be unseeing. Warren knew that was an illusion, though. The man was aware of what was happening to him. The Nester demons' secretions didn't deaden everything. Inside, the man was screaming.

"He's not unconscious," Warren said.

"We believe that he is. His eyes may be open, but that's just a reflex."

"He's screaming," Warren said. "I can hear him."

Naomi looked at him. "You're sure?"

"Yes."

"No one else can hear him." Naomi excused herself and went to talk to one of the Cabalists.

Warren continued watching the man, listening to his screams. Looking at the X-ray view of the pockets of Nester demons scattered throughout the body, Warren couldn't help thinking about the creatures that had been in the IV drip.

Naomi returned to him.

"What would have happened if one of those Nester

demons in the IV bag had gotten into my bloodstream?" Warren asked.

"That didn't happen. They helped heal you. Concentrate on that." Naomi glanced at his hand. "Since your body isn't rejecting the hand, there's a lot to hope for."

Warren didn't say anything, but he kept his hopes small. He wanted to kill the man that had taken his hand from him. Every time he thought that, he could hear Merihim laughing quietly in the back of his mind.

Keep thinking that way, the demon encouraged. *Hate will make you grow strong. And if you hate enough, I'll make you powerful enough to do anything you want to.*

The poultice across Warren's wrist had been made from the slime of yet another demon that had been found within the parts of London where the Burn had caused alterations. That one had looked like a snail, but it had been three feet tall and equipped with a tongue capable of striking over a distance of ten feet. The tongue-strike carried lethal toxins. The Cabalists still didn't have the proper name, but they were calling them Death Darts at present.

Instead of a secretion, though, the Cabalists had learned to scrape the mucus-based body from the shell and mix herbs in with it. Then they used more arcane powers to blend the snail's body with the herbs and energy. They'd learned to use that concoction to enable host bodies to accept transplanted materials like horns. Evidently whatever property that protected the Death Darts from the toxins they carried also allowed the grafts to take.

No one had ever tried to graft a limb to anyone before Warren, but they had tried since. So far, those who had suffered the amputations to attempt to take on demon limbs had rejected their new appendages.

Warren's body never tried to reject Merihim's hand. Instead the scale line from the hand crept past the heavy scarring at the wrist, growing almost as Warren watched. The scales stopped at mid-forearm.

"I think the scales have added a layer of reinforcement," Dr. Metser told Warren on the morning of the seventh day. The physician was in his fifties and sported a white coat, heavy tattooing, and ram's horns that he'd had grafted on immediately following the invasion of the demons. "I'm certain that your body isn't going to reject it. How does it feel today?"

"Fine," Warren answered. That was what he always said.

"Can you move it?" The physician always asked that.

"No." Warren never tried.

"Perhaps we could take off the halo." Metser referred to the hardware that encircled the demon's hand. Rigid metal spikes pierced the fingers, holding them straight and steady.

"No," Warren said. He didn't intend to let them remove it.

"I see." Metser struggled to disguise his impatience and his curiosity. "I think it's healed well enough to experiment with the range of movement you may have left to you."

"And I don't."

Metser sighed and nodded. "Have you tried to move it?"

"Yes," Warren lied. "I can't." In truth, though, he could wiggle each of the fingers a little. He never did so with anyone watching.

It's time, Merihim whispered in the back of Warren's head. *The hand is healed. It's yours now.*

Then I can use it—or not, Warren replied.

Don't you want your revenge on the man that maimed you? the demon taunted.

Warren didn't say anything. He tried not to let his thoughts betray him.

You want revenge, Warren. I know that you do. I can feel it burning inside you.

The physician was speaking. Warren tried to focus on the man's words but couldn't.

I've given you a gift, Merihim said, *unlike anything my kind has ever given before. You don't even know the full extent of it.*

Warren was afraid to find out. A demon's price was usually a man's soul.

I wouldn't want anything so tawdry, Merihim said. *I want you to work for me.*

To do what?

To help me. This is a new place for us. There are kingdoms to be carved out here. I want everything that I can get, and you can help me.

Warren tried not to think about that.

The Cabalists are proving powerful, Merihim said. *They will be a deciding force in the coming struggles in this world. Most of the demons don't want anything to do with humans.*

But you're willing to make an exception?

I am. I want you to lead that faction I will take from their ranks. You will grow strong among them, because I will help you, and then—when the time is ripe—you will lend your strength to mine. You will be my champion, and I will let no one ever hurt you.

Memory of the pistol shots that had ended his mother's life then wounded him and ended his father's life echoed inside Warren's head. They sounded so close that he could smell the gunpowder.

No one, the demon repeated. *No one will ever be able to hurt you.*

Warren stared at the demon's hand. *I've already been hurt.*

It will be the last time. You will be stronger than any of them, Warren. You will be mine.

Warren closed his eyes. He heard the physician asking him if he was all right, but he ignored the man.

The man that took your hand is fleeing the city as you sit here, Merihim said. *Do you want to let him escape?*

You're lying. Pain stabbed through Warren's temples and he knew the demon was angry with him. But as suddenly as the pain hit, it disappeared. In its place was a vision.

The armored man—*He is a Templar,* Merihim said— stood in an underground tube with other armored men. Around them were several homeless people dressed in ragged coats and huddled around small fires. The armored men—*Templar,* Warren corrected—and some of the men worked on the pulling engine.

What are they doing? Warren asked.

Working on their escape, Merihim answered.

They're going to use the train?

Yes.

For a few moments, Warren watched the Templar work, crawling through the engine and attaching new parts. *How long has he been doing this?*

Since he took your hand.

The vision started to fade. Warren tried to hang on to it, feeling again and again the cold bite of steel slicing through his arm. That man—that Templar—had hurt him.

He can be the last one to ever do that, Merihim promised.

What good is a demon's promise?

I gave you my hand.

And you grew another.

I could have killed you. I could still choose another. Reject me and I will.

The vision faded away but Warren couldn't forget that

the man who had hurt him so badly was getting away. He would be gone from London and then Warren would never see him again.

Warren couldn't stand that.

Take the hand, Merihim said. *Make it yours and it will give you the power to destroy him.*

Warren took a deep breath, scared of what he wanted so badly to do. Accepting the hand would mean crossing over to the darkness. Everything he'd read warned of that. But he looked at Kelli sitting by the door like a puppy, her mind almost a blank now, and knew that he'd already crossed over before he'd noticed.

What's one more step? Warren asked himself. But he knew that he wasn't stepping over because he'd already come so far. He was afraid. And he wanted the power that Merihim promised. If he had enough power, he could protect himself.

Even from the demon.

Opening his eyes, Warren stared at the demon's hand at the end of his arm.

"Warren?" Naomi asked.

"I'm fine," he said, and even in his ears his voice sounded stronger than it had in days. In fact, it sounded stronger than he'd ever heard it.

The miasma that had gripped him since his maiming left him, like winter fog blown off a radiator-heated window. He stood up from the hospital table.

"Do you want me to take off the—"

The physician never got the chance to finish his question. Warren flexed his hand, then made a fist. The halo that had been protecting it snapped into pieces and dropped to the ground. Then the spikes that had been stabbed into his fingers shot across the room and stabbed into the wall. They quivered and smoked.

Warren turned to Tulane. "I want transportation."

"For what?" Tulane looked wary and irritated at the same time, obviously sensing things were beyond his control.

"I don't have time for your questions."

"You'll bloody well have time for—"

Warren gestured without thinking, using his demon's hand.

Tulane suddenly stopped speaking. Then he held his hands to his temples and screeched in pain.

"Don't question me," Warren said. "I don't have time. Give the order for someone to bring a vehicle around to take me back to the city. Do it now and I won't explode your head like rotten grapefruit. Do you understand?"

Wracked with pain, nose bleeding, Tulane nodded.

Warren lowered his hand.

Tulane fell to his hands and knees and started retching.

"What are you doing?" Naomi demanded.

Warren looked at her, noticing that she unconsciously took a step back. "You can go if you want to, but stay out of my way." He walked toward the door, hearing Tulane rise and shuffle along behind him. By the time he walked out into the cave tunnel, Tulane was already calling for security.

They arrived on the double, rifles drawn and aimed at Warren.

For a moment fear touched Warren, but he brushed it away, feeling the power surging within him. He drew back his hand and threw it. Liquid fire materialized and flew toward the ceiling, clinging there and dripping down in long burning ropes.

Warren turned to Tulane, daring him to say anything other than what he'd been told to say.

"Take him," Tulane said, eyes filled with pain. "Take him wherever he wants to go."

FORTY-SIX

Tired and covered in grease, wearing coveralls instead of his armor, Simon sat on the Virgin Cross Country's pulling engine's fender and spooned stew from the paper bowl he'd been given. Through eyes burning from lack of sleep as well as grit, he gazed at the homeless he and the other Templar had spent the last week gathering from the broken buildings and tube stations. They'd guided them from wherever they'd found them, promising food and a way out of the city.

After the first few days, some of the men and women they'd rescued went with them to help with the scavenging. In the beginning, Simon had been worried about them, not certain they could protect them from the demons. But in the end the extra help had become necessary to gather all the food and supplies they needed to take care of the intended evacuees.

At first, the survivors hadn't wanted to come with the Templar. They'd been more afraid of leaving what little shelter they'd managed to find than conscious of the inevitability that the demons would soon find them.

They'd found thirteen the first night who were willing to come with them. It had been an inauspicious number, and one that Wertham had considered unlucky. But they'd brought in double that number the next night. And the numbers had grown exponentially from there. Paddington

National Rail station was in the heart of a residential area that also had a lot of hotels where people from other countries had gotten stranded.

At last count this evening, they'd had one thousand eighty-nine people housed in the Paddington tube station. Lack of food and water was increasingly a problem. The Grand Union Canal was nearby, though the levels had shrunk there and Simon didn't trust the water, and they lacked the resources to purify any appreciable amount. So far the demons hadn't found them.

But Simon knew that was going to change. Their luck couldn't hold forever because there were more people awaiting rescue than he would have imagined.

Wertham walked over to join Simon, carrying a bowl of stew and a bottle of water. The old Templar popped his faceshield open, revealing his tired and haggard features.

"More volunteers arrived tonight," Wertham said as he settled in beside Simon.

Volunteers were what they called the people that managed to wander into their sanctuary on their own, without being guided in by a Templar. It was good that people were hearing about the *Knight Train,* as it was being called, but Simon knew that such knowledge being so widely spread would mean their undoing as well. If that many people knew about them, the demons would discover them before long as well.

Simon gazed down the long tube. The people huddled in small groups around tiny fires that barely staved off the chill that permeated the ground even as deep as they were. Many of the people curled up in blankets or big coats.

"How many volunteers?" Simon asked.

"Thirty-two."

"Did we have enough to feed them?"

Wertham nodded. "We did. But we can't keep scavenging enough by hand to feed a group like this. We're going to need a fleet of lorries before long. And go farther to get it."

"I know."

"If we don't run out of food, we're going to be found out."

"I know."

"And we're running out of space on the train."

Simon sighed and felt exhausted. Hopelessness flickered within him again. When the idea had first occurred to him—to update one of the abandoned pulling engines in one of the storage spurs in the Paddington Nation Rail line and use the train to take survivors from London—it had sounded easy.

Now, with the successful arrival of every newcomer, it edged back toward impossible.

"I know that, too. Is there any good news?"

Wertham grinned. "We're still alive." He offered a toast with his water bottle. "To luck and pure hearts."

Simon echoed him, touching his bottle to Wertham's briefly before they drank.

Knuckling stew from his beard, Wertham looked at Simon. "Have you slept?"

"Yeah."

"When?"

Simon shook his head. Ever since he'd stopped going outside the tube and had concentrated on making the necessary adjustments to the pulling engine, he'd lost all track of time. He figured the HUD could tell him, but he couldn't remember the last time he'd been inside his armor, either.

"I can't remember."

"You need to get more rest."

"I will," Simon said. "As soon as we get these people out of here."

"How soon before they have the engine converted over?"

"A few hours. A few days." Simon shook his head. "I don't know. McCorkleson doesn't know either."

Ian McCorkleson had proven a godsend. He was an old man, in his late seventies, but still had a mind as sharp as a tack. He couldn't do all the physical labor himself now, but they'd recruited able bodies from the volunteers to help with the engine refitting.

All his life, McCorkleson had worked on the trains as a mechanic. He'd even been one of the first to help design the MagnaPUSH electromagnetic engines that were supposed to be the wave of the future. Japan and other countries had already started using maglev trains, but those depended on current running through the rails.

Instead of being powered by electricity, the MagnaPUSH engines operated by accessing the natural electromagnetic fields of the earth, cutting the operations costs dynamically. Plans had been in motion to start converting the pulling engines over the next ten years. The technology had still been on the drawing boards in the commercial shops.

But Templar technology had always been more developed than the rest of the world. The Templar had planned to fight the war against the demons if they ever came, and they'd enlisted the brightest minds to their cause. The Templar designers had been using NanoDyne technology a score of years before MagnaPUSH had become a reality.

Simon had worked with the NanoDyne engines, experimenting with them on skateboards he'd built. Some of the maglev skateboards had been released on the market, but none of them were anywhere near as powerful as the ones Simon had designed. But he had learned nearly everything there was to know about harnessing the power available through them.

The Templar had gotten the NanoDyne engines from some of the unmanned Templar Underground. After the massacre at St. Paul's Cathedral, several of the area's Templar compounds were seriously undermanned. Or totally abandoned. That had been part of the intent as well, making sure there were enough supplies left behind for the survivors to be able to stretch over a period of years if they had to.

McCorkleson hadn't believed how sophisticated and compact the engines that Simon had provided had been. Part of the problem was figuring out a way to properly balance and place the engines so they wouldn't tear loose of their housings the first time they were powered up. They'd had to reinforce all of the structures.

"McCorkleson wants a few more days to test the engines," Simon said.

"You had it up off the rails yesterday," Wertham said.

Yesterday. Simon couldn't believe that had been yesterday. It seemed like only a few hours ago.

"The balance wasn't right. We've got that corrected, but he wants the housings tweaked."

"Personally, I don't think we have days," Wertham said. "We're going to run out of resources for these people, get discovered by the demons, or get overwhelmed by refugees."

"If we have to wind the engines up, and escaping the city will probably mean that, they could leave us behind. Or self-destruct."

Wertham thought about that for the moment. "I can see the problem with that." His brow wrinkled. "But if we don't leave soon, we're either going to be discovered or we're going to have to leave people behind when we go."

Simon nodded. Neither one of those alternatives appealed to him.

"Sir? Excuse me, sir?"

It took Simon a moment to realize that the woman was speaking to him. He crawled from beneath the pulling engine and picked up the grease-covered rag lying on the ground. The rag didn't help cut the crusted grime on his hands.

The speaker was a middle-aged woman with a bandage over her left eye.

Simon started to get to his feet.

"No, you don't need to get up now. Just stay as you are. My family and I just got here today."

Simon tried to remember which *today* it currently was, but couldn't.

"I didn't want to interrupt," the woman went on, "but I had to come tell you how much I appreciate what you're doing."

Simon felt embarrassed. Somehow he never got too tired to feel that way. "It's not just me," he said. "There are a lot of people helping."

"I know." The woman smiled. "Truly, I do. But they say you're the one that started all of this."

Simon didn't know what to say to that, so he just nodded. He felt that was what his father would have done.

"I just wanted to thank you, you know. For caring enough about us to do this. If not for you, my three children would have died in that city, perished at the hands of those monsters."

We're not out of the city yet, Simon wanted to point out. But he didn't. Hope was the commodity they had the least of, and he didn't want to take it away from anyone because he knew it was a fragile thing, too. Most of them had come to the tube tunnel for a last few meals.

"Bless you," the woman said. "That's all I wanted to say." She took his grease-grimed hand in hers and squeezed. Then she walked away.

Simon stared after her for a moment, at a loss for how he was supposed to react. More than anything, he supposed, he was afraid. It was one thing to find strangers murdered in their homes by the demons, but if he lost these people it was going to hurt.

It's also going to be your fault that they're here to get caught, he told himself. He drank some water, then climbed back under the pulling engine.

"You doing okay?" McCorkleson asked.

Simon picked up a battery-operated drill and slid his safety glasses on. He started drilling holes for another support lattice strut.

"Yes." Metal bits struck Simon's face sharply enough to sting.

"Right or wrong, however this things turns out," McCorkleson said, "you've done all you could. The rest of it will just have to take care of itself."

"I know."

"No," the old man said gently. "You're just saying that now. You don't know it yet. But you will."

Simon hoped so, but he hoped most of all that everything turned out well.

"Clear!" McCorkleson yelled from the pulling engine's control center.

"Clear!" Simon yelled back. Three other men standing guard around the pulling engine yelled out the same, letting McCorkleson know that he was clear to engage the power.

The NanoDyne electromagnetic engines were charged by solar power or by cranking them with a special lever.

The engines were about the size of scuba tanks and had been mounted just under the pulling engine's housing. Simon and McCorkleson had managed to put sixteen of them on the unit. He hoped it would be enough to move all the people depending on them fast enough to make their escape.

The engine shuddered as McCorkleson engaged the power. There was little noise as the engines created the magnetic lift that caused the pulling engine to glide up six inches above the rails. Even though the power to the tubes had been lost during the attacks over the first few hours of the demon invasion, the NanoDyne engines generated enough power to accelerate the pulling engine to unbelievable speeds on their own. That had been part of the attraction of the design.

The engines balanced out easily, each working well with the others. At the controls, McCorkleson grinned like a loon. Then he sat the engine back down on the tracks.

"She's as ready as we're going to get her," McCorkleson declared.

A cheer exploded from the men, women, and children lining the tube tunnel. Word was passed along the line and further celebration came in waves.

"All right then," Simon said. "Let's get the cargo cars bolted up and see how it responds then. We'll get moving after full dark tonight."

Being inside the armor helped take away some of Simon's fatigue. The computer took over caring for him automatically even though he hadn't been taking care of himself. Once he'd climbed inside, the armor had tended to his needs, using slap-patches to chemically adjust his physical awareness back up to full alert. He'd pay for that later, he knew, but at the moment he needed the assistance.

The train was ready as they could make it. They'd packed the space with as many supplies as they'd had on hand, which had been precious few, then packed the passenger cars. In the end they'd had to add one more than they'd anticipated, but McCorkleson was confident the pulling engine would have the energy to get it moving.

Only one problem remained, and Simon had left it in place on purpose.

When the power had been cut in the tube, one of the trains had gotten stranded out in the main tunnel. It sat now, blocking the access tunnel of the spur where the out-of-service pulling engine had been stored.

Simon and McCorkleson had located a fuel-powered engine that was used to haul broken trains to service areas. Thankfully it had been functional.

One of the other men who had tube experience climbed into the engine and powered it up. The ripping roar of the massive engines filled the tube. Other than the possibility of running out of fuel, the sound was another reason Simon had wanted to use the NanoDyne engines. The Nano-Dynes were nearly silent.

Running loose through the tube and the city, the sound from the fuel-powered would have been a siren call the demons wouldn't have been able to ignore. As it was now, the only sound the train would make would be the passenger car wheels turning on the rails. There was nothing they could do about that risk.

Slowly, by fractions of an inch at first, the stalled train started moving northeast, toward the Edgware Road station.

"Simon," Wertham called over the HUD.

"Yes."

Wertham was stationed at the northeast end of the rail where it emerged from the Underground for a time. On its

route through London, the train ran above ground inter-
mittently. Simon had guessed they were going to be at their
most vulnerable during those times.

"We've got trouble. A group of demons has just entered
the tunnel here."

Fear stirred within Simon, fighting off the effects of the
drugs the armor had put into his system. "Have they seen
you?"

"Negative. But there's no way they're going to miss hearing that locomotive. I can hear it up here without the suit's
audio booster."

Panic started to rise inside Simon. He fought it back and
tried to think clearly. Even with the drugs in his system
making him sharper and more clear-headed, it was hard.

But all they could do was proceed with their plan. It was
too late to turn back now.

"We stay with what we're doing," Simon said. Then he
called to the Templar, bringing them to him, and started
running northeast, toward the end of the Paddington tube
and the demons. If they got lucky, they could attack the
demons and create enough confusion to allow the dead
train to be pulled clear and allow McCorkleson to ease
their escape train out onto the main track.

Then it was just a matter of surviving long enough to escape.

Simple, really. But he had to force himself not to think
of the people he might lose.

Or that they might fail.

Simon checked his weapons out of habit, then he began
to run.

FORTY-SEVEN

"Stop the car," Warren ordered.

The driver applied the brakes and brought the SUV to a halt near the Edgware Road tube station. It sat in the middle of other midsize buildings that lined Edgware Road and Bell Street. The broken windows were dark but the skies were still light gray from the evening sun sinking in the western skies.

"What are we doing here?" Naomi asked. She'd acted somewhat reluctant about coming, but she had.

Warren wasn't sure if she was there because she wanted to be, because she was curious, or if she was there to spy on him for Tulane, who had stayed behind. Warren didn't think it mattered, nor did he think he cared.

"The man who took my hand is here." Warren opened the SUV's door and stepped out into the falling snow.

"How can you know that?" Naomi stayed on his heels.

"Because I saw him here," Warren replied, focused on the strong impression that quivered inside his head. "Because I can *feel* him here now." He started walking, crossing the shattered debris that littered the area in front of the tube station.

Naomi followed him, pulling her coat tight against the freezing wind. "What are you going to do?"

"What am I going to do?" Warren snorted mirthlessly, not believing that she couldn't figure that out. He'd lived with images of his stepfather beating him for years before the man had shot himself. During his recovery, he'd been haunted by nightmares about the knight that had taken his hand. The old fear had returned, and he knew the only way to rid himself of it was to destroy what he feared. "I'm going to kill him."

"By yourself?"

Warren looked around, feeling a little uncertain when he saw that the Cabalists and the security people had remained with the car. He started to call out to them.

"There were a lot of them the last time we crossed their path," Naomi said. "Do you think the handful of security guards we brought with us are going to be able to stand against them?"

Frustrated, Warren gazed at the tube station. He hadn't thought to bring more people, and he doubted he would have gotten more volunteers.

Don't worry, Merihim said. *You don't need them. I will give you an army.*

"I'll go alone," Warren said, answering Naomi's question.

"You didn't come here to die," Naomi accused.

"No." Warren continued across the rubble. Suddenly he was aware of others' eyes on him. Feeling threatened, he glanced around and saw shadows moving along the edges of the buildings.

Stop, Merihim said.

Warren did.

"Demons," Naomi warned quietly as she drew back. "They're all around us."

Recognizing the demons as well, Warren felt a worm of fear slither through him. There were Darkspawn, Imps, and Gremlins in the hunting pack. Above them, a dozen Blood Angels clung to the sides of buildings. Warren couldn't help wondering if Merihim had intentionally set him up to get killed.

No, Merihim said. *I didn't betray you. I brought you an army. These serve me. Just call to them and they'll be yours.*

Why aren't you here?

This is your battle. I have my own. Tonight you can prove my investment in you, or you can die. Either way, I'll know what I need to about you and your abilities to be part of my plans.

"Warren," Naomi said softly. "Maybe we can get back to the car." She put a gentle hand on his shoulder and pulled. "Come on. Before they rush us."

In the next moment, the demons broke free of the shadows and came running at them.

Warren wanted to run, but he couldn't move. Naomi yanked on his shoulder twice, then she abandoned him and ran back to the SUV.

Command them, Merihim encouraged.

Fear ran rampant through Warren. It was the most familiar emotion he had. All his life, it had been his constant companion. Fear had driven him to live a small life, to take abuse from people he'd offered friendship to, to be taken advantage of by people who were nowhere near as smart as he was. Fear had chased him to bed at night and awakened him with a pounding heart in the morning.

To command them, Merihim said, *you must first command yourself.*

"Warren!"

The demons came on, gnashing their teeth and waving their weapons. Miraculously, none of them had yet opened fire.

The SUV door closed behind Warren. He heard the sound and immediately recognized it for what it was. Then he heard the engine accelerate over the din of demonic growls and knew that they were pulling away. By then it was too late to run because the demons were on top of him.

"Stop!" Warren said, feeling his heart pounding in his chest.

The demons, dozens of them, halted immediately. Two of the Blood Angels flapped their wings and came to agile landings atop the Edgware Road tube station canopy. They eyed him with cruel interest.

Warren felt their hunger and excitement and knew that they scented his blood and lusted for the taste of it. Forcing himself into motion, he walked toward the demon pack. The fear was frozen inside him, held in place by the fascination he got from seeing the demons standing before him. They shifted as he neared them, making room for him to walk among them.

They didn't like him. Despite his ability to command them, Warren knew they'd tear his throat out in a minute if they were allowed to. Merihim controlled them through fear, Warren felt that, and he was the demon's favorite.

They hate you for that, too, Merihim said. *And the day you fail me, I'll let them have you.*

Warren almost grew afraid again, especially standing in the middle of all the demons. But he kept himself strong. Whatever fortune had favored him so far, it had brought him to this point. If he had powers as the Cabalists seemed to agree, and the way his stepfather had died bore that out, then he could somehow reach more deeply into that power.

I can learn and get stronger, he told himself, *and I will. I won't live in fear of anyone.*

Merihim laughed. *Go carefully, whelp. Ambition is a good thing, but it can border on insolence.*

Warren ignored that, enjoying the feeling of power he got from knowing he controlled the demons around him. "I'm hunting a man," he told them.

The demons listened, but many of them growled and spat, eager to be running and chasing prey.

Warren pictured the armored knight—*the Templar*—in his mind. "I want this man. And I want him dead."

More of the demons shifted, anxious to be moving.

"He's in that tube," Warren said. He pointed at the Edgware Road tube station entrance. "Find him and bring him to me."

Immediately the demons turned and charged toward the station. They tore down the doors and raced inside.

Warren followed them, running after them, moving with a demon's speed and knowing that too was part of Merihim's gift. Dark anticipation filled him. He couldn't wait to see the look on the Templar's face when he wreaked his revenge.

Braced and ready, worried that McCorkleson and the others wouldn't get the train onto the tracks in time, Simon stood with his sword in one hand and his Spike Bolter in the other. Wertham was to his right. The other Templar, and there were forty-three of them now because more of the Templar had abandoned High Seat Booth's command, stood in a ragged line behind Simon.

All of them had wanted to help clear the city of survivors as much as they could before they concentrated on battling the demons. None of them were convinced that the Houses yet had a plan for dealing with the demons. Most of the ones who had taken up arms with Simon had lost family and friends at St. Paul's.

In the distance, lit up by night vision, Simon saw the first of the demons as they came into the tube tunnel. Wertham ran ahead of the pack, reaching the Templar easily.

"Bloody hell," someone swore.

"I told you there were a lot of them," Wertham said.

"We can't hold them," Simon said. "We can only slow them."

"We wouldn't have to slow them as much if the train were up and running," someone grumbled.

"And it would have been better if we'd left an hour ago," Wertham said. "But there's no use complaining about that now."

None of them, Simon noticed, suggested they leave. While they'd been tending to the survivors they'd pulled from the wreckage of the city, Simon had seen that the Templar had shown more spirit while surviving on lean rations than in living in the relative lap of luxury within the Templar strongholds.

They were born to fight, Simon realized proudly. But that also meant dying in battle.

A few tentative blasts from the demons' weapons struck all around them. Then three of the Templar were struck, but their armor protected them.

"Hold," Simon said calmly. "On my mark."

They held.

The demons came closer, bearing down quickly.

Paddington Station was wide and tall. Shops lined the walls on either side of the rail lines. Most of the glass had been broken and the goods stolen over the last few weeks.

"Ready," Simon said, *"now!"* At the same time, he sent a signal through his armor, broadcasting to the detonators they'd placed at that end of the tube.

All of the Templars had the same signal coded into their HUDs. That way the explosives they'd seeded the mine with would go off as long as any one of them survived. They'd mined the tube at that end as a defensive line. The other end of the tube past the train spur had been mined as well, in case they'd needed to shut down an attack from that end.

The explosives detonated in waves, throwing debris and clouds of dust into the air. In an eye blink, that end of the tube was obscured and littered with wreckage. Rocks pounded Simon's armor but he ignored it. Part of the high ceiling sagged and came down, dropping across the advancing line of demons.

"McCorkleson," Simon called over his HUD frequency, patching in to the radio the man carried.

"Yeah," McCorkleson answered. "I guess they're on us, then."

"They are. Where's the train?"

"We're almost out of it. The other train took longer to move than we'd thought."

Simon had known that from what he'd seen before he'd had to leave. "Hurry."

"I will."

"We'll hold them here as long as we can."

"Take care of yourself, Simon."

The first of the demons burst through the roiling dust cloud, clawing over the debris-covered bodies of those that had fallen. Without hesitation, they launched themselves at the Templar.

"Fire!" Ethan said, pointing the Spike Bolter and squeezing the trigger. He held the pistol on target despite the yammering recoil.

The other Templar opened fire as well. Palladium spikes, flames, and toxic liquid covered the distance separating the two groups. At first the Templar fire ground the demons to a halt, dropping bodies to the ground whole and in pieces. Then more of the demons kept coming.

Two Blood Angels flew overhead, streaking forward and attacking before anyone realized they weren't just shadows streaking the high ceiling. They swooped down at once, firing powerful bolts of spectral energy that blazed yellow-white. The bolts struck four of the Templar and blasted them from their feet.

Simon lifted his Spike Bolter and tracked one of the Blood Angels as it passed in front of him. Before the first of the Templar had landed on the ground, he was firing palladium spikes that knifed through the Blood Angel's body and perforated the wings, turning them into leathery rags.

Screaming in pain and defiance, the Blood Angel collided with a wall only a few feet away. One of the Templar rushed forward with his sword as the demon tried to get to its feet. The Templar swiped twice, cutting through the Blood Angel's neck and again across the midsection, spilling the demon's insides.

The demons established a line and opened fire. Their flames, rounds, and toxic spew struck the Templar. Some of the human warriors dropped in their tracks, and a few of them—Simon knew—wouldn't be getting up.

FORTY-EIGHT

Taking more deliberate aim, Simon chose his targets, watching as the palladium spikes slammed into the demons. But there were too many of them. They kept coming.

"Look out for the ceiling!" Wertham yelled.

Glancing up, Simon saw that the Stalkers had scuttled up the side of the tube walls and had clambered to the ceiling, hanging upside down as they prepared to drop onto the Templar.

"Break!" Simon yelled. "Form Fists!"

Immediately, the Templar broke into small combat teams. Most Houses trained for that style, allowing the Templar to form four- to six-man units to cover each other's backs during hand-to-hand fighting.

Simon joined the three Templar he'd assigned himself as a Fist member. He sheathed his sword for the moment and scooped up a Scorcher from a fallen Templar. Using both pistols, he peppered the nearest wall with palladium spikes and fiery balls that spread on impact, striking several Stalkers in quick succession, dropping them like flies.

"McCorkleson!" Simon yelled, slipping and sliding through demon gore at his feet.

"Almost!" the man replied. "Almost, Simon. Just hang in there."

The Templar on Simon's right got hit by an astral blast

that tore him in half. Simon aimed the Scorcher at the Gremlin that had fired the weapon, then squeezed the trigger.

The Greek Fire round that belched from the Scorcher struck the Gremlin in its ugly face. The round detonated, engulfing the demon's head in flames. It screamed and clawed at its head, but the efforts didn't last long and it collapsed.

The wall shattered, then spilled inward, followed by a huge, bulky shape. When it shook the debris off like a dog emerging from a lake, Simon recognized it as a Carnagor. Two others tore through the wall on the other side of the tube. One of them tore into the demon ranks and left dead scattered behind it.

Tossing its massive head around, the Carnagor nearest Simon roared and charged, maw open. Simon stood his ground, firing steadily, piercing the creature's face with palladium spikes and filling its gullet with explosive rounds that detonated on contact and gave it fiery breath.

"Break!" Simon ordered.

Several of the Stalkers had taken advantage of the Carnagor's presence to scuttle forward again. They hung from the ceiling, shifting back and forth as they tracked their prey and pounced.

Simon darted to the side, drawing the Carnagor's attention. The huge creature tried to turn its body to pursue him, but its forward momentum was too much. Its taloned feet tore through the pavement on either side of the rails.

Running as fast as he could, Simon ran up the wall to avoid the Carnagor's gnashing fangs. His boots automatically extended the spikes that grabbed traction on the wall. He ran up until he felt gravity overcoming his momentum nearly ten feet up. Then he kicked hard and propelled himself into the air away from the wall.

Holding the pistols pointed in either direction, using the 360-degree view afforded by the HUD, Simon fired at the demons. The palladium spikes chopped into the Stalkers on the ceiling while the fiery explosions ate into the Gremlins on the floor. Dead Stalkers fell from the ceiling and Gremlins dropped where they were hit.

Arching his back, Simon leathered his Spike Bolter and reached for a grenade. He landed on the Carnagor's back and called for the spikes to lock him down. His armored boots jerked with impacts at the force required to tear through the demon's thick hide. Several demons' weapons struck Simon with projectiles, fire, and toxic liquid. His armor took a beating but held. He ignored the onslaught, feeling the huge demon beneath him twist and turn.

Rearing on its hindquarters, the Carnagor reached for Simon with its hands. Kneeling quickly beneath the grasping fingers, Simon pulled the pin and shoved the grenade into the Carnagor's left ear hole. Then he vaulted from the brute's back as it started scratching at its ear.

Simon didn't think the thing was intelligent enough to know what he'd done, but somehow it sensed that he'd gotten the upper hand. It roared with rage, stamped the ground, and started to dig through the ground. Before it got very far, the grenade exploded and turned the massive head into a gory mess of steaming, cooked flesh and burned bone. The Greek Fire continued to burn, consuming more of the creature.

Several of the demons jumped on Simon, bringing him down with their sheer numbers.

"Simon," McCorkleson called. "I've got the train on the tracks. Should I wait for you, or—"

"Get out of here!" Simon roared. He put a hand on the ground and shoved himself up, throwing as many of the demons from him as he could. He reached over his shoulder and drew his sword. Focusing the arcane power he had, he said a quick Prayer of Conflagration.

Immediately a flaming nimbus appeared around him, setting several of the demons on fire. They squalled and peeled away from him. By then the tide shifted and Simon had both hands on his sword.

Simon swung, cleaving bodies almost effortlessly. He slashed again and again, not worrying about skill. All he needed for the task at hand was brute strength. There was no need to finesse when targets tried to envelop him like a cocoon. Despite the damage he was inflicting, the demons continued to try to drag him down. They'd succeeded in taking some of the Templar down.

"Retreat!" Simon yelled to the survivors. "Retreat!"

"You heard him!" Wertham crowed. "We've got a train to catch!"

Simon fired the Scorcher into the face of a Darkspawn that shot at him. All of the Templar that were able to, disengaged from the demons and ran down the tube. Simon waited for just a moment, then ran after them. With his enhanced strength and speed, he surprised the demons and managed to get a head start.

He hoped it was enough. Hell dogged his footsteps.

Dragging himself to the top of the dead demons, Warren looked around in disbelief. He'd seen the Templar. They'd been seriously outmatched, outnumbered. Even now nearly half their number lay scattered across the tube floor. Those that still lingered in life wouldn't last long.

Standing, swaying, his eyesight showing double now because a chunk of ceiling had fallen and clipped him in the head, Warren knew he'd never be able to catch up with the Templar. The one who'd taken his hand was still alive. He screamed in helpless fury, then an idea came to him.

He looked at one of the nearby Blood Angels. "Come. Obey me."

The Blood Angel glided over to where he stood. She hissed and snapped at him, but she didn't come close to him in spite of her efforts.

"Down," Warren ordered.

Kneeling, the Blood Angel was only inches from Warren's feet. Wiping blood from his eyes, Warren threw himself on top of the demon.

"Get up," he ordered, wrapping his legs around the Blood Angel's waist and leaving her enough room to use her wings. "Fly."

The Blood Angel rose to its haunches and threw itself forward. It flapped hurriedly, struggling with the extra weight. Then it was airborne, streaking over the carnage and pursuing the Templar. At her best speed she barely made headway against her quarry. Warren knew then that the armor gave its wearer extra speed and strength.

Glancing down, he saw that the chase continued. The demons weren't going to simply let the Templar get away. They were in hot pursuit, and they weren't going to stop until they overtook the Templar.

Looking forward, Warren felt the Blood Angel's muscles contract and loosen as it winged through the air. It shot over the leading demon hordes and caught the attention of the Templar.

Then, ahead in the darkness, Warren spotted a bright light headed away from him. *A train!*

He recognized the train for what it was almost at the same time he realized that it was moving under its own power when it should have been stalled. Somehow the Templar had arranged an escape.

The Templar caught up to the last car and pulled

themselves up. They scattered across the train car at once, lying prone and filling their hands with pistols.

Several energy bolts and flaming explosions whizzed by Warren, ripping into the ceiling and the walls around him. The Blood Angel never wavered, but she threw bolts that struck the train and knocked one of the armored men off.

Summoning the power he felt within him, Warren created a glowing ball of force in his hand. When he felt, instinctively, that it was the proper size and strength, he threw it at the train.

Two of the knights dodged away, fleeing back along the train car, but a third wasn't so lucky. The ball of crackling blue-white energy smashed into the knight and blasted pieces of his armor away as it knocked his body from the train to the nearest wall.

The train continued on its way but hadn't reached its top speed yet. The demons closed on it.

Warren guided the Blood Angel with his thoughts, causing the demon to dip down low enough so that he could see what the armored men had sought to protect. When he looked through the broken glass windows and saw men, women, and children huddled fearfully on the floor of the train car, he was surprised.

He was even more surprised when something whipped out of the darkness and wrapped around the Blood Angel's neck. Then the demon was yanked sideways, brought into a distinct collision with the side of the car.

Dazed, Warren tried to hang on to the Blood Angel, then he saw the demon's feet slide under the train car's wheels. Recognizing the danger, he jumped for the side of the train car just before the churning wheels yanked the Blood Angel beneath them. Before he could pull himself up, a knight stood at the edge and peered down at him, pointing a large pistol straight at his face.

Running hard as he could, Simon caught up with the train with the last of the Templar. His HUD informed him that nineteen of the warriors had been lost. The number shocked him. He'd expected some losses, but nothing like this.

Don't think about that, he told himself. *You've still got over a thousand people to save.*

Taking three more steps, pulling to within five feet of the train car, Simon reached for the safety bar surrounding the platform. Something hit him in the back between the shoulder blades and threw him off-stride. He lost ground for a moment, then recovered and ran again.

When he was close enough this time, he jumped as hard as he could, propelling himself forward and aiming for altitude, using all the strength the armor gave him. He spun in the air and pulled his other pistol, filling both hands, then firing at the wave of demons trailing the train.

Palladium spikes and the Greek Fire rounds staggered the advancing demons but didn't stop them. But the train was finally gaining more speed.

Simon landed on his feet on top of the train car, feeling it cave in slightly under the impact of his weight. He was tilted too far forward, though, and couldn't stop himself from falling on his face. He skidded across the train car top for a moment, watching helplessly as a Blood Angel swooped in and the rider on its back threw a glowing energy ball that slammed into a Templar only a few feet away.

FORTY-NINE

In disbelief and horror, Simon watched as the glowing ball of energy ripped the Templar to shreds and knocked his scattered remains from the train car. The doomed Templar's Grappler sped across the roof of the train car.

Releasing the Scorcher, Simon grabbed for the Grappler and barely caught it. The Scorcher slid off the side of the train car and disappeared.

Grappler in hand, Simon stood and anchored his boots to the train roof. He shoved the Grappler toward the Blood Angel as it overtook the train and glided alongside. Simon aimed at the demon's rider at first, then realized that would leave the Blood Angel still able to attack. Behind the train, the demons were finally losing ground, falling back as the train raced on.

They were almost free.

Simon shifted his aim to the Blood Angel and squeezed the trigger. The nano-molecular line crossed the distance between him and the demon, then looped around the Blood Angel's neck. Triggering the Grappler's reel, Simon braced himself as the line tightened. He yanked, pulling the Blood Angel into the side of the train.

The impact vibrated through the train car. Simon held on, then felt the Blood Angel pull back with impossible strength. Realizing that the creature was getting caught under the train car's wheels, Simon released the line from the Grappler. A moment later, he saw torn and bloody hunks of the scattered Blood Angel along the train's wake.

Then he saw the demon's hand holding on to the side of the train.

Simon stepped to the train's edge, listening to the scream of metal along the tracks, and saw the man attached to the demon's hand. He was surprised to find that it was the same man he'd encountered while searching for Balekor's Hammer.

Leveling the Spike Bolter, Simon aimed between the man's eyes. He didn't know how the man had gotten there or why, and he didn't know what had moved him to conspire with the demons, but it was going to end now. The Templar had left too many dead behind them to let them go unavenged.

He pulled the trigger as the man threw up a hand. Arcane energy gathered in front of the man and the palladium spikes froze in midair. Undeterred, Simon holstered the Spike Bolter and plucked a grenade from his gear, pulling the pin and dropping the grenade into the man's face.

As Simon had expected, the grenade froze in midair as well. But the grenade would also explode. Before Simon could move, though, the man gestured at him.

An invisible wall of force slammed into Simon, tearing his boot anchors free of the train's roof and throwing him across the train.

"Simon!" Crouched on the train car, Wertham reached for him. Their gloved fingertips touched for just a moment, then Simon was gone, sliding out over the side.

Warren swung his free hand at the grenade suspended in the field of force he'd instinctively summoned to keep the palladium spike from shredding his face. Before he made contact, the grenade exploded. Detonating so close to the passenger car kept the deadly force from the Templar on top and managed to rock the car a little, but the explosion came back on Warren. The impact and following second wave tore Warren from the train and knocked the air from his lungs.

He was barely cognizant of striking the ground. Fear steamrollered over him. He couldn't imagine the ruin his body had taken this time.

Or what would be left of him.

Unable to get control over his fall, Simon struck the ground and rolled. Dazed, he tried to get up but couldn't move for a moment. He knew the demons trailing the train would be getting closer with every second he lay there.

And the train would be getting farther away.

It didn't matter, though. The train was no longer an option. The demons couldn't catch it and neither could he. It was safe. He just had to hope he would be. He rolled over onto his stomach and decided to wait before he tried climbing to his knees.

"Simon!"

The HUD immediately flared to life. "Warning. One of the communication bands available to this unit has been appropriated by an unknown source."

But Simon knew the feminine voice. It belonged to Leah Creasey. He didn't know what she would be doing hacking into a frequency they were using.

"Get up."

That surprised Simon. How had she known he was lying down?

"Get up! Now! I'm coming for you! We don't have much time!"

Simon groaned as he pushed himself up. He looked back toward the demons, then dodged back to the nearby wall as they opened fire. Explosions, projectiles, and fires rained all around him.

Then the familiar rumbling noise of a powerful motorcycle engine came through the audio. Tracking the sound, Simon glanced back in the direction the train had gone.

A BMW R 1200 GS Adventure Enduro motorcycle specially built for off-road travel roared toward Simon. It didn't have a light, which meant the driver had some kind of night-vision wear.

"Leah?" Simon asked.

"Yes. Get ready."

The motorcycle slid around, reversing the way it was headed when it came to a stop in front of Simon. The figure astride it looked impossible.

Clad in some kind of matte black armor that consisted of overlapping sections, the rider looked almost insect-like, but the armor was so close-fitting that she was undeniably female. An abbreviated full-face helmet covered her head, offering only goggle-looking eyes and a singular antenna jutting up from where her left ear would be. Other armor components, more dense to offer more protection at neck, shoulders, elbows, thighs, and knees, looked slightly lighter in color.

"Leah?" Simon asked again, still not believing what he was seeing.

"Yes. Now climb on before the demons reach us."

Simon slid onto the motorcycle behind Leah Creasey. There wasn't much room, but there was a secondary set of pegs for his feet. "What are you doing here?" he asked.

Leah twisted the throttle and the rear tire ripped across the ground, then caught traction. Evidently someone had done some work on the motorcycle, increasing horsepower, because it took off almost effortlessly even with his extra weight. He slid his left arm around her waist and leaned into her.

"Saving you," she responded. She sounded completely calm, not as he'd remembered her when he'd met her on the plane from South Africa. "And I shouldn't be doing that. My X-O isn't going to be happy about that. I was here to observe. Not get involved."

"Your 'X-O'?" Simon knew from his study of military commands that X-O stood for "executive officer." But Leah wasn't in the military.

Still, he remembered how skilled she'd been at using the rifles they'd picked up after their arrival on the coast of England. He also remembered how she'd been constantly asking questions about things. *Everything*.

Until she disappeared from the Templar stronghold.

"We don't exactly have time to talk about that," Leah replied.

"Are we going to have time later?"

"No." Leah handled the motorcycle like it was a part of her. She roared through the darkness, weaving across the tracks and around debris that littered the tube. "I'm not supposed to be here."

"But you are."

"Foolish weakness on my part. I was trained better than that."

Trained? Trained by whom? For what?

The train took shape in the darkness ahead. The surviving Templar had taken up positions along the passenger car.

"You might want to contact your friends," Leah suggested, "and let them know we're not the enemy. It would be ironic if I saved your arse, then we got blown up by your mates."

Simon agreed and called for Wertham.

* * *

Stunned, partially from the impact against the ground and partly from the fact that he was still alive, Warren stood in the darkness of the tube tunnel. He wasn't using the night sight he'd learned, so he focused just for a moment and made the change.

Turning toward the roaring motor over to the right side of the tunnel, Warren saw the knight that he had knocked from the train as he slid onto a motorcycle. Then the rider twisted the throttle and the motorcycle sped forward.

Drawing a breath with effort, feeling the pain of something broken inside his chest and hoping it was only a rib, Warren examined his hands. Nothing appeared to be different or injured. The grenade blast hadn't been an antipersonnel one filled with shrapnel.

He'd read about grenades in games he'd played. From what he had seen, the grenade the knight had dropped had to have been a high-explosive munition, capable of doing damage through blunt force.

He'd been lucky.

Then he realized it had been more than that. He'd been powerful enough to escape the blast relatively unscathed.

He gazed ahead, watching as the motorcycle grew smaller. Then he called to another Blood Angel and climbed aboard her as the demon horde swept by him. A moment later, he was once more flying, hoping to find the knight that had taken his hand.

"Were you following me?" Simon asked. "Is that how you found us?"

"I was assigned to you in South Africa," Leah said. "I followed you from there." She leaned the motorcycle and avoided a huge chunk of mortar. "Finding you here tonight was just a fluke. I was assigned to something else."

Simon decided not to ask her why she was there because he got the impression she wouldn't answer. But his mind was already spinning from all the possibilities. "Why did you follow me from South Africa?"

"We needed to know more about the Templar."

"Who is 'we'?"

"That's one question you don't get to ask."

Simon felt certain the question was only one of several he couldn't ask. "Why were you told to follow me?" He leaned with her, automatically moving with her on the motorcycle.

"Because we needed to know more about the Templar."

"How did you know I was a Templar?"

"Your father was identified."

"My father?" Hope dawned within Simon. "You've talked to my father?"

Leah was quiet for a moment. "No. I'm sorry, Simon. His body was identified. He was in his armor. That's how they knew him. That's how they knew you. They knew your father was a Templar. They didn't know if you were, but the bet was that you were. You were also the only link we had to the Templar, so we had to exploit that."

Exploit. The term sounded offensive.

"If you hadn't saved my life, I'd be tempted to throw you off this motorcycle," Simon growled.

"You wouldn't. You're too much like one of Lord Robert Baden-Powell's Boy Scouts." Leah juked around another mass, then raced up on the train. "But that's one of the things I like about you."

"Why did you need to know about the Templar?"

"Because you knew more about the demons. Until the invasion, the people I'm with believed they were just myths propagated by the Templar and other people."

"Why didn't you just ask?"

"We couldn't ask. That's not our way. Now be quiet. I broke cover tonight—and I'm going to pay bloody hell for it—for a reason. Those demons back there aren't the only problem you have."

Simon leaned into Leah again as she sped up and started passing the train.

"Simon," Wertham said.

Glancing at the train, Simon saw Wertham sitting atop the car with his sword and a Blaze Pistol naked in his fists. Simon also saw the frightened faces in the shattered windows of the passenger cars. With all the damage there, he didn't know how there couldn't have been casualties. He turned his thoughts away from that.

"I'm all right," Simon said.

"Who are you with?"

"Leah Creasey."

"The woman you brought with you?"

"Yes."

"What's she doing here?"

"She claims she's helping."

Wertham cursed. "Is she?"

"She may have saved my life back there."

"Well, that's a start. And it's not like we're going to be picky about who helps us here tonight."

Leah pulled in front of the train, feathering the throttle to jump the rail and land in the center of the track. She sped up, the motor roaring loudly.

"You said there was another problem," Simon said.

"There is." Leah leaned again, making the exchange at the Oxford Circus tube station and roaring on toward Charing Cross. "A demon named Merihim has set up an ambush for your train on the Hungerford Bridge."

That immediately caught Simon's attention. All rail lines crossed the River Thames over the Hungerford Bridge.

There was no other way by train to reach South London. The Bakerloo tube line ran under the river, but they didn't have access to those rail lines.

If what Leah was saying was right, the demon stood in the path of their escape.

FIFTY

Warren clung to the Blood Angel as it pursued the train whizzing through the Underground tubes. Other Blood Angels joined the one he rode. Like a mass of bats, they screamed through the tube after the train.

Thinking furiously, Warren guessed that the train would head for Charing Cross Rail Station, and from there across the Hungerford Bridge into southern London. When it came out of Charing Cross and raced across the bridge, the train would be vulnerable.

All it would take was a few moments to overtake the train. Then, if the Blood Angels could overcome the engineers in the control compartment, the train could be shut down. He felt certain the Templar he was after would come back to help.

Warren felt badly about the people that would be hurt. He didn't want to injure them. But if his life hung in the balance against theirs—and he knew that it did—then they would have to die.

No one in London had ever cared about him. Now, with his life on the line, he wasn't about to be foolish enough to care about them.

Patience, he mind-whispered to the Blood Angels. *We'll soon have our chance.*

* * *

Leah halted the motorcycle inside the Charring Cross Station. Behind her, Simon shifted and peered out at Hungerford Bridge. Elevated from the station, the bridge spanned the River Thames. Dusk, not true night, colored the gray sky. Snowflakes came down steadily, obscuring his vision.

But the thermographic vision in his HUD allowed him to see the bright orange figure standing in the middle of the bridge.

"Is that him?" Simon asked. He knew they were only minutes ahead of the train. "Merihim?"

"Yes."

"How did you learn about—"

Leah turned the blank mask she wore to look at him with her goggle eyes. "Simon, we don't have time for a Q&A. Not if you want to save that train. Those demons you met back there aren't going to give up. If the train stops, they'll catch up and those people will still die. Even then they'll have to beat out other demons that will be drawn to this. Do you understand?"

"Yes." Resentment vibrated through Simon. She sounded so professional, so sure of herself. And he . . . well, things weren't turning out the way he'd thought at all. The rescue attempt was turning out to be a mess. He'd planned hard and worked hard, went sleepless for days. *And all for what? To lose at the end? By inches?*

"We've been observing Merihim," Leah said.

Simon resisted the impulse to ask who *we* was.

"There's been a shift in the demon hierarchy since they arrived," Leah went on. "Merihim is a late arrival, but he's staging a power play among the demons as far as we can tell. We had a . . . someone in a Cabalist organization when Merihim came through into this world. Merihim's playing his own game. Tonight he intends to make your rescue attempt part of his scheme."

"How?"

"He's going to blow up the bridge while the train passes and send everyone in it into the river to drown."

"Why?"

"As part of a sacrifice to satisfy some blood ritual. That's all we've been able to gather. We don't understand as much about the demons as the Templar do."

"Even we don't understand everything," Simon admitted. He watched the orange figure waiting on the bridge. "How is he going to blow up the bridge? Explosives?"

"We don't know. We tracked one of the Cabalists—like the guy riding the flying demon back there—"

"It's a Blood Angel," Simon said automatically.

"—who's managed to spy on Merihim." Leah shook her head. "They're foolish and pathetic, all of them. Children playing with unknown monsters that can devour them all."

Simon didn't quite agree with her assessment. He thought the Cabalists were just too smart for their own good. Smart enough to get themselves in trouble. Or dead.

"When we questioned the Cabalist we had in custody under heavy drugs, the man told us what he knew. Unfortunately, what he knew was limited. So now is the time you choose whether you want to fight the demons back in the tube, or you figure out some way to break Merihim's threat."

Simon only thought about it for a moment. That was all the time he had anyway. The train was bearing down on them. Brief communication with Wertham confirmed that.

"I'll need to borrow your motorcycle if I'm going to get there in time," Simon said. Simon slipped out of the backpack he'd used to carry extra ammunition and explosives in. He had seven grenades left on a bandolier. He considered seven to be a lucky number, and he hoped it would be enough. Even if he couldn't destroy the demon, he could at least hope it would be distracted long enough for the speeding train to go by. There was no way they were going to get all of the survivors safely out of the area without the train.

He slid the bandolier over his shoulder, making certain where the cord was that would allow him to pull all the grenade pins at one time. The resulting explosions would take place at relatively the same time.

"What?" If the mask Leah wore had possessed features, Simon was certain he would have seen shock written heavily there. "You can't go out there—"

Simon moved quickly, shoving his hands under her thighs and hurling her from the motorcycle with the armor's augmented strength. Flying through the air, she twisted like a cat, coming down on her feet thirty feet away. By then Simon's hands were on the handlebars. He kicked the gear shift lever into first, twisted the throttle as he let out the clutch, and shot out of the rail station.

"Simon!"

Ignoring her, Simon called out to Wertham. "Where are you?"

"Almost upon Charing Cross Station."

Simon roared along the rail, aiming for the demon standing at the middle of the bridge. "Keep a weather eye peeled," Simon advised. "If the bridge blows up before you get there, be prepared to stop."

" 'If the bridge blows up'?"

"Just stay ready, Wertham. And wish me luck." Simon stayed low over the handlebars. Leah's voice was in his ears, cursing him for being a fool, then pleading with him to come back. Simon ignored it all. Instead, he thought about his father, about all the lessons his father had given him, and how he was never going to be able to tell his father how much all those memories meant to him now.

He knew, Simon reminded himself. *There wasn't much that got by him. He knew.* Simon took some solace in that. Even if he died, he would die the way his father had taught him to.

Something was wrong.

Warren knew that when he saw the train was slightly slowing down. They were almost up on Charing Cross Railway Station now and he thought that might have been part of the reason.

The flock of Blood Angels raced on.

Fear rattled around inside Simon's head as he raced toward the demon. Shadows stood behind the demon, partially hidden in the falling snow and the thick fog that covered the river below.

If the demon was one of the Eldest, or even a Dark Will, Simon might not be able to kill it. And if he didn't kill it, he was certain that it was going to kill him.

You don't have to kill it, Simon reminded himself. *You only have to destroy whatever means Merihim intends to use to blow up the bridge. Or manage to keep him from doing it long enough for the train to get by.*

Simon took some heart that Merihim wasn't a name known to him. Maybe the demon wasn't as strong as he could have been. Maybe through whatever course he'd chosen to follow, Merihim hoped to become one of those.

If so, he was still weak enough to be destroyed.

But he's more than powerful enough to defeat you.

Less than eighty yards away, the demon turned to face Simon. Taking heart in the fact that the demon was only a couple of feet taller than a normal human being, Simon drew the Spike Bolter from its holster and took aim, firing as soon as he had target acquisition.

The demon roared and covered his face with an arm as he slightly turned away from the onslaught. Then Merihim whipped back around, his fist engulfed in a whirling fireball that he threw at Simon.

As the train reached the more open area of Charing Cross Station, Warren urged the Blood Angels into greater speed. He drew his power into him, filling both of his hands with blazing balls of energy.

The Blood Angels swooped forward, gaining on the train with difficulty, but gaining all the same. Warren looked for the motorcycle and the knight but saw neither. He threw the balls of energy at the pulling engine.

Juking the motorcycle, Simon managed to evade the fireball the demon threw at him. Heat seared his skin as it approached. The fireball splashed against the ground where he would have been had he not changed directions. Immediately, the pavement puddled, turning semiliquid and bubbling.

Twenty yards away, Simon deliberately lost the motorcycle, turning it over on its side and sending it skidding across the rails toward the demon. He didn't know how fast he'd been going, but it was fast enough that the motorcycle caught the uneven surface and leaped like hooked fish into the air.

Incredibly, Simon's aim was true. Even whirling and flipping, the motorcycle stayed on course. It struck the demon in the chest, breaking apart, then exploding as the gas tank caught fire. The flames enveloped the demon, but Simon doubted that it would do anything to the creature.

By that time, Simon was sliding across the pavement as well. Out of control, he tumbled and skidded, willing himself to relax and let the armor take care of him the way it was supposed to. Trying to stop himself with an arm or a leg could get it broken even inside the armor's protection.

The world turned insane for a moment, filled with whirling images and near-nausea. The armor slap-patched him and the sickness went away.

Then he crashed into the side of the bridge and came to a halt. He struggled to breathe, only then realizing that he'd had the wind knocked out of him.

Glancing at the HUD, Simon saw that the train was only then emerging from Charing Cross Railway Station. He spotted the flying demons swirling around the pulling engine. Tracer-fire from Templar weapons burned brightly.

Hungerford Bridge took on a whole new vibration as the train hit the tracks.

Simon pushed himself to his feet, drew his sword from over his back, and ran toward the demon as it brushed the last of the motorcycle from its chest. Only then did Simon realize the shifting shadows behind the demon were real.

Hideous corpses stood packed tightly across the bridge. With the shadows and fog ripped away, an army of undead stood revealed. All of the zombies looked fresh from the grave, but Simon doubted any of them had ever been properly buried. The walking corpses shambled forward hesitantly, as if the vibration of the train shooting down the bridge had an effect on them.

Then Simon was on the demon, firing the Spike Bolter and swinging the sword.

Warren watched as the energy balls struck the pulling engine, actually strong enough to rock the heavy locomotive to one side for an instant. Then it tilted back down, churning wheels once more on the rails.

The people inside the passenger cars screamed fearfully.

They scrambled to resume their prone positions on the floor.

In the next moment, the train and Warren were outside the Charing Cross Railway Station. Warren urged the Blood Angel to greater speed as he reached for more of the reserves of his power. Two of the Blood Angels actually established holds on the pulling engine, but before they could do more than take a few ineffectual swipes at the men inside, Templar fire cut them to pieces and they dropped onto the pavement.

Just as he was about to throw the energy balls, a Templar fired a steady stream of palladium spikes at the Blood Angel Warren rode. The spikes struck the creature in the head, killing it almost instantly.

Flailing weakly, the Blood Angel sailed over the side of Hungerford Bridge and promptly died. Directionless, the demon dropped, twisting like a broken kite.

Upside down, hanging on for dear life, Warren saw the black surface of the river coming up fast. He hit hard and his senses went as black as the water.

The demon growled at Simon and threw out its hand. Almost instantly, the demon rocked back on its heels as a trio of rockets from a Cluster Rifle slammed into it. Simon felt the detonations as he rushed toward his opponent. He kept firing the Spike Bolter, aiming for the demon's eyes. Some demons could regenerate, but even if the blindness were temporary, he hoped that it would be enough.

Another trio of rockets hammered the demon again, driving it back a couple of steps. Before it recovered, Simon was on it, slashing with the sword and opening large wounds to join those suffered from the rockets.

Through the HUD, Simon was aware of the train rocketing toward him, knowing that when it reached him it was going to pass him by in a second.

The demon caught his sword on the next blow, trapping his arms so he couldn't put much force into it. Simon kicked the demon in the crotch and yanked the sword free.

Instead of going down, though, the demon backhanded Simon, catching his helm. Even though the blow seemed weak, it still felt like he'd been hit by a truck. He spun away, barely able to keep on his feet. He'd never fought anyone—any *thing*—so strong. He was almost out on his feet from the impact alone.

Lifting the Spike Bolter again, Simon fired it point-blank at the monster in front of him as the zombies lurched into the fight. Turning the pistol on the zombies, Simon mowed them down. They were gross, blue-faced and vacant-eyed. Simon hated the idea of blasting the zombies because they'd once been human. The demons never had been.

The demon's attention turned back to the train. It lifted its hands and traced symbols in the air. Then it growled, or provided some verbal commands.

By that time, the train was already out over the river, racing toward them. Redoubling his effort to get to the demon, Simon slashed his way through the zombies to reach Merihim.

More rockets sizzled past him, but these struck fire from the bridge and not the demon.

Growling again, the demon swatted at Simon. Leaping at once, Simon cleared the blow, tucked, and flipped, firing the Spike Bolter the whole time. Then he holstered the pistol, seeing that the train was rushing at them, growing larger and larger.

Other weapons fire from the Templar aboard the train

joined Simon's efforts. The demon staggered back, roaring with rage.

Landing on his feet, Simon took a two-handed grip on the sword and leaped to the top of the zombies nearest him. He ran across the undead army that had swarmed protectively around Merihim. Skulls crunched, necks snapped, and shoulders shattered beneath Simon's weight, but he reached the demon.

Merihim threw another fireball at him. It hit him, slowing his approach and setting several of the nearby zombies on fire. Simon drove himself forward, trusting the armor to hold even though the HUD was filled with warnings.

Then he reached the demon and his sword came alive in his hands. He slashed at the demon's head, driving it back. Runes carved into the demon's scaled flesh burned molten scarlet. The sword opened grievous wounds that revealed more scarlet, only this trickled down the demon's body.

Roaring with rage and pain, Merihim curled his hands into fists and struck back. The impacts shook Simon to his core, and for a moment he felt certain that he was about to die.

Then, on the HUD, he saw one of the Templar on the train raise a grenade launcher and fire a volley into Merihim. The grenades drove the demon back.

Taking advantage of the distraction, though he'd been buffeted as well, Simon stepped forward and plunged his sword through the demon's chest. Moving swiftly as the train reached him, Simon grabbed the bandolier of grenades from his shoulder and pulled the cord that popped all the pins. He looped the bandolier around Merihim's head, letting it settle over the demon's shoulders like a lethal necklace.

"Die, hellbeast!" Simon shouted, grabbing his sword hilt and kicking Merihim in the stomach to drive him backward.

The demon tripped over one of the rails and went down in the midst of the zombies. Merihim reached for the grenades, but they went off before he could yank them away. The explosions ripped his upper body to shreds, but he remained alive.

Simon couldn't believe it. Even if Merihim wasn't one of the Eldest or the Dark Wills, the demon was hard to kill.

The communications band crackled to life inside Simon's HUD. "Simon!"

On the HUD, Simon saw that the train was on him then. A few of the Templar shot down a handful of Blood Angels that had continued pursuit.

"Give me your hand!" Wertham shouted.

The train plowed into the zombies, shuddering from the impacts that threw undead bodies and pieces of undead bodies in all directions.

Wertham stood at the last car, one hand dug into the side of the car, the other extended to catch Simon's hand.

Simon turned and shoved his left arm out, thinking that Wertham was mad and they were both about to get killed. Their hands closed around each other's forearms, locking tight. Simon barely realized that before the train's momentum yanked him from his feet.

Confusion filled Simon's world for a brief instant as he collided with several zombies that the train had missed by inches. Then Wertham pulled him to the platform behind the passenger car and they fell in a heap.

By the time Simon forced himself to his feet, the zombies and Merihim were behind them, growing smaller as the train sped on. But the demon stood, weakly it was true, but it stood nevertheless. There was, however, no pursuit.

Now if we can just get out of London alive, Simon thought. He stared at the horizon through the swirl of snowflakes. London looked dark, like an infected body part that had died from gangrene and needed to be amputated. Dark clouds roiled around the Hellgate near St. Paul's. Blood Angels claimed the skies, sailing over the buildings.

Looking at the city, Simon couldn't help thinking that no one would ever again escape the death trap that London had become.

He hoped that wasn't true.

EPILOGUE

Two days later, a convoy of rescue ships picked up the survivors the Templar had delivered from London to Bristol. One of the Templar had managed to find an outpost that sent the message out to the rescuers.

The ships sat at anchor out in the harbor as longboats powered back and forth to pick up the survivors. It was early morning and the day seemed full of promise. For the first time in days, the sky was clear.

Captain Webber, a seasoned veteran who had once lived in London himself, stood with Simon and Wertham as they watched the survivors climb aboard the ships.

Simon stood on the shore in the sunlight, not minding the winter chill on his bare head. He held his helmet under one arm.

"You could come with us," Webber suggested.

Gazing at the people boarding the ships, Simon knew that he couldn't leave. He took a deep breath and let it out. "No, but thanks all the same. My place is here."

Webber turned and glanced north. Even in the distance, the smudge in the sky left by the presence of the Hellgate could be seen. A gray winter morning might have covered it up, but not the clear weather of today.

"London isn't a place for anybody these days," the captain said. "I grew up there, but I was in the city when the demons came. I was lucky to get out." He shook his head. "I don't want to go back there. I don't know if I ever will." The older man's eyes looked haunted.

"I've got to go back," Simon said.

"Even with all the demons?"

Simon showed the man a grim smile. "That's my calling, captain. Just like the sea is yours. I know men who would never set foot on a ship to cross a sea."

Webber shook his head. "Well, those demons are one sea you can have to yourself. From what I gather in the news, nobody knows what they're supposed to do with them."

"The answers are there, captain," Simon said. "We've just got to look for them."

But he knew there were more questions than before, too. He was certain Merihim wasn't dead, and he'd wondered about the demon's agenda ever since Leah Creasey had told him what she knew.

And then there was the mystery of Leah as well. Who was she really? And who was she working for? It was a lot to think about, but it also meant that a lot of pieces were in play in London.

But one of the keys was Merihim. That was why Leah and her mysterious group had locked on the demon. If Merihim was disruptive among the demons, if he was working at cross-purposes to them in some kind of power play as Leah had suggested, there was a good chance more information about the demons would pop loose.

When Simon returned to London, he intended to find out as much about the demon as he could. But first he had to get his team rested and healthy again. Thankfully Bristol hadn't yet been invaded. There were still plenty of supplies inside the city, and they were relatively safe there. Except for the demon patrols that ranged the English coastline.

But it would be enough for a few days' respite. He intended to make the most of them. They would mourn their dead and care for their wounded, then—when they were able—they would head back to London.

The war for the city had just begun.

A high stone and wrought-iron fence protected Good Saints' Cemetery from vandals, but the gates exploded inward at Warren's gesture. Part of him didn't like what he was about to do, but another part looked forward to it because he'd never done it before.

Three days had passed since he'd fallen into the River Thames and been thwarted in his attempted vengeance on the Templar that had taken his hand. He'd managed to save himself. For a time, though, he'd feared that Merihim would finish what the Templar had not.

But the demon's wrath had passed and Warren had received further instruction. He was amazed at how quickly his power continued to grow.

Walking through the graveyard, Warren didn't worry about the demons prowling through the area. He was marked, to their senses at least, by Merihim's protection and knew they would give him a wide berth.

Demon-claimed, they called him. Warren wore that name willingly. Demon-claimed was demon-protected. Here, with the power he had and the demons in control of the city, he was a lord.

And he was getting stronger.

He walked through the graveyard, looking for one marker in particular. When he found it, he sat on crossed legs and unleashed the spell that Merihim had given him to use.

An electric-blue fog rose up from the frozen ground, providing a foot-thick layer of cover over a large section of the graveyard. Then, after a long time, the dead began to crawl from their graves.

Since the cemetery was hundreds of years old, the zombies Warren awakened stood in all manner of dress, from knickers to modern khakis. Some were soldiers and some were slackers. Dead and mindless, they were just a force Merihim could use to build his army.

But the one Warren waited on took a bit longer, as if reluctant. But then that zombie too rose and stood before him.

The mortician had done a good job of putting the dead man's head back together after he'd shot himself, but Warren could still see where the bullet had gone through.

Standing, Warren extended his demon's hand toward the corpse of his stepfather. "Not you," Warren said softly. "You're not going to come."

Flames jumped from Warren's fingertips and wreathed the zombie. It howled and beat at the flames. Sinew popped and cracked as it exploded from the heat.

Warren held his hands out, warming them in the heat given off by the demon. Then it fell. Warren stood there, watching as his stepfather's body burned down to ash on the frozen ground.

When the last ember had flickered out, Warren turned and led the undead army from the cemetery. It was time to get on with his master's work. Warren was looking forward to it. The more power Merihim gathered, the more that Warren got as well. Being independent, being strong and powerful, was worth every dark and dreadful thing Warren had to do.

But part of him still burned for vengeance against the Templar. He wouldn't let that need go unanswered. He would find the Templar, and he would kill the man in the most painful manner he could manage.

Soon.

THE *HELLGATE: LONDON* SAGA
CONTINUES IN BOOK TWO:
GOETIA

ABOUT THE AUTHOR

Mel Odom lives in Moore, Oklahoma, with his wife and children. He's written dozens of books, original as well as tie-ins to games, shows, and movies such as *Buffy the Vampire Slayer* and *Blade,* and received the Alex Award for his novel *The Rover*. His novel, *Apocalypse Dawn,* was runner-up for the Christie Award.

He also coaches Little League baseball and basketball, teaches writing classes, and writes reviews of movies, DVDs, books, and video games.

His Web page is www.melodom.com, but he blogs at www.melodom.blogspot.com. He can be reached at mel@melodom.net.